INFERNO
BENEATH THE BLAZE

LUNA MASON

Cover Design: Coffin Print Designs

Formatting: Peachy Keen Author Services

Author's Note

INFERNO is a stand-alone, DARK Irish Mafia Romance with a BDSM game of survival. It does contain content and situations that may be triggering to some readers.

This book is explicit, intended for readers 18+.

The FMC is in an abusive marriage (not with the MMC). Don't worry, that asshole gets a very satisfying end.

Please enter Decadence at your own risk. For a full list of triggers please see my website:

www.lunamasonauthor.com

Note, for anyone who has read Beneath The Mask and Beneath The Secrets series previously. Part one of Inferno is set 5 years ago, which would be the same time as the end of Detained (BTM Book 4) and when we switch to Present Day in Part Two, that then directly takes us to after the events in Claim (BTS Book 4) – If you haven't read my previous series, do not worry, this is a complete standalone, it's just part of the 'Beneath' universe.

To keep up with Luna's chaos, find her on social media:

Instagram: @authorlunamason

Her FB Reader Group- Luna Masons Mafia Queens

This one is for my spicy Queens who read this list and think fuck yes!

- Hot Irish Mafia Boss with a **huge dick.**
- Pretends to hate you, but he's secretly <u>OBSESSED.</u>
- Hosts a **BDSM game of survival** in his chocolate factory.
- **Reads smut** to learn what women crave.

You liked that list, didn't you? Such a good girl.
*Mr. Quinn is ready to open the gates of Decadence **just for you.***

PLAYLIST

https://spoti.fi/3RipRmW

- Insanely Illegal Cage Fight - Dal Av, Jackson Rose
- Animals - Architects
- The Offering - Sleep Token
- WONDERLAND - Neoni
- Hide and Seek - Klergy, Mindy Jones
- Descending - Sleep Token
- Pretty In The Dark - Ashley Sienna, Ellise
- Indigo (feat. Avery Anna) - Sam Barber, Avery Anna
- everything i wanted - Billie Eilish
- the crown - take luck
- Meet you at the Graveyard - Cleffy
- Young And Beautiful - Lana Del Rey
- The Apparition- Sleep Token
- eat me ! - Holywatr
- beartrap- Holywatr
- Wonderwall - Spotify Singles - Bring Me The Horizon
- let me fall - Ex Habit, BURY
- Better Off - VOILÀ
- Scream My Name - Thomas LaRosa
- Wicked Game - Chris Isaak
- Empty Bench - David Kushner
- Blasphemy - Bring Me The Horizon
- F E R A L - Bad Omens

- Silver Swarm - Thornhill
- Tattoos - Artemas
- Hospitals for Souls - Bring Me The Horizon
- Aphrodisiac - KIRRA47, Desire4u
- Dreams - SKUM, Meisym
- How Villains Are Made - Madalen Duke
- OFPP - conscience
- Go to Hell, for Heaven's Sake - Bring Me The Horizon
- SAW TRAP - Jackson Rose, Dal Av
- Obey (with YUNGBLUD) - Bring Me The Horizon, YUNGBLUD
- more than friends - Isabel LaRosa
- Just Pretend - Bad Omens
- Sugar - Sleep Token
- Candy Shop - 50 Cent, Olivia
- Fuck Me Like You Hate Me - Jutes
- Vicious - Bohnes
- Who I Was - V.I.P.N
- Emergence - Sleep Token
- GODDESS - Written by Wolves
- Sleepyhead - Jutes
- Red Velvet (with Ari Abdul) - Jutes, Ari Abdul
- Love, Touch, Thrill - ORGAVSM
- Delirium - CHVRN
- A Grave Mistake - Ice Nine Kills
- Caramel - Sleep Token
- Second Sight - Arankai
- Something in the Orange- Zach Bryan
- Play with Fire- Sam Tinnesz, Yacht Money
- Vore- Sleep Token

*A special thank you goes out to **take luck** who have kindly provided a direct link to go inside on their chapters so you can click, listen, and read for the full experience of their banger, **the crown.***
  https://takeluck.komi.io

A NOTE FROM THE MASTER OF INFERNO

The gates are now open for you…
Please leave your inhibitions behind.
You are entering a world like no other.
To many, it's simply a chocolate factory, but as you descend deeper,
you'll see Decadence is so much more.
It shall lead you to Inferno, a place for your dark, sinful and utterly
twisted desires to come true.
The rules are simple and there is only one golden ticket for the
surviving contestant.
But not everything is as you may first believe.
Sometimes it's in the darkness that one shall find their own light.
Be warned, you must step into hell to get a taste of heaven.
Have fun and let's see who makes it to me, shall we?

With Love From,
The Master of Inferno.

PROLOGUE

CHARLOTTE

10 years ago.
Chicago.

Just as Mom is cutting into my chocolate birthday cake, a resounding knock batters on our front door. I jump up and my father's face pales.

"No," he whispers.

"Who is it?" I ask. I don't have time for distractions, today is my black belt grading day.

A stern look washes over his features as he hunts through the cupboard, retrieving a gun.

"Dad! What the hell? You're scaring me."

Mom wraps her arm around me and hugs me close, just as another flurry of aggressive pounding echoes through the house.

"I need you to listen to me very carefully. In my dressing room, behind the shoes, there's a keypad to a safe room. The code is your mom's birthday. Go." His voice almost cracks.

"Tell me what's happening! Why do you have a gun?" Tears stream down my face.

All my life I've been sheltered. Homeschooled. Martial arts was my only escape to a normal teenage life. We moved to Chicago after my sixth birthday. I always wondered why I was different. I was

1

kept away from the real world. I used to watch kids playing outside and get upset that I couldn't go.

But the fear on my father's face tells me everything as he brushes a shaky hand through his graying hair.

He steps forward and grips my shoulder tightly.

"I love you, Charlotte. I'm proud of you."

It sounds so…final.

"Go!" he bellows and points to the ceiling.

Holding on to Mom tightly, we race through the hallway. As we reach the stairs, we come to a halt as the air vibrates from the heavy blows.

"Shit. Run!" I shout, dragging Mom behind me.

I'm just to the top of the landing as the front door crashes open. My mother's screams rip through the air. I feel leather gloves on my bicep, and I use all my force to rip my arm away from his grip.

As I turn, I stare into devious black eyes. His hand shoots out and I duck. Swiping his feet from under him with my leg, he tumbles down the stairs. My lungs burn as I run as fast as I can to my father's room, slamming it shut behind me. Flinging open the doors to the wardrobe, I head to the shoes.

"Fuck, where's the keypad?"

Taking a breath, I scan the surroundings from top to bottom, looking for something out of place.

The gray shelves stand out from the white ones. As I look closer, they come out further than the others. Standing in front of it, I shove the boots from the center onto the floor, revealing the number pad and start to jab in the digits with my trembling fingers.

"Come on, Charlotte," I hiss.

As I hit the second to last button, the door creaks open.

"Little bitch." The distinctive Russian accent turns my blood to ice. I step back, holding up my arms when I see the gun in his right hand.

"Please don't hurt me," I whisper.

A sadistic smirk spreads on his lips as he stomps towards me, grabbing me by the back of the neck and pressing the muzzle against my temple.

He leads me out of the room and down the stairs. I keep my breathing steady as I am pushed into the kitchen.

I let out a scream when I find my mom and dad on their knees with their hands behind their head.

Tears run down my father's cheeks, my mother is shaking in fear as she looks at me.

A tall man stands behind them, he must be in his mid-twenties. His eyes are like the first guy's, almost black, except he has a defining scar over his left eyebrow. His gaze drags over my body, almost with satisfaction on his face.

He jabs the pistol into the back of my dad's head.

"Pretty little thing, your daughter. I'm going to have a lot of fun. This is a very rewarding deal for me after all."

The Russian guy runs his tattooed finger along his lip, and I want to throw up as I watch him. Blood pulses in my ears and the room starts to spin.

"Vlad. No. Take me. I'll do whatever you want. Don't harm my girl," my dad pleads, and Vladimir simply laughs.

It's menacing. It's evil.

"No more chances, Damien. You're lucky I'm not burning your house to the ground with you all tied up inside."

My mouth falls open as the guy behind me tightens his grip. I am frozen in fear.

"You aren't taking her!" my mom yells. Jumping to her feet, she launches herself at *Vlad*. The guy behind me throws me down, my head smashing against the tiles. As I look up, I hear the shot go off, and she falls to the floor. My father's cries rip through the air.

"Charlotte, run!" he bellows.

I scramble to my feet and wipe my tears as I run. Before I can grab the door, a hand clamps down on my shoulder. I thrust my elbow into his ribs and spin to face him so I can block his next move.

When his fist flies towards me, I snatch his arm, moving out of the way and twisting hard enough to elicit a growl from him. I smash my foot into the back of his calf, dropping him to his knees. I push him forward until he topples and use my weight and force to hold him down by the back of the neck, pulling back his left arm, waiting for the pop of his shoulder.

"You cunt!" he grunts out in agony. He tries to shake me off, but I hold him in position. Grabbing him by his chestnut hair, I smash his face into the tiles as hard as I can, not once, but twice. As his body relaxes under mine, I leap off him and race for escape.

As the door opens and the air hits my face, gunfire makes me jump and glass shatters next to my head.

"Do not take another step or my next bullet will be in the back of your skull, Charlotte."

I hold up my hands. He knows my name.

"Turn around," he commands.

I do, slowly, keeping my head down.

"Look at me."

As I slowly bring my chin up, he looks at me with amusement. And then down to his man on the ground.

"Is Emil dead?" He raises a brow, his pistol pointing between my eyes.

"P-probably not, I don't aim to kill." My voice shakes.

He slowly nods as he moves towards me, I instinctively step back.

I suck in a breath as his aftershave assaults my nostrils and I shiver in fear as he runs his fingers along my bare arm.

"We will have a lot of fun, Charlotte. I can see it now. You will make the perfect wife."

My heart stops. The blood drains from my face. I snap my eyes up to him and he laughs.

"Daddy didn't tell you that?"

I shake my head and he presses the muzzle of the pistol between my breasts.

"You could now be my most valuable asset. He's paid off his debt and more. Perhaps I will keep him alive if you behave. Can you do that for me, printsessa?" he whispers in my ear. The acid burns my throat as I take in his words.

I'm frozen.

I hear my dad's faint whimpers coming from the kitchen. He's injured. But alive.

I look into the devil's black eyes and my fate is sealed. Visions of my mom falling to the floor terrorize me. There's no escape. But I can play a clever game perhaps, my dad's words of warning fresh in my mind.

I'm trained to survive.

This might be the worst eighteenth birthday in the history of birthdays.

But if my years in martial arts have taught me anything, it's that I can fight.

So I nod.

CHAPTER 1

DECLAN

Five Years Later…
Song- Insanely Illegal Cage Fight

With fists clenched and my eyes locked on my brother, Conan, inside the cage, I can hear the frantic beating of my heart above the sounds of the arena.

He's known for being unpredictable, both in and out of the fight. The youngest of the three of us.

Six feet six inches of pure muscle.

Lethal.

Hence why me and Finn are in this dingy hell hole in Birmingham. We've learned to always bring backup to his fights.

We might have a peace truce with the Bowen's, but a single punch can change that.

This fight is different. It's fixed. As long as Conan listens to my orders, he will be allowed back in the cage to compete. He's been given one shot. By proving to the organizers he can listen to instructions and fall when he needs to.

Show them that he isn't the same man that beat a guy to death after Mom's death. It might be underground, but there is a limit. And Conan needs the cage like he needs air to breathe.

A sharp impact against my ribs announces Finn's arrival, making me stagger slightly to my left.

"The fuck?" I turn to him and notice his long fingers wrapped around the scrawny neck of some guy.

"I told you once to get out of my space. Bump into me again, I'll knock all your fucking teeth out," Finn seethes.

I grip his shoulder to calm him down. I can't have both brothers fighting tonight.

"Enough, Finn," I say under my breath, but loud enough for him to hear.

He releases the wide-eyed man, who gasps for air, clutching at his throat.

"Sorry, man," he says in a London accent. I roll my eyes in response.

Probably one of the many Bowen cousins.

We run our operations in Dublin, the Bowen's rule London.

Right now, our father and theirs have an agreement that's hanging on by a thread. The thread being this fight. They don't want Con back in the cage, so they pushed the organizers to make this fixed. A test they thought Con would fail.

Finn flips him off and shoves one hand in the pocket of his black overcoat. The other runs through his hair, sweeping it back into place.

"He goes down next round, right?" Finn asks discreetly.

I fiddle with the knuckle dusters in my coat.

"Yeah. He better fucking do it, too."

Finn shakes his head. "Perhaps you should have let me drug him a little. He might not get as angry in there."

"Not. Happening. Finn. Father's orders. What would he have said about us drugging our little brother before a fight?"

He winces, almost in pain, and I know I've struck a chord. We protect each other. Even from ourselves sometimes.

"Calm down, Dec. I was joking. He'd beat my ass if I tried anyway."

I wince as James, Conan's opponent, the youngest son of our lifelong enemies, knocks his fist into Conan's nose. Of course it had to be a Bowen he's fighting. The best they've got too.

Even though it's fixed, they'll be gloating James beat Conan fair and square.

Blood pours from his nostrils that he furiously wipes away, and a chilling switch flickers in his eyes.

"Declan," Finn warns, knowing that deadly look Conan has as well as I do.

The cold metal of the cage bites into my skin as I reach the edge and grip the bars.

"Don't you dare fuck this, Con," I almost scream, trying to snap him out of it.

He looks over to me and his crimson stained teeth appear as he smiles.

"Lose your head. I'll kill you myself," I shout.

James hurls himself at Conan, his grip like a vise on Conan's waist as the impact sends Conan's back crashing into the cage with a sickening thud.

Conan lets out a ferocious roar, the raw power in his voice mirroring the brutal force of his fists pounding into James's skull.

The blows echo through the basement.

The crowd erupts into a flurry of cheers. As I glance across the other side of the room, my eyes lock with Arthur.

The eldest brother of the Bowens. His face is serious as he slowly shakes his head at me.

A warning.

"Conan!" I bang my fists against the cage frantically.

He has one more round.

I let out a shaky breath as the bell's clang, and James is roughly pulled from Conan's grasp.

"I'm going to fucking kill you!" James spits blood next to Conan's feet.

Fuck. Those are the last words Conan needs to hear. He takes threats very seriously.

With a pounding heart, I run to the entrance with Finn hot on my heels, and together we storm towards Conan.

As he wipes the damp sweat clinging to his skin, I grab his face, forcing his gaze to meet mine.

"I need you to listen to me, very fucking carefully, brother."

His nostrils flare as Finn patches him up with petroleum jelly and ice on his eye.

"You go down on your ass in the next round, no fucking around. You don't get a choice here, Conan. You want to keep fighting in the cage, listen to me for fucking once in your life." I warn.

He grunts, spitting out his mouthguard.

Mom's death hit him hard. He was her little boy. Even when he towered over her, she was the only person to tame him.

Now, no matter how much me, Finn, or our father try, it falls on deaf ears.

He's a tank of anger waiting to erupt.

"I said I'll do it, so I'll do it."

I slap his cheek in an attempt to bring him back.

"Don't let me down, brother. We can't afford a war."

Not yet, anyway.

He nods, avoiding eye contact with me as I release him and step back.

Finn's worried frown and the furrow in his brow are clear as we head down the creaky, old wooden stairs.

"How armed exactly are we, Declan?" Finn asks from beside me, retrieving his flat cap from his inside pocket.

We have men dotted around the venue, a getaway driver, and enough blades on us to have everyone in here bleeding out.

But you can never underestimate the London guys.

They fight dirty and they fucking hate our guts. The feeling is mutual.

As we resume our positions at the side of the ring, I slide the cool metal over my fingers. Better to be safe than sorry.

When the bell rings, my heart races.

Don't fuck this up, Con.

The fight resumes. Two minutes is all he has to fall on his ass and tap out.

Conan clenches his bare fists and charges at James. Pulling back his arm, his fist connects to his nose again. Blood sprays out, making me grit my teeth.

"He's just making it look believable, Dec."

I shake my head. We're fucked.

James reacts instantly, a left hook followed by a straight right to Conan's gut, the impact audible even from across the ring.

He doubles over and takes a step back.

James's stellar uppercut lands with a sickening thud on Conan's jaw, making him wobble.

Go down. Go down. I'm almost praying.

"Your mom was a dirty, useless whore."

Those will be the last words James ever utters. I rub my hand over my face and take a deep fucking breath.

Conan straightens his legs and smirks at James.

"Shit," I hiss.

A quick yet powerful jab lands on James's cheek. Followed by another, and another.

It's almost too easy for my brother.

James stumbles back and I close my eyes.

I can't even hear the crowd over the blood pounding in my ears.

"The asshole is going to get us killed," Finn says, drawing me to watch.

Conan's fists become a blur as he unleashes a flurry of punches on his opponent.

It's a fucking bloodbath.

James collapses to the ground and Conan jumps on top of him, easily shrugging the ref off.

Sliding my flip knife from my pocket, I hold it in my right, while my left is covered with a pair of brass knuckles.

There's a strict no gun rule down here.

Fury engulfs me as I set sights on my asshole brother. Racing into the ring, I stop when I see James' mangled face, the ref nursing his own after an elbow to the cheek. Conan sits back and I grab him by the neck.

"Your ass should have been on the canvas before this point, you cunt," I hiss. "Get up."

I square up to him, asserting my place. He might be a couple of inches taller than me, but I am above him in authority.

Even if he challenges that every day.

I'll continue to remind him who the hell he is in the pecking order.

"I'm sorry—"

I hold up my hand.

"Don't fucking talk to me," I dismiss him.

No matter how angry I am, this can wait until we're all safe.

I scan the room. Arthur is no longer in his original position. He's our major concern.

I toss the flip knife to Con. The room is in utter chaos.

Fists flying, men cheering, chairs beating against the cage.

"Defend yourself only. This is not our territory. Follow me."

Grabbing another blade from my pocket, I quickly jog down the stairs. As a fist hurtles toward my face, I snatch the guy's forearm, twisting it and sending a hard blow into his face. The impact sounds like a dull thud.

We're going to have to beat our way out of this hellhole. I spot Finn nearer the exit with the twins, Rowan and Reggie. With adrenaline fueling my every move, I barge my way through the fighting crowd.

"Oi. Irish cunt." I hear from my left in a Cockney accent. Clenching my fist with the duster, a brawny man, smelling of sweat and stale beer, barrels into me, the impact jarring my teeth. I grab him as I'm propelled backward, my muscles screaming in protest. I unleash a flurry of punches into the back of his head until his grip loosens. As he charges again, I instinctively step back and then grab him by the face, digging my thumbs into his eyes.

His screams rip through me, only fueling my fire further.

He digs his fingers into my arms as I spin us around and push him headfirst into the brick wall.

He's down for now.

Straightening my jacket, I reenter the brawl. Keeping my wits about me, but monitoring Conan and Finn as best I can, I make my way to the exit.

I punch my way through to Con, who is using his sheer power to pummel through the crowd.

"Fuck you!" He grabs the guy by the shoulders and smashes his forehead into his, then drops him to the ground.

"Good job, you've got no fucking brain cells." I grin at him.

Before Con can reply, he winces in pain. I cringe seeing the knife shoved in his side.

Blind rage consumes me. Moving swiftly, I grab the slender blond man by his hair and forcefully push my blade beneath his chin. As I slide out my weapon, I drop him to the floor, looking back at Con.

"Let's fucking go! This way!" Finn shouts.

"Shit, this stings." Conan moans. He breaks into a jog and I follow towards the side exit.

The freezing air hits my face, stinging my cheeks, and I suck in a sharp breath. Finn and Con jump into the truck, their laughter echoing in the frosty air.

As I take a step forward, I'm stopped by someone clearing their throat to my left.

"Mr. Declan Quinn."

Arthur-fucking-Bowen.

Clutching my blade tightly, I turn to face him. He's leaning against the brick wall, slowly dragging on his cigarette.

"Quite the performance. I knew that beast didn't have the brains to listen." He pushes himself up and steps in front of me. His dark eyes are full of pain.

"The truce is over."

"I gathered," I respond, deadpan.

"I hope you're ready for war, Declan. I've been waiting a long fucking time for you to screw this up. We're coming for your empire."

He pauses, taking another drag.

"And we will burn it to the ground and bury you all alongside your whore mother."

My jaw ticks.

I know better than to react. Their words don't hurt me.

I know we won't be defeated, nor will they take shit from us.

Our operations are bigger. We have more men. These assholes are a thorn in our side.

"I look forward to it, Arthur. Just be very careful. You may believe you are larger than life, and you may well be." I square up to him, flicking the cigarette out of his hand.

"In a single city. But no one outside knows who you are. You are meaningless. You have no allies. Our empire is more secure than yours. Remember that before making threats."

I brush off the stray ash from my coat and step back.

"Anyway, it's up to our fathers to decide."

He grunts in annoyance. I know his game. It wouldn't surprise me if this sick fucker wanted his own brother dead for power.

"You owe us. We lost a lot of cash from your brother's failure."

I roll my eyes.

"Give me the number. I'll wire it across personally once we're home."

Everyone has a price.

"You think money can fix this?" he scoffs.

A casual shrug is my only response.

"That's all you lot are after, ain't it? More money so you can sniff it up your nose and forget all your posh boy problems, ay?"

He lets out a deep chuckle, pulling out his packet of cigarettes.

"You better hope James pulls through," he tells me, the threat evident in his tone.

I keep my facial expression neutral. It does not look promising.

I'd guess brain damage. I'm sure our doc, Finn, can give us a better idea. But he's right. Their father, Charles, will declare a war for this.

I told my father this was a stupid idea, that Conan wasn't mentally ready to be let loose in the ring yet.

He didn't listen, and look where that got us.

CHAPTER 2

CHARLOTTE

The rhythmic thud of my fists against the heavy bag fills the air as I unleash punches. My arms burn until spots dance before my eyes.

This is my escape.

The violence flows through my veins. I let out a scream as I swing back my leg and propel it onto the leather.

Every punch. Every kick. I release some of the pain inside me.

Today more than most. The five-year anniversary of my mom's death.

The day I watched the life drain from her.

The last day I was ever Charlotte.

Now, I am Vlad's property. His spy. His assassin.

The first month I was here, I was locked away in a basement. Just after our 'wedding', Drago found me. That moment marked the change in my role here. That is how I became an important player in Vlad's operation. Drago saw my skill and he forged a deal to let me use it.

But I had to stay a secret from the outside world. Even Tatiana. The woman who rules this family has no idea I exist.

Today also marks one thousand, eight hundred, and twenty-five days of plotting his demise.

I've learned a lot. I've listened and crept through the house looking for my perfect escape plan.

Nothing has fit into place that wouldn't risk my father's life.

That's even if he is still living. I draw in a deep breath. He is alive, Drago told me so. I trust him.

Mocking slow clap cuts through the silence as I press my head against the bag, gasping for air. The fabric smells faintly of sweat and dust.

Relief washes over me as Drago's deep Russian accent fills the gym.

"I see your shoulder has healed nicely."

With a grunt, I push myself upright, wiping the sweat from my forehead, my muscles aching, and turn to face him.

"Wanna fight?" I ask, putting up my fists.

He grins, a flash of white teeth against his tanned face, as he closes the distance.

He slides his tattooed hands down the front of his navy suit jacket.

He's a beast of a man. Ripped, dangerous, and a master of the martial arts.

That's how our friendship blossomed. He took me under his wing to train me to become a force to be reckoned with.

Yet, by day, he chooses other business activities. Boring ones that required tailored suits and acquisitions.

"I don't have time. Busy schedule."

I huff and roll my eyes.

"Sounds utterly dull, Drago. You should come on a job with me." I grin, rubbing my hands together.

I've been trying to get rid of Misha as my outside handler for months.

He's an asshole. A fucking sex pest and someone I want to add to my tattoo collection one day.

Drago chuckles a low rumble in his chest as he approaches, slamming his fist hard into the punchbag making a satisfying thud.

"Impressive for a business boy," I tease.

He holds it still, his light green eyes bore into me.

Great. That means there's news.

"I take it I have a job?" I tilt my head.

That brief rush runs through me. I get to leave this mansion. Even if it's temporary, it's something.

Away from my husband.

Even if it means the greasy-haired Misha is breathing down my neck.

I shudder.

"You do. You might enjoy this one." He grins, running a hand through his dark blond hair.

"Why? There's an escape plan?"

He glares at me.

"Patience, Charlotte. There are lots of pieces at play here. You and your father are alive. Outside, you won't be."

I sigh. I know damn well that's the case. I live every day with this carrot dangled in front of me.

In an ideal world, I run and get a new identity and save my dad.

But I'm too valuable to Vlad. Especially now that I've been trained to kill.

There isn't anyone else in his force that has the wits and the skills, unfortunately for me.

"I'm alive, but I'm not safe here."

I look down at my bare feet on the mat. Vlad is clever. He doesn't leave physical marks often. No, those scars are inside.

He's my tormentor.

And one day, when the time is right, he will suffer.

What I've learned so far is that the Kovalyov family is powerful. Especially under Tatiana's reign. Although, there is another family, the Volkov's, who seem to cause issues.

Drago is right. On my own, I would not survive. I would be dragged back here, my father would be killed, and my life would be worse than what I have to endure now.

For now, my freedom is in these jobs.

If that was taken away, I would have nothing.

"I know, Drago. But how long? I've been here for five years. I can't do another five."

His face softens.

"You can because you're a warrior, Charlotte."

"One day, you're going to have to tell me why you want to help me."

He smirks, holding the bag in place, and nods at me to go.

So I do. I let out a barrage of punches. Quick and sharp.

"Like I said. Lots of pieces in this chess game, Charlotte. Just be thankful I am on your side."

"Fine. What's the job then?"

"Italy. A five day trip. We're tracking a guy, one who doesn't want to be found."

Ruffling my hair through my fingers, I straighten my spine.

"So extract and bring to Russia?"

Drago's eyes go wide and he shakes his head.

"He is not our mark. Do not even let him know you're there. This is one chess piece we do not fucking touch."

I groan.

"But that's my fun. Have I been demoted to tail work?" I frown. I haven't stepped a foot out of line.

"No. You'll have your fun. You will stay in the shadows and identify the person he is meeting. And then, that person is the one you take. We have a unit set up. You take him there, you find out what the meet was about and why. Anything you can get on the purpose of their relationship."

I tap my finger against my lips.

"Still sounds boring, Drago."

He chuckles and shakes his head.

"Once you have the information. You kill him."

I smile brightly at him and run my palm along the ink on my forearm. An array of beautiful flowers on branches wrapped around my skin.

His vision follows my hand.

"Yes. So another tattoo is required. What flower this time?" He nods at the ink.

I raise my shoulders in a nonchalant gesture.

"Depends on the personality and type of kill. I like them to have meaning."

He raises an eyebrow. I have lots of fun hobbies. Because of boredom and keeping my brain busy to forget the hell I live in.

Tattooing is a hobby that stuck.

Each kill is rewarded by a flower. A representation of the lives I've taken and made into something beautiful.

And a reminder of the monster I've become. But killing these men takes some of my pain away.

"Okay, so follow, extract, interrogate, and kill. Easy. I take it I have the asshole, Misha, with me?" I ask, crossing my arms over my chest.

"Unless you kill him, which will raise many questions I may not be able to cover up, you're stuck with him."

I pout my lips in annoyance.

"Don't give me ideas, Drago."

He pulls up his sleeve and checks his Rolex.

"One day, he will get what's coming to him, voitelnitsa, *warrior*. Just don't let it be you who lands the blow."

He straightens his tie and gives me a nod.

"Don't overwork that shoulder. Italy is an unpredictable place. You can't have a weakness."

Instinctively, I rub the area. It was only a small wound needing a couple of stitches.

"Is Vlad returning before I leave?"

I hold my breath, hoping the next word to leave his mouth is no.

He chews the inside of his mouth and my heart sinks.

"He will be back in a few hours, according to Emil."

I have kept my distance from the family. Vlad and his brother, Emil, are evil. Not that I have gathered any information on him. Only that he has a son.

"I'll check in as usual throughout the trip." He pulls out a cell from his pocket and holds it out in his palm.

"You'll have a day or two. Use it to relax. Be Charlotte for a day?" He offers me a sad smile.

"I don't know who she is anymore, Drago."

His hand clasps down on my good shoulder.

"She's in your heart. She's there. You're fighting to keep her there until it's safe again. Never lose your spark. It's keeping you, your dad, and probably me alive at this point."

My breath hitches.

"He's fine, Charlotte. Vlad may be evil, but he keeps his word so long as you keep this up."

With that, he releases his grip and I clutch the phone in my hand.

"I'll see you on the other side." I grin before adding, "Maybe."

The constant threat of me running away keeps him on his toes.

It also helps me assess his reactions. If he's hiding anything from me, I'll read it in his eyes.

"You are many things, Charlotte. But running away in fear is not who you are." His fist hits his enormous chest.

"Only teasing." I stick my tongue out and hear his laugh as he walks down the hall. I turn to look into the floor-to-ceiling mirror and stare into my dark blue eyes.

Charlotte is in there somewhere.

I pull my hair over my shoulders, letting it cascade down my front, stopping just over my breasts.

A smile twitches at my lips as the sun beats on the deep purple strands scattered through the ends.

The first color I've actually stuck with.

Maybe I can fit in one more round in the gym before Vlad's home to ruin my day.

CHAPTER 3
DECLAN

My knuckles turn white as I brace myself and knock on my father's door, the wood cold beneath my touch.

"Come in, son," his deep voice booms through.

I'm angry at him, but he's probably more furious with me.

Twisting the knob, it creaks open, revealing him sitting behind his desk, a glass of amber whiskey swirling in his hand. The scent of aged oak and leather hangs heavy in the air.

Losing Mom last year has aged him.

She was the better half of him. The good part. That made him the father we needed him to be.

Perhaps it was the shock. One minute she was fine, cooking us our Sunday dinner. Within an hour of us leaving, her heart gave out, and Dad couldn't save her. Nor could the doctors.

She was gone and our family has been left with a gaping hole.

"You don't need to fuckin' knock, boy," he tells me with a grin, pouring my glass of whiskey as I take a seat opposite him.

"It's ten a.m." I joke.

"Shove it in some coffee, then. Us Quinns are made of steel."

I nod, accepting the fiery drink, and knock it back in one gulp. The burn chases away some of my anger.

I can't be mad at the old man. He made me who I am today.

"James's dead, Declan." There's a hint of worry in his voice.

"I thought that might be the case. He was mangled."

Dad looks down at his wedding ring and sighs.

"I got off the phone with Charles Bowen this morning. It ain't good, son. We need to make the moves now." He gives me a knowing look.

Meaning our alliance with the States. We have an opening to set a fresh path there, through a guy named Enzo.

We haven't seen the need. Our shipping routes are well established, with enough guns and drugs being moved to fund our empire. And we funnel it through our whiskey distillery. It's a neat cycle. It's worked for generations.

"What's our plan?" I ask as I roll up my sleeves and lean back.

He shakes his head.

"Son, it's about time you oversaw this. I'm getting too old, and the likelihood is we're about to have a war on our doorstep. I need you and your brothers out of the way. I don't want an American empire for myself, I want it for my sons. And only you can do that for me."

I swallow the lump in my throat. He's trained me my entire life for this role.

Everything has been calculated. I am the strategist. The leader. Conan, the muscle, fearless and loyal, and Finn. He's our superpower. Unimaginably clever and devious. A trainee surgeon by day, and lord knows what he gets up to at night.

Nothing gets past him. No one crosses him. It's like he sees the future. He knows what will go down before it does.

"You know I've got this, Dad. But how?"

He shrugs, pouring himself another glass.

"I've set you a meeting with Enzo. He has, let's say, opportunities for you boys. It's a whole new world over there. And once you're set up, we can merge the Irish branch with the American branch. The Quinns will be unstoppable."

Scratching my stubble, I let the ideas swirl around in my brain. There's always a fucking cost.

"At what price?"

He throws his hands up in the air.

"I don't know. Enzo isn't a man of many words. But he has connections, he has power. If we are aligned with him, you boys will be safe."

"You want me to sell my soul?" I chuckle, but he doesn't join me.

He frowns, running a hand through his white hair.

"Maybe part of it. Being a boss is a ruthless game. There is no time for weakness, boy. I know you have it in you. Let the world believe the Quinn brothers are true embodiments of evil. The villains of this game. It will give you respect. You want them to fear you. That's the only way you can play to win. But just never lose that golden heart your mother gave you. Keep her alive through her boys for me."

Fuck.

I rub at my chest as the pain radiates. I miss her so damn much.

She was the light in our dark lives. There was nothing a hug from her couldn't solve.

There was even comfort to be found when she slapped us on the back of the head.

She was our safe space. And now she's gone. All four of us are lost.

Maybe this new start is what we need. Build a new empire.

"I understand."

"Good. I'm confident you'll do well. Just keep an eye on Conan. His temper is your only weakness that I see."

"He wasn't ready to fight again, Dad. I told you."

A sadness washes over his face. I can sense his disappointment.

"I know, son. I know. I just thought maybe going back to the one thing he found joy in would be the answer."

I can't help but laugh.

"You let a killing machine in a cage and expected no blood?"

That gets a smile out of him.

"Lapse in judgement. I'm getting old. All he had to do was fall on his ass and we'd have a boatload of cash right now."

My eyes roll, a clear sign of my exasperation.

"We don't need money. And since when has Conan ever listened to us?"

He chews his lip, deep in thought. Almost as if he is reminiscing as he smiles.

"He only listened to your mother. Remember that time at school when he nearly strangled that boy to death for stealing his sandwich?"

I shake my head, a chuckle rumbling in my chest.

"How the fuck could I forget that? Mom was furious. I've never seen her that mad. I vaguely recall a saucepan being thrown at the wall."

"Yep. That was her. Sweet as pie until you pissed her off, then all hell broke loose."

That glimmer in his eye appears. It's there every time he talks about her.

"She was angry because he publicly embarrassed the family name. Not because he defended himself. That was her motto. She wanted you guys to be respected outside. Not thugs. But behind the scenes, she had no issues with seeking revenge. If Conan would have gone to the boy's house in the middle of the night and then taught him a lesson, without a crowd, she wouldn't have batted an eye. It's about being feared for the right reasons."

I solemnly nod. Even talking about her, the memories, as much as they bring joy, bring pain alongside them.

"Good job we have you, then. We can get through to Conan."

He looks up at the clock and back at me, his dark blue eyes burning into me.

"This old man won't be around forever, son."

"You're sixty-eight. Plenty of years left."

He spins the glass on the wooden table.

"I hope so. But honestly, just know when I go, I'll be at peace with it. I miss your mother, and you boys have each other."

"You ain't going anywhere."

He can't. We need him.

"Now, back to Enzo. You three are going to take a little trip." He smirks.

I raise a brow. "To where?"

"Italy," he replies.

"When?"

"Tonight. Jet is ready. You just have to pack."

He pulls out a burner phone from his desk drawer and slides it across to me.

"His men will meet you on the landing strip. You will have to pass a test first to secure the meet."

I twirl the cool, smooth ring on my index finger, feeling its weight.

"A job in Italy? That sounds fun."

"Be prepared for anything, son. Use your brothers to your advantage, but I suspect it will be mostly on you. You represent the Quinns to Enzo."

My heart pounds a rapid rhythm of excitement and apprehension, a mixture of anticipation and dread.

"You trust Enzo?"

"I would not send my eldest son to meet him if I didn't. He's a businessman. But he's far more than that. Do not underestimate his power nor skill. If you win him over, the world is at your feet. If you piss him off, he will destroy everything we've built. For the love of God, do not cross him. Ever, Declan. There isn't a place on this earth he couldn't hunt you down. The man sees and knows everything."

"Perfect. He's omnipotent. What could possibly go wrong?"

"Nothing if you keep him on your side. Mr. Testa is the God of the mafia underworld. If he allows us in, that power is shared."

I slide the phone into my jacket pocket.

"I have faith that once he meets you, he will see what I see in you. Powerful. Ruthless. A born leader. It's natural to you, son. You will make the Quinn family great again."

"No pressure," I chuckle.

There is. A lot of it. The weight of our empire is on my shoulders.

"Diamonds form under pressure, boy. That's how we got here, and that's how we move forward."

I nod.

"How come we never heard of him before this point if he's that big of a deal?"

He lets out a deep chuckle and shakes his head.

"Only he decides who knows of his existence. The mere fact we know his name, means he sees value in us. If he asks you to get on your knees and kiss his fucking boot, you do it."

I scoff.

"Let's hope he doesn't have a thing for boot kissing," I joke.

Pushing myself up out of the chair, I stand.

"Conquer the world, son. You'll do me proud. I know you will." He taps his fist over his heart.

"I'll do everything I can, Dad." I nod to him and head towards the door.

I've had twenty-nine years to prepare for this.

"I don't say this enough, but I love you, Dec. You and your brothers mean everything to me."

The sincerity in his voice makes me stop.

I turn to face him one last time and smile.

"We all love you too."

CHAPTER 4
CHARLOTTE

I shove the last black swimsuit in my duffle bag. Drago told me I'd have a few days to relax while we wait for intel.

I'll take it. My body is exhausted. I know I'm damn good at my job, but he has plenty of men trained to kill. Yet, I seem to be the one constantly hunting.

No, they probably aren't as skilled as me. But if they worked harder, they could be.

I dedicated my life to martial arts. And now he's molded me into a killing machine.

Taking the life of another is the only thing keeping my own heart beating.

And the more jobs I take, the less time I have to spend with Vlad.

I freeze as I zip shut the bag. That's how I know he's in the doorway. My body alerts me to danger. It goes into protection mode.

I turn to face him, his gaze locking with mine across the dimly lit room, a strange silence filling the space between us.

Six feet tall, his dark hair cut short, and a long, thin scar sliced across his left eye. A pale line against his tanned skin. To most women, he's probably attractive. But it's what lies behind his eyes that gives the real version away.

There is a dark evil that lies beneath them.

Tatiana might be the head of this family, but the awful shit they do, that's all this man. The puppet master and he controls us all.

"How dangerous is he? This Enzo guy." I ask.

Vlad swipes his thumb across his lip. His eyebrow with the slit twitches. That's how I sense his fear.

"Dangerous to you? Probably not unless you are caught. It's not what he can do, it's what he knows."

Jesus fucking Christ, the riddles of this family.

I pinch the bridge of my nose to try to reduce my annoyance. I know what happens to me when I have an attitude. And I don't want that.

"What does he know?"

With a careless shrug, he dismisses the comment, the sound of his jacket rustling faintly.

"That's what I'm trying to find out, malyshka. We stole something he wants back. We have to ensure he never finds out it's here."

"So what am I asking? What do you have?"

My head shakes involuntarily as I try to make sense of the situation.

"It's better for interrogation purposes that you don't know."

Fuck, I want to punch him in the throat.

He's probably making the right call. I'd throw my "husband dearest" under the bus to save myself.

Vlad knows I'll never love him. I make that damn clear every day.

The second I have an opening to escape, I will make time to shove his wedding ring down his throat.

"Okay. Fine. Got it. So find out who Enzo is meeting, intercept them, interrogate, and then kill them."

Another flower to add to my forearm. That makes me smile, but not in front of him. He doesn't deserve to see that. He never has and he never will.

"Correct. Then report straight back to Misha with the information. Should be easy for you. You should thank me, actually, for this vacation."

I choke on a cough. A vacation.

"It's work, not a holiday."

He steps forward and my stomach sinks as I watch that darkness take over his eyes.

His rough fingers dig into my cheeks, his stale, smoky breath is hot on my face as he hauls me off of my feet.

"Get on your fucking knees, malyshka, and thank your husband for keeping you alive. Thank him for giving you a purpose in this world. And when I shove my cock in that tight pussy, that is you thanking me for this vacation."

The reason it's tight is that it's so damn dry because I hate him and every time he touches me.

I hiss out a breath as he throws my back against the wall and he grabs my throat so hard my lungs burn.

"What do you say?"

Bile rises into my throat.

"Y-yes. Sir."

I know when to pick my arguments. Now is not the time to, not when I'm unarmed, on my own, and vulnerable.

Not when with one call he can kill my father.

He shoves me down to my knees and I look away.

I'd rather he cut me up than do this to me. Every time it tears away parts of me and replaces it with evil.

I am the evil that he created. Exactly how he wanted, so he could use me to build his empire.

The woman in the shadows everyone is afraid of. The woman who rips out hearts.

When actually, I'm just a woman fighting to save herself.

I wasn't born evil.

I was molded, shaped, and twisted into this monstrous form.

And one day, I'll use every ounce of pain he's inflicted on me to destroy him.

We will both burn in the fires of hell for our sins, but I will make sure he suffers the flames before me.

It's just a waiting game.

As he rips open his pants, I recite that line in my head to get me through this.

One day, it will all be over.

He can't break me.

I won't let him.

My husband. My abuser. The only way I'm leaving this earth is by taking him with me.

CHAPTER 5

DECLAN

Finn leans over Conan, who's nestled between us, his eyes questioning mine.

Yes, being bundled into the back of a truck by two Italian guys when our jet arrived was not how we pictured this going.

But we have to prove our worth to Enzo.

A pothole causes the truck to lurch, and I instinctively tense up as a protective reflex, Conan's head hitting the roof.

"Jesus fuck," Conan hisses.

I whack his arm.

The driver grunts and carries on, the vehicle slowing down on the gravel.

I keep facing forward, even when my door opens to reveal the blinding sunlight and its warmth on my skin.

I turn to a new face, one with slicked-back black hair shining with an oily sheen. Probably mid-thirties.

He extends a strong hand, his grip firm as I accept the handshake.

"Declan, I'm Romeo. Second in command to Enzo," he says, his rich Italian accent coming through.

"Nice to meet you, Romeo."

"Please." He gestures for me to get out of the truck.

Stepping out into the scorching sun, I brush down my dark suit jacket, already damp with sweat.

As Conan shuffles out, Romeo holds up his hand, his head shaking slowly, a silent command to stop.

"No. Just you." He looks at me sternly.

Conan's face begins to redden.

"It's fine, Con," I say calmly.

He visibly relaxes and I turn to Romeo.

"Just me today?"

He nods, the metallic click of the truck door lock echoing in the stillness as he shoves the keys into his pocket.

"Trust is earned. Three of you and one of me?" He shakes his head with a laugh. "I don't think so. I've seen what you Irish are capable of."

I frown. But I understand.

Enzo and his men are smart.

"And leverage. If I fuck up, you have my brothers. You know I won't do anything out of line to harm them."

He taps a finger against his temple, a slow grin spreading across his face.

"Ah. You get it. Now follow me." He turns and takes his gun from the holster.

"You're not armed, but you've got a blade, correct?" he says over his shoulder.

How the hell?

"Yeah. That's right."

He stops in the gravel and turns to me, his face serious.

"You know a knife makes you armed? Correct?"

I nod.

"And Enzo specifically instructed you to come unarmed."

Straightening my spine, the extra inches giving me a commanding view over him.

"So why did you defy his order?" He continues.

"Trust. Romeo. You don't walk into a war zone unarmed when you don't know who you're up against. I don't step foot outside of my house without a blade on me. That never changes."

I shove my hand in my pocket, my expression remaining neutral.

"Being unarmed is reckless."

A slow smirk, revealing a flash of white teeth, spreads across his lips. He's amused, maybe impressed.

"What's to say you don't slice that across my throat?" He tilts his head.

"Because you know we need Enzo more than he needs us. And you have my brothers locked in a scorching truck."

Everything today is a test.

"Let's go," he tells me and stalks off.

Following him to the metal unit at the end of the track, I watch as he shoves the door open with a loud screech of metal and fires an echoing bullet into the ceiling.

"Miguel. Get the fuck out here now!" he bellows.

A man in his fifties storms out of the back office, the weight of the world dragging down his shoulders. Sweat drips from his thick, dark brows, and he wipes it away with a trembling hand, like the truth he doesn't want to say is already burning his skin.

"Declan, go check the back, make sure no one else is inside. Count the crates."

"Got it."

I head further through the warehouse. Stacks and stacks of crates, up to the ceiling. Retrieving my knife, I check behind each one and count, the temptation of opening one of the wooden boxes eating away at me.

By the time I get that done and head back to Romeo, a cacophony of shouting in Spanish hits me. As I round the corner, I stop when I find Miguel on his knees with his hands behind his head and Romeo pressing his gun against his forehead.

I approach slowly.

"Thirty-nine," I tell him.

Romeo's eyes darken as he glares at Miguel.

"We save you. We pay you well. We give your daughters a new life in Italy. And this is how you repay us? By fucking stealing?" Romeo shouts in his face.

Miguel squeezes his eyes shut and shakes his head, his body trembling.

"I-I didn't. I promise. That is all the deliveries."

Romeo nods, taking a step back. An evil chuckle escapes him as he runs his fingers through his hair.

"You think I'm fucking stupid?"

He shoves his hand out and grabs Miguel by the neck, slamming him into the wall.

"I had my men watch over that delivery. We saw exactly who

you handed it over to. We tracked it down and retrieved it. Fifty thousand? You really risked your life for a measly fifty thousand? On a crate worth a hundred? You are the stupid asshole."

With a grunt, he releases his grip, sending the man sprawling to the ground, and then brings his foot down on his throat.

With my arms crossed tightly over my chest, Romeo thrust the gun toward me, his wild brown eyes filled with manic energy.

"Show me," he demands, his voice sharp and cutting through the silence.

"What?" I step forward.

"I'd like to see what you would do, as a boss to a traitor."

A slow, sly smile curves my lips as I carefully retrieve the heavy pistol, its weight familiar in my hand. Romeo slowly takes his foot off the man's neck, and he gasps, clutching at his throat.

I stand over him, his eyes wide with terror, his lips trembling as he whimpers.

"Please, sir." His voice trembles.

He looks at me for pity, and I laugh.

As he tries to sit up, I pull the trigger. The bullet rips through his shoulder. He collapses onto his back, his hand clamping down on the wound as scarlet blooms between his fingers, staining the ground. His wails fill the room like music to my ears.

Stepping over him, I position myself with one foot on each side of his waist, taking careful aim between his eyes.

"I'm sorry. Tell Enzo, I'm sorry. I will do better," he whimpers.

I don't even bother looking at Romeo.

"There are no second chances, Miguel."

His eyes go wide as I shoot a bullet right into the center of his forehead.

The blood, thick and dark, flows across the floor as I step over him, the gun feeling slick and cold in my hand as I hand it back to Romeo.

He purses his lips and nods in approval.

"Quick. To the point. No flinching. No second chances. I like that."

I shrug.

"Once you lose trust, there is no going back."

He clasps a firm hand onto my bicep.

"You'll work well with Enzo." He slides out a phone from his inside pocket and hands it over to me.

"He will contact you later with a time and location for your meet. You arrive unarmed, on your own, and on time. He doesn't do slacking. Understand?"

"Yes."

Sliding the phone in my pocket, I follow him back out to the truck. He opens up the door and I see the relief in Conan's face when he sees me.

Or maybe it's the fresh air, now that he can breathe.

"My driver will take you to the resort. Declan, you have the penthouse suite, your brothers are close by. Sit tight until you hear more."

I extend my hand to him. He accepts.

"I appreciate it, Romeo."

He steps back and nods to my brothers.

"Look forward to working with the Quinn brothers in the future."

With that, I hop in the truck and he slams the door closed behind me.

Finn leans forward with a grin. "All good?"

"As good as it can be for us, brother."

CHAPTER 6
CHARLOTTE

I hammer my fist on Misha's door, the sound loud enough to shake the frame.

"Evan!" I shout, banging harder.

We have cover names for this operation. Evan and Brittany. Brother and sister.

I shiver, just the thought of being related to this buffoon makes my skin crawl.

Stepping back, it creaks open, and there he is, his wet hair clinging to his forehead, water streaming down his skin, a white towel precariously covering his modesty.

He gives me a slow smirk, his eyes crinkling at the corners, and leaning casually against the frame.

"Can I help?" he mumbles, and I frown.

"I was going to the grocery store to pick up stuff for my room. Want anything?"

"Evan! Get back here, tiger!" a squeaky female voice shouts over the noise of the shower.

"Oh."

His creepy gaze rakes over my body. I slipped into a sleek, black bikini top and a flowing skirt earlier. I regret my decision.

His tongue darts out and licks his bottom lip.

"Condoms," he replies.

"I meant water, food. You know, stuff we didn't pack ourselves," I spit back.

God, he's vile.

And how the hell, in the matter of an hour, did he get a woman in his room?

Probably paid her.

As I turn, the rasp of his throat clearing stops me. A silent roll of my eyes is my only response.

"You know, you can always join if you'd like. Alice would be more than happy to service you too. So would I, gorgeous."

Spinning to face him, I slam my foot down, the force rattling up my spine, fury pulsing through every vein like wildfire.

This motherfucker knows he can get away with it because I am Vlad's property.

He knows I'm kept in line. That I can't kill him, but holy shit, do I want to.

My fists clench tight, the pressure building in my forearms.

"We are here on a job, Misha. I've told you before and I'll tell you again. I. Am. Not. Fucking. Interested. Grow up before you get us killed."

His laughter, a cruel booming sound, fills my face as he jeers.

"Such a stuck-up princess. I guess Vlad must be giving it to you good, for you to not stray," he growls.

Disgusting.

Just mentioning it, I can feel my husband's disgusting hands on me.

Before I erupt and blow our cover, I flip him off with a sarcastic grin and stomp down the hall, taking my anger out on the elevator call button.

Fuck him. Fuck Vlad. Fuck men.

I take a deep breath and calm my raging thoughts, primarily of strangling them both to death and watching the life drain out of their eyes.

My dream.

As the elevator doors slide open, revealing a smiling couple, cooing over their fussy baby in a pushchair, I step in, pressing myself against the cool metal wall.

Looking at the buttons, the ground floor has already been pressed.

"Isn't she so sweet?" the woman whispers to her husband.

"Just like her momma." He kisses the side of her head almost proudly.

It's like the walls are closing in on me. My chest is heavy with sadness.

A grief over a life I'll never have.

A dream that I won't ever get to pursue. Because when I escape, it will never be safe to have a child.

I'm not even sure I'll find love, or if I even know what it is, for that matter.

As the elevator dings, I shake my head and let out a breath.

I just have to keep fighting and surviving.

That is enough. It has to be.

I gesture for the couple to go first. They give me a smile as they exit, and I hug my purse closer against my side.

Drago told me it's a "safe-ish" area, but to keep my wits about me. Like I ever let up.

I'm constantly in fight or flight. Usually fight.

Rushing through the bright white marbled reception area, I head out into the street. I look left and right, nothing.

I frown. Maybe the shops are on the other side of the resort.

I open up my bag and slide my hand in, rummaging for my cell.

There's a tug on my shoulder. I look up, and I'm staring into a set of unfamiliar, bloodshot eyes, his stale breath ghosting my face.

Probably mid-forties. Scruffy as hell.

I gaze down and find both of his filthy fingers on my bag. Dirt coats his nails and dried blood covers his skin.

I tug it back, but the thief doesn't let up, only tightening his grip.

"Lady. Give me the bag and I won't hurt you."

I bite back a grin, doing a quick scan of his body.

I don't see any weapons and both hands are on my belongings.

"You have three seconds to back the fuck up. If you don't, I'll show you what real pain is," I say, looking him dead in his dark eyes.

I am not afraid of him.

He should fear me.

CHAPTER 7

DECLAN

"**F**inn, keep an eye on Con at the bar. I'm just going to check if your room is ready yet at reception," I call out as I slide my sunglasses back over my eyes and get up off the lounge chair.

Finn has made it clear he isn't staying in the same room as Conan. And the resort didn't have both of their rooms ready when we arrived.

Some sort of mix-up with a brother and sister needing two rooms, not one.

Makes sense. I won't stay with my siblings either.

As I head in, I'm greeted by the young receptionist, offering me a bright smile as she wiggles her fingers at me.

I flash her a grin, but something catches my eye moving out the front through the windows.

I hold up my finger.

"I'll be back in one minute," I tell her, intrigue getting the better of me.

The closer I get, I blink, pushing my sunglasses to the top of my head.

Is that?

The electric doors open as I jog outside.

"Like a pretty little thing like you could hurt me," the short man laughs, and rage consumes me.

As I step forward, the dark-haired woman grabs him by the neck and puts him in a headlock.

45

I'm too stunned to move.

In awe but panic and confusion, too.

In one swift move, she jabs her hand into his arm, making him release his grip on her purse, and I swear to God, his body goes limp.

I quietly take a step forward. She knows what she's doing.

"Fucking men," she mutters, and I try not to laugh.

Her sweet voice. Her dainty yet athletic figure.

She drops him down on the ground with a sigh. When he starts to groan, I step closer.

Lifting my foot to hold him in place by the throat, but as I do, I see her clenched fist—hurtling straight towards my dick.

She lands it before I can protect myself.

"Fuck," I cry out. Doubling over, I grab hold of my manhood for dear life.

The pain.

It's in every vein, muscle, and bone. All of me.

I suck in a breath through my teeth.

"What the fuck?" I hiss.

Still unable to stand up. It's throbbing. My dick has a pulse in the worst possible circumstance.

Why is that kind of hot?

"Oh, shit. Are you okay?"

Her voice soothes me.

She spins to face me and she steals all the breath from my lungs. Magnificent.

Her big, round, deep blue eyes captivate me. A perfect contrast to her pale skin and jet black hair that blends into a deep purple in the curls at the end. Unique, yet stunning.

The air around us crackles. Time goes slow.

If I wasn't turned on already watching her beat that guy's ass, I sure am now.

Husky, well-spoken, a twinge of an accent I can't place. Almost American but not quite.

I cough, clearing my throat, and stand upright.

Those damn eyes.

Thick black lashes and the dark eyeliner just draws more attention to those pools of deep blue.

I'm fucking lost in them.

"Sir, are you okay?"

The sternness in her voice makes my cock twitch, and damn it, it hurts.

She just punched me in the dick. Yet, the way the word "sir" rolls off her pretty lips is captivating.

A twisted smirk appears as I look her up and down. A black bikini top, just about covering her full breasts, a toned stomach, but her ass is covered by the skirt. Dammit.

I take a step towards her and take a deep breath. Vanilla. Sweet. Of course she is.

"I'm fine."

I loom over her, my height emphasized by the way she tilts her head back, one eyebrow arching in curiosity.

And when she bites that glossy bottom lip, I lose it but keep my hands stuck to my sides so I don't touch her. I can't help but notice the beautifully intricate ink that spans her forearm. I wonder what else she is hiding?

"You want some ice for that?" Her eyes glance down at my crotch and then back up to me.

And just like that, my heart flutters. The hell is happening to me?

"Ice? I don't think I need that. Maybe something warmer and wet?"

I lick my lips, and she does the same.

"Something that will get you absolutely soaking?"

Jesus Christ.

"Yes. The wetter the better." I wink at her.

She twirls her black curl around her finger. In the light, I can see the strands of deep purple shining through, her nails pointy and sparkling silver.

Everything about her is hot as sin.

She taps on her lips with her pointy nails.

"Come with me?" she offers.

A playful grin stretches across her face as she holds out her open palm to me.

The second I slide my hand in hers, the air around me crackles, and a bolt of something sharp shoots up my arm, to the point I almost flinch.

She feels it too. She frowns and looks down at our interlocked fingers.

I let her lead the way, sneaking a view of her ass as she walks.

"You fight, I take it? Martial arts of some kind?"

"Umm. A mixture of a few."

I have visions of her snaking herself around me and taking me down to have her wicked way with me.

She pushes open the doors to reception and then takes the first door on the right.

The aromatic smell of chlorine almost makes me cough.

As we get to the second set, she stops, spins to face me, and pushes on my chest so my back hits against the wall.

Her nails drag down my abs and I let out a groan.

I lean down and hover my lips over hers.

I've never wanted to kiss a woman so badly in my life.

She brushes her nose along my stubble and her warm breath beats against my ear.

"Have fun in the Jacuzzi. You'll get nice and warm and absolutely soaking in there. Should fix you up nice."

I blink a few times. A chuckle escapes me, a soft, rumbling sound that feels good in my chest.

As she brushes her hair away from her shoulder, a sharp intake of breath escapes her lips when I gently lick her earlobe.

"I know for a fact what I actually want is soaking for me. I can smell your desire from here."

"We can't always get what we want in life, pretty boy." She smacks my ass, making me jump, and steps back.

Adjusting myself in my shorts, I pin her against the wall. My fingers snake around her throat, and her eyes go wide.

Yet she smiles. A deadly grin.

"What's your name, sweetheart?"

"Why? You need it to add to the list of women who have rejected you?"

I tighten my grip.

"You would be the only one on that list."

Her fingers delicately trail up my chest, and then she grabs my throat. Putting just the right amount of pressure on each side.

Pressing my nose against hers, we stare into each other's eyes.

"I can feel your heart racing, pretty boy. Rejection turns you on?"

I laugh.

"This is rejection? I can see your nipples through your bra. I bet if I slide my hand under that skirt, I'd find exactly what I'm looking for. Warm and soaking. All for me to feast on."

I swear a little moan escapes her lips.

Just imagining her screaming my name in my ear has my dick twitching so painfully.

CHAPTER 8
CHARLOTTE

Holy hell.

Who is this man?

I squeeze my fingers tighter around his neck, and that just makes him grin.

He's dangerous. Everything about him—the tattoos that span from his jaw, covering his entire body, even his fingers that are perfectly placed around my throat.

Those eyes are captivating, I could get lost in them. I've never seen a light blue so piercing.

And that grin. That smug, shit-eating grin I don't want to wipe off his face.

"You want me," he says confidently.

I do. But I'm not admitting that.

"Actually, I really want a chocolate milkshake."

He pushes my legs open with his thick thigh and presses his body against mine.

He's making pushing him away extremely difficult. So instead, I dig my nails into his neck as I squeeze.

"Maybe I want to lick chocolate milkshake out of your pussy and spit it in your mouth. There, we both win that way."

My body is becoming an inferno. His lips hover over mine, and I'm so close to saying fuck it.

The air crackles with anticipation as our lips near, only to have him pull away, his fingers ghosting along my cheek, leaving a trail of warmth.

"Think about it. I'm room five-oh-two. Penthouse. The code on the elevator is six-six-six. I've got an extremely bad sweet tooth and a dick that now requires CPR. It's only fair that the woman who injured it, heals it."

I don't know what to say.

I can't take my eyes off the enormous bulge in his shorts.

This cannot be happening.

"I'll see you around, heartbreaker."

"My name is Brittany." I smirk.

A grin spreads across his face as he shakes his head, his eyes crinkling at the corners.

"Lies. I'm Jimmy."

I hold on to the wall behind me as he turns and bashes open the door.

When I hear the splash of water, I let out a breath.

I have a job to do. I look up at the clock on the wall, watching it tick away in silence.

All I know is I need to go cool down and clear my head.

CHAPTER 9

DECLAN

"What the hell is up with you?" Finn snaps at me. He unloads another box of guns from the van into Romeo's truck.

"It's fucking boiling!" I tell him.

Wiping the sweat from my forehead as Conan easily picks up a box and tosses it in with a grunt.

We got a call early this morning about assisting with a job for Enzo as they're a couple of men down. What we didn't realize is we were the only ones on this job.

And we've been here for hours.

"Careful!" Me and Finn both shout at Con.

Conan brushes his hands together and slides down his sunglasses.

"Why don't you both just stop bitching and get on with it. Faster we do it, the quicker we can have a beer."

Finn shoots me a look, and I nod.

Conan has a fair point.

As I put my final box in the truck, we hop back in the van to return it to the warehouse.

"Not even a fucking thank you." Finn seethes.

As I turn the key in the ignition, the van jolts.

"It's all a test, brother. We're at the bottom of Enzo's food chain right now. We gotta work to be on top."

He taps his fingers on the dash as Conan turns up the air conditioner.

"Or… we stay in Dublin and fuck the America plan off? We don't need to expand here. We have the perfect setup back home."

As I drive onto the main road, I chew on my lip.

"Look, with everything going down with the Bowens, who knows how long our empire will stand? Dad wanted us here, this was his dream. He wouldn't have sent us for no reason, we gotta trust his gut."

Conan hums to himself so I turn up the music, and Finn smacks Conan on the arm.

"It's your fault we're fucking dying of dehydration here, you left the damn water I asked you to bring," Finn grumbles.

Conan laughs, but then his face drops to being dead serious.

"Wait, we're dying?"

I hold in the laughter and keep my eyes on the road.

"That's what you took from that sentence, Con?" Finn says, clearly irritated.

"Well, yea." Conan shrugs.

I look at him and give him a warning glare not to wind Finn up anymore.

"What? He's the fucking doctor here. If he tells me I'm dying, what the hell else am I supposed to think?"

As I indicate to take a left, heading on the straight back to the hotel, I zone out as those two bicker. I'm the eldest, they both listen to me. But they argue constantly between themselves.

As I pull up into the back of the lot, I hide the keys on the tire for Romeo to collect and grab my black T-shirt, putting it back on, it clings to my sweaty skin.

My dick aches and I adjust my pants.

"You caught something?" Finn laughs.

"No. I got punched in the dick earlier," I tell them quietly.

They both stop and look at each other, then back to me.

"What? Who? Did you kill him?" Con says, trying to hide his laughter.

"No, they're alive. And not a 'he', a 'she'. A very beautiful she."

Finn's eyes almost pop out of their sockets.

"Beautiful, hey? Someone's got a crush. Careful, you might actually end up with something."

I shake my head and slap his arm.

"Enough. Beer?" I ask my brothers, redirecting the direction of conversation.

They both look at me sporting the same menacing grin.

"Fuck yes," they say at the same time.

I rub my hands over my face in frustration. These two will be the end of me.

As they go to walk off, I put my hand out to stop them.

"Silence. I want the first drink in absolute silence. I don't want to hear a fucking word from either of you until I've finished. I don't even so much as want to hear you breathe. Clear?" I tell them.

"Whatever." Conan strolls off and Finn walks next to me.

"Somethings getting to you, Declan," he presses, and I sigh.

"I thought you were training to be a surgeon, not a psychiatrist."

"Ha-ha. Smart ass. It's that girl. Ain't it? The dick-puncher?"

My jaw ticks as I picture her. I can't explain it. Why did it feel like I was about to pass out when she looked at me?

It wasn't just looking at me. She saw through me.

No fear. No judgement.

She pressed my buttons and tricked me.

I rub my hand along my throat, right where she grabbed me.

There's something about this girl I can't put my finger on.

"I'll take your silence as a 'yes'."

I grunt, wanting to ignore my feelings. Or the fact I've been thinking all day about how I could get her to go on a date with me.

Something I never, ever do. But I want to learn more.

Like how she learned to fight.

And why there's so much pain behind her eyes.

"It's nothing, Finn. Don't worry," I tell him and walk ahead.

"Denying it only makes it worse," he calls out.

Denying what?

I just met her. It's not anything.

CHAPTER 10
CHARLOTTE

"Just go to the bar or something. I've got plans tonight." Misha brushes me off and opens the bathroom door.

"Plans? You had me scoping out the potential meet areas on my own today. You are meant to be *my* handler, not the other way around."

I stomp towards him and he spins to face me, his nostrils flaring.

"What're you gonna do about it, little princess?" he mocks, running his hand through his hair.

When he chuckles and shakes his head, I glare at him.

"Nothing. Just as I thought. Now run along. Go have a cocktail. Might loosen you up. This whole uptight, stick-up-your-ass thing you've got going on is not hot."

My fingers twitch by my side.

"And this whole manwhore thing you've got going on is doing you real good, isn't it?" I laugh.

He's a fucking useless mess.

"Shit at your job. No woman stays more than one night. Well, not even that if you pay them." I count on my fingers for dramatic effect.

"Shit haircut," I say, staring at him.

"Bitch," he hisses, and his hand flies towards me. I grab his forearm, digging my nails into his flesh as he cripples over.

Plunging my knee with full force into his gut, he cries out in pain.

I don't let go but tighten the grip. If I'm not careful, I'll dislocate his shoulder. Then he will be completely useless to me.

So I hold it where it is, enough not to do full damage.

"What was it you called me? 'Little princess'? How's that looking now? Huh?" I whisper in his ear.

"Get off."

"No," I snap back.

God, this feels good.

"Say sorry." I bite back a grin.

He growls, so I tug back just a tiny bit more, and he screams out like a little bitch.

He knows not to fight back in this position.

"Fine. I'm sorry."

I release him and he almost stumbles into the wall, and I can't hide my laughter.

"Asshole. I'll see you in the morning," I chirp.

I flip him off and stroll out of his door, slamming it behind me.

Adrenaline fuels me as I jog to the stairs.

Now I do need a drink so I don't go back in there and shatter his skull.

By the time I get to the bottom, I've calmed down slightly.

I'm less murdery.

Tugging my black dress down, I fluff up my long, big curls with my fingers and head to the restaurant area.

I hear the deep laughs and chattering from the main doors to my left, and as I take another step forward, I collide into something.

Holding out my hands to break the impact, I look up, completely flustered—into those beautiful blue eyes.

The air gets trapped in my throat, my mouth falls open, and it's like my brain turns to mush in his presence.

"S-sorry," I stutter.

His eyes track up my body, not in a creepy way, but in an appreciative way.

Especially when a smirk tugs on his lips.

"We need to stop meeting so aggressively, sweetheart."

God. His Irish accent melts me. My heart rate spikes as I take another step back.

I need space from him to think.

"I didn't punch you in the dick this time. Improvements."

I grin as I speak.

My cheeks start to flush, he clearly notices as he shoves his hands in the pocket of his black shorts.

I can't help but stare at those muscular arms, smothered in dark ink. And those veins that protrude from his hands and forearms. He clearly works out.

"Heading in for a drink?" He points behind him.

I nod, but words don't follow.

"Would you care to join me?" he asks.

And I freeze.

Rubbing my hand along my forearm, I open my mouth, everything inside me is screaming to say "yes".

To loosen up as Misha said.

Then Vlad pops into my head. It not only risks me, it risks Jimmy.

I'm Vlad's property. If my life were different, I'd jump at the chance.

It feels so right. Sparks crackle around us. He is the first guy I've crushed on since I was a teenager.

"I won't bite. Just a drink," he says with a soft smile.

But his eyes dart down to where I'm rubbing my arm, and he frowns.

"I can't. Thank you for the offer, though."

I swear he's disappointed as he chews the inside of his mouth.

Well, so am I.

He seems cool. I bet he has good banter. And he makes my stomach flutter.

He simply nods and steps to the side and I rush past him in a hurry.

I clutch my purse tighter against me and perch up on a stool.

I look back and steal another glance. The other guy looks similar to Jimmy.

They have the same slimmer face with a chiseled jaw. Except he has tattoos all the way up to his jawline and up around to his ears.

As he turns, I see the ink spanning on his head where his hair is shaved at the sides.

As his gray eyes meet mine, I look away.

"What can I get you, Miss?" The petite bartender asks.

"What cocktail do you recommend?" I ask, grabbing the menu and scanning the words.

"Sex on the beach?"

I find the details on the page and it sounds sickly sweet.

"Okay. I'll take one of those. Thank you," I tell her.

Rubbing my hands along my thighs, I feel safe with my blade under my dress.

I've learned to trust no one. That's why I instinctively picked the barstool with the view of the room and my back to the wall.

No one can get to me without me noticing.

I can't resist stealing a glance over at Jimmy and his, I assume, brothers.

I expected them to be downing beers and laughing, but instead, they're staring at their drinks in complete silence.

A burning fire heats my core as his eyes lock with mine.

I've been caught ogling him. But it's hard not to.

He's, by far, the sexiest man I've ever seen.

He has an aura about him, commanding his space.

Even down to the silver rings over his fingers, the mean tats, and the all black outfit.

As he winks at me, I cross my legs as pressure builds down there.

What the hell is happening to me?

I'm captivated, but I attempt to tear my gaze from his. I can't.

And when he scowls, I arch my brow.

"What's your room number?" A soft voice asks.

That shakes me out of my spell.

I turn to the bartender and pick up my bright pink and orange drink.

"Three-oh-two."

Taking a sip, I'm pleasantly surprised. It's not too sweet, with a hell of a lot of booze.

"Is this seat taken?" A husky Italian voice distracts me from my drink.

As I look at him, he grins, pointing to the stool right next to me.

"Without sounding rude, I'd quite like to be on my own. The other stools are empty," I tell him.

I point to the other ten available out of my personal space.

"You're too pretty to be sitting at a bar all by yourself. Let me join you. Please." He fake pouts and I hold up my hand to cut him off.

"No. I'm perfectly fine. Thank you."

He taps his fingers on the red leather of the chair and doesn't move.

His dark eyes glare at me. A shift from rejection.

"Can I at least buy you a drink?" he asks, this time smiling fully and revealing his gray teeth.

Ew.

"No, I'm good, thank you." I hold up my glass.

Get the fucking hint.

As he steps around the stool, I stand, placing my drink on the bar.

"Do not take another step forward, sir." I keep my tone harsh.

He tilts his head, running his gaze up my legs and pausing on my breasts.

Absolute creep.

"Let me buy you a drink." This time, his tone is less welcoming, more aggressive.

"No."

He takes another step and I suck in a breath, scanning the room to work out how many witnesses would see me beat his ass down. I'll have to downplay my skill slightly.

I wait as he leans in. It's then I hear my drink start to fizz, and I see him pull his hand back from the bar down to his side.

Slowly, I slide my hand under my dress and put my fingers on the handle of my knife.

"Fine. I'll leave," he whispers and steps back, holding up his arms.

As he does, he crashes straight into a furious Jimmy, who grabs each shoulder and holds him in place.

My mouth drops and my heart hammers.

CHAPTER II
DECLAN

Song- Vicious. Bohnes.

Her hand twitches by her thigh. She was about to go for him. And I want to know why.

"Is he bothering you?" I ask, voice low.

Scum like him deserve more than a beating, they deserve to be buried in the dirt.

"Yes," she replies, firm.

She glares at him, picking up her drink like it's a weapon. She holds it out to him with deliberate calm. He shakes his head.

"You wanted a drink, didn't you? Well, this is my treat," she tells him.

She thrusts the glass into his chest, and fuck, she's beautiful. Even more so with that murderous look carved into her features.

She's fire, fury, and survival in heels. And still, there's a softness beneath the blaze, like she's terrified of anyone finding it. Especially me.

"Drink the drink." I follow her lead, tightening my grip on his shoulders.

"I'm not thirsty," he whispers.

She grins, slow and dangerous, and slides the straw up to his lips. He tries to bat her away, but she grabs his wrist. Hard.

"Open your mouth and drink it. Every single drop," I order.

Her eyes flick to mine. And my heart fucking somersaults in my chest. There's that twinkle, and it damn near undoes me.

He starts squirming, so I switch tactics, my hand sliding up to grip the back of his neck. My other discreetly unholsters my gun and presses it into his spine.

I lean in, low and cold. "Do as she says or you'll never walk again."

He starts shaking. Good. She shoves the straw into his mouth.

"Very good. Now drink," she chirps, and I could swear I've never seen anything sexier than her in this moment.

I hold him still, gun firm in his back, grinning at her like we're sharing a secret no one else in this place could survive. Time slows. Just her and me, smiling like maniacs.

Then the idiot starts slurping, and the spell breaks.

She sets the glass down, eyes fierce. "You can let him go. See how far he gets," she tells me.

I conceal the weapon and let him go. He stumbles like the coward he is.

"Lightweight."

"Hmm," she hums, watching him with narrowed eyes.

She leans in suddenly and grabs a fistful of his greasy black hair, yanking his head back.

"Be careful out there on your own, you sick fuck."

My brows lift. That venom in her tone? It's real. She's not bluffing.

She pushes him off and he crashes into a table, limbs flailing.

I step closer. I need to be near her.

"You okay?" I ask.

We sit, our eyes locking again. Electricity. No bullshit.

"Yeah."

But her gaze is somewhere else, teeth nibbling at the edge of her nail.

"You've taken down two guys in one day. Pretty impressive."

She doesn't respond.

"And you punched me in the dick. Anyone would think you hate the male species." I try to tease, but her walls shoot back up.

Her face sharpens. She snaps to look at me.

"The first guy tried to mug me and that one drugged my drink. Tell me, what the hell is there to like about your kind?"

I clench my fists. That's what I didn't want to hear, because now I want to murder the fucker.

"I'm sorry," is all I manage to get out.

And she laughs. It's a sound that splits through the tension and damn it, I want to hear it again. I want to hear all her sounds.

"What, on behalf of all men?" she asks between giggles.

"If that makes you happy, then yes. On behalf of the entire male population, I apologize for our scumbag behavior."

But inside? Rage. "He drugged your drink?" I ask, already planning how I'm going to make that bastard disappear.

"Yep. I rejected him. He didn't like that. So, he thought he could take what he wanted instead."

There's something hollow in her voice. Sadness, masked in steel.

"Can you give me a second?" I ask, needing to go fix this before it eats me alive.

"Sure. You want a drink?" she asks, and fuck, her voice hits me low.

"I'll take a beer, please. Ice cold. No drug additions, please." I grin, trying to keep it light.

"Maybe this is my chance to get my revenge against men."

She winks, and I'm toast.

"I'll be one minute," I tell her, praying she doesn't vanish when I turn around. I have a feeling she's a runner. I have to keep her close to keep bashing down these walls.

I head straight for my table and slam my hands down.

Finn's head snaps up.

"What's up?" Conan asks.

"That guy, the stumbling buffoon," I say, jerking my thumb back.

Finn glances past me and spots him.

"Yeah?"

"He just tried to drug my friend."

Finn's brows arch, a slow grin spreading across his face. Conan starts rubbing his hands together.

"You want us to deal with him?" Finn asks, already sliding out of the booth.

"Deal with it in a sense he will never do that again. Yes," I say, voice cold.

"You got it, boss."

They disappear, and I head back to her.

I don't even know her real name. But I feel like I've known her forever. It's unnerving.

She's ordering our drinks when I get back. And when she turns to look at me? I'm fucked. That smile.

"Ice cold beer, no drugs, ordered," she says, saluting. Then takes a seat, legs crossing like she's doing it just to kill me.

I lick my lips before I embarrass myself. I'd get on my knees right here to worship every inch of her.

"Thank you, heartbreaker." I wink.

"Why heartbreaker? Surely it can't be broken that easily?" she asks, tilting her head, that little smirk playing on her lips.

"I've only experienced it once," I reply as the beer slides across the bar.

"Oh, I'm sorry," she says, lifting her espresso martini.

"I lost my mom. That broke my heart."

I don't even know why I'm telling her. It just falls out. Like the truth doesn't want to hide from her.

She nods and sips her drink.

"It hurts, doesn't it?" she whispers, eyes flicking away.

I want to touch her. Make her look at me again.

"That it does," I mutter, taking a long swig from the bottle.

"But it also hurt being rejected by you."

A flicker of a smile curves her lips.

"Did it?"

I nod, pressing a hand to my chest.

"Deeply. And then you rejected me again earlier. So it's official. You are my heartbreaker."

My heartbreaker. Mine.

The words settle into my bloodstream and don't leave. It makes my cock twitch.

I see the red creeping up her throat. And I remember how it felt with my hand wrapped around it.

God, I want more. No. I fucking need it.

"Well, you've got your drink now. Does that make up for it?" she asks, batting those thick lashes at me.

"Not even close. Have dinner with me? That might fix my broken heart."

She pouts, nails tapping the bar like a siren's call.

"Okay. On one condition."
Anything.
"Let me hear it."

CHAPTER 12
CHARLOTTE

I watch his brothers follow the guy who tried to drug me and lead him towards the elevator.

Having Jimmy with me as I forced that asshole to drink the drugged cocktail made my heart swell.

It's always me fighting for myself. Having company felt good.

There's something about him, something that tells me he's dark, brutal.

But also soft for the right people. Like me.

"You let me design a tattoo for you."

It's the first thing I can think of.

He smirks and pulls up his shirt at the hem, revealing his toned stomach, covered in tats.

"Where do you think it should go?" He asks.

Instinctively I put my hand across his chest. I almost tear it away, but it feels so right.

"Many here?"

"A few. Make it small, and I'll find it a home." His voice drops almost seductively.

I nod, the temperature rising.

He stands up, which only shows off his height over me as he offers me his hand, and I take it so he can help me off the stool.

He squeezes my hand as he leads me over to a table, secluded in the far left corner. He stops and lets me in the booth first and follows in after.

"I feel like champagne is in order," he says as he shuffles closer to me. Our thighs touch and I almost melt against him.

"We celebrating the fact I didn't get drugged and raped?"

His eyes darken, his lips a thin line.

"Don't say that. He won't ever come near you again." The danger in his voice excites me.

I bite my tongue and refrain from telling him I could have killed him with my bare hands.

He's already seen too much of who I am.

"Good."

"Now what are we celebrating?" I question, resting my chin on my hand.

"You."

"Me? Why?"

He leans back, snaking his arm over the chair rest behind my head.

"For being kickass. And for agreeing to have a date with me." He winks and my stomach does a flip.

"This isn't a date." I can't hide the smile.

Even if the fear is inside me, for once I want to let loose and do something for me.

And I want to have dinner with him and chat.

It's refreshing to have a normal conversation with someone outside of Vlad's circle.

"You don't want champagne?"

"I would love one." I smile.

"Say it then."

I roll my eyes and his hand twitches on the table.

"You don't like eye rolling?" I question.

His deep, rumbling chuckle makes me clench my thighs.

"Instinctive reflex. I wanted to grab you by the neck and kiss you when you did it. Bratty behavior really gets to me."

I'm intrigued.

"What would you do after that?" I whisper.

He clears his throat and leans in.

God, he smells divine.

"I'd take you back to my room, tie you to my bed, and gag you, so I could enjoy you in peace."

I shiver against him. My face must be bright red.

"Enjoy me?" I ask, my voice shaky.

"Hmm, mmm. In so many ways. But I'm not telling you how. You'd have to find out firsthand." He sits back as the waiter appears.

"A bottle of your finest champagne," he orders.

The waiter hands us both a menu, but I can't tear my eyes away from Jimmy.

"Of course. Coming right up."

I scan the page, but I'm not reading the words, I keep gazing over at him as he studies it.

His sharp, chiseled jaw. The ink that runs up his neck.

What the hell am I doing here?

The waiter returns with the bottle and pops it open, pouring us each a glass.

I take a sip and the bubbles dance on my tongue. It's creamy. Delicious. My first taste of it, actually.

"Mmmm."

"That's one of the sounds I'd like to hear," he tells me with a mischievous tone.

Hiding my face behind the menu, I decide on the steak salad.

"I make you nervous." His voice is low.

It's a statement, not a question.

I look down at my leg bouncing.

"I don't know if that's the right word."

Excited. Relaxed. I don't know. I've not felt like this before.

We order our food and slip back into chatting. About everything and nothing.

I've learned he loves fixing cars. Whiskey. His favorite color is black.

He wants a dog.

He loves chocolate. Or anything sweet.

As I finish up my last glass of champagne, I'm all giggly. He slides me a napkin and pen; he must have got that on his way back from the bathroom.

"You owe me one tattoo design, heartbreaker."

His eyes focus on my ink.

"Yours are pretty." He nods at them.

If only he knew what they represented.

"Thank you. I can't help but keep adding to it." I hiccup as I speak.

"You do your own ink?"

"Taught myself. Although, I've always enjoyed drawing. But you can see as it goes up the arm, they get better."

I hold out my arm to show him.

As his fingers wrap around my wrist, my heart beats so rapidly, and my pussy also has a heartbeat.

"Gorgeous," he whispers, looking directly into my eyes.

How many times can this man make me blush?

As our meal arrives, I study him, trying to get some sort of inspiration for his ink.

Selfishly, part of me wants something he will remember me by. I just know he is going to stick with me for a long time.

The perfect man I could never have.

"This food is so good. Tasty. I haven't had a meal out in forever," I tell him.

As I finish my sentence, my harsh reality topples over me. I don't have friends to go out with. I haven't lived a normal life in five years. Have I ever really?

This man has no idea what he's blessed me with tonight.

He stops before taking his final mouthful, and his fork clatters onto the plate.

"You okay?"

"You know what? I am. Thank you for dinner. I needed this."

Just to feel normal for an evening.

"We could do this again?"

He looks at me warily, not wanting to push me.

"Maybe."

I give him a sweet smile.

Once our plates have been cleared, I'm given the dessert menu.

"Oh, chocolate strawberries." I used to love those as a kid.

"My mom used to love those. A Friday treat, we'd have a fondue with all the fruits and candies. She loved chocolate, actually," Jimmy tells me, I can hear the grief in his voice.

"Hey! My mom was the same. A whole cupboard full of all varieties!" I smile thinking about my mom for the first time since her death.

My eyes glass over and Jimmy puts his hand on my shoulder and squeezes lightly. I bury my feelings away. They make me weak. I want to forget.

"Any memory is a good one, heartbreaker. Don't let the bad overtake the good ones." He nods to me and I fight the tears.

"Shall we order some? Start some new memories too?"
He brushes my hair away from my face and I lean into his touch.
"I'd like that," I whisper.
"I'm just going to the restrooms, I won't be long."

CHAPTER 13

DECLAN

"You better not be running on me," I tell her as I pull my phone from my pocket.

"And miss dessert? It's the best course."

My cock twitches. I shift in my seat, adjusting the tension pressing against my zipper. "Damn right it is. Be quick."

I wink, and satisfaction curls in my gut as that pretty flush climbs her chest. She tries to act unaffected. But she's not.

But neither am I. I'm here with an aching dick.

She's not used to kindness, not used to being looked at like this. And it shows.

There's something else, too. Something just out of reach. A shadow behind those sapphire eyes. I shouldn't be this comfortable around her. I sure as hell shouldn't be offering up pieces of myself like confessions. Yet here I am.

While she's gone, I wave down the server and order the strawberries and more champagne. My eyes catch the napkin she's been doodling on all night. I pick it up and study the design, the delicate lines and sharp curves.

It's her. All wrapped up in ink and intention. A heart pierced by a blade, but the handle is laced in soft, floral detail. Feminine. Deadly. *Mine.*

I fold the napkin and tuck it into my wallet. By the time I do, I hear her heels.

She slides back into the booth, eyes dropping to the table with a frown. "I wasn't finished drawing," she huffs.

Christ, she smells like sugar and sin. I want to drown in it. "I love it exactly how it is."

She smiles, and my goddamn chest tightens, but then she slaps me in the arm. "That was sickly sweet," she teases.

I lean in, not touching, but close enough to feel her breath. She's looking at me, not like she wants to run. Like she's bracing for impact.

And I want to crash into her.

Those full lips, parted slightly. Her pupils blown wide. I lean forward another touch, just as the server sets down the tray of strawberries.

I force myself to sit back, take one, and hold it up. "Open up."

She hesitates. I see the fight flicker in her eyes. So I pin her there with mine.

She opens her mouth. I slip the berry past her lips. "Good girl."

She stops chewing and I try to fight my grin.

I say nothing. Just take another berry and lick the juice from my fingers. "Damn, this is delicious."

"Very."

After we finish, I toss the cash on the table, stand, and offer her my hand. Her palm slides into mine, and it shouldn't do a damn thing to me—but it does.

As we walk toward the elevator, she suddenly stops and turns to face me.

"Thank you," she breathes, eyes scanning the room like she is looking for someone.

My spine goes rigid. Someone's watching her. Or she's watching for them.

I step closer and curl my fingers under her jaw, guiding her gaze back to me.

"No. Thank you," I whisper.

This was the best evening I've had in a long, long time.

I tilt my head and lower my voice, brushing my lips close to her cheek.

"Can I kiss you?"

And fuck, I already know if she says yes, I'm never letting her go.

CHAPTER 14
CHARLOTTE

I want to say yes.

I imagine his lips on mine, and fuck, I want that.

A man this insanely gorgeous, who sat and chatted about everything and anything with me. Who helped me drug a guy.

If I was single and free, I wouldn't even question it.

Here? I can't trust anyone. Certainly not Misha.

The risk isn't worth it.

My bubble has burst, and the weight of my life crashes over me.

"I'm sorry. I can't." I whisper, looking down at the marble beneath my heels.

"Don't apologize. I've clearly got more work to do to get my kiss, ay?"

He pulls back and his face is soft with a smile.

Which throws me.

Quickly before I retreat, I press my hands on his chest and place a soft peck on his cheek.

"Goodnight," I whisper.

I turn away to the opening elevator before I change my mind.

As the elevator closes, I let out a breath, still tasting the sweet chocolate on my tongue.

I wish things were different.

But I have a job to do.

Maybe, one day, once I'm out of this mess, I'll try to find him.

Or someone who makes me feel this good.

I couldn't sleep. All I could picture was Jimmy. So I went to the only place I know I can clear my head.

The place I can unleash the monster festering inside of me.

But with every punch and kick to the bag, I imagine Vlad is there.

For every time he's pinned me down.

For shooting my mom.

For taking me away from my family.

For making me a goddamn murdering monster.

And now, for stopping me from kissing Jimmy.

Letting out a scream that feels like my ancestor's pain is also being released, I swing my leg around and beat it into the bag.

Resting my hands on my knees, pain rockets up my shin. Taking deep breaths, my lungs heave.

I wish they had a target here I could throw some knives at.

All this pent-up aggression can't be good for me. No matter how many guys I kill, it's never enough because it's not him.

My monster.

And I see no actual way out.

But what I know is that the only escape I can see so far his death.

And I've contemplated it many times. Those nights where I just lie there and he takes what he wants from me.

The only thing that keeps me alive is Drago's promise.

He witnessed the after effects of what my husband does to me behind closed doors.

He knows who they are.

That's how he became my handler. But how long can I survive in this nightmare?

Fuck. Vlad.

Fuck. This.

I will find a way out, even if I have to burn the estate to the ground and take those sick bastards out. This is how I survive. Fueled on the thought of revenge.

The world's a better place without them.

Slow, loud claps from behind me make me jump. Clenching my fists, I spin to face whoever it may be.

I know exactly who it is, just by the aftershave.

And the way my heart is beating.

As our eyes lock, that smirk appears on his beautiful face.

"She could give you a run for your money, brother."

I don't even notice the tatted beast behind him. The one with him last night.

Pulling out my hair from the ponytail, I shake it out, sizing up the guy.

Yeah, it would be a challenge. He has that dangerous look in his eyes. Unhinged.

"Careful of your dick, though. She likes to aim for that first."

He winks at me and the guy's face screws up. But then amusement grows on his face as he looks between us.

I sidestep, feeling the ground shift beneath my feet as I move out of the way.

"All yours. I got shit to do, and I don't fancy embarrassing you again, Jimmy."

I wink at him as I scoot past him.

His fingers close around my wrist, a jolt shooting up my arm, and I gasp, stopping abruptly.

Oddly, his touch doesn't make me angry. It kind of feels safe. The grunts of Jimmy's brother beating the shit out of the bag fills the room, and Jimmy leans in. Shivers run down my spine as I slowly turn to face him.

Those damn eyes steal the sense from my brain again.

"If you want to fight me, all you gotta do is ask. I won't aim for your dick this time."

His deep chuckle makes my pussy clench. I've been taught never to submit.

But the way he looks at me, it isn't just at me, it's through me. His lips graze my jaw and my eyes flutter closed.

"The kind of fighting I want to do with you very much involves my dick," he whispers.

His fingers trail down my arm. The delicate touch of a man is alien to me. But this sensation I crave more of.

"Are you flirting with me? There are hundreds of beautiful women staying here. Why not one of them? Why me? The one you can't have..."

He chuckles and interlinks our fingers, and electricity jolts up my arm. I squeeze his hand, not wanting to let go. Almost forgetting who I am when I'm near him.

"Of course I'm flirting, heartbreaker. I made it clear I want *you*. And you know exactly why. Why would I go after a Porsche when I could have a Bugatti?"

I chew the inside of my lip.

"Because a Porsche is more easily available, a Bugatti you have to work *very* hard for."

He runs his hand through his dark hair.

"You get it. And imagine how much better the *driving* experience would be. It's worth the hard work for the ultimate reward."

My cheeks heat. In fact, my whole damn body is on fire.

"Well, I hope one day you get your dream car, sir."

I tap my hand on his cheek, and he holds it there, dragging it to his lips and placing a delicate kiss on my skin—his eyes burning into mine with desire.

Just picturing him looking up at me from between my legs and...

Fuck. I need to find my escape, out of Italy. I don't think I can resist him otherwise.

"I always go after what I want, heartbreaker." He drops my hand and steps back.

"And what I want is you."

His words hit me straight in the chest.

"I-I ca—"

"Jimmy! Hurry up, I need a sparring partner."

My lips curve into a mischievous grin, while his expression morphs into a deep frown.

"Time to go." I pout at him.

"Are you going to tell me your real name yet, heartbreaker?"

I shake my head. I was surprised he didn't press at dinner. I guess we were so distracted in conversation, it was so natural.

"Brittany. Like I told you."

I give him a small wave and back away.

"I'll see you around, heartbreaker." He winks at me before heading off to the mats.

Holy fuck.

CHAPTER 15

DECLAN

"Jimmy? Really?" Conan's grin widens as he tosses the pads at my chest, and I quickly shove my hands into them.

"First name that came to my head."

I knew she was lying about hers. She is not Brittany. It doesn't fit her at all.

"You seem different around her. Like you're trying to impress her."

The prickly stubble on my jaw itches, and I scratch it with a sigh.

"Probably 'cause she punched me in the dick, Con."

I play it cool, but the truth is, my heart pounds like a drum solo whenever she's near.

And when we touch, I get pains running up my arms.

Or when I look in her eyes, I lose myself. Love at first sight doesn't exist. But lust does. And so does intrigue. Something about this girl has me wanting more.

"I take it we won't be going for a drink later then?" Conan huffs, launching a glove at my pad.

"That, I don't know."

If I had it my way, I'd lock her in my room with me for the next three days and bury my face in her pussy to see how many ways I can make her scream with my tongue.

But I fear I'd never let her leave me.

I just know she would submit beautifully, yet push enough to give me an excuse to punish her.

And I bet she can handle pain. There is more than meets the eye with that little menace.

You don't learn to defend yourself to that level for no reason.

Nor do you come to Italy on your own.

My gut is telling me to stay away. But my dick, my head, and a bit of my heart are telling me to keep going.

"I'm about to knock your jaw off your face if you don't concentrate, brother. Either go get your dick wet or fucking help me train."

My jaw ticks as he hits one of my nerves and I can't hold back.

I lunge forward and smack him on the side of the head before he can get a defensive arm up.

"Remember who the fuck you're talking to," I spit out.

I've always been hotheaded.

All of us are, hence the scars we all have from beating the shit out of each other.

I rip off the gloves with my teeth and toss them next to his feet.

"So you wanna get your dick wet?" Conan smirks, rubbing the side of his head.

"Abso-fucking-lutely."

I just have to come up with an elaborate plan to break down her walls and drag her into my lair for the night.

But even thinking about her like that, tricking her almost, doesn't sit right with me. I want her to willingly come to me and leave all her inhibitions behind.

Like how she was at dinner, that softness under the surface. Like the blade wrapped in flowers.

GRABBING my towel from the locker, I head to the pool bar and order up a bottle of beer. I need a game plan, and I need to clear my head without Conan goading me.

Heading to the nearest sun chair, I stop when I hear the splash of water.

The cool drops hit against my bare back and I turn around.

And my heart pounds as I lock onto her blue eyes.

And that smile. Those perfect white teeth. Those full pink lips.

"Are you following me, Jimmy?" she asks, spraying me again.

I want to be soaked with something, and it sure as hell isn't water.

I step towards the ledge of the infinity pool, resting my forearms on the tiles.

"You flirting with me, heartbreaker?"

I tilt my head, assessing her reaction.

She pouts and shakes her head.

I'm kinda into the different personalities she has. Sometimes vulnerable, other times vicious. I really like the one who tried to choke me.

But I'm also really into this fun, lighthearted, almost menacing version of her.

"Nope. Just simply asking if I should make security aware of my stalker problem. Wouldn't want you sneaking into my room to watch me sleep. Would I?"

As she goes to push away from the ledge to swim off, I grab her arm and lift her slender frame out of the water. Enough so her nose is against mine.

The droplets of water run down her collarbones and over her breasts.

I want to lick them off her.

"I wouldn't worry about me watching you sleep, gorgeous. What you should worry about is me breaking in and fucking you back to consciousness. But no one will be able to hear your cries, because you'll be tied and gagged, so I'll stay there for as long as I wish, doing whatever the hell I desire."

Her mouth drops open and I chuckle, closing it with the tip of my index finger under her chin.

I lean in, brushing my lips along her jaw, feeling her shiver under my touch.

"Don't forget the milkshake."

She chews on her lip, not fazed by the way I'm holding her. Yet I can feel her heart thrash against my palm.

"But if that's what you want, tell me your room number and that can be arranged. You know where to find me, heartbreaker," I whisper before dropping her back into the water.

I don't usually play games, but with her, I'm all for it.

CHAPTER 16

CHARLOTTE

Gasping for air, I push myself back up to the surface of the water, flicking my hair out of my face, and swim to the stairs.

The way he speaks, so filthy, so raw. I want everything he says.

Stomping over to the chaise lounge, I grab my towel and dry myself off. As I scan the area, I can't see him, but I can feel his eyes on me.

This burning heat just doesn't go away.

Every touch lingers.

I barely know the man, yet, when he looks into my eyes, it's almost as if he knows me.

He brings out *Charlotte*.

The carefree one. The one who laughs and jokes. The girl I used to be once upon a time.

Once dry, I shimmy on my skirt and head to the bar. I better check in with Misha soon.

As I approach, the blonde lady smiles at me and waves.

"Hi." I plonk my butt down on the stool.

She slides a chocolate milkshake in front of me, and I frown.

"How did you know that was just what I needed?" I laugh, taking a sip.

It's delicious.

Sweet, yet not too much. I don't indulge often, but I am on vacation after all.

"The drink comes with a message. Jimmy says to enjoy and think of him while you suck on that straw."

As I choke on a cough, I nearly spit out my drink all over her.

My cheeks are burning from embarrassment. The bar lady joins me in amusement.

"He seems smitten with you. Very kind."

She offers me a nod and goes back to serving the next customer.

I stare at the thick brown liquid and swirl it around with my straw, imagining all the things Jimmy said he would do with this on me.

The ice would cool my hot skin.

His tongue would burn at my core. I almost let out a moan. What is happening to me?

I only live romance and sex through literature. It blocks out the nightmare I have to endure in my own bedroom. Drago manages to smuggle them in for me occasionally. Much to his displeasure.

It helps me create a fantasy in my head, almost to get me through it.

I wonder what it would be like if I had my own memories to go off of. Just for once feel pleasure, not pain, embarrassment, or like a piece of property.

What if I felt like a woman?

I shake my head. It's too dangerous. If I get caught, or if Misha sees, so many things could go wrong, and everything seems to in my life.

I rest my head on my hand and finish my drink, watching the world go by around me.

"Another?" the bartender asks.

"I shouldn't have even had that one," I reply, not being able to hide the sadness as I hand her the empty glass.

Sighing, I slip off the stool. Maybe I am just not meant to have nice things.

MY HEART FLIPS as there's a knock at my room.

Is it him?

Anticipation sizzles through me as I approach; checking through the spyhole, my mood sinks when I see Misha.

With a sigh, I open it and let him barrel through without even a hello.

"I assumed you'd be busy?" I slam the door shut and make my way into the living room, finding him slouched on the couch with his feet up on the table.

Running a ring-filled hand through his long blond hair, he grins.

"I'm free for ten minutes. Vlad wanted me to check on you. Make sure you're behaving."

I roll my eyes.

"You managed to take your dick out of someone for ten minutes to be my handler. How kind of you. I'm fine. Off you go."

I point to the door and he jumps to his feet.

He towers over me probably by a foot. I know I could take him out, Drago taught me well in that aspect. It's not the size of my opponent, it's the skill.

And Misha's skills apparently are restricted to bedroom activities.

"If you want, sweet cheeks, you can be my ten minute appointment. Vlad never has to know."

I pull away abruptly as he tries to stroke my face.

"Get the fuck out," I seethe.

He smirks at me, and it reminds me of Vlad. That darkness. Evil lying beneath his eyes.

I step back to get some space from him. He's one of Vlad's top men.

That doesn't mean I'll bow down to him. He doesn't own me.

"You want me to tell Vlad what you just said?" I tilt my head and return a smirk.

I can play with the best of them.

"Like he'd give a fuck. You're merely his property."

"Ouch." I hold my hand over my heart.

I hate my husband with every bone in my body.

"Okay, well, how about this?" I step forward into his space.

"You touch me without my consent, I'll slice your fucking balls off and feed them to you."

He chuckles but I harden my stare. This dumb asshole has seen me fight. He knows he would lose.

"You've seen what I can do, Misha. Your battle skills do not match mine. We are not equal. I will make you suffer. Now, get the fuck out of my room. I'll see you for the meet tomorrow when we have word from Drago."

I watch his face redden and the vein in the side of his head pop.

"Go on. Be a good boy and fuck off."

"You're a bitch, Charlotte." He points at me, his jaw clenched.

I smile sweetly at him.

"You're lucky I'm being a bitch. I could be your nightmare. Goodbye, Misha."

I wave at him as he retreats, swearing in Russian under his breath.

Over the last five years, I've picked up words and phrases. Important ones anyway.

I'm a girl from Chicago. But I'm a fast learner, especially when it comes to survival.

My phone pings on the side and I pick it up, recoiling as my husband's name flashes across the screen.

V

check in.

ME

All fine.

V

good. Can't wait to get you home.

God, he makes me feel physically sick.

As I sink down on the bed, I can feel his hands on me. Suffocating me.

I'm a toy to be used. And when he's pissed off, I'm there to be punished.

No safe words. No way to escape. I just have to take it.

And if he thinks I'm not enjoying it, he makes me act like I am.

I hate every second of it.

I'd rather be strung up and tortured.

I wonder what it would feel like having Jimmy touch me. The way he is so open about what he wants.

The fact he wants to give it to me, not take it.

I believe everything happens for a reason, no matter how shitty it may be. And I am certain I was meant to cross paths with this man.

My soul is telling me to go to him.

Fuck it.

Just this once, maybe it's my turn to take what I want from a man.

One night to experience real pleasure.

Life can't get much worse for me, maybe I need one night to be free from my chains.

Experience a normal life, even if it is pretend.

Maybe this is what I need to survive.

A real man.

I take a quick glance in the mirror and wrap my fingers around the bottle of milkshake I bought on the way back to my room.

To hell with it, I'll go in a black bikini set and skirt.

Pulling my hair out of the ponytail, I let it cascade down my back, ruffling out the curls, with the dark purple shining in the light through the black.

He can take me as I am.

And I think that is exactly what draws me to him.

He simply wants me. Just how I am.

CHAPTER 17
DECLAN

I thought I had her. The heat on her face in the spa room when I had her throat in my hand, it did something to me. And the blush that stained her cheeks when she got that milkshake? Yeah, I clocked that too. I waited. Watched.

So when she turned toward her own room and not mine, the disappointment hit me like a fucking sucker punch.

I yank my black shirt off, tossing it on the couch, and stride to the balcony, throwing the doors wide open and stepping into the sun-soaked air.

The view's something out of a movie, ocean glowing, sky on fire.

I glance down at my Rolex. Still early. No message from Enzo yet, not even a fucking time.

Maybe I should go find her. I need to see her. Taste her. I can't even think straight, let alone focus on a business meeting.

If Enzo picks up on that? He'll smell blood in the water.

Fuck it. Maybe I just eat her out on the floor and leave her tied to the bed while I go to the meeting.

I could do it. Easy.

Then come back; finish what I started.

But even an hour wouldn't be enough.

If I had my way, I'd keep her chained to the bed the rest of the damn trip.

I don't believe in love at first sight, and I don't even know her fucking name. But I've never wanted anything the way I want her.

And the thought of walking away without knowing what this could be? That might be the one thing I can't stomach.

My phone vibrates in my pocket. I pull it out and unlock it.

UNKNOWN

11AM tomorrow. Location incoming.

Perfect. I'll have all night and most of the morning with her.

I pocket my phone and head toward the elevator. Press the button, step inside, and hit "G."

The doors slide shut and I catch a glimpse of my reflection in the mirrored walls. Ink swirling over my bare chest, across my arms.

It's Italy. Shirtless works.

Plus, if she's gonna dig her nails into me, I want to feel every goddamn second of it.

The elevator dings, doors gliding open.

And there she is.

Blue eyes. Chocolate milkshake. Bikini top barely holding it together.

"I was just coming to find you, heartbreaker."

She bites her lip, eyes sliding down my chest.

I catch the door before it closes again.

"Are you coming…"

She licks her lips.

"Shut up."

That wicked little grin plays across her face and I blink. Did she just tell me to shut up?

This menace. Hot as hell.

Before I can speak, her hand wraps around my throat and she slams me back against the elevator mirror.

And then she kisses me.

No. She claims me.

Fucking fire.

I thread my fingers into her hair, fisting the silky strands, holding her exactly where I want her.

"If you're gonna choke me, sweetheart, I like it rough. Let those pretty nails dig in. Take what you want."

My hand wraps around her neck, squeezing, just as she tightens hers around mine.

"You got it, heartbreaker. Such a good girl for me, aren't you? Are you going to let me take every damn thing I want from you tonight?"

Her hips roll and she sucks in a breath.

"Hmm. Just like that, baby."

I spin her so her back hits the wall, hiking her leg up and pressing my cock hard against her center. My finger slams the close button and I punch in the penthouse code.

My mouth never leaves hers.

Lifting her effortlessly, her pussy grinds against my shorts.

"Fuck, heartbreaker. Keep doing that and I'll come in my goddamn pants."

She's moaning into my mouth and it's everything.

Her head tilts back as I lick up her neck and down her collarbone, tasting her.

I squeeze her breast through the bikini top and she moans so fucking loud.

The elevator dings and I grin against her lips.

I carry her through the suite, crashing her back against the first wall I find, devouring her lips again.

Her legs tighten around me. Every sound she makes is a dagger to my resolve.

But I need to taste her. Worship her.

I set her down on the dining table and grip her throat, easing her onto her back.

Softly, I tug her skirt off, resting her heels on the edge. Her calves tremble, just a little and I stop.

Pulling her to sit, I cradle her face in my hands, eyes locked on hers.

"I need you to use your words. Beg me for it, even. But this doesn't go any further without it."

The confusion on her pretty face is cute but concerning.

"I came here and kissed you, isn't that me telling you to do it?"

I shake my head, twirling one of her dark purple curls around my finger.

"No, baby. You kissing me, as hot as that was, is not consent for the things I want to do to you."

I tip her chin up to me.

"I-I just thought…" She trails off.

I press my lips to her cheek and her eyes flutter closed. Just that small notion has her brain starting to switch off.

Fuck, I'm going to blow her damn mind.

Holding her cheeks in my hand, I delicately stroke her soft skin with my thumb, my eye contact never wavering.

I want her to see how desperate I am for her.

"Your voice matters. If you are willing to submit to me, we have to communicate. Your pleasure is more important to me than my own. But I gotta hear you say it, heartbreaker. Just tell me you are mine."

This is her first important lesson.

Even though she's giving me control, she is always the one with the true power.

"Just tell me you're mine. Beg me to ruin you, and I'll do just that. If that's exactly what you want. If not, we stick to a heavy petting session because I'm not letting you out of my room until the sun rises."

My heart races. I feel like she needs to know I will respect her body and her mind.

"I want this. I really do. Can we—" She pauses, her cheeks flushing red.

"Can we, what? Use those words, heartbreaker," I urge her softly.

"Can we go slow into it?"

"Of course. I want to savor every second with you. Taste every inch. I want you to come so many times you forget your name."

Her eyes go wide and I laugh, brushing my fingers through her hair. She seems to like that.

"Don't worry. I won't ask for your real name." I wink.

She's cagey. Like a woman who has had her wings clipped but is desperate to be free.

Maybe tonight might help her with that.

I've seen her badass side. I want her vulnerable, submissive side.

"So, you're happy for me to take the lead; if you tell me to stop, I will. If you want more of something, you tell me. I want to hear exactly what you like. See what makes you scream. I need to be in control, I like to be rough. Can you handle that?"

She nods, and I pull her bottom lip back before ducking my head and capturing it with my own and sucking.

"Words."

"Yes. I can handle it."

"Good. Be a good girl, lie down and spread those legs for me. Let me see all of you," I whisper against her cheek.

I glance down at the milkshake placed next to her and her eyes follow mine, and she smiles.

A promise is a promise.

I bet she's sweet enough without the milkshake, though.

She slowly lays down and opens her thighs, letting her knees rest on the wood, and my god, am I salivating.

Untying the bow on either side of her skirt, I rip them off, toss them over my shoulder, and release her glistening pink pussy.

"Beautiful and so ready for me, aren't you?" I trail a finger along the inside of her thigh, brushing past the edge of her smooth pussy, and she wriggles.

She reacts to every touch, every breath. She's fucking perfect for me.

Her lips part as I press a finger on her clit. Working in small circular motions, I keep my vision fixed on her. I want to see what makes her tick. Explore her.

For some goddamn reason, I want to make this perfect for her.

More than a fuck.

I want to give her something to remember, because this nagging feeling in my gut tells me she's never been worshipped.

I don't want her to just come. I want her to explode.

"So beautiful, heartbreaker," I say softly, dragging my finger back to her entrance.

Her body starts to shake and I pause, gauging her reactions to me.

She's trembling and I've barely touched her. I frown and move my hand, stroking her thigh in reassurance.

"All good?" I ask.

"Yes," she replies quickly.

As I slide one finger inside her, her back arches slightly off the table and she sucks in a breath, biting down on her lip. I love watching her reactions so I can work on my next move.

A puzzle that I want to fit together perfectly.

"Feels good, doesn't it?" I ask, and she nods.

"Open your eyes, look at me, see how much I'm enjoying watching you," I command, and her blue eyes snap to mine.

"Good fucking girl. Another one?"

That makes her cheeks heat a bright red.

"Yes." That husky, breathy whisper sends my heart wild as I sink in another finger. Her tight pussy squeezes me, when my dick is inside, I'm going to explode in two minutes.

With a few deep thrusts, I study her as the blush spreads all the way up her neck and to her cheeks. The sound of her wetness coating my fingers fills the room.

"M-more," she cries.

"More what?" I smirk.

"Please, please, give me more."

Her breathing gets heavier and I slide my fingers out. Her brows furrow, the disappointment clear as her body relaxes against the table.

She goes to close her legs and I push them back down, tutting and shaking my head.

"Remember who is in control here, heartbreaker. Did I say I was done?" She shakes her head and I push down harder on her thighs, digging my fingers into her skin.

"You don't want me to get on my knees and taste you? Fuck you with my tongue and drink chocolate milkshake out of your sweet cunt? Hmm? Patience is rewarded. You want to be a good girl for me, don't you?"

She sucks in a breath as I release her, stepping back.

"I do. I want to be good," she says quietly.

Grabbing the container from the counter, I flick off the lid, letting it drop to the floor. Tipping back my head, I pour some in my mouth and swallow.

"Pretty nice. Usually I'm a whiskey man. But it appears, for you, I make exceptions."

Placing the bottle next to her, I bend over, grabbing her by the neck to lift her face to mine and slam my lips over hers, letting her moan in my mouth as my tongue explores hers.

I'm hungry for her. Starving even. I lean back and rip off her bra, groaning as I look at her perfect tits; her nipples are already begging to be sucked.

Laying her back down flat, I begin exploring her. Dragging my tongue down her smooth neck, down to her breasts, taking one rosy bud in my mouth and biting. She hisses as my teeth sink in, I glance up and she's watching my every move.

With curiosity, but also desire in those beautiful eyes. I move over to give some attention to the other, letting my hand slide down her toned stomach and cupping her throbbing pussy.

I smirk as I continue my journey down her body, letting my tongue run over her skin, watching her heat up beneath my touch. Her breathing becomes more frantic, but she's relaxed and hungry for more.

Stopping just as my face is positioned in front of her sweet, glistening cunt, I look up at her and smirk.

"You good, baby?" I ask, looking for her reassurance.

"Better than good." She grins, showing me those perfect white teeth.

The more I relax her, the more she comes out of her shell. Ideally, I want to get to that badass I saw taking down a man outside the hotel. A niggling feeling catches in my chest.

That will take time. More than one night. I shake the thought away. I can enjoy her and worry about that later.

"Good. Now, prop yourself up on your forearms and watch. See how much I fucking love eating you. And trust me, I'm going to enjoy seeing you react to my tongue."

Her eyes go wide the second my mouth connects with her pussy. With my hands on her hips, I start off slow with circles on her clit.

"Oh my god," she whispers under her breath.

"You've never been eaten out before?"

She shakes her head and I frown.

"You've had sex before, right?" I ask and give her another lick to calm her down.

She nods her head, not enthusiastically. I don't like her reactions to these questions.

"You had an orgasm before, from this?" I sit back slightly and replace my tongue with my fingers.

She chews on her lip, so I slide a finger inside her. Fuck, my dick is begging to get inside her.

"No."

"Oh, baby. I am about to shatter you." I smile at her, resuming my position between her legs.

A real man eats. He worships her. He gets on his fucking knees where he belongs and makes sure she comes first, multiple times, before he even gets his dick wet.

I'm about to show her exactly what it's like to be respected and equally disrespected in the bedroom. But first, I'm going to have her coming on my tongue, shaking around me and screaming my name. And try my hardest not to come in my pants while I witness her undoing.

I eat her out like she's my last damn meal on this earth, keeping one finger slowly thrusting in and out, her juices dripping down my hand.

I suck on her clit and her moans grow louder, I can't help but grin.

"You like that? A little bit of pain?" I ask.

"Y-yes," she says, almost breathlessly.

Good.

"Yes, what?" I lower my tone.

"Yes, sir."

I grin against her pussy. "That's my good girl."

Adding another finger, I grab the milkshake with my free hand, and the surprise on her face is a picture.

"I'm a man of my word, angel. I said I'd drink chocolate milkshake out of your pussy, and that's exactly what I will do."

"I think you're missing the final step that you promised." she replies mischievously.

I chuckle, thrusting my fingers deeper and her mouth falls open as I hit her G-spot.

"No. I'm fully aware. I'm going to spit it straight back into that sassy fucking mouth of yours. But for now, you let me eat, and the only noise I want to hear is you moaning or panting out my name. Anything else, I stop. And it would be a mighty shame for only me to enjoy such a delicacy."

CHAPTER 18

CHARLOTTE

An unexplainable sensation washes over me, pleasure gripping every inch of my body the moment he hits that spot.

I cry out as he wriggles his fingers inside me, the pressure building low in my stomach. Fuck.

I blow out a shaky breath as he pours the milkshake onto my lower stomach, the cold liquid a jolt against my overheated skin. I shiver in response.

My eyes lock on his, and the hunger burning there, it gives me confidence. When he questions me, the truth falls out. This is the most exposed and vulnerable I've ever been. But I trust him with it. He's given me no reason not to.

I tremble around his fingers as he licks me clean. The sight of chocolate rolling down my stomach, smearing over my pussy, it's sinful. It's his. He leans in to claim it.

"Fucking delicious, heartbreaker," he groans.

"Just as greedy as me, aren't you?" he winks, and my heart stutters in my chest.

My eyes flutter shut, head tipping back as I surrender to it. This wild, unfamiliar sensation. Bliss. Peace. Pleasure.

My toes curl as he feasts on me. The contrast between cold sweetness and the heat of his tongue pushes me over the edge. Screams rip from my throat, hips moving on instinct.

"So fucking hot," he groans. I like that sound. I want to make him do it more for me.

He doesn't stop, his fingers pumping faster, his tongue flicking my clit.

"Give me your orgasm, heartbreaker. They belong to me. I want it. Now." His voice is rough and possessive.

A thrill tears through me as he hits that sweet spot inside me. His tongue and fingers moving in sync until I unravel.

For the first time in my life, I fall apart for someone. For him and only him.

My body shakes, orgasm crashing through me as I cry out, fists clenched, my pussy pulsing on his tongue.

"Beautiful. So fucking beautiful," he mutters, slowing down as I collapse against the table, gasping for breath.

When I look down, he's watching me in awe. A slow smirk curves his lips.

"I think you deserve a taste now."

I blink, trying to piece myself back together.

He licks my sensitive pussy and then pours more milkshake over it. Oh my god.

My leg jerks, my body reacting before my mind catches up. It's overwhelming. But I can take it.

He pours a fair amount this time, holding it in his mouth. Then he stands, his grip tightening around my throat, lifting me just enough to bring our faces level. He nods.

Ah.

I tilt my head back, mouth open. He spits the contents of his mouth into mine.

It's warm. Sweet. Intimate in a way that makes my heart stop. His gaze is molten as I swallow.

He leans in, licks the corner of my mouth, then crashes his lips against mine. He steals the breath right from my lungs, with his hand tightening around my throat just enough to make my head spin.

"How does it taste? Sweet? Sinful? Delicious?"

He pulls back, grinning, licking his lips.

"Hmm," I hum, running my fingers up the planes of his abs. "Decadent."

He raises a brow, slowly nodding.

"I like it. Decadent. Your pussy certainly is."

A beat passes. The world fades.

I lose myself in his bright, burning eyes. The air between us crackles. He must feel it too, because he pulls me closer and kisses me, hard.

"I can't stop, fuck. I need to be inside you, sweetheart."

I wrap my legs around him as he lifts me off the table and I lace my arms around his neck, deepening the kiss, our mouths never parting.I want him just as much. Every second with him drowns out the nightmares. He's a light switch to my darkness, flipping it on so I can feel again.

He slides the balcony door open. The low hum of the hot tub buzzes through the air, followed by a wave of heat.

He steps in, submerging us in the warm, bubbling water.

As he sits, the heat bites at my oversensitive skin. His hard cock nudges against my bare pussy.

I help him shove his shorts down, straddling him, nuzzling my face into his neck. But he tuts, gripping my jaw and dragging my face in front of his until our noses are touching.

"I want to see your pretty face as you take every inch of my cock, heartbreaker. I want to see how far I can push you. You tell me everything in those beautiful eyes."

I blink, speechless. His words? They light me up. Make me feel seen.

This is different. This is what being alive feels like.

He guides the tip of his cock to my entrance and my lips part. With my hands braced on his shoulders, I dig my nails into him and start to sink down.

"Fuck," he grunts.

His fingers grip my ass, helping me lower slowly.

"Keep going, there's more, baby." He winks, and I grin through the stretch.

"I'm so full," I pant.

It burns, but the way he kisses my throat, pushes my hair up, and pulls at the roots like he's worshipping me…It makes me take every inch.

"So fucking tight, baby. I'm going to explode inside you," he whispers, breath hot in my ear.

I tremble. He rolls my hips against him, and every time my clit brushes him, I moan.

"Let yourself feel, heartbreaker. Feel how good it is. How my cock fills you perfectly. Hmm?"

I nod, eyes fluttering shut as he dips down to suck my nipple between his lips.

His moans feed mine. The confidence he gives me has me riding him, taking what I want for once. Like I have some power here.

I want everything. More.

I want him to lose control. To throw me around and wreck me.

"Tell me, baby. You want more?"

I pull back and he lifts his head and chuckles.

"I can tell your brain went off there," he says, cupping my cheek. His hips jerk up—sharper this time.

"Shit," I hiss.

He nods knowingly.

"Yep. You need it harder. Don't you?" He swipes his thumb across my cheek.

His other hand squeezes my thigh, holding me down on his cock. I clench around him and his eyes slam shut for a beat as he groans.

"I need to fuck you properly. Let me give you what you need? Let me loose, and I'll take you right to the fucking edge and let you fall over it."

My blood pounds in my ears. Orgasm building again, faster this time. He keeps thrusting.

He leans in, his stubble grazing my jaw.

"Don't worry, I'll be flying right off that cliff with you. I don't want to just ruin you. I want you to destroy me too. Neither of us are leaving this room as the same people we stepped in as."

His eyes burn into me, so real, it makes me ache over the fact I am lying to him. I am not the woman he thinks I am.

"I want it all. Everything you have."

His hand grabs my throat. Hard.

I drag my nails along the lines of his shoulders, my breath hitching.

"You think you can handle pain and pleasure? I think that's what you really want, sweetheart. A little bit of both. Balance. The ultimate combination to have you seeing stars."

I bite my lip.

It makes sense. Maybe this is how I work.

Pain not to break me, but to build me. To wake me up.

"Do it."

That smirk spreads across his face.

He pushes down on my shoulders and thrusts up into me at the same time.

I cry out, and his arms wrap around my waist as he lifts us out of the water.

CHAPTER 19

DECLAN

Do it. Those two words turn me feral.

As fast as I can, I rush us out of the hot tub and into the bedroom, my dick being squeezed by her pussy. It is the closest thing to heaven I think I'll probably ever get to. Lifting her up, freeing my throbbing cock, I toss her onto the bed. She almost bounces off the bed from the force.

She giggles as she centers herself on the mattress, and my chest swells. That bright smile almost turns me on as much as her face when she comes.

I climb on the bed and flip her onto her front, snaking my hand around her hips and bringing her up onto all fours.

Running my tongue along her spine, she parts her legs for me. I slap her ass, causing her back to arch as she hisses out a breath. I pepper kisses over the slight red mark forming.

"Grab the headboard."

I smack her ass again, jolting her forward.

She crawls forward and places both hands on the headboard, leaving her ass in the air on display for me.

"Good girl," I praise her.

I settle between her legs, stroking my dick as I admire her. Ready and waiting. Trembling in anticipation for me.

Pushing down on her back to bring her ass up slightly, I tease her entrance with the tip.

"Such a perfect little slut for me. How do you want it? You want it nice and slow so you feel yourself stretch around every inch?" I say in a low tone, pushing into her soaking cunt and stopping.

"Or do you want it hard and fast? Want me to grab your hair and make you take it all like my good girl?" I trail my fingers up her back and grab a handful of her hair at the roots, but I don't pull.

I wait. But I'm not a patient man.

"Hard."

Before she even finishes the word, her screams rip through the air as I thrust into her all the way to the hilt and yank on her hair to pull her head back.

With one hand holding her in place on her hip, as she tries to move forward, I hold her in place and I pull out before thrusting in again.

"Fucking heaven." I tip my head back, pounding into her from behind.

"Oh my god," she cries out, and I smack her ass.

"None of that. Scream for me and only for me."

After a few more thrusts, I lean over her and grab the headboard above her, using that grip to propel forward. Deeper, harder.

Fuck.

My body tenses up as her cries rip through me and her walls clench around me, strangling my cock.

"Damn, heartbreaker. Your pussy is divine," I grunt between thrusts.

"Decadent," she manages to get out.

I chuckle, smacking her ass and tugging her hair harder.

I know she's close as her body shakes, so I pull out and grab her, tossing her down on her back. I stand and position myself at the edge of the bed. Pushing open her thighs, I grab her hips and drag her to the edge. She wraps her calves around my hips and I lean over her, taking her hands and holding them with mine above her head, my other hand positions my cock at her entrance and I slide right in.

"So fucking good," I groan as her slick heat smothers my dick.

"Mmmm." Her eyes flutter closed. I take her swollen lips with mine and kiss her, squeezing her wrists as I almost reach my peak.

"You ready to jump with me?" I whisper against her lips.

She smiles, and my heart races.

"Yes. Take me with you," she says softly.

Keeping one hand firmly on her wrists, I slide my other up her toned body and grip her throat and squeeze the pressure points on either side.

"Come all over my dick, like the good little filthy slut I know you are," I command.

With a few final pumps, her back arches as she falls apart, crying out and shaking against me, and that throws me over the edge. I come so violently inside her I swear I'm seeing stars.

But I don't take my eyes off her. As hers lock with mine, I give her everything. Filling her up with all I have.

"Good girl," I rasp, slowing my pace.

Rather than withdrawing from her, I hold still. I want to stay inside her for as long as I can. I gather her in my arms and get on the bed, lying on my back and keep her on top of me.

Brushing her hair off her face, she nuzzles into my neck, her breathing still erratic.

"Don't hide from me, heartbreaker," I whisper, suddenly wanting to comfort her.

I press a kiss to the top of her head and she hugs me tighter.

CHAPTER 20

CHARLOTTE

I close my eyes and press myself hard against him.

Everything overwhelms me at once. Is this how it is supposed to feel?

Listening to his fast heartbeat soothes me. He strokes my head and holds me tight.

"You okay, baby?" he whispers softly.

He strokes my face and takes my chin between his thumb and finger, dragging me to face him. The concern on his face is evident as his brows furrow.

"Talk to me. Was that too much?"

I shake my head. He doesn't know me. Not really. I can't tell him the full truth. Although, I actually wish I could. Not that he could help me.

"You can tell me, heartbreaker. I won't bite," he says, licking his bottom lip.

"Well, I'd take a bite of that fine ass of yours."

He runs his hands over my ass and up my back in reassurance.

"I've never come—" I pause. "—like that before."

He blows out a breath.

"Did you enjoy it?"

I nod.

"I never knew it could be so… intense?"

He chuckles.

"We've barely even scratched the surface. But yes, with the right man, all sorts of things are possible."

I pout my lip. If only he knew. I shake my head, not wanting any thoughts of Vlad to appear. I repress that shit and take it out in anger and one day, revenge.

"Would you like to come again for me?"

I feel his dick harden inside me, and I grin.

"Maybe. What do you have in mind?"

He pulls me forward, capturing my lips.

"How about you clean up your mess on my cock while I think about it?"

He steals another kiss.

"How do you like it, sir?" I ask.

Chewing on my lip, I watch as he raises an eyebrow. I think he's impressed?

"I love it when you suck on the tip. And really use your tongue, lick it clean. And once you've done that, relax your throat and see how deep you can take me. That mouth of yours is sinful, I will be coming in no time."

I suck in a breath, just imagining the new heights he is going to take me with this.

"And if you're a good girl and do that for me, I'll drag you in the bath with me, clean you off myself, and maybe even give you a massage."

I lick along his jaw towards his ear.

"Deal. I'll give you the best blow job of your life for that," I whisper.

Pushing myself upright, I crawl back and position myself between his legs, looking up at him through my lashes.

Sticking out my tongue, he keeps his fingers entwined in my hair as I lick the tip.

"Just like that. Good job, baby," he praises, and my cheeks heat.

Taking the tip in my mouth, I keep using my tongue, gauging his reactions as I suck.

His eyes close and he moans, giving me the confidence to try to take him deeper. I relax as best I can and take him as far back as I can before I gag.

"Oh fuck," he coughs out.

"I thought you screaming was my favorite sound. But you gagging on my cock just won. Go deeper, baby."

I do as he says, and he pulls my hair at the roots tighter.

"Mmm, yes."

I keep watching him as I bob my head up and down. It's a weird sensation, but seeing how turned on he is has me wanting more.

"Keep going. Don't stop. You're doing such a good job, baby," he says through gritted teeth.

He puts slight pressure on the back of my head to hold me in place and moves his hips. His eyes catch mine and they darken with pure hunger. Enough to make my pussy ache for him.

"You look so beautiful when I fuck your face. Next time, I'll film it so you can see just how pretty you are. And if you're a good girl, I'll let you watch it while I eat you out."

I wish there was a next time.

I pick up the pace, working with the thrusts of his hip, my scalp stinging from where he's pulling. Pain and pleasure are perfectly entangled.

"I'm gonna come down your throat." His voice is husky and so fucking hot with that Irish accent.

I nod, and he holds me there. His thighs tense up and I dig my nails into his skin as he coats my throat with his cum.

"Fuck," he roars out.

It would be better if he was growling out my name. I swallow, and before he can pull me off, I lick him clean as he strokes my cheek.

"Where have you been hiding?" he asks, and I look away.

"I've been living in Italy with my brother." I lie with the first thing that comes to my head.

It sounds better than I was kidnapped at eighteen and forced to marry a monster who forces me to kill for him.

"What's in Italy? Other than the sun and decent food."

"I have a waitressing job by the sea, and my ex doesn't live there."

"You weren't meant for him," he says seriously.

I raise an eyebrow.

"How so?"

"Because if you were mine, I would make it my mission to make sure you were relaxed enough to turn your brain off. I'd make sure you had unlimited orgasms every day, whenever and wherever you want them. I'd take the time to learn and explore your body, mind, and soul."

That will never be my life.

He sits up and pulls me up into his arms.

"Let's get cleaned up, shall we?" He leans in and presses a kiss to my forehead.

I nod as I run my hand through my hair and frown when it feels sticky. I look down at my fingers and his chest vibrates as he laughs.

"I need to wash my hair," I giggle, wiping my hand on his chest.

"Yes, baby. I'll wash my cum out of your hair, no problem." He winks, and I nearly die of embarrassment.

As he carries my spent body into the huge bathroom, once the tub is filled, he lowers me in the bubbles and I let out a moan, every muscle relaxing.

The water spills over as he gets in behind me and lays me back onto his chest, which vibrates as he sighs.

"You okay?" I ask, feeling his racing heart.

"Yeah, baby. This is just… different."

I swallow the lump in my throat. It's perfect. Lying with him is the most relaxed I have ever been in my life.

"A good different?" I question, and his arms tighten around my waist.

"The best kind."

He grabs the sponge and tips my head back, gently squeezing the warm water over my hair.

And when he massages my head, I nearly lose it. That is orgasm worthy in itself.

"Keep moaning and I can't be held responsible for what I'll do next," he growls, and a grin twitches on my lips.

So I let out an even louder moan as he washes out my hair gently.

He pours the water over my face and I squeeze my eyes shut.

The next thing I know, he lifts me in the air, ducks under the surface of the water, and my ass hovers above his head. Using my hands, I lean forward and lift myself up so he can breathe.

"Let me tell you something now. If I want to drown in this tub while eating your sweet pussy, that's exactly how I'll go out. Sit the fuck down and let a man eat." He slaps my ass and I do as he says.

He must have lifted his head slightly out of the water, because this man devours me.

Sucking, biting, and licking until I'm seeing stars, gripping for dear life on the side of the tub.

"Oh, my god," I pant out.

"Come on, heartbreaker. Drown me. Soak me. Come all over my tongue and let me clean it all up again."

So I do. I let my hips roll to his rhythm, and I climax again. Earth shattering to the point I'm shaking.

I almost want to cry. Not from sadness, just from feeling totally and completely worshipped.

Once we finish up in the bath, he helps me dry off and gives me one of his t-shirts, which ends up looking like a dress on me.

"I said 'till sunrise. That means, we get to cuddle," he tells me, wrapping his arm around me from behind and resting his chin on my shoulder.

"I didn't have you down as a cuddler. Let me guess, you want to be the little spoon too?" I lean my head back on his pec and look up at him, pressing a kiss on his stubbly jaw.

"My dick wants to be wedged between your asscheeks all night, so no, big spoon for me."

He presses a kiss on my throat, and my eyes flutter closed; the faint sound of the waves crashing fills the room as we watch them from the glass window.

Turning in his arms, I wrap mine around his neck and pull him down for a kiss. His hands find their place on my throat as he deepens it, moaning in my mouth.

"Fuck. I don't want this to end," he mutters between kisses, and my heart sinks.

"Me neither."

"Let's talk in the morning. We need some sleep," he whispers against my lips.

Part of me wants to stay in his arms forever.

It feels like home. Like the other half I've been searching for.

Someone who sees me. Beyond who I was forced to be.

But the rational part of my brain knows this is a fantasy.

My father's life depends on it, and so does my own.

Vlad will scorch this earth to find me. I will never be free.

Jimmy deserves better.

CHAPTER 21

DECLAN

I roll over and go to wrap my arms around my heartbreaker. But as my hand flops onto a cold pillow, my eyes open, and I sit up.

That fucking pain radiates in my chest.

She's gone.

Jumping out of bed, I know this search is pointless, yet a tiny part of me hopes she is still here.

Checking my phone, I have one text.

I open it up and it's Enzo with the location pin.

I look at the time. It was sent exactly ninety minutes ago. Shit. I look at the time and find some relief in the fact I still have forty minutes to get to that location still.

Dialing Finn, I rampage around the penthouse, and I'm right; her clothes are gone, and so is she.

No note. No text. Nothing.

Fuck.

"Meet me in the lobby in ten minutes," I tell him as soon as he answers and throw my phone across the room.

I'll get this done, then I'm going to find her.

That was more than a fuck. Having her in my arms, the world felt right. I don't want to lose that feeling.

I don't want to lose her.

I look up at the wooden beam door frame, covered in Hawaiian-style colorful flowers, and frown, double checking the address on my sat nav.

I'm definitely in the right place.

A text pops up.

E

Go through the main bar and out the double doors
at the back.

Okay then.

I follow the instructions, the bartender keeping his eyes laser focused on me as I slide open the door.

"Close it behind you," he grunts behind me.

So I do.

An array of wooden tables and red hammocks fills the beach-style courtyard. I find Enzo sitting on his own, head down looking at his phone with a frown.

I clear my throat as I approach and he looks up.

His eyes, almost as blue as my own, almost looking right through me, with a tailored navy suit and slick black hair.

He looks every part the Italian mob boss.

"Mr. Quinn. Pleasure." He extends his hand as he stands, and I offer a strong handshake in return.

"Take a seat, we have a lot to discuss and little time." His Italian accent, like Romeo's, comes through.

I sit opposite him and notice the pile of paperwork on the wooden table.

He looks around and laughs.

"Good venue, right?" He holds up his hands.

I chuckle.

"Different, I have to say."

He nods.

"Different throws people off," he says almost seriously and slides a piece of paper towards me.

I look down and frown as I stare at what appears to be a rundown factory behind huge iron gates.

"Tell me what you see, Declan."

I look up at him, hiding my confusion.

"A factory."

"Hmm."

He hands over the next piece of paper, a bird's-eye view of the factory.

"And now?"

I study it for a moment.

"A fuck lot of woodland, a mansion, and the same factory," I say, placing the paper on top of the other.

Another piece is handed to me. Words cover this sheet. I scan it quickly, my eyes stopping on the word "chocolate".

"Anything interesting?" he asks, continuing to read as I get to the interesting bit, profit reports from before it closed.

"A chocolate factory with a very decent turnover."

Enzo interlocks his hands, placing his elbows on the desk, his Rolex shining in the light.

"Now, I've seen the books for the Quinn Distillery. You boys know how to run a factory, or should I say, use one to your advantage. Correct?"

"Of course. It's our bread and butter."

We grew up running around that damn place, no matter how dangerous Mom warned us it was. It fascinated us.

Little did we realize at the time, it would become our laundering empire.

"Whiskey is a little different than chocolate."

Enzo shrugs.

"But nothing we couldn't learn fast."

He hands me another, smaller piece of paper.

The listing price. I blink a few times at the amount of numbers.

Eight fucking figures.

As if on cue, the door opens behind us and a bottle of whiskey and two tumblers are placed on the table.

Enzo throws down wads of cash and pours the glasses.

My brain is too busy doing financial calculations. He leans over and picks up the overhead view again.

"Do you want me to tell you what I see here?"

I pick up my glass and take a sip, letting it coat my throat. I need this.

"Please."

He rubs his hands together and grins.

I've heard he is the ultimate mastermind here.

He places the paper in the center of the table and points to the mansion behind the factory.

"You may not be aware, but I own an empire within the sex industry. Specifically, high-end clubs, only for the mafia or the elite in society."

Now that gets my heart racing.

Money, guns, and sex. This sounds like a dream job.

"Okay."

"Look closer, behind the mansion. There are houses placed in the woodlands, one giant mansion in front, see?"

I lean in and take a look and nod.

"What I see is the ultimate enterprise here. This is where we maintain order within our world. The factory, the perfect front to launder, to get our deliveries and disperse."

"Agreed. Easily done."

"I'm thinking, this mansion could be the center of my club. Only those who we want to know shall know of its existence. A place we can vet future members for other clubs across the globe. Managed by you and your brothers. Weed out the dirt, so to speak."

He hands me another piece of paper, images of inside the mansion.

I flick through them.

It's huge. In need of a revamp, but easily done.

"Lots of scope here for rooms, a bar. I see where you're going."

He leans back and knocks back his whiskey.

"I assume this area of my business is something you and your brothers would be interested in pursuing?"

I tap the side of my glass.

"I've never thought of owning my own, but I am very much involved in that lifestyle, yes."

He nods.

"I know."

Fuck, what doesn't this guy know?

"You know my blood type?"

"O negative."

I chuckle and finish the remains of my drink.

It's a no brainer. Its genius, is what it is.

"How do we move forward?" I ask, resting my calf on my thigh.

"You purchase the factory, I will remain a silent investor. We work together in partnership to get it up and running."

Flashbacks of last night whirl through my brain.

The chocolate milkshake.

The way she looked up at me through her thick lashes.

Her taste on my tongue still.

Decadent.

Her voice fills my head.

"Decadent. That's what we call the chocolate factory. The brand."

Enzo's eyes light up.

"I like that."

I nod. But it needs more of a flair. I tap my finger on my chin and a grin forms on my lips.

"So do I. But actually, Decadence sounds better."

My skin almost itches, feeling her scratches on my back. I can still smell her sweet scent. And that little niggling pain in my chest returns at the fact she left.

"You good?"

I shake my head, trying to rid that beautiful heartbreaker out of my mind.

"Yes. Sorry."

It's almost like he knows as he leans forward.

"There is no room for distractions here, Declan. I've seen it go wrong, I've lived through it too. Our game here, it's dangerous. Much worse than what you deal with in Ireland."

A shiver runs down my spine.

"The people I intend to test at—" He pauses. "—Decadence, will be the worst scum on the earth. We treat it as a means to an end. But Romeo and I will teach you the ropes as we go. You see, there is a clear order within my empire, one that is expanding rapidly throughout the states now. I need you." He taps his head. "In the fucking game twenty-four, seven."

"I will be. We are ready."

He leans back, pulling a cigar from a tin, offering me one.

I take it and spark it up with my lighter.

He holds out a small card, I take it and investigate. A name and a number, on the back, a price. Lower than the one on the piece of paper earlier, but still a staggering amount.

"Tomorrow, you call this number, you offer that price, and he will accept."

I frown.

"How do you know?"

A mischievous grin forms.

"I know everything, Declan."

Kinda adds up at this point.

"Once you secure ownership, we will start work on making Decadence everything we could possibly dream of."

I can't help but laugh.

"It's gotta be a first, hasn't it? No one will ever expect what lies behind the gates. Indulging in pussy and chocolate."

That earns me a chuckle from Enzo as he blows out his cigar smoke.

"A boss with a sweet tooth," he retorts.

"We gotta come up with a good slogan." I tell him.

The opportunities are endless.

A chocolate factory and a sex club. What more could we need?

"So, I take it we have a deal?" He extends his hand, and I gladly accept.

"The Quinn brothers are in."

He squeezes my hand hard, his blue eyes locking onto mine.

"Loyalty is rewarded highly in my world, Declan. This deal will make you the new boss of Pennsylvania. You will be in contact with Frankie Falcone, the New York boss, and Mikhail Volkov in Las Vegas. Are you ready for that?"

I've heard of both. I admire both. They're as ruthless as they are cunning.

"More than ready, Enzo. You have my word, we won't let you down."

CHAPTER 22
CHARLOTTE

"**A**nything on the cameras?" I snap at Misha.

I've been looking out of these damn binoculars for an hour. I saw Enzo walk in on his own, or a guy matching his vague description we've been given.

Italian, over six foot, and dark hair.

The camera feed went down two minutes before he stepped foot through the door.

"We should have got an apartment lower down," I grumble, looking back at Misha, who is laughing at his phone.

"I swear to fuck, if you're watching stupid videos again, I will smash that over your damn head, Misha."

His dark eyes snap to mine and he growls.

"It's dead, Charlotte. He's hacked the system and we can't override it. Just keep looking pretty with what you're doing. I'm almost in the cameras across the street."

I huff and get back to it.

"I'm in," he calls out.

"Good."

Not many people pass by here. There's a few loitering at the bar, but I can't really see it through the windows. Whoever the mark is, they'll likely be the next person entering. Seeing as the meet is set for one minute's time, I bet whoever they are won't leave this Enzo guy waiting if he's this important.

My breath hitches, and my heart almost stops.

Jimmy.

He is looking down at his phone when he gets to the door, then he stops and looks up.

I close my eyes and pinch the bridge of my nose. Hoping to God Misha isn't going to put two and two together of where I was last night.

"Gottcha," he shouts out cheerily.

Putting the goggles back on my eyes, a sinking feeling happens in my chest.

How am I supposed to kill the one guy who has ever made me feel… anything.

Why did it have to fucking be him?

"Hold up."

I cringe, refusing to turn around.

"Charlotte. Get your ass here."

I squeeze my fists and slowly turn. Leaving the binoculars on the table, I pad over to Misha on the kitchen island.

He points at the screen and looks up and smirks.

"Your face tells me exactly why I caught you running in the hallway at sunrise."

His eyes flick between my face and the screen. He tuts.

"You dirty fucking whore, he was where you were last night? You slept with the fucking mark?"

Silence fills the room before he slams his palm on the counter and erupts into laughter.

"No." I keep my voice flat.

"Liar. Well, well, well, you naughty girl," he mocks.

My blood starts to boil when he stands and leans in, taking a deep breath.

All my hairs stand on end as his nose touches my bare shoulder.

"You know I can't keep this information from Vlad, don't you?"

I shake my head and step back, keeping my chin up.

"Nothing to tell. You're wrong." I keep my gaze on him. I do not back down.

A sly smile erupts on his face.

"You smell of sex, baby. There is one way this can all go away. I will keep quiet and kill the mark, your identity never revealed."

My heart accelerates as he says the word "kill" so flippantly.

I remain still, assessing my options. There has to be another way. Fight, Charlotte.

"How's that then?" I question, tilting my head, reminding him I do not fear him.

He slumps back on his seat and taps his lap.

"Easy. Ride my fat dick, baby. Show me what you gave this asshole." He points at the still of Jimmy filling the screen.

Even like that, he makes my heart race. He doesn't deserve this. Not because of me and this bastard family.

"Oh, yeah? Is that all it would take?" I twirl my hair around my index finger and bat my lashes.

A growl erupts from Misha's chest as he swipes his greasy hair back from his face.

"God, I've wanted a taste of you for a long time."

With a slow step forward, I slide one strap of my cami down my shoulder. He spreads his legs and I shake my head.

Placing my hand on his thigh, I lean in and whisper, "If you want me to ride you, I have to straddle you." I pull back and bite my lip. The hunger in his eyes is repulsing me, but I keep this show up. He leans back and starts to unbuckle his belt.

I take a breath, trying to calm my erratic heart. He cannot lock on to my plan. Just as he's whipping his dick out, I grab the knife from the stand. He looks up, and I don't hesitate.

I drive that blade in the right side of his neck. Level with his Adam's apple, hoping I hit the right spot.

He jolts forward, his eyes bulging out of his head and mouth dropping, and right on cue, the blood rapidly spurts out of his neck.

He grabs hold of the handle, the crimson pouring through his fingers as he drops to the floor.

I step back and watch him bleed out. It happens so fast, the blood spilling over the white floor.

He tries to take a breath but gurgles, his eyes going wide, staring right at me. I can't move. I don't want to.

When he starts to wobble as his body goes limp, and all the color drains from him, I jump back when he falls face first on the tiles.

Fuck.

With shaking hands, I grab my phone out of my jean pocket and tighten my grip on the knife with the other. Calling the only person in the world who can help me.

The moment of truth about where he aligns.

I hit dial, and he answers on the first ring.

"Charlotte?" Concern is clear in Drago's deep voice.

I suck in a shaky breath, him being on the line calming my rapid heart.

"We have a problem. A big one."

"Let me check the line."

I hear a couple of clicks and he's back.

"It's Misha, he's dead."

Silence. I swallow the lump in my throat. My hands trembling.

"How?" he finally asks.

"Knife to the throat."

He swears under his breath.

"You did this?"

"Yes."

"Fuck. Fuck. Let me think."

I keep quiet, like a kid being told off at school. I glance up at Jimmy's face on the screen.

"The mark. Have you identified him yet? I assume you didn't make yourself known?"

"Identified. We are in the apartment across the street as directed."

"You got enough to ID him? We need someone to pin this on, pronto."

I look at the laptop and hold back the tears.

"Charlotte. Talk to me. You fuck this up, you're as good as dead."

"I know him. I know who he is, which room is his, and how to get to him."

I really don't want to do this. But it's me against him. If I fuck this up worse than I have already, I will die, and so will my father. And probably Drago.

"How do you know him?"

I cringe.

"I slept with him. Last night."

I flinch as he shouts over the phone.

"Jesus. Fuck."

"There is no other option. We pin this on the mark. We tell Vlad that when you attempted to capture him, he turned, stabbed Misha in the neck, and turned on you. You fled."

I nod. It makes sense.

It keeps Jimmy alive.

"Will Vlad buy that?"

I can hear him scratch his stubble.

"We get the cops on his tail. I have someone I can call in, it will get us the paperwork we need to back us up. You know what that means?"

I chew on my nails, dread pitting in my stomach.

"I can get into his penthouse. I can have it done in fifteen minutes. I'll hack into the CCTV, alert you when he's going to his room so you can get the cops in. I have no idea when he's leaving the resort. It has to be done now."

"Leave it somewhere he will pick it up, without thinking. His prints need to be on the knife."

My heart is almost beating out of my chest. I shouldn't care this much. I should be thinking about myself. But I can't help it. He had an effect on me that I can't shake.

"Will he actually get arrested? Like, go to prison?"

"He's part of the mafia. Even if he doesn't run, he will get out, especially if he's linked to Enzo. We just gotta hope he doesn't come after us with those connections."

"Won't Vlad go after him? The mark?"

He groans.

"Don't ever catch feelings from a one-night stand. And no. Not if we make clear he is dealing with Enzo. He's wary of Enzo. He won't start a war he can't win yet. We just have to stick with our story without the evidence and hope Vlad falls for it."

I let out a shaky breath.

"I don't give a fuck about him. I am here to protect you and your father, and myself in some respects. It will be fine. Your mark killed Misha. I'll arrange a clean-up. Now go. Do your job. We can discuss your behavior when you get home."

"I'm sorry."

I hate letting him down. I look down at Misha's dead body and feel no remorse. In fact, I want to get my tattoo gun and draw his flower on me now.

"I appreciate you telling the truth. I'll arrange your jet. Keep the phone close for details and call me when the knife is planted."

He clicks the call off. I swipe the laptop up, ready to delete all traces of Jimmy from the laptop and dump it.

It's the least I can do for the shit storm my actions are about to cause.

CHAPTER 23

DECLAN

A s the elevator to my penthouse opens, I sigh. It still smells of her in here. She's everywhere. I'm half tempted to ask Enzo to find her once we get this deal through.

Shit. I've gotta call Dad back.

I take a step out and my foot slides. Without thinking, I look down and see a slither of silver. I blink a few times, bending down and picking it up, and my heart stops.

Blood and a knife.

In my fucking penthouse.

Silently, I take out my phone from my pocket and dial Finn, resting it on my shoulder as I pace the penthouse.

"Dec?"

"You didn't butcher someone and drop the knife in my place, did you?"

"No."

I push open the balcony doors, nothing.

"Pack your shit. We gotta get out of here."

"Heard."

"Meet me at reception in ten minutes. I have a call to make."

Going to the kitchen, I grab the bleach and a cloth. Using my phone for Enzo, I hit call and pray he answers.

"Hello?"

"I need a favor."

"So soon?"

"Can you get the security footage into my penthouse in the last two hours?"

"I can. Hold on. What am I looking for?" he replies immediately.

"Someone's left a fucking bloodied knife on my floor."

"Wipe the prints."

I roll my eyes. I'm not a dumbass.

"I am as we speak."

Placing the knife in the drawer with the others, I slam it closed and ball my fists. Whoever did this, they have no idea who they are playing with.

"Sending images now. You might not like this."

My brows furrow as I put him on speaker and open the attachment. A face I will never forget.

The night of my life with the woman of my dreams.

Turns into a fucking nightmare.

I wanted to track her down to claim her as mine. She was perfect for me.

Now, I want to find her, and I will break her.

My fucking heartbreaker.

"Did you get her name?" Enzo asks, shaking me out of my fury.

"No. Not her real one, Brittany is all I have." I grit out.

I've been fucking stupid. Never again. It wasn't anything at first sight. She fucking tricked me.

"I'll see what I can do. Um, Declan, you have a further problem."

I sigh, resting my palms on the counter and lowering my head. This is a headache.

"Tip off to the cops. ETA ten minutes. Get your brothers, head to the trail just towards the beach, there's a road that leads off there on your right. Go there, and I'll have Romeo pick you up. Take the knife with you and dispose of it when you're home. For now, we will put you in a safe house and get you back to Ireland as soon as we can."

I slam my fist against the counter.

"What do they want with me?"

Enzo sighs.

"I'm unsure if it's you or me, Declan. There was someone trying to push us out of the security earlier. It's connected, and I will find out how. Now go. You have nine minutes to get the fuck out."

I frantically shove all my important shit in the bag and leave. My rage has tempered for now until I'm safe.

Fuck going to an Italian prison.

And fuck having a heart.

As I get in the elevator, I take another look at that image. The pain in her eyes is almost haunting.

"Mark my words, heartbreaker, your nightmare has just begun. I don't give a fuck what it takes, I will become your nightmare," I whisper.

Closing my eyes, no doubt about to walk into carnage with my brothers, all for the sake of some pussy.

Not just any, though, that night will live in my brain forever.

Now, it's tainted with hatred.

CHAPTER 24

CHARLOTTE

Five months later…

Shoving the last of my clothes in the backpack, I grab the stack of cash Drago gave me and put it in, zipping it closed. This is finally it.

Putting it on my back, I jog down the stairs. Even that now makes my breath heavy.

My hand instinctively goes to my little bump as I reach the door and I come to a stop.

Quickly retreating back to the kitchen, I hide a small-flip knife in the back pocket of my jeans.

This is the first opportunity, albeit, short notice, that I've had to make a final attempt to run.

Once I got back from Italy, everything changed.

It's not just me I'm protecting now, it's the baby growing in my tummy.

It sucks leaving my father here to rot, but this little beam of light is my priority.

And if it hasn't dropped in Vlad's head yet that he isn't the father, it will soon, especially when I give birth.

This baby will, I'm sure, look just like their daddy.

I have to leave, and Drago agrees.

Today was the first time Vlad has given me space to breathe since I found out I was pregnant. He got called to an emergency and that gave me the window I need.

Even if it hurts my heart abandoning my father. I shake my head, I can't dwell on that, I have to push forward. I can't save my father, but I can save my future.

Opening the door slowly, I step out into the gray air.

"Going somewhere?" Maxim asks, sitting on the bench on my porch.

"Just for a walk, being cooped up in here all day is driving me crazy." I say, keeping my tone sweet.

He huffs and stands.

"Against bosses rules. Back inside." He points at the door.

"I-I don't feel well, I just need air." I make my voice shake.

He shakes his head and steps forward, I see the wariness in his eyes.

"Vlad won't mind. Ask him for me." I rub my growing belly with my free left hand and smile.

"For fuck's sake, Charlotte," he grumbles and pulls out his phone.

Perfect day for a new recruit to be on the door. It's as if Drago planned just that.

Of course he did.

And he told me clearly, "get out of the house by any means possible."

As he frowns looking at his phone, I seize the opportunity to retrieve my blade and flick it open. Lunging forward, I plunge the blade directly into the artery in his throat. I've been practicing my knife skills more recently, getting ready for this.

His phone tumbles onto the deck, and he reaches out, so I bury it deeper and twist, making him fall to his knees with a grunt.

His face pales and he gasps for air, grabbing his neck as blood spills out.

He falls on his front with a thud, crimson now pooling near my feet.

Bending down, I maneuver him so I can unholster his pistol and I run for the gates.

I can almost taste freedom.

Where do I go next?

I don't know. But as far away from here as possible. I have the coordinates for a meeting spot Drago has set up.

Who I'm meeting is a mystery. I don't care. This risk of staying here far outweighs the dangers outside this compound.

This fucking hellhole.

The gravel crunches under my boots as I sprint as fast as my legs will take me.

I know this place well enough to know where the guards could be.

As I get closer to the black iron gates, I hide in a bush, assessing the situation.

One guard in the booth.

Ducking between the hedges, I find my way to the stairs and climb, flicking off the safety of my pistol as I near the top.

Keeping myself below the window. I take a breath, grabbing onto the seal, I pull myself up with my left hand and aim with my right.

He's busy tapping away on his phone and I grin, pulling the trigger straight into the side of his head.

My heart races as I slide open the window and jump in, searching for the button to open the gates.

"Sorry, Dan." I whisper.

I don't really feel remorse for these monsters anymore.

Hitting the green button, the gates slowly open. Excitement runs through me as I descend out of the window.

I let the adrenaline flood me as I sprint through the open gates.

I'm so close. So fucking close.

Whatever part of the universe took Vlad out on a job today with the majority of his men was clearly looking out for me and my baby.

A new life; I can almost taste it.

Just me and my baby.

The faint sounds of engines rumbling makes me come to a halt. I edge backwards up against the wall and duck behind the oak tree.

Four blacked out vehicles slowly drive by; I keep my guard up, holding my breath as the last car passes and enters the compound.

I don't have long before they see the bodies.

Or notice the gates were left wide open.

Pushing myself up to stand, I hold onto the tree and wait for the dizziness to pass in a few seconds.

As my vision returns, I gasp when the sound of heavy clapping appears behind me.

Fuck.

I Squeeze the gun tighter in my hand.

Maybe I get to kill two birds with one stone.

Spinning to face him, I aim at my husband, that disgusting smirk on his lips as he continues to clap.

"Quite the performance there, Princess."

His eyes darken as he stops, holding up his arms in surrender.

But that smirk remains.

"You think you have the power out here?" He tilts his head.

"Maybe I do. I'm the one with a gun aimed at your chest." I shrug, not breaking eye contact.

He takes a step forward and I release a bullet that scrapes his jeans.

"Don't come any closer or I will kill you, Vlad," I shout.

"Silly girl. There's nowhere for you to run. We have you cornered now. So power is back to me. You kill me, I'll have my brother rip that disgusting baby out of your stomach, and have you watch as he ends its life before it even begins. Then he will let you bleed out over the floor like a fucking pig."

"You think I can't take on your men?" I spit.

"Not in your condition, no. Shouldn't have been such a whore, cheating on your husband and getting yourself knocked up." The hatred in his tone has my heart racing.

He fucking knows. Of course he does.

I wonder if he knows who?

He chuckles.

"When I find out who he is, don't worry, I'll skin him alive, and then you can make a mannequin for your kid of their father."

I feel sick.

Shaking my head, my finger twitches on the trigger.

"You shoot me, you'll be the worst mother in history. Kill me, you kill your baby."

"What's the alternative? You kill me anyway? I think I'd prefer to just take you down to hell with me."

He swipes his thumb across his lip.

"Because you're so useful to my organization, I'll offer you a deal. Or, well, your child, a deal. It's not their fault they have the unfortunate luck of you being their mother."

Resting my hand on my bump, I lift my chin. His words won't break me.

"You come back to the house, you have your kid, and they will be overseen by Drago and remain safe. You, however, will not only be my prisoner, but also my assassin. For fucking ever. You step one foot out of line, a bullet from that gun goes between your kids eyes.”

I suck in a breath hearing the crunch of leaves behind me.

I feel the barrel of a gun connect to the back of my head. Fuck.

“Emil will escort you back to the house, Princess,” Vlad says softly and steps forward.

Gripping my chin harshly, my gun hits against his chest and the click of Emil’s safety makes my blood drain.

“Well? Death or duty, Charlotte?”

Reluctantly, I spit out “Duty.”

“That fire in your eyes. I can’t wait to take it from you,” he whispers, stroking my cheek, and bile rises up my throat.

He peels my fingers from my weapon and my arm goes limp as the gun is removed from my skull.

“I won’t be long. Me and your father have some unfinished business. His welcome here has been overstayed, don’t you think? Your child has taken his space.”

Tears well in my eyes.

“Please don’t.” I beg, and his evil laughter penetrates through me.

“I can and I will. I’ll make it quick. And tell him the good news. And how you sacrificed him.”

Emil roughly grabs my hands and shoves them behind my back. I don’t fight back.

These men are dangerous and their threats real.

“I’ll see you soon.” He leans in and presses a kiss to my forehead, I resist the urge to slam it into his nose.

What the hell do I do now?

CHAPTER 25

CHARLOTTE

5 Years Later.
Moscow

A searing pain rips through my face as Vlad's deep, gravelly voice slices through my sleep. My body shakes as I open my eyes. My wrists sting and burn as I tug on the rough, cold chains, the metal biting into my skin.

"Time to wake up, whore," he spits in my face.

I keep still and quiet. If I behave, I will see my daughter. If I fuck up, I stay chained here.

My limp arms fall, and before I can sit up, his rough hand closes around my throat, the pressure pinning me to the mattress.

"Today is a special day; isn't it?" he asks, stroking his index finger over my lip.

I search his dark eyes. He looks at me with pure hatred.

"What do you mean?" I whisper.

I have to be careful. It's not just myself that I have to fight for now.

"How could you possibly forget, maylshka?" He pauses, and his jaw ticks. I choke on a cough as his fingers tighten around my throat.

"Today is the anniversary of Isabella's conception. Or shall we call it the date my slut of a wife bedded another man?" He says her name with such malice, it almost makes me feel sick.

Pulling me up by my neck, he forces his face close, his stale, smoky breath a suffocating wave.

This isn't going to go well for me. It hasn't in the past four years. He won't kill me, not yet anyway.

He made that clear the night I tried to escape. Even with a blade plunged through his stomach, there was no getting out.

He has more hold over me now than he ever did. Despite my father being gone, the threat over my own daughter outweighs that. I get sent out on the most treacherous jobs; why? Because he knows I will always return to Isabella.

There is no way out for me from this prison.

A sinking feeling appears in my gut. Today is the anniversary of the last day I felt alive.

I wonder what happened to Jimmy?

The jarring impact of Vlad's hand on my head snaps me out of it, my skull protesting with a dull ache as it is forced to the side.

"What do you have to say to me today?"

As he yanks back my hair and licks my throat, a shiver runs down my spine before he parts my legs.

"I'm sorry." I make it sound as genuine as I can. I've almost perfected this scared, innocent act.

I'm begging for forgiveness when, in fact, all I want to do is slice open his chest. This time, fatally.

"Whore," he whispers, his fingers digging into my thigh. I resist cringing. I am numb to this now.

A sharp intake of breath escapes me as he snakes his arm around my waist, his grip on my tender wrists a burning brand. Welts on top of scars. I gave up begging him to stop chaining me to the bed.

He doesn't trust me not to kill him in his sleep. I suppose he's clever in that respect.

Instead, now if I have a job coming up, he won't do it as tight. It might impact my work.

I close my eyes and take myself back five years to the day. How it felt to have Jimmy's hands on me.

How he set me on fire with his words, with his touch, with everything.

He cared about me.

He, even now, is still the light in this nightmare I live.

I TUG down on the sleeves of my hoodie when I open the door to Isabella's room.

"Mommy!" she squeals excitedly, jumping into my arms.

"Hey, baby." I hold her tight, breathing her in.

"Uncle Drago said we are doing maths today," she says in a grump, and I laugh.

"Math is important."

A deep frown creases her forehead as her face scrunches up in a pout, her lower lip jutting out.

"Can we do fighting after?" She gives me a cheeky grin. She reminds me of her dad when she does that.

She's mischievous like him and knows what she does and doesn't want. Just like him.

"If you do your math, we can do some training, yes." I place her down on her feet and she slides her hand in mine, dragging me over to her painting bench.

"Wow, that's pretty, baby."

She takes a seat and gives me a brush smothered in pink paint.

"I drew you and me."

"I love it. I can put it in my special notepad."

She looks up at me.

"Can you tell me what my daddy looks like?"

I sigh and sit cross-legged on the floor next to her. Vlad wants nothing to do with her, so I told her the truth that he isn't her daddy as soon as I thought she could comprehend it.

I never wanted her to think her father could be so evil.

I feel sorry for her, never being able to leave this house. But it's best for everyone she's kept a secret, much like I am. Vlad is scared of Tatiana; that is something I am sure of, that is why our lives rest on the fact she does not know we are here. To her, I'm just a childless contract killer. She has no idea what her brother is really up to. That alone keeps us alive.

The second she does find out, we die. That is the agreement Drago managed to secure with Vlad. And that is why we have to find an alternative.

Drago's influence and power between the siblings has been enough to keep us alive, but for how much longer, I don't know.

"How about I draw him with a pencil in my special journal?" I ask her.

I wonder what Jimmy looks like now.

Sometimes I wonder if she would be better off with him and just let me rot here.

But then she smiles at me and she keeps me alive.

Grabbing the black leather pad I keep in a draw, it's how I make notes of important contacts, dates, names. Anything I can use.

And it's locked up in Isabella's school room. We can't leave the property, so Drago has become responsible for her learning, on top of keeping tabs on me. A pain shoots through my chest. He never asked for this life. He stumbled on me in the basement and ever since has held the burden.

"Did someone say numbers?" Isabella's bright blue eyes light up when Drago's voice booms through the room.

"Mommy said I can fight after!" Isabella sasses back.

I sheepishly turn to face him, and he raises a brow.

"Did she now? And is Mommy in a fit state to fight?" He tilts his head. He's worried about me. I know that.

I almost lost my mark last week. My task has been to remove any remaining men that were once part of Ivan Volkov's army. It's safe to say a few of them know how to fight, and I got caught between a wall and a knife.

Instinctively, I rub on my sore wrists. This is not helping.

"I'm always ready."

He nods, stepping past me and crouching next to Isabella.

"How about you go get the whiteboards and pens, sit at the table and wait for me? I just have to speak to Mommy real quick." He taps her shoulder, and she nods, jumping off her little seat.

I wait for her to be out of earshot.

"Talk to me about?" I ask, pushing my feet into frog pose to try to relieve some tension in my hips.

"A job."

I shrug. The usual.

"Anything interesting?" I ask, almost uninterested. I'd rather be here, homeschooling Isabella and plotting my escape.

"We need to talk in private later." The vein on his temple protrudes. That's never a good sign.

"How?" I throw my arms in the air.

"I'll speak to Vlad. Meet me in the office after Isabella goes to bed."

Drago stands and brushes off his suit jacket.

"That's good. Like life can't get any worse," I mumble under my breath.

"Charlotte. Suck it up. You are alive and so is your little girl. Not a hair on her head has been harmed. I am doing my best, and so are you. Stop this fucking pity party. You'll get yourself killed, and then what happens to her? What kind of mother does that?" he hisses, his eyes darkening, and I jump to my feet.

Within a second, I'm in his face, fists clenched by my side.

"Say it again, Drago, and I'll fucking drop you on your ass. I might be a bit defeated at the moment. It's been a rough few weeks. But I'm still in there."

A slow smile spreads on his lips as he steps back.

"There she is. Keep going. Find her again. The fighter who takes no shit. I need her."

I blink a few times.

"What has he got me wrapped up in?" I ask quietly, and Drago shakes his head, looking at Isabella.

"Not here."

I suck in a breath. Here we go.

I'm trapped worse than ever before. Even after he murdered my father after the birth of Isabella—my punishment for getting pregnant and running from him. He knew he now had someone more important to keep me in place.

My daughter.

And the threat that she would suffer the same fate.

The seriousness on Drago's face tells me this isn't good.

CHAPTER 26

DECLAN

"Fuck, I hate today," Conan whispers beside me.

I clap him on the shoulder and squeeze.

"Even after five years, it doesn't get any easier," I say, looking down at our father's grave on our estate. Right next to our mother.

Even though they both died in Dublin, we buried their ashes here, together. How it was meant to be.

"He's with Mom. I bet they're having a grand ball up there, aren't you, Da?" Finn tips his cap to the gray stone.

He died protecting us. I shake my head. The old man knew what he was doing.

Sacrificing himself to stop the war.

He gave himself over to the Bowens and let that cunt Arthur lodge a bullet in his head.

It should have been for Conan. Clenching my fists by my side, anger radiates through me. If I wasn't running from the cops in Italy, I might have made it home in time to stop him from making that decision.

My father may still be alive if she hadn't planted that bloodied knife.

"We are doing him proud," I tell my brothers, a lump in my throat forming.

Conan should have been the one. He killed James. We should never have let that happen. But we would have fought a war.

Our father knew that, so while we were in Italy, he took it upon himself to end it before it started.

It stopped the war from beginning and gave us our roots in Pennsylvania. All the money, the distillery, and his army all became mine.

"I can imagine he's watching us now and laughing. He would have been amused by our Decadence games idea," Conan mutters.

I laugh, looking at the name on the grave.

"Da only ever had eyes for one woman. He wouldn't have got it," I reply.

Perhaps that's my own problem. My eyes are firmly looking in the past at one woman. My fists clench just thinking about her. Those eyes haunt me. That still image of her planting the knife haunts my dreams.

While I was on the fucking run from the cops in Italy, our dad was killed. I'm standing here at this gravestone, placing flowers for my father, and I blame her for that.

Her first mistake was betraying me. Her second, the one I can't forgive, is this.

For the first year, I did everything in my power to hunt that bitch down. Grief and anger consumed me to the point I became a monster.

Whoever she is, she's damn good at hiding. Not even Enzo can find a trace of her.

I know in my gut, one day, I'll get my answers as to who she really is.

"I can hear you scheming, brother." Finn grins at me.

"Pointless scheming." I shrug.

Conan shakes his head.

"Well, maybe next year will be the year she turns up at the resort and you can drag her ass back here."

I roll my eyes.

It was a dumb idea, but one I couldn't shake.

"At least I get a vacation and a tan every year before the fun begins here."

Every damn year, to the date, I return back to that Italian resort. Waiting. Hoping. That my heartbreaker comes back for me.

If what I believe is true about her, that she's part of another group, then she will be far too clever to return. She knows it's a death wish.

Yet part of me still thinks that night we had was real.

You don't fake that. You don't fake that hurt behind her eyes. That was raw and real. Someone is causing her agony.

And now, five years have passed; every year, more fury is added to my fire.

I want to be the one inflicting the pain on her.

She is mine to destroy.

CHAPTER 27
CHARLOTTE

Song- Indigo, Sam Barber, Avery Anna

She has his blue eyes.

Much like he was for a brief period, she is my bundle of light in this hell.

"Mommy, can you read me one of your stories?"

She throws herself into my arms and snuggles against me. I stroke her black curls out of her face.

"What kind of story would you like, baby?" I whisper onto the top of her head.

This is our thing, sometimes we read books, most of the time Isabella wants stories I make up on the spot.

"The love one. The Queen and a Prince. Finish where you left off yesterday."

I nod slowly.

There's one story I want to find the words to write properly. The story of us. But the ending isn't my reality now; this is the what if.

What if I wasn't who I was?

What if it wasn't just one night?

What if he was the love of my life and we lived happily ever after?

That will never be my life, but I can dream, I can write about it.

I can tell my daughter stories to make her believe in love, that outside these four walls there is better.

I take a deep breath, feeling my chest expand with the cool air.

"The Queen cried herself to sleep, locked in the small room while the wicked man left her there for days on end. He knew of her betrayal and he would never let her leave."

Isabella gasps, and I stroke her shoulder.

"She was starting to think there was no way out of there. Years went by, and no one could save her, not even herself. Her only light in the world was her little princess."

I press a kiss to the top of my baby girl's head.

"But Mommy, isn't the Prince going to save her from the bad man that locks her up?"

I fight back my tears. How do I find the words to tell my four-year-old that there isn't always someone to save you?

That the love of your life may never return for you.

"No, baby. Because sometimes, the Queen has to save herself and her little princess first." I press a kiss into her dark curls again.

"But this is your story, Mommy. Make the Prince come and save her, please?"

I shake my head and smile sweetly at her beautiful, little face.

"Nope. You want to know why?" I whisper.

She nods excitedly.

"Because after the Queen takes down the bad man, she can find her Prince. Queens don't always need a prince to save them. They are strong on their own."

Stroking her soft cheek, I just about manage to keep it together.

And sometimes the Prince doesn't know the Queen is in so much danger. He doesn't even know her real name.

"But will she? Will she find the one she loves again?"

"Yes. She will search for the rest of eternity for her soulmate. I promise. It's my story, remember?"

I swallow the lump in my throat. I will find him.

I just hope it's before it's too late.

"But, you'll have to wait for another day to see what happens. It's time for you to go to sleep, baby," I whisper, picking her up in my arms and taking her over to her bright pink bed.

I smile, a quiet contentment settling over me, as I tuck her in, listening to her soft breaths.

She's healthy, she's happy, and she has no clue what goes on past her own little world here.

Drago and I protect her, and I take the brunt of all the pain.

And I'd do it every day for the rest of my life to ensure Vlad never touches her.

"Night, night, my gorgeous girl."

I press my finger on the tip of her nose, and she giggles, melting my heart.

As I stand, she grabs my wrist and I flinch, wincing in pain from the fresh cuts from the chains under my sleeves. Despite the stinging pain, a smile stretches across my face. I will be her shield.

"Mommy, do you think the Queen and the Princess will escape? Maybe live on their own one day?"

She looks so deep into my soul. She's a clever little thing. No matter how much I shelter her, she will know there is a world beyond these walls.

It's what she gets taught every day.

"Yes. The Queen will make it happen. I promise." I squeeze her hand, and she sniffles.

"Good."

She cuddles her unicorn teddy and closes her eyes, and tears stream down my cheeks.

"I love you," I whisper and walk to the door, taking one last look at her before heading to my room.

Tonight is an escape for me. Vlad and Emil are away on business for the night. It means I can sleep in peace and heal my wounds.

Before Isabella, I might have seen this as a chance to escape. Now, I've learned not to. There are guards everywhere and I am monitored constantly. One foot steps out of line, that sick son of a bitch will take Isabella.

The chains aren't used to actually keep me here. He knows the threats against my daughter do that on their own.

The chains are to break me down. Make me weak, vulnerable, and exposed.

Wiping away the fresh tears streaming down my cheeks, I open the laptop, staring at the blank document. Any search history is monitored, but I doubt he'd check a document saved in between Isabella's homeschooling folders. And if he does, it's simply a story.

Maybe I can rewrite my story and get lost in the words on the pages.

An escape so I can forget the nightmare I'm living in.

I can tell the story of Charlotte that was meant to be. The story where she isn't sold and forced into a life of murder.

No. This can be my happily ever after, where I find my Prince again. Where our story doesn't end after three days.

This is my "what if".

What if I save myself and find Jimmy again?

I type those two words on the screen, and it feels right. Visions of our night together replay on a loop.

It's like I can still feel his touch all over my body.

I picture him kissing my scars. Telling me it's going to be okay. I rest my head in my hands and let the tears fall.

No matter how many times I get knocked down, I get back up.

But each day it's getting harder and harder to do.

I need an escape, and I need it soon. I'll speak to Drago. Perhaps this last mysterious job is my way out. This will not be how my story ends.

As I picture Jimmy's piercing blue eyes staring into my soul, I smile.

I look at the screen through my tears and run my hands over the keyboard.

I can't rewrite my history, but I can decide my future.

Fiction or not, I have to believe one day, our souls will be brought back together and I can reign hell on this house.

As I start to type, the words flow so freely as I describe the Italian hotel. I don't know how much time passes. The world doesn't exist currently outside my laptop.

In this world, I am a badass martial arts instructor, away for a competition. My only care in the world is winning my fight. That's how I dreamed my life would turn out.

A knock at the door throws me back into reality. I take a deep breath and slam the laptop shut. Drago knows what happened and who Isabella's father really is. He doesn't need the full details.

"Come in," I tell him.

Without a word, he steps through the door, his worn sweats and faded black t-shirt hanging loosely on his frame, the shadows under his eyes deepening my worry.

"You good, Drago?" I ask as he silently hands me a stack of paperwork.

I know he's been tied up helping Tatiana recover from her head injury. Not many people survive a bullet in the skull, but she did. That's all I know and all he will tell me.

"Look, before you read this, just remember your end goal." He scratches at his stubble, and I snatch the paper from his hands.

I frown, reading the bold title in a fancy-ass font.

You are invited to participate in the Decadence Games.
Please ensure you read the rules and contract carefully.
One must step into hell to get a taste of heaven.
Upon signing, you shall become property of Decadence.
We look forward to welcoming you soon

"Drago. What in the fuck is the Decadence games? Property? Games? What?" I can't take my eyes off the words.

I can't be reading this properly.

I'm seeing BDSM, pain, and pleasure. Lists of things I've never even heard of.

I blink at the last page.

Death.

"Drago, I suggest you tell me what this job really is other than some fucked-up sex game."

I look up at him and he cringes.

"Words." I press, throwing the paper on my desk.

"Vlad was given an exclusive invite. Men are invited to sacrifice their wives or daughters to the games. Every year it's hosted, apparently. Only one woman survives and gets a ticket to freedom with some cash; the family of the winner is granted entry into Inferno. That's what the real prize is."

"Hmm."

I don't know what to say. Vlad wants an 'in' to America, and I'm the fucking bait.

"And I am what? Vlad's golden ticket into America?" I shut up as my voice raises.

"Am I his fucking sacrifice?"

I slam my fist on the table, the sound echoing in the sudden silence.

"I'm not doing it. I'm not walking into my death."

Drago steps closer. I hold my hand up and shake my head.

"No. That isn't your job."

I flick my head up.

"Your job is to go in, win the games, and get that fucking ticket to the Master. Once you're taken to him, you interrogate him."

I tap my nails on the wooden desk.

"Interrogate him, why? No more secrets, not like Italy. I need everything. Who even is he?"

Drago frowns. He's hiding something. His pupils dilate. Ew. What if it's some sick, creepy old man?

"It's linked to Italy, sort of. Vlad mentioned Enzo extended the invite especially for him. Whoever is behind these games is running it for Enzo. We need to know who and why. We need to know what the purpose of the games are."

I look at the scattered paperwork.

"To fulfill some fucked-up fantasies they have?"

Drago shakes his head.

"There is more behind those gates, Charlotte. Read the contract and the terms in full. Fill out the questionnaire. I've included a sheet with your alias details. There are some, umm, preferences."

"Preferences?"

He clears his throat and shuffles on his feet.

"Sexual. Do some googling after you read the terms. Make sure you hit the points he wants."

A shiver runs down my spine and I look down at my hands on my lap.

Is this all I'll ever be? A man's fucking property?

"I'm sorry, Charlotte. But this could be our last resort to get you out of here." His voice is laced with pain.

He knows what I endure.

He crouches beside me, and I force myself to look at him.

"You think I can honestly win this? I fight, Drago. This isn't my speciality."

Running my hands through my hair, I tug it to relieve some tension building in my skull.

"You can do anything, Charlotte. I think this could be your way out."

My heart almost stops. My eyes snap to him.

"How?"

"Whatever information Vlad is after, he's desperate for it. Find it out, use it to your advantage. Something has him rattled. And while you're stateside for a couple of weeks, I can work on an evacuation plan for Isabella."

"You're not coming with me?"

He shakes his head.

"I can't. You have to go alone. Part of the terms. We don't even know where it's held. You'll be collected via jet. You will be on your own."

I take a deep breath.

"You reckon you can get Isabella out?"

He nods.

"But how? Why now? We haven't found a way in four damn years, Drago." I throw my hands up in the air.

Right now this just seems like a suicide mission for me, not an escape plan.

"Get the information and proof you've killed the mark. Yes, I think this will give us the advantage we need. Isabella's freedom in exchange for information. You'll already be out of the damn country, unattended, untracked."

I scoff.

"Wait. I have to kill the owner? That's signing my own death warrant. In his house? His army? On my own? What makes you think Vlad will even go for a deal?"

Dragos' firm hand claps down on my knee.

"Remember how we said we might need to sacrifice ourselves to save Isabella? I think that is the way it has to go. The risk is worth the reward here. Tatiana is vulnerable now, and Vlad is after a takeover. We just need something good enough to give him to make him think it's possible. There is a link here, we need to find it and use it. I truly believe the key to freedom is inside these games. I see no other reason why Vlad would entertain this otherwise."

Tears well in my eyes, and I shake my head.

"And what if I don't win? I won't see my baby grow up," I whisper, my hands trembling.

He pulls me into an embrace.

"I'm not saying it will happen. It's a possibility you need to be prepared for. This job is more than any other before. The games are a survival mission, your task after is dangerous. But I know you, and I know how bad you want out of here. You can do it."

My tears soak into his shirt.

"How will I even contact you with the information?"

He hugs me tighter.

"We will figure it out. We have another week before you leave. We need to be smart. If we can pull this off, you and Isabella will be free. Just remember that."

I pull back and wipe my eyes.

"If there's a chance, I have to take it." I rub my fingers over my wrists.

"I'll start the paperwork tonight."

"This information could be the key to all of this, Charlotte," he whispers.

"What about Tatiana?" I ask as I pull back.

"What do you mean?" He frowns.

"You'd still betray her, even now? While she's recovering from a bullet in the skull."

He looks down at his loafers and sighs.

"Tatiana isn't a monster like them. She's a lost soul, Charlotte. Just like you. I'm helping her, just as I am you. This isn't a betrayal, it's helping you both. Okay? That's why I can't tell her about you or Isabella, the threat is real to you both. You have to trust me on that."

I process the information.

She's our leader. How is she lost?

I don't bother pressing. He gives nothing up about her. She's a mystery I won't ever solve.

I know parts. Things I've overheard from Vlad and Emil.

"She needs to remember who she really is, the same way you need to remember who Charlotte really is."

With a gentle tap on my shoulder, he silently leaves.

Which just has my mind spinning.

CHAPTER 28

DECLAN

The door to my office inside Inferno flies open with a loud bang, making me sigh in frustration.

This club is our haven inside Decadence.

Hidden behind the factory is four floors of sin—only for the elite. And the only way to get to Enzo, Mikhail Volkov, and Frankie Falcone.

Between us, we run the largest Mafia operation in the States. Those who aren't part of Inferno want to be part of it.

In fact, they're so pathetically desperate they're willing to sacrifice their wives and daughters for just a chance to rub shoulders with us.

If you know about Inferno, you're invited in, or it will be the last thing you learn before you're six feet under.

"You look stressed, bro," Conan tells me as he heads straight to the cigar cabinet.

I am rattled. It's the same every year. I go to Italy and come back and immerse myself in the Decadence games.

Part of me believes one day she will turn up and I can taste her again.

There isn't a chocolate that could even be invented that would taste anywhere near as good as her cunt.

And our chocolate is good. The best even. With some of the wildest flavors on the market.

I can't satisfy myself anywhere else. And God, I've tried. That's how Inferno was born.

Yet no matter who I indulge in. There's always only one woman on my mind.

A fucking thorn in my side at this point.

Rubbing the tattoo on my chest, I swear it burns every time I think of her.

With every year that passes, my lust is replaced by fury.

If we ever cross paths again, I vow to break her and drag her into the depths of hell with me.

I am not the same man I was five years ago.

She is best staying wherever she is hiding.

The acrid smell of Conan's cigar filled the air as he approached, his throat clearing snapping me back to reality.

He looks just like Dad.

"Good trip?" Conan's sly smile means he knows exactly what he's digging at.

"The games are still going ahead then?" he asks as he swipes a bottle of whiskey from the shelf.

"The games are on every year," I reply dryly.

"Why don't you just go find that woman you're obsessed with and marry her? Why make her come to you without an invite? I mean, come on, you could find her if you really wanted to. Ask Enzo again. You say you hate her, and I believe you, but I also know you better than that."

I could ask Enzo again. But truthfully, I don't know how I'd react.

He couldn't find her the first time. Why would he now?

I've played it over in my head, us meeting again for the first time again. Each time, I believe her lies.

She could make me weak.

Or she could plunge me so far into the darkness that my last shred of humanity is gone.

And my brothers need me.

"Excuse me?"

I don't know who the fuck my brother thinks he's speaking to. Just because he fights in a cage doesn't mean I won't crack his skull open.

"I don't want a wife. I want a slave."

"Oh, fuck off. You're too nice to your submissives. You ever left one in the woods all night?"

"Just because you're deranged doesn't mean I'm nice. I do my punishments differently, each catered to the woman."

He rolls his eyes and slumps down on the velvet couch in front of me.

"I don't mean it like that. I mean, it's been five years. I don't think the women that work at Inferno are what you want."

I swirl the ice in my whiskey and the clinking sound fills the quiet room.

"Well, she doesn't exist."

"Hmm." He knocks back his own drink and slams it on the table in front of him, then kicks his feet up. I smack them straight off.

"Feet off, you filthy fucking pig."

"No wonder she did a runner. Get that stick out of your ass, bro."

Before he can continue, I dart my arm across the table and grab him by the neck.

"She didn't run away. She fucking betrayed me and nearly landed me in an Italian jail to rot. So unless you want to live in the fucking woods and forage for food for the rest of your life, I suggest you shut that fucking mouth and go do some work. The chocolate factory still has to run, you know? That's the whole idea of a fucking front."

A wicked smile forms on his lips.

"It's running, isn't it?"

I squeeze my hand tighter.

"Maybe I enjoy being choked. Get your hands off me, Declan, before I nut ya and break your pretty face."

I release him, and he slumps back in his chair.

"Pretty good grip. You been training like I told you to?" he says, rubbing his neck.

"I train every day."

He sniggers, and I lean back in my chair.

"So, who are your contestants this year?" He claps his hands together, looking at the paperwork in front of me.

We never receive photos. Just backgrounds, tests, and preferences.

These families want an in to Decadence, well, they want the mafia ties we have across the country.

That is exactly the point of the Decadence games. Weeding out the bad in our world for Enzo.

Not everything behind these gates is as evil as we want them to believe. We lead them to think the winner will become my submissive for a year, and the losing contestants end up in a grave. If only they knew the truth. The winner, in fact, ends up with one million dollars and a ticket to a brand new life. Far, far away from their abusive families or husbands.

"Same criteria as the previous years. Hot, dark hair, can handle pain, won't talk back." I flick through the pages and stop on the one that instantly caught my eye.

"Sounds good. I'm still waiting for my final contestants from Enzo." Conan cracks his knuckles.

"Yeah, I had to wait longer for mine. Something to do with a Russian family he's wanting to create ties with. He was waiting for their response before offering out the final space."

I rarely question it. Each year he just slaps the final contestant's papers on my desk. He made it clear that was his role. We aren't looking at the women. We are hunting the families responsible for the applications.

Men desperate enough to sacrifice their daughters or wives to get a way into our club.

Inferno isn't just a sex club.

It's a whole other world. Only those who are worthy of knowing about it are aware of its existence.

It doesn't just open you up to sex.

But to arms, drugs, laundering, hitmen. You name it, the Quinn brothers provide it.

These families are giving a sacrifice to me for their membership.

Little do they realize they are about to lose far more than they could ever imagine.

That's where Finn and his menacing, arguably evil, ways come in. Death is involved in the games; that is a fact.

But for the family of the woman who receives the ticket, they get the ultimate prize. It's their ticket to our inner circle, which extends to mafias in Vegas, New York, Chicago, London, and Italy.

Again, it's a very short-lasting arrangement.

I don't know who is more sick in the head. Us, or the fathers who sell their daughters to the games.

"They look good. A good variety. It will be interesting to see who wins this year."

I slide my hands over the one report that sticks out to me.

Ebony West.

She sounds sexually inexperienced in the BDSM world.

Likes: spanking. Being tied up. Blindfolds.

Hard limits: none.

Everyone has a hard limit in this game. Not that they exist during the games themselves. But in the end, the winning woman gets a choice. Take the money and run, or if we both so choose, they can become my submissive for the year. Yet, I haven't come across a woman who interests me so far to offer her that deal.

Now looking at Ebony's answers, I want to find her hard limit. This gut instinct wants to take her, break her, and mold her into the perfect submissive for me.

There is nothing better than breaking one in to be mine.

"There's one you like, isn't there? You know the rules, Declan. We can't have favorites."

I bite the inside of my lip.

"I'm the head of the family. I can do whatever the fuck I like, Conan," I growl in annoyance.

Maybe this is just what I need to finally get over my mystery girl.

Someone else to shatter instead.

That's how I get my pleasure now. Inflicting my pain on others.

Those who are hurt, hurt other people. And that's the harsh reality of my world.

"Let me see." Before I can swipe it out of the way, he grabs it from my fingers.

"Oh, sexy name. Ebony."

A pang of jealousy shoots through me.

"Enough."

"And she likes spankings. Pretty bland other than that. What caught your eye?"

He scans the report, and then I watch the light switch go off as his green eyes look up from the paper.

"No fucking hard limits. Brother, this girl has to win. Imagine the shit you can do to find them. I want her in my games. I'll give you one of my girls. Do a swap?"

"Exactly my thoughts. And no. Fuck off."

I snatch it back and place it with the others.

"So, you gonna influence the games? Or take part this time? You should. It's fun. Just wear a mask so no one sees your face."

Maybe I could watch from the sidelines this year rather than from a monitor screen. Both Conan and Finn immerse themselves in their own versions of the Decadence games. Finn's, well, we stay well away from that.

But if this woman is that inexperienced, I have no hope of her winning. Unless she really is telling the truth and has no hard limits.

But that's about as likely as a magical chicken shitting out golden eggs full of cocaine at this point.

"No. We never influence the games. That's the entire point, Conan. They have to survive by their own right to earn their ticket to freedom."

He chuckles.

"Someone should look inside our brains. We're all fucked up, Dec. Even our precious doctor, Finn. I bet his contestants are like a test experiment."

He clears his throat and gets into his "Finn" character. Those two are like chalk and cheese. Conan, the cage fighting lunatic that never shuts the fuck up, and then Finn, the brooding doctor, intelligent as hell. He's quiet yet won't even blink when slicing someone up. Possibly the truest psychopath you can get.

"Spread your legs, baby. I need to get a good look up in your cunt to make sure you're tight enough for me. If not, I'll add some stitches," Conan mimics our brother's deep, yet well-spoken voice.

"Fucking hell, Conan." I toss my pen at his head. Now I have visions I don't want playing out in my brain.

"Never bother trying doctor role play."

He frowns, as if he's deep in thought.

"I do enjoy a bit of blood and knife play. I might have to give it a go. I'm sure Finn won't mind me using his kinky medical room."

"Good luck getting the keys from him," I tell him.

Finn is the most secretive out of the three of us. Neither of us have seen inside there, not sure I even want to.

He has an important role in our games. Whatever keeps him satisfied is no concern to us.

I glance back down at Ebony's file. Something about her is making my chest ache. I'm excited to watch her arrive. Contestant number three will be high up on my watch list.

CHAPTER 29
CHARLOTTE

I lean on the counter, breathing in the rich, dark aroma of the freshly brewed coffee, the warmth of the mug a soothing contrast to my fingertips.

With a loud bang the kitchen door swings open, and the sound of Vlad's boots echoes across the wooden floor.

"Sign the contract. Today," he commands, tossing the paper down on the dining table.

I nod, my gaze drifting away from his intense stare.

I already sent in the application after some thorough research. It was eye-opening, to say the least. We must have had confirmation I've been accepted, guessing by his abrupt tone.

A sense of unease washes over me, making me instinctively walk next to Isabella and place a protective arm around her.

She's terrified of him.

Mostly, he ignores her. She disgusts him.

"Get the brat out of here, or I'll send her to the pig farm." He wiggles his finger at her.

She shivers against me, almost plastering herself to my leg.

As long as I behave, she stays alive and unharmed.

Ultimately, I couldn't save my father. Vlad took my mother from me, too. He isn't taking my baby.

I will never let this man touch my daughter.

Speaking of, I look up at the clock, and it's two minutes past eight. Drago is late.

Unusual.

Crouching down to Isabella, I brush her dark curls away from her shoulder.

"Why don't you go wait in the living room and pick out a book. I'll read it while we wait for Uncle Drago. Okay?"

She nods, and I give her a kiss on the forehead.

"Good girl," I whisper.

I keep my eyes pinned on her as she skirts around the table and runs past Vlad.

"You don't trust me?" Vlad scoffs and steps forward, clenching his fist.

"Me? After what you did, you dirty whore. You don't trust me?" he shouts.

I don't flinch as he pushes the chair away from the table and it knocks against the floor.

I lift my chin. I won't shrink from him.

He picks up the paper and shoves it into my chest.

"Sign it. The perfect assignment for a slut like my wife." His saliva hits my cheek and I wipe it away with the sleeve of my cardigan.

I take the paper and back away until my butt hits the cupboard.

"Surprised you aren't jumping for joy. Time away, and you get to be a whore." His lips twist into a grin as he twirls my hair around his finger.

He pulls it, and I wince.

"You're lucky you're an asset to my family; otherwise, you'd be dead by now," he seethes.

Pulling back, his evil eyes stare into mine as he grips my jaw.

"And, I like having you as my pet. Locked up and under my thumb. Turns me on." He grabs his junk, and my nose scrunches.

I wince as he leans in and slaps a sloppy kiss on my cheek.

"Make sure the brat is in bed before I get home. I want an evening with my wife. It could be one of our last." He releases me and winks, stomping towards the front door.

I grab the counter after throwing the contract down and take in a shaky breath.

Hatred. That is all I feel.

Every time he touches me, I imagine the joy it would bring me to stab him through the throat.

One day.

"Mommy? Can we read now?" Isabella asks once the door slams shut.

"Coming, baby," I call out.

I fluff my hair back out, grab my coffee, and head in to see her.

She's happy, giggling away to herself as she plays with her dolls in their sparkly pink dresses.

I don't care how much pain I have to endure if it means that smile stays on her face forever.

"Which book?" I ask. She looks up at me with her enormous blue eyes, all bright and full of life.

She pouts and taps her lips.

"I was thinking, your special one again?" she says, giving me a cheeky grin.

"Didn't we finish it last night?" I tilt my head.

She's desperate for me to change it.

I wish I could rewrite my past.

"Yes. But we can do a different version. Please?"

Expertly, she bats her lashes and gives me a sad pout.

"Fine. We can make some tweaks," I tell her.

Taking a seat on the leather couch, she jumps up next to me and snuggles in.

If I'm not training or on jobs, I'm writing my book. The perfect escape for me. But it plagues my thoughts all day and night of Jimmy.

I don't even get halfway through before Drago knocks on the door.

"Go let him in," I tell her, looking at the camera and checking it is him.

Heading into the kitchen, I pour him a coffee and hand it to him as he carries Isabella in.

"You okay?" he asks.

I nod.

Picking up the contract, he frowns, putting Isabella on her feet.

"I'll sign it today," I tell him, finishing my drink and washing it out in the sink.

"Thank you. I've been working on contacts to have near the area. I've done some digging. I'm fairly certain I have a close enough location."

"Fine. How's our other plan looking?"

"I think we can find a way; just get the job done. Okay? Trust me. Whoever is behind those gates is the key to this."

I nod.

He's never given me a reason not to.

After giving Isabella a kiss goodbye, I take the contract and curl up on the couch.

My morning read is quite something.

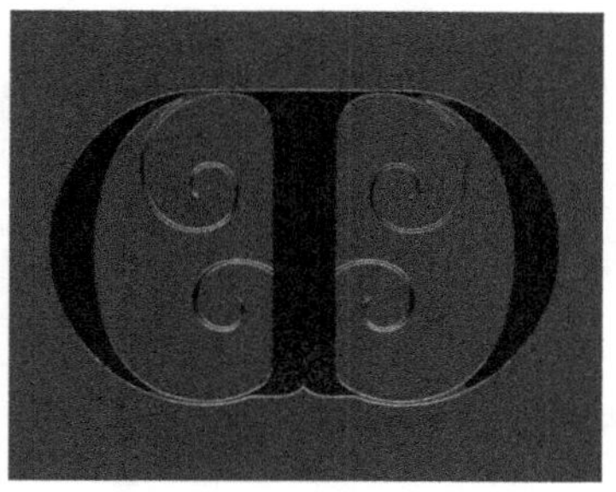

The Decadence Games Contract

The agreement is entered into between The Master of Inferno **(hereby referred to as 'The Master')** and Ebony West **(hereby referred to as 'The Contestant)**.

PARTICIPATION:

This contract binds the contestant to The Master. Once the contestant enters the gates to the property, they willingly give full control to The Master.

The Contestant understands this is a game of survival. She shall compete with SIX other women.

There shall be five rooms total to complete. Only ONE woman receives the golden ticket.

THE REWARD:

The Contestant understands that a golden ticket is the reward if she should win.

The golden ticket shall be issued and must be given to The Master to accept.

In return, The Contestant shall receive **one million dollars.** Their family shall be invited into Inferno. There are further winning perks, those shall be discussed directly with The Master on collection of the ticket.

CONSENT:

The Decadence Games are designed to establish and test The Contestant's tolerance of both pain and pleasure.

Therefore, The Contestant consents to the below, but is not limited to:

- Spanking (using various tools)
- Hair pulling
- Restraints (of entire body)
- Use of sex toys
- Food play
- Sensory play
- Branding
- Anal
- Vaginal penetration
- Choking
- Biting
- Spitting
- Rough play
- Role play
- Self-gratification
- Edging
- Orgasm denial
- Torture
- Degradation
- Humiliation
- Death

The Contestant agrees to allow her designated guard/handler to lead her around the property. She must not go anywhere without her guard.

She must follow orders.

She must dress as required for the games. Outfits shall be provided by The Master.

She must not climax in the games unless it is specifically instructed by The Master.

She must respect those who are part of Decadence the same as she would her master during the games.

CONSEQUENCES:

The Contestant understands the survival element of these games. Therefore, The Contestant understands that once she enters the gates of Decadence, if she is unsuccessful in the games, she consents for her life to be ultimately terminated.

If The Contestant makes any attempt to harm a member of Decadence, or escape her fate, she is also consenting to a punishment of death.

One must step into hell to get a taste of heaven.

SIGNATURE AND DATE:

By signing this agreement, The Contestant understands she is signing her mind, body, and soul over to Decadence.
The parties hereby agree to the terms and conditions set forth in this agreement and such is demonstrated by their signatures below:

....

Holy fuck.

I read it over and over, until eventually I sign that dotted line. As I forge my fake name, it seals my fate.

With everything riding on this last attempt, this is my last chance for freedom.

A million dollars can't solve my problems, but killing The Master could.

CHAPTER 30
DECLAN

His face bright red and slick with sweat, Conan jogs toward me, wiping his forehead with a strained expression.

"I told you not to be fucking late."

I slap him on the side of his head, and Finn glares at Conan.

Con scowls, his frown deepening as he checks the time on his Rolex.

"I'm only two minutes late!" he protests.

A snicker comes from Finn next to me.

"And this is why we told you a time ten minutes earlier than Enzo was actually arriving," he tells Conan, who smirks in response.

He's so invested in reviving his cage fighting career, we hardly see him. He lives and breathes the cage.

But the Decadence Games bring him out to play.

He kicks his sneakers on the gravel and looks back at the front doors to the factory.

"What is this, show and fucking tell? He knows how we run our games. What makes this year different that he needs a damn tour?" Finn snaps.

I lift my shoulders in a nonchalant gesture. "We will never understand how Enzo's brain works."

Clearly annoyed, Finn lets out a derisive scoff beside me, making me turn to him.

"This isn't very 'silent partner' of him. The games were our idea. We've run two; I've done what I had to do after. Con is right. Why is he suddenly so interested in it now?"

"I don't know. Maybe it's linked to the Russian family he invited? We know the game has changed in Russia recently. Maybe Mikhail is behind it?"

Finn bites his lip, deep in thought.

"With Ivan dead, that makes sense. Although, I'd have thought Mikhail would want to be as far away from Russia as possible after killing his own father."

Pain twists in my chest thinking about our own father's sacrifice. But his was different. Ivan tried to kill his own family first. He deserved it.

We've met Mikhail occasionally. We keep our alliance with him and his family in Vegas tight, and also with Frankie Falcone in New York. Seeing as we facilitate bringing in most of their arms and drugs now, they have time for us.

Silence falls as the gates to Decadence open, and we all crane our necks to see the sleek, black Bentley glide in, its tires humming on the asphalt.

"Here comes our King," Conan whispers, full of sarcasm.

"He made us who we are today. This fucking empire was built with his help. Now play nice," I hiss at Con.

As the Bentley smoothly comes to a stop, the quiet hum of the engine fades as his driver opens the door, and I head over.

"Enzo. Welcome back to Decadence." I extend my hand, and he shakes it firmly.

"Good to be back."

He nods curtly to my brothers, who stand silently behind me, their faces grim.

"The full family tour today, I see," Enzo says, straightening his navy tie.

"Yes. Now, you want to see this year's games?" I smirk.

"I do. Then I have some things to discuss with you."

The sound of his fingers dragging across his five o'clock shadow accompanies my nod.

"Of course. Follow me."

I swipe my card to the main doors of the factory. As we walk in, the sweet smell of chocolate hits you.

"Any new flavors?" Enzo asks beside me.

"AK-47 with a hint of honeycomb."

He chuckles as we pass the loud machinery. Our workers are part of the mafia families or directly under me.

Sworn to secrecy.

The twins, Rowan and Reggie, appear from the side office, and I nod, hearing the soft click of their shoes on the polished floor.

We stop, and Enzo looks between them, studying them.

"Hang on." He holds up his finger. "Don't tell me."

We all stand in silence as Enzo holds out a hand to Reggie on the left. They are identical, even down to the dark green streaks in their black hair. Same style, shaved sides, swept over on top.

"Reggie," Enzo finally says with a grin, and Reggie bursts out laughing, accepting his handshake.

"Got it. What gave it away?" he asks Enzo.

"You have a slight speck of amber in your eye."

Reggie looks at me, impressed. The twins are our right-hand men. Down to do anything. They mainly oversee the non-chocolate operations we have here.

"You don't miss a thing," Rowan says, and Enzo nods.

"Sir, we have a delivery coming today. We are going to split it between Mr. Volkov and Mr. Falcone and deliver one each tomorrow. Then we will be back in time to run the games," Rowan tells me.

"Good job. Everything is ready for the games, yes?"

They nod, their eyes losing their light, a chilling darkness replacing the usual spark.

"Yep. I have to say, I'm looking forward to this. Whichever woman wins is a total badass."

My lips curve into a broad grin, showing my teeth. That's the plan.

"I said I wanted this year's games to push them to their absolute limits."

"Oh, it will." Reggie grins.

Pain and pleasure. The premise of my games. A way I can find a woman—to inflict some of this torture I feel inside on.

No emotions. A clear deadline. No ties.

It's perfect.

The games give us exactly what and who we need. But it's far more than that. These games establish who the Quinn brothers are to the world.

They must believe the illusion that we are the true villains so we can be their saviors.

Once one steps into Decadence, there is no way out.

The illusion is real. In a sense, we make them walk through hell to get a taste of heaven.

"Are you ready?" I push open the door and turn to Enzo.

"Now you have me all excited."

The group trails behind, their footsteps echoing softly as I lead them down the long corridor. We created this as an add-on to the back of the factory, completely separate with security to get through. Only to be used for the Decadence games.

Two secret exits exist.

One is for the winning girl to lead her to me.

I scan my finger on the pad and then type in the code, causing the bolt lock to turn. The first room to my left is the holding room.

Where the losing contestants are held before they meet their fate.

"New floors?" Enzo asks, looking down at the shimmering purple marble under his feet.

"Easier to clean up the mess," I tell him and smirk.

I take him to the first door and look back at my brothers, who are holding it together. I can tell Conan wants to laugh.

I let Enzo go in and wait next to Finn.

"Jesus fucking Christ, Declan."

That sends Conan over the edge. He bends over, clutching his stomach, tears streaming down his face as he laughs uncontrollably. The cool air makes me shiver as it beats against me from the room.

"It's fucking freezing." Enzo rushes out of the room and closes the door behind him.

"Gotta keep the molds in perfect condition. Chocolate melts." I bite back my grin.

A low chuckle escapes Enzo's lips as he shakes his head, a smile playing on his lips.

"I am lost for words. Creative. But an easy start for them?" He frowns. I can hear the cogs turning.

I clasp my hand on his shoulder.

"It only gets worse from here. False sense of security. I want to see how they behave. If they take it seriously or not."

Enzo blinks at me. Taking in what he's just seen, Conan finally stops laughing.

"Show me the worst room," Enzo asks.

"As you wish."

CHAPTER 31

CHARLOTTE

"Dimi, behind," I shout. He's too slow.

With a sharp intake of breath, I heft a throwing star, its weight familiar in my hand, and take aim at the man rushing toward Dimi.

It lands right on the back of his neck. He grabs it and falls to the ground. Finally, Dimi turns and finishes the job by slashing his throat.

"You're fucking welcome," I mutter.

Moving forward through the woods, the last cabin comes into view, a lonely structure amongst the towering trees, where Ivan's remaining men wait.

They've been in hiding since his death after his son, Mikhail, slaughtered him last month. Obviously, no one wants to take over his father's vile operations. Vlad tasked us to wipe the rest out.

This way it's easier for them to establish full control over Russia.

So here I am.

Ending their lives.

Flower by flower.

As the wind blows, I shiver, coming to a halt by the oak tree.

"You take the back, I'll take the front," I tell Dimi.

"How many have you counted?" he asks from behind me.

He's there to keep an eye on me, a replacement handler while Drago is busy, but like every op I lead. He's almost as useless as Misha was.

Except this one is less creepy. He fears Vlad, and that keeps him far away from me.

"Well, one armed guard is out front. Inside is anyone's guess. You got enough ammo?" I turn to him, and he scratches his head.

"Yea. You?"

I nod, retrieving my gun and flicking off the safety.

"See you on the other side, I guess. Wait till my shot to go in," I tell him and crawl close enough to get a shot on the guard.

Once I line it up, a wave of guilt washes over me as I watch him light a cigarette.

I wonder if he has a family?

Taking a deep breath, I shake my head. He's a piece of shit like the rest of Ivan's men. He wouldn't hesitate to blow my head off, either.

The recoil jolts my shoulder as I pull the trigger, and I watch him crumple to the ground in slow motion.

One.

Two.

Three.

Bang.

Dimi is in.

The sharp crack of gunshots fills the air, and I react instantly, sprinting for the front door, snatching the guard's AK-47 as I pass.

A heavy, expectant silence greets me as I push open the front door, the only sound the faint creak of the hinges. Two dead bodies in front of my feet.

Dimi grins and rubs his hands together. Of course he will be the one who gains from all of this.

As he opens his mouth to speak, a deafening shot rings out, sending him diving for cover.

Fucking pussy.

I fling myself behind the nearest wall, the sound of my breath echoing in the sudden silence, and peer around the corner, my eyes straining to see.

A tall, dark-haired guy emerges from one of the bedrooms, his presence filling the hallway.

With a ferocious roar, he lunges at Dimi, who, in response, immediately issues a bear hug to tackle him to the ground, the impact jarring. He's also a fucking beast of a man.

I rush over as Dimi slams him to the floor, his neck pinned beneath Dimi's weight, and the breath whooshing from his lungs.

His eyes are wide and filled with terror, pleading with me as I point the gun between them, the cold steel pressing against his skin.

"I'll tell you everything," he croaks.

I look at Dimi. Maybe we should listen. I wonder what tales he has about the organizations.

Any knowledge to me is power.

"Shoot him," Dimi shouts, as the guy struggles.

He's young. Probably only twenty.

I'm a monster, but part of me wants to leave him to battle Dimi.

What if he got the better of him? Another one of my husband's men would be gone. The world would be a better place.

Then I remember what Vlad could do to my baby girl. I never know who is watching me anymore.

As I pull the trigger, I look away.

I'm a fucking monster, and I hate it.

"Took you long enough," Dimi spits.

"You'd be dead if I didn't help you earlier. Remember that before you speak again," I tell him, tossing the AK next to the body.

"We're done," I huff, heading to the front door.

I want to get home and see Isabella and wash away my sins.

I wish survival wasn't so damn hard. As we jog to the truck, I jump in the driver's seat and start it up.

"If you're nice to me, I won't tell Vlad you almost got me killed."

Visions of slicing Dimi's throat flash through my brain.

I'm being sent away from my daughter on a fucking death mission.

Dimi is one of Vlad's top new recruits.

"I'm sorry. Okay?" It hurts me to say it. But I did nearly leave him to die.

He sighs as I pull away.

"It's fine. Let's call it quits, seeing as you saved my life."

I nod, heading back to my prison.

"Appreciate it."

I had no idea I'd be going out on jobs so close to the Decadence Games. I want to spend every waking moment with Isabella. I have no idea how long I'll be gone for.

And yet, here I am. In the fucking woods, freezing my ass off. I need to be in top shape to win these games, not exhausted and beaten up.

It's almost like Vlad wants me to fail.

CHAPTER 32

DECLAN

Holding my phone against my ear, I rest my other hand on the cool windowsill, the crisp morning air brushing my skin as I gaze at the still, silent woods.

Jesus. Christ.

My patience is wearing thin.

"What do you fucking mean?" I yell down the phone at Conan.

"Exactly what I said the first time. Where do you want us to take him?"

I rub my temples, feeling the dull throb behind my eyes.

Today of all days, when the girls arrive, one of our truck drivers gets a tail on an arms delivery.

So he brakes, smashes up the guy's car, and drags his unconscious body into the truck to deliver him to me.

"How certain are we that he was being tailed?" I ask.

"Asher doesn't bullshit. He's one of Enzo's best."

"We can use my cabin?" Conan suggests.

I nod. Actually, a good idea from him. His setup in the woods on our estate has its uses.

For Conan, it's his hunting ground.

But it keeps us protected.

"Good plan. I'll head there now."

Shoving my feet in my boots, I light up a cigarette and trek through the woods to Conan's cabin. Nestled right at the back.

I see the markers on the trees and chuckle.

He's already begun the prep for his own Decadence Chase.

Pushing in the passcode, the door creaks as I enter. Inside, it's pretty decent. Wooden furnishings, a cozy log fire, and leather couch.

And a bar. A fully stocked bar of our dad's whiskey.

I pour myself a glass and wait for my brother's arrival.

He bursts through the door, the heavy weight of the bleeding man a burden on his shoulder, with Finn hot on his heels.

Con drops him on the couch, the impact muffled by the cushions. Finn immediately starts assessing his vitals, his fingers deftly checking a pulse.

"Well?" I ask Finn.

The guy doesn't look well at all.

"He's breathing. Heart rate is very low. If we wanna keep him alive, I'd need to get him to my medical room pretty quick."

"Check his pockets," I tell him as I step closer.

His face is pretty unrecognizable at this point.

Probably should put the fucker out of his misery.

Finn tosses me the wallet.

I open it up and pull out the license.

Igor.

Russian.

Interesting. What are they doing here? It wouldn't be one of Mikhail's men. But he might know who this fucker is.

"I'll make some calls. Is it worth trying to keep him alive?" I ask Finn.

"Honestly? No. Waste of our time. Hit to the head like that. He ain't gonna be telling us shit."

With a curt nod and a sharp intake of breath, there is an unmistakable metallic click of my pistol snapping free from its holster.

Finn moves well out of the way as I pull the trigger.

"I liked that couch," Conan whines behind me.

"Burn it and him. Get a new couch." I brush him off. I don't have time for distractions.

This whole thing is driving me insane, another piece in a chaotic puzzle that makes absolutely no sense. The uncertainty is a suffocating weight.

Something ain't right.

Today is not the day; I have games to play.

CHAPTER 33
CHARLOTTE

Song- Dreams, SKUM, Meisym.

The truck screeches to a halt, tires spitting gravel. Drago cuts the engine as moonlight streams through the trees.

Cliché assholes. This is probably the first time I've felt some sort of fear before a mission.

It's not just my life that depends on this. It's my little girl, and Drago, too.

A nervous throat-clearing sounds as I fixate on the thrumming helicopter.

"You know this isn't your typical sex club, right?" His voice is low.

"No, Drago. Please tell me more."

I roll my eyes. I read the damn contract. Told them my sexual preferences and consented to my own fucking death.

"The games. You're going to need to remember your training."

"I don't recall learning how to fuck as part of my assassin 101."

A shudder runs through my body and my fists clench. That statement is wrong. Marrying Vlad tied me to a life of sex that I didn't want. So if I can deal with that, I can deal with anything.

"I'm fine. I can handle pain. What's the worst they can do in a sex club?"

They won't kill me. I won't let them. If my husband has taught me anything, it's that consent doesn't matter.

So that Decadence contract I signed means shit. I do not consent to my own death. I'll burn the entire place down.

"You dealing with torture isn't my concern. Can you deal with pleasure and pain? I'm thinking your best way to win is to immerse yourself in the games. You have to find your way to The Master."

Hmm. That I don't know. I've only ever been with one guy who focused on my pleasure.

That didn't just take from me.

There's one man on this Earth that values my voice, and once I'm done with this, I will find him again.

"I'll be fine. I can cope with a bit of spanking."

Drago chuckles, which makes me less tense. But then his jaw clenches and his eyes darken as he turns to me.

"There is one of you. You are unarmed, and they're clearly deranged fuckers to be hosting this. Don't fuck around, Char. Win the games. Do your job."

I twiddle my thumbs on my lap.

"Make sure he doesn't hurt her, Drago. Please."

"You have my word. I will do everything I can. Just like I have done her whole life. No matter what, you both are my family, even if not in blood. Remember, it's just waiting for the right time. Everything will turn out okay in the end."

I acknowledge with a nod.

It's been ten fucking years of hell. I can wait longer if it means we're finally free. I'm clever enough to know if I ran away with her, there isn't a corner of the world I'd be safe. Even with Drago on my side.

Every bone in Vlad's body is malicious. Evil.

I rub the welts on my wrists. You'd think after five years of being handcuffed to a bed to sleep at night, the skin would toughen.

That bitch still hurts.

Once I'm free, I'll tattoo over the scars. And adding his flower to my tree will be the best one yet.

"You'll be fine, kiddo. I trained you well. Keep focused. Breathe through the pain. You aren't there to withstand the storm, Charlotte. You're there to be the fucking storm."

I take a deep breath to recite the most important mantra from our training.

"A fighter's soul never weakens. Even if my body is beaten to the ground, my soul will stand tall."

It doesn't matter what they do to me. There is nothing that can battle the spirit of a mother protecting her child.

Five rooms. One golden ticket. One kill.

And then I come home and obliterate my husband's empire.

Whatever gold mine this ticket leads me to, I'll make damn sure it's enough to get me and my daughter out safely.

I've played games for long enough.

Now I'm ready to fucking win.

"Remember. There's no way out. Not if you want me to watch over Isabella. But I have a couple of people on standby nearby. Or did. I've lost contact with Igor."

"What do I do? Send a fucking smoke signal?"

I can't help but laugh. I know I'm walking in alone. It almost sends a thrill through me.

"No. I've got eyes in Pennsylvania, don't you worry."

I glare at him, my eyes burning with intensity.

It makes me wonder why an invitation was even extended to us. I'm not kept in the know of the business; I just fix their problems.

"Don't overthink it. There is a plan, but the safest way is to just not fuck it up."

I smack his arm.

"When have I ever fucked a job up? If I did, I wouldn't be sitting in this car with you."

Drago holds out his hand to me.

"Take off your necklace."

My mouth drops open.

"Oh, I'm really going in free."

I've known all along it was a damn tracker. That's how the asshole found me when I did escape.

"I fear they would easily spot it's a tracker, then your cover's blown." He pauses.

"Well, that's what I told Vlad," he says with a menacing grin.

"Thank you."

It gives me a shot. A real one. After Tatiana was shot, the dynamics have changed in the house. Vlad is away more. Distracted. The timing is right, hit him when he's weaker.

"What is this, some sort of cult?" I frown.

Looking at the five guys in balaclavas, tailored black suits, standing with fucking AK-47s around the helicopter.

"You're positive you've got nothing that can be classed as a weapon?" Drago asks, keeping his eyes on the men in front.

"I mean, my boot laces are about the only weapon I have now."

I can disarm just about anyone with a weapon at close range. I don't need one myself when I can beat them to the ground and take theirs.

"Good luck, Charlotte."

"Who really is Enzo? Vlad wanted him in Italy, and now this? Wouldn't it be better for me to be going after him? The actual source?"

It's the one bit of information my husband wants and could be my key to freedom if The Master talks.

This guy is a threat. I can tell by the way my husband says his name. There is fear in his eyes.

I like that.

I want to find this Enzo guy.

Drago stills.

"What about Enzo?" He scratches at his stubble.

"I don't know. That's the whole point." I throw my hands up and quickly shove them back down.

"Do not under any circumstances go after Enzo in there, Charlotte. Fuck!"

He slams his fist against the dashboard, a sharp cracking sound echoing in the otherwise silent car.

"Okay. Okay. I won't hunt him down."

But maybe I can snoop. Or find the information out for myself and keep quiet.

"You swear? This is important. All our lives depend on that. We don't want him. We just want the intel. The more we have to threaten Vlad with, the stronger our position."

I swallow the lump in my throat. I feel like I'm missing some important puzzle pieces here, and it's pissing me off.

"Once I get out of here, you and I need to talk. You gotta fill me in so I can take that bastard out. I can't keep doing this blind. Intel is everything. You told me that!"

With a sudden movement, I fling my arms out, only to have him seize them. His grip is strong, holding my arms tightly at my sides.

"Do not make them think we're arguing. I promise we will talk. There is a reason why I am where I am in that family. It's given me enough power to keep you alive, but it isn't enough yet to make our final play for your freedom. We need the information, but we must not involve Enzo, okay? We have to stay off his radar."

He knows something more, or he's protecting someone that isn't me.

I don't like this, not one bit.

"I'm going to end this."

He nods solemnly.

"Hey, don't be so glum. I'm coming back."

I offer him a soft smile.

In these ten years, not only did he save me, he became my family. He took me under his wing. Without him and his training, I'd probably have thrown myself off the roof by now.

A friend that always has my back.

"Isabella will be safe."

Fuck.

Tears threaten to spill, but I hold them back, just like I always do.

"Thank you, Drago."

I open the passenger door. The cool morning air rushes in as I slide out, grabbing my heavy rucksack from the seat beside me. The bare essentials to survive.

Slamming the door shut with a loud bang, I gave him one last, curt nod before leaving. My heart pounds a frantic rhythm against my ribs as I approach the armed guards, their weapons gleaming menacingly in the dim light.

I toss my bag onto the damp grass and offer my hands in surrender before them.

The large man at the front, his muscles bulging beneath his shirt, gives a slight nod to his companion. I glance down and notice the black bag in his tattooed hand.

Great.

I close my eyes as he steps forward and secures it over my head, but I can still breathe fine.

He leads me up the steps and sits me on a leather seat.

"The games begin now, Contestant Three. Get some rest. You'll need it," a deep voice says through the mask.

A wave of exhaustion washes over me as I drift off, the surrounding noises fading to a dull hum.

These motherfuckers.

CHAPTER 34

DECLAN

"**M**r. Volkov. It's Declan Quinn. Do you have a minute?" I tap my lighter on my desk as he grunts over the phone.

"Mikhail. Call me, Mikhail." His deep Russian accent is enough to elicit fear.

"Mikhail. How are you? I hear there's quite the mess in Russia." He chuckles.

"Cunt deserved it. I'm sure it will resolve itself."

Hmm.

"Do you recognize this name? Igor Popov?" I ask.

"Off the top of my head, no. I can check the records we took from my father's estate. If he worked for Ivan, I'll be able to tell you."

"Appreciate it."

"He alive?" Mikhail asks quietly.

"No. Tried to infiltrate Decadence. I wanna know who is behind it."

"I don't see any Russians coming for power in the States. They'd have to get through me first. I'd say it's unrelated to my father. They're being wiped out every day. Hardly any remain from my sources."

I rub my temples, feeling the tension slowly melt away with each circular motion.

So who the fuck is behind this?

"I'm sure I'll get to the bottom of it."

"There's always someone. If you need me or my men, let me know. We're pretty sweet here now."

"Thanks, Mikhail. Same goes for you."

We say our goodbyes and cut the call.

Taking a picture of the ID card, I shoot it over to Enzo and Mikhail.

I try not to pester him too much. We want to establish ourselves as our own unit.

But he'd be able to find out who this is.

Checking the security feeds for Decadence, I see the front iron gates, their stillness hinting at an eerie quiet in the pre-dawn light.

Three contestants, each carrying a backpack and looking determined yet full of fear, have already arrived. I'm eagerly awaiting the final two to put faces to the names.

Ebony is who I'm looking forward to. Contestant number three. The first woman to ever catch my eye enough to think about offering her the alternative deal.

My phone vibrates, and it's the man, Enzo himself. I lock my computer as I head back to my house.

I need to get ready for the games to start.

CHAPTER 35

CHARLOTTE

The drive from the airport was a welcome reprieve since I wasn't forced to endure a suffocating, blindfolded journey. But the blacked-out windows mean I still can't see anything outside.

I've got two heavily armed guards on either side of me in the Escalade.

Neither have said a single word to me, or hardly even looked at me.

Distracted, I nervously twist the rope binding my hands, the rough hemp scratching against my skin, a dull ache growing in my wrists. The car slows down, and the driver opens his window. Not that I can see through the black partition, but I can hear him.

Italian possibly. They're so muffled it's hard to make out.

I keep as still as possible as the guard on my left opens his door. Taking in a deep breath of fresh air is a relief. My head is still kinda fuzzy from the way over here.

The light almost blinds me as I look outside.

"Come on," he grunts.

Nope. American?

Shuffling out, my legs are unsteady, and he holds out a hand to keep me up.

I go to thank him, then I stop, remembering what I'm walking into.

The car drives off, and I'm left with my two guards on either side of me, staring down a gravel pathway that leads to an enormous set of iron gates with the same letter "D" pattern as on the invitation and contract.

Smoke billows out of the brick factory behind the gates. They weren't fucking around.

A chocolate factory. The bright purple Decadence sign is branded on the front. I look at the guard on my left as we approach the doors. But he continues ignoring me.

As my boots crunch on the gravel, we approach the gates. A gigantic water fountain, its spray a shimmering arc in the sunlight, stands behind the gates, marking the entrance to the imposing factory.

The purple-branded delivery trucks to the left idle, their engines a low thrum against the morning air, exhaust smelling faintly of diesel. Shivering, I wrap my arms around myself, hugging my torso tightly despite the warm air; a deep chill still permeates my bones.

Dread consumes me as the words on the contract replay.

I'm stepping right into hell, and there is no turning back.

Whoever is behind this has me trapped. There's also a chance I'll never walk back out of here.

I tip my chin up, remembering Drago's words that this place could set me free.

I've already been to hell. It's my time to taste heaven.

As the gates open electronically, I'm frozen on the spot.

"Come," the guard grunts.

I can't walk.

I can't move.

Torn between one hell and another.

"This is your last chance to enter the games," he says in a low tone, and it's the kick up the ass I need.

I have no choice. My daughter needs me.

It's hard to comprehend everything as I follow him through the main doors.

It's a normal factory. Huge steel machinery. Workers all dressed in white coats. Ignoring me like I'm a ghost.

And the smell. It really is decadent. It makes my stomach rumble and my eyes go wide.

Decadent. A word I've not heard in five years. A word that makes my stomach flutter. I almost want to laugh. What are the chances of that?

"Do I meet The Master before the games?" I whisper.

The guard stops and spins to face me; his deep green eyes bore into me.

"Rules. You do not speak unless spoken to. Now move. Follow orders." He nods before striding off towards a set of double doors. He enters his thumbprint, and I store that in my brain.

Okay, definitely American.

And I'm gonna need to cut off someone's thumb if I'm going to escape at any point.

Following them down the corridor, the smell of wet paint stings my nostrils as I trail behind him to a door on the right.

"In here," the man grunts, and I hear the click as it opens.

As we moved away from the doors, the rich aroma of chocolate fades, replaced by the sharp, sterile scent of cleaning chemicals, the faint smell of leather, and the fresh, slightly acrid tang of paint.

I step inside and he clears his throat behind me, and I turn, taking in the giant in front of me covered with a black balaclava. His dark brown eyes burn into mine, intense and unwavering, as I scan his body clad in a tight black top that hugs his arms.

I'm looking for markers. A sign of which family they belong to. Nothing. Covered from head to toe.

"Tonight is preparation night," he tells me, nodding behind me.

I follow his line of vision, a plush double bed with satin purple covers. A bathroom. And a black duffle bag on the bed.

"Preparation?" I ask, turning back to him.

"Shower. Get yourself clean. You've traveled far. Get some sleep. Dinner will be served in thirty minutes. The games begin at sunrise."

I nod.

"And where exactly am I? You know, so I can work out my jet lag situation." I bat my lashes at him.

"Pennsylvania. In a chocolate factory."

I choked on a sudden, unexpected laugh, my face turning red.

"I'm sorry. It just sounds like a joke when you say it out loud."

His eyes darken, and he scratches his, I assume, beard beneath the mask.

"We don't joke."

I snap my mouth shut. Why does he suddenly sound less American?

"Okay. So you'll come get me at sunrise. How many hours?"

He looks at his shining watch; as he lifts up his arm, I get a peek of his pistol.

"Seven hours," he says flatly.

I bite back a yawn. Whatever they knocked me out with is clearly having its effect still.

"Okay," I say, and take a step back.

"What's in the bag?" I point to it. I wasn't allowed to bring a single thing with me. The guards must have my rucksack.

"Your outfit for the games."

"Like a costume?" I shake my head in disbelief. What the hell is going on?

He steps forward and towers over me.

"Nothing here is a joke. You read the contract. You signed on the dotted line. You belong to Decadence now."

I blink at him, the harshness of his voice sending shivers down my spine.

"Sorry," I reluctantly whisper.

"I'm nervous." I'm not completely lying. A lot rests on these games.

And it's exactly that, one big sick game.

One I fully intend to win.

With an indignant huff, he slams the door shut, the sound echoing through the room, and the heavy lock clicks into place. Once his heavy footsteps disappear, I sit on the edge of the bed.

I just want my little girl back.

Letting out a shaky breath, I grab the bag and tip it upside down.

"Outfit?" I mutter to myself.

All I see is an array of black and purple leather straps.

I pick up one section and hold it up, tilting my head.

I'm going to be barely covered.

There are lots of gold hoops.

I rummage through the rest, picking out two purple leather cuffs with hooks.

"How the hell do I get into all this? Are there instructions?" I mutter, shaking the bag again.

Great. A puzzle of lingerie.

My first test.

I best wake up two hours before so I can work this out. Right now, I need a hot shower and some rest.

Rule one of battle: be physically ready.

CHAPTER 36

DECLAN

"They're all in," Reggie tells me as he takes a seat opposite me.

"Good job. First impressions?"

He tugs at his collar. Someone has riled him. I can see it in his wild eyes.

I've been on calls with Enzo about our mystery Russian intruder that I missed the last two entering.

"One is a complete brat. Contestant two."

I roll my eyes and pick up the decanter of whiskey. If I remember correctly, contestant two is Tara. Comes from a very wealthy family of arms dealers and human traffickers.

The absolute scum of the earth.

"Taming can be fun." I shrug, pouring the first glass.

"No, boss. She's irritating. Daddy's money. She wouldn't shut the fuck up. Daddy this, Daddy that. And not in the sexy way, in the 'needs psychological testing' way."

His Boston accent really adds a flair to that statement.

"You can drop the accent, Reg." I chuckle.

"I'm keeping in character. Do you know how long it took me to perfect this?"

"You've perfected it?" I smirk.

"Fuck off." His Dublin accent shines through, and I lose it, bursting out into laughter.

"Ah, there he is."

"Fuck, that feels better. My **accent is better** than Conan's. Have you heard that shit?" He rubs at his neck and leans over to grab his whiskey.

"And that, Reggie, is exactly why Conan is under instructions to not open his damn mouth." I smirk.

As hard as Conan tried, that Irish accent wouldn't leave him.

"Why can't we be Irish anyway? No one has a clue it's us," Reggie asks.

To start with, it was to conceal us, protect us in a way. We're the new empire.

"Well, now, purely for my own fucking entertainment, Reg. Now, tell me more about my contestants." I tap my rings against my glass and sit forward.

"My personal favorite is Contestant Three. She's sassy, in a different way."

My ears perk up at the clink of my whiskey glass as I take a large gulp.

"Different?"

"She's intelligent. Asking the right questions. Assessing everything and the calmest of the six. She even fucking laughed that we're in a chocolate factory."

I wonder if it's the one that caught my attention initially.

Miss no hard limits.

"Fearless? Or stupid?"

He shrugs.

"I can't get a read on her. Absolutely stunning, though," he gushes, and my fists clench.

"Ah. The best kind of submissive. The ones who crave it. Naturally fierce, but demand to have control ripped from them in the bedroom."

My cock throbs.

"I think she has a good chance. Physically, she's perfect."

I chuckle.

"Well, you and Rowan keep up the good work. Maybe you'll host your own games one year."

"That's the dream."

The worn leather of my chair creaks softly as I recline, with my hands clasped loosely in my lap.

"I don't know what a dream is anymore," I say, accidentally out loud.

"You don't dream?"

I shake my head, a sigh escaping my lips.

"Nope. Nightmares."

The same woman's face every time. The bloodied knife. My father's body. Everything merges into a hell loop every damn night.

The fact she vanished without a trace. I'll never know the truth. Why did she try to frame me? Why did she hunt me out in Italy?

Was that night as real for her as it was for me?

Sighing, I reach for the bottle of whiskey, its smooth glass cool against my fingers.

Burn away the pain. The embarrassment.

Since that day, I became as cold as ice, numb from my father's death. I'm every bit the angry mafia boss Enzo wanted me to be.

I fill my days with distraction. And the Decadence games are perfect for that.

My gut tells me she's still out there somewhere. Probably laughing that she got one over on me.

I wonder if she still thinks about me?

If I haunt her nightmares like she does mine.

"You okay, boss?"

I crack my knuckles and stretch my neck. Fuck, I'm tense.

Pouring out a generous second serving, I toss it back and stand.

"Yeah. I'm heading off to get some rest. Big day tomorrow."

CHAPTER 37

CHARLOTTE

I pull up the lace panties, feeling the soft fabric against my skin.

"The fuck?" I hiss.

Crotchless thong.

Grabbing the leather straps, I stand in front of the full-length mirror in front of the bed.

I spin to look at my ass.

She's good. All the squats pay off.

Holding up the contraption in front of me, I play around with it, trying to figure out which bit goes where.

It looks too small. I frown, staring at all the gold buckles.

I get to work undoing one side and step into it. As I pull it up, it gets stuck on my thighs.

"Jesus."

Taking it off, I try again. I can feel my anger sizzling as my face reddens with frustration.

On the second attempt, it's still not right.

This time, I rip it off and let out a scream as I throw it against the wall.

This is step one, and I'm already showing my weakness.

Taking a few deep breaths, I walk over and pick it up.

Okay. It looks like there's a garter to go around my stomach that unclips from the straps around my leg, and the hoop from the garter must connect to the one hanging down from my bra clasp.

"I can do this."

I keep my cool and concentrate, and ten minutes later, I'm in. I even have the black leather cuffs on each wrist.

Finishing it with the killer black heels, I swipe on some clear lip gloss and ruffle my long curls before looking in the mirror.

"Damn." My mouth drops open.

I've never looked or felt this drop-dead sexy in my life. I've never had a reason to.

The straps, almost like a thin collar around my neck, go down over the sheer black bra. The waist garter pinches me in.

As I turn, my ass looks perfect.

It almost distracts me from the games.

If this is the outfit, then what the hell am I going to be doing?

Or who will be doing it to me?

I've focused so much on the thought of escape, and the games themselves, I've looked at it as more of a battle. But looking at myself now, this could be the least prepared I've ever been.

I rush to the bathroom, the cold porcelain of the sink a shock against my clammy hands as I turn the tap.

Bile rises in my throat, thinking about Vlad's hands on me. The first time. The way I screamed for him to stop, but it only made it worse.

It felt like an eternity. Like it would never end.

That murderous feeling returns as my blood boils. I have to win these games so I can kill that asshole. That drives me. Ten years of suffering are my fuel.

I was eighteen. The more I fought, the worse I was punished.

For years.

And now, I'm numb. These men cannot hurt me more than my husband does.

I close my eyes and splash the icy water on my face to calm myself.

"I will end this," I whisper, over and over.

Jimmy's face flashes in my mind, calming me. I can hear his soft praise in my ear.

It's almost like he's here.

His touch, his tongue, his everything reminds me there is more outside of my cage.

That one night with him altered my entire outlook. It gave me hope.

He proved that there are men who respect consent.

That will worship their women rather than break them.

I just need to survive a little longer, then perhaps I'll find someone who can help me heal.

Until then, I will keep fighting.

CHAPTER 38

DECLAN

The third annual Decadence Games are finally here.

A new submissive for a year.

And more scum obliterated from this earth.

I do a last check on the monitors in each room. We've already checked the voice-altering system.

Everything is ready to go, and the women are being led down to the first room now.

I keep my stare locked on monitor one as contestant one is ushered into the room.

She's nervous. I can see her hands trembling in front of her.

Petite frame, long red hair, plump lips. But she looks like a scared rescue puppy.

I grumble as the door knocks.

"Yes?" I call out in annoyance.

I'm starting to sound like my dad.

"You excited?" Conan is rubbing his tattooed hands together as he tosses something black on my desk.

"Why?" I ask, holding up the black balaclava.

"Just in case you wanted to take me up on my offer. I just got a look at one of the contestants on my way up here. You might wanna look at the screen, brother."

He nods to my computer, and I frown, scrunching the mask in my fist. Every time I go to check, something comes up for me to deal with.

The door swings inward, revealing Reggie, who smells faintly of woodsmoke and something sweet. A gasp escapes my lips as my heart threatens to leap from my chest, my mouth is agape in disbelief.

"It can't be," I mutter.

My sight begins to fade, but even through the haze, the intricate details of those flower tattoos are unmistakable.

There's more. A lot fucking more than there was five years ago. It's to her shoulder.

The hair. The purple and black curls.

Every memory of her floods my mind, each one accompanied by the sweet, lingering scent of her vanilla perfume.

Decadent.

I slam my fist on the desk in a fit of rage, sending my coffee crashing to the floor in a dark, bitter puddle.

"Look at the monitor," I shout to her, even though she can't hear me.

I won't believe it until I see those blue eyes. The ones that haunt me.

The ones that show the pain deep in her soul. She strides confidently into the room, the click of her heels echoing, and my jaw clenches in response.

"Calm down before you have a heart attack," Conan tells me, resting a firm hand on my shoulder.

With a sharp movement, I knock his hand away, a frantic rhythm of my heart echoing in my ears. Fuck, are the walls closing in on me?

My world stops as she looks up directly at the monitor.

It's like she's burning into my veins, and I stop breathing.

"No. This can't be happening."

I run my fingers through my hair.

"This is good, right? We've finally got her. We can find out why she did it? Who she is?" Conan says nervously.

I shake my head slowly, a pit forming in my stomach.

"This isn't a fucking coincidence, Con. This is dangerous."

This could be the end of us.

"Call Finn. Get him in here now," I order Conan.

I switch my attention to pulling up the contestant's sheets.

"Ebony. Not Brittany," I scoff.

The measurements fit.

"Fuck!" I roar.

I can hear her in her words. As I scan the documents, I frown.

"This is fucking bad."

Pushing myself away from my desk, I stand, resting my hands on the wood.

"What do you want with me this time… Ebony?"

That name sounds wrong. I'd bet it is another fake.

Running my finger over the warm screen. As her eyes dart around the room, she almost looks nervous, but she hides it well.

Except from me. I can read her. I know her body.

I've run my tongue along all of her curves.

"He's on his way."

Clenching my fists, I want to be the one who inflicts agony on her.

I deserve it.

I should be ecstatic. I've finally got her in my grasp, but my gut is telling me this is very fucking bad.

CHAPTER 39

CHARLOTTE

Song- Aphrodisiac, KIRRA47, Desire4u.

What. In. The. Hell.

In all the fucked up shit I've seen in my life, this tops it.

Crossing my arms over my chest, I start to shiver, the cold seeping into my bones. It's freezing in here. My breath plumes out before me, a visible mist in the frigid air.

I blink, momentarily stunned by the sight before me.

The vibrant purple wall was adorned with six massive chocolate creations shaped like dildos.

And I mean gigantic in length and girth.

I turn to my handler, Richard—I've given that nickname to him because he was such a dick—and my stomach plummets as I see the black flogger in his hand. The sight is sickening and smells faintly of leather and sweat.

"Head down until The Master gives you your instructions," he whispers.

With a sharp turn, I immediately follow his instructions, the air thick with anticipation.

"Welcome to the third annual Decadence Games. We are delighted to have you here. Now, you're all probably wondering what your first task is," the robotic voice booms through the room.

Even disguised, I can tell it's deep. Every time I hear the word decadent, I feel instant regret thinking about what I did to Jimmy.

"Each of you are property of Decadence now. This is a game of survival. Only the winning contestant shall receive the golden ticket. That ticket will not only change your life, but your family's, the ones who signed you over to us. The games are all simple yet effective to find the perfect winner. This is about pain and pleasure, finding the perfect balance between the two can be euphoric. But the question is, can you handle what I can give you? Are you worthy of it?"

I swear I hear the girl next to me sniffling, a tiny, almost imperceptible sound.

"On to the first game. As you can see in front of you, there is a wall, and each of you have your own piece of chocolate to attend to. How deep can you go?"

I gulp.

A low chuckle vibrates through the air, making me clench my fists in response.

"That's the pleasure element. Perhaps the sweetest dick you'll ever have. For some of you, your last. But don't forget, where there is pleasure, there is pain."

I squeeze my eyes shut. The flogger.

"The guards will give you a score out of ten for your performance. The woman with the lowest will be eliminated. Your Master wishes you luck in this sweet hell. Now, get on all fours. It's time to see how much you can take."

Scrunching up my face, I look at the chocolate dildo on the wall in front of me.

This is embarrassing.

Of all the things I've trained for, this is something I don't have a clue about.

With numb fingers tapping a rhythm on my ice-cold thigh, I considered my options.

I'm unarmed, six guards, and no way out. Cameras are everywhere, I just have to suck it up, literally, and move on to the next game.

So I'm the first woman to step forward, as I drop to all fours a position both humbling and strangely empowering.

The other girls quickly follow suit, not wanting to be the last one.

Who knows how we're being scored?

The Master said, "how deep can we go?"

Taking a deep breath, I realize that this isn't being forced upon me, it's about my self-reliance and pushing my limits. No force. No slamming me against a wall.

I block out the world, returning to Italy in my mind. The smooth texture of the chocolate shaft against my hand brings him instantly to mind.

As I part my lips and slide the chocolate into my mouth, I realize it's kinda similar in size to him, too.

As the tip hits the back of my mouth, I jolt forward and choke, feeling the flogger crack down hard on my ass.

And again on the other side.

My eyes stream with hot tears, blurring my vision, but I keep going, relaxing my throat to ease the tension.

This is no different from torture training techniques. I breathe through my nose and endure the pain.

Even as it rips through my skin.

Stinging, burning, aching. My heart races as I go deeper.

Disconnected from the room's chaotic noise, I'm hyper-aware of the maddening ringing in my ears and the periodic, guttural sounds of my gag reflex.

The warmth from my mouth melts away the chocolate as it drips down my throat.

Dammit. It's delicious.

"Good girl. Another inch and you'll get the perfect score," Richard mutters beside me. Flicking my eyes to my left, I find him standing over, watching me intently.

As I inch closer, the tension in the room is palpable, and the taste of adrenaline floods my mouth just before he delivers the final, intense spank.

Fuck, I'm going to be sick.

"Now, lick all the chocolate off with your tongue," he orders.

It's a relief as I pull back and my throat is free, and I get to work on licking it. It's actually distracting from the fact that my ass is burning.

The chocolate melts easily. Smooth, sweet, indulgent.

No wonder it's called Decadent. It truly is. A delightful contrast of bitter and sweet notes created a complex and satisfying taste. Almost creamy as you swallow.

A violent shiver wracks my arms as the air bites with an icy ferocity. My nipples are so hard they might cut through the lace fabric soon.

Sitting back on my ass, I wince, a sharp, burning pain shooting up from my cheeks.

"All clean."

He runs the soft, supple leather down my back, the warmth of his touch a stark contrast to the icy fear that grips me, a fear that melts into unexpected heat.

Maybe I'm not as bad at this as I thought. I smile to myself and wait.

CHAPTER 40

DECLAN

I'm mesmerized by her, and I cannot take my eyes off her.

The thought of being in there makes my hands twitch uncontrollably, a cold sweat breaking out on my palms.

If I had the flogger in my hands, the things I would do to her…

Would I have enough self-control to refrain from dragging her out of the room?

Fuck.

The way she licked it at the end was teasing and tantalizing. Her sinful fucking mouth.

Remembering how good it felt when she came apart for me, my body ignites with desire.

I lift my glass, the cold condensation clinging to the outside, and drink deeply, the liquid fire burning a path down my throat, mirroring the inferno within.

Five years I've let her consume my thoughts.

The why, the how, the everything.

I want my answers.

But I also want to sit back and watch her suffer.

As her eyes scan the room, my lips twitch into a grin as she winces sitting down.

"Oh, heartbreaker, this is only the beginning of the end for you," I whisper.

Assess and analyze my enemy. Those are my next steps.

And try to contain myself for when I do finally come face to face with my nightmare.

CHAPTER 41

CHARLOTTE

"**K**neel in a line in the center of the room. Hands on your thighs and heads down. We will wait to hear from The Master," the big masked guy tells us.

He has big green eyes, and at one point I swear I caught a glimpse of his hair peek through, a really dark green.

We shuffle into line in order, and I drop to my knees into position.

As I swallow, I can taste the chocolate. It's annoying because it's really fucking good.

The silence is deafening apart from the girl to my left with her erratic breathing.

She needs to calm down before she has a panic attack.

Beside me, the blonde who'd earlier sized me up with disdain, snickers, her platinum hair catching the light. She has a slow, knowing smirk spread across her face; the sound of her quiet laughter echoes faintly in my ears.

"That was easy. I enjoyed it," she whispers, and I cringe.

"What, you didn't? You aren't into kinky stuff, I take it?" she continues, and I squeeze my fists.

"Oh, whatever. I'm going to win these games, anyway."

I roll my eyes, a silent expression of my disbelief.

I keep my head down as the manipulated voice comes from a speaker in the ceiling.

"What a group of good girls I have this year. I've started you off easy, haven't I? That was almost a treat."

He chuckles, and my skin crawls.

"Now, you all read the contracts. You know one of you has to go. Your time in Decadence is unfortunately over."

I swallow the lump in my throat and close my eyes. I hope I did enough. I try not to think of Vlad and the things he does to me. But that bit of fury might come in useful.

"Contestant three. Please stand."

A wave of dizziness washes over me as I push myself upright, my head bows low, my heart hammering in my chest.

"Congratulations. You have made it into the second room. Please let my men escort you to the door."

I nod, feeling the guy's surprisingly firm grip on my bicep as he stands next to me.

"What do you say to The Master?" he growls under his breath.

Boston. That's the accent. I think.

"Thank you," I almost whisper.

"Thank you, what?" the voice from above says.

I let out a breath.

"Thank you, sir."

"Good job."

I'm escorted to the door in front. He gets his keys on the chain of his pants and unlocks it. Okay, so my guard has a key. I'll need those and his thumb.

"Find table three and sit," he orders.

I wince at the thought. My ass stings like a bitch, I really don't want to sit down.

As the door slams shut behind me, I look up straight into the camera. My eyes go wide. Almost like being caught snooping as a kid.

I rush over to the table and pull out a chair.

There's three items.

A purple toy device, almost U-shaped with buttons. A sharp, pointed blade and a drawing. The entwined D's, the same design on the raw iron gates as I arrived at the factory.

I tap my finger on the white, wooden desk, playing out different scenarios as I take the knife in my hand.

The guard assesses me, keeping his eyes neutral. I wonder what he's thinking?

I could slit the guard's throats and run. But that doesn't help me or Isabella. I clench my fists as the door opens again. This time, three more girls are shoved through the door.

One nearly falls on her trembling legs.

"Get your hands off me," the irritating blonde girl hisses.

I roll my eyes.

I can't wait to see her lose. Spoiled brat.

They move silently to their desks. The nervous girl with the red hair looks to me, and her eyes water.

"It's okay," I mouth to her.

Although I don't have a clue if it is or not.

As the door clicks shut, only four guards re-enter, meaning two are with the first losing contestant. I frown at the door.

They can't be—

The sound of a gunshot rips through the silence from the room in front of me, making my ears ring.

The girl beside me erupts into a fit of hysterical crying, her sobs echoing around us; it's distracting. I keep my eyes fixed on my guard, squeezing my blade handle tighter.

Not even a flinch. Emotionless.

Psychotic.

Every hair on my body stands up. This truly is a game of survival.

Part of me believed it was bullshit to elicit fear. Yet, that gunshot confirms that is not the case.

That changes everything.

I cannot lose. There is no way I am dying before I get to The Master.

CHAPTER 42
DECLAN

Her face, a mask of shock, is a priceless painting I long to capture and hang on my wall.

Fear.

She realizes now this isn't a joke. A glint of steel catches her eye, and her gaze snaps to the cold, deadly blade.

She's assessing everything. Just how I expect she's been trained to.

Once all the girls are sitting at their desks, I slide the microphone in front of me and hit the red button.

"Welcome to the second game."

I spin the rings on my fingers and focus on her. I speak directly to her, making sure my next words are carefully chosen.

"This game is important. Where you officially become the property of Decadence. Both in life and in death, your soul shall be marked to belong to me and only me, your Master. Through your pain, there shall become a new beginning."

I pause, watching as she sucks in a breath. Slowly, she looks up at the camera in the corner of the room, and it's like all the air is knocked out of my lungs.

As if she too is stealing my own soul right out of my body, a chilling emptiness spreads through me.

Shaking my head, I try to clear the fog from my mind, the lingering scent of cigar smoke still in my nostrils. I can't let her get to me.

Bringing my mouth back to the microphone, I continue.

"But let's not forget, when I inflict pain, I also provide pleasure. But none of you deserve the full extent of that yet. I suppose you've all noticed the toys on the table. The rules are simple, and listen closely. First, you will insert the toy into yourself and turn it on. You will then be given sixty seconds to memorize the drawing in front of you. Your guard will blindfold you and hand you the knife. You then have five minutes to carve the design into your thigh."

I hear the audible gasps, sharp intakes of breath that fill the silent room.

I've not told them how big or small, how deep, realistically; if they're clever, it doesn't need to hurt too bad.

But alongside the toy sucking at their clit, it should provide an enjoyable experience… for the right woman.

My real winner would be squirming in her seat, begging to come. Begging me for more.

And I'd lick the blood off her thigh and kiss her, letting her taste herself.

My dick strains against my pants, imagining her, my heart-breaker, dripping with blood and aching for my cock.

To excel at Decadence and be worthy of entering Inferno, one must be fearless but trusting.

Trust that I can take care of them.

If they can put their trust in the games, thriving under real, immediate fear, then I have found my woman. One that I offer a deal to, to become my submissive.

Rubbing my palm over the dull ache in my chest, I stare at her on the screen.

I fear I found the woman five years ago.

"I shall be watching you all closely. There is one final rule: you are not, under any circumstances, allowed to orgasm."

They all frown, but Ebony, no, she arches a brow. I'd guess she doesn't believe it's even possible to want to come.

I chuckle, picking up the remote to her toy.

"The guards are in charge of the intensity of your toys. You go over the edge, you're out of the games. As soon as your design work is complete, to a high standard, you can remove the toy. Are we all clear?"

They all nod, except Ebony. She's too busy eying up the toy. Is that confusion on her pretty face?

Clapping my hands together, I lean back in my chair.

"Never used one before, gorgeous?" I mutter under my breath.

God, I can't wait to see her suffer under my own hands. For now, I'll take control of her toy. I have the power to take over any game should I so choose. I never have, until now.

Pressing the earpiece to the group, I clear my throat.

"Reggie, I'll lead on this one."

With the remote firmly in my hand, my cock twitches against my zipper.

"Give her a little guidance on how to use the toy, she seemed confused." The words are out of my mouth before I put thought into it.

Oh, what fun we could have had together.

CHAPTER 43

CHARLOTTE

Drago's words echo in my ears. Can you handle pleasure?

As I pick up the toy, my body shivers in anticipation of my turn for the guard to add the lube.

As Richard walks over, I hold it up as he adds the clear liquid.

He leans in, the scent of his cologne filling my senses, and my body instantly tenses. Are those specks of amber in his eyes?

"Bigger end goes inside you, the other end is a suction, put that over your clit," he whispers.

I frown. Why the hell is he helping me?

And his accent, it seems…less now? I pull back and look into his eyes.

Nerves and shame rock through me. As I open my legs and pull my panties open, my handler quickly turns his head away.

With trembling hands, I continue to pull the toy open, and a gasp involuntarily leaves my lips as I feel the cool object slipping inside.

I stop fighting the feelings swirling around in my body.

This is a game. This is not real. A means to an end. Just like everything in my life.

Breathing out through my nose, I insert it fully and relax, adjusting to it being inside of me. After completing that step, I carefully adjust the suction end to my clitoris.

I don't feel anything yet, not a tingle, not a vibration, nothing.

As I squirmed in my seat, trying to get comfortable, a sudden twinge of pain in my cheeks makes me flinch.

A hard wooden seat with a spanked ass is a test in itself.

With a huff, I pick up the picture and study it. Easy.

Two D's connected at the line and a couple of swirls.

My tattoos are far more intricate. I place the paper back down and put on my blindfold, picking up the blade before my vision goes dark.

"You were meant to wait for me to do the blindfold and hand you the knife," a low voice grumbles in my ear.

I stiffen. Shit.

"I'm sorry."

He grunts, and my stomach drops. Like any war, you need allies. Richard doesn't seem to hate me, in fact, he's helping me.

While I wait, with my left index finger, I practice on my right thigh the shape of the tattoo on my skin.

They never specified how large. An inch should do it.

About the same size as these guard's cocks, most likely.

A few minutes pass, and I hear my guy clear his throat in front of me and then his heavy footsteps.

I wish the girl next to me would stop hyperventilating. I want to assess my surroundings, not listen to her gasp for air.

"I-I can't," she whimpers.

"Can I start?" I say loud enough for my guard.

"No. We wait," he grunts back.

"You can do it," her guard tells her under his breath, and she starts to sob.

"I don't like blood. I'll pass out," she whines, and I tighten my grip on the handle of my blade.

I want this over with.

"The knife is sharp enough you won't feel it too bad. And you have a blindfold on, you won't see it," I tell her, trying to hide the irritation in my voice.

"But, if it looks ugly, I'll never be able to post it on my social media. I'll lose so many followers."

I choke, a rattling cough seizing my throat and stealing my breath.

Is she serious?

"How do you plan on posting from the grave?" I say coolly.

My guard chuckles and shivers run down my spine.

She's the girl I want to be up against in the final. If I can get her there, this will be an easy win.

"Do it small," I whisper.

The room falls back into silence, and I steady my breathing to calm down.

"You have five minutes. Starting now," the distorted voice commands.

I jump in my seat as my toy comes to life. The low vibrations make me squirm painfully on my seat. I swear my lack of sight is heightening everything.

"Oh, shit." I almost jump out of my seat as the suction part on my clit turns on.

I can feel it heating every part of my body.

My hands shake as everything quickly bubbles up inside of me.

"Remember the rules," Richard tells me, and it's like an icy bucket of water has been tossed over me.

I can't come.

But how the hell do I stop?

Clenching my thighs, the pleasure intensifies, a deeper, more electric current surging through me.

I want to scream until my lungs burn and rip my hair out in clumps.

Squeezing my eyes shut, all I see is Jimmy. The pleasure building, that was the only time I've ever felt this sensation wash over me.

Shaking my head, I jab the tip of the blade into my thigh. The pain is distracting me from everything else.

A warm, fuzzy feeling washes over me as I tune into the stinging.

Even as my pussy throbs around the toy, I make my first line in my thigh.

Carefully. Delicately. But deep enough to really feel it.

As I finish it up on one side and remove the blade, I let out a moan and heat rushes to my cheeks.

Everything is more intense. Almost unbearable as my body begs for release.

I quickly get to work on the second side, finishing on the straight line in the middle. Lightening the pressure on the blade, I add the swirl details inside of the letters.

"I'm done," I pant the words out.

As I do, it turns up again. Tossing my blade to the side, I put my hands on the edge of the table and squeeze, gritting my teeth.

I can hear the blood whooshing in my ears. It's as if a million jolts of electricity are being injected into me.

I can feel everything.

With every tap of my feet on the ground, I fight to control the powerful rush of pleasure. The pain in my wound is so faint, it's almost nonexistent. Just a dull throb beneath the surface. Pleasure, forceful and consuming, sweeps through me, igniting a fire within.

Squeezing my eyes shut, I see fireworks of color explode in the darkness behind my eyelids.

"No," I whisper.

And it cuts out, right on the verge of orgasm.

Exhausted, I let my head fall onto the wooden table, the rough grain scratching my skin, while a flurry of tingling erupts across my body.

I feel weak and on the edge of exploding.

"Sit up. Blindfold off." I hear him over the ringing in my ears and reluctantly drag my body up.

Squinting as the bright lights hit my eyes as the blindfold is removed, I look down through one eye at my handiwork.

The blood, a crimson stream, drips down my thigh. I lick my finger, tasting the coppery tang as I smear the blood away.

"Not bad," I praise myself.

Clean lines. The swirls are not my best work, but I'd like to see how anyone could perform under those circumstances.

I pause as screams rip through the room, and I look to my left.

Panic girl is pale as hell looking at the mess she's created on her thigh.

"You haven't finished," her guard says with annoyance.

The guard, a towering figure with hands clasped tightly in front of him, looms over her, and I feel a nervous lump form in my throat.

"I can't do it anymore. Please. No more. It looks atrocious, and it hurts so bad."

I lean over discreetly and take a look.

God damn.

It's just a bunch of scattered lines and she cut deep too.

A heaving sob racks her body and tears stream down her face.

"The blood. Make it stop," she wails frantically.

I can see the annoyance in the guards' eyes. He glances at me, and I look away.

Frantically wiping the blood from her skin, she smears it, making a bigger mess as she watches it drip from her hands.

Too deep. Too messy. I shake my head.

"Contestant four, your time in the games has ended, and your fate is sealed. Please follow your guard out of the room," the robotic voice tells us, and the other girls gasp.

I don't flinch. I just watch.

I'm more pissed off that she didn't make it through. The other three girls are tougher than her.

And these games aren't easy. My weakness is the pleasure, for the rest of them it's the pain.

Depending on the next rooms, I could be screwed.

The guard slips her blindfold back on and I look away as she's taken through the door back into the first room.

Clever, killing them in the ice room.

It's not long before the gunshot rings out. You can feel the fear in this room. It's palpable.

"Congratulations. Please stay seated. Our doctor will fix you up now. Please enjoy some light refreshments before the next game. You'll need the energy."

A cold dread grips my stomach as the guard returns, the clinking of the bottles and rustling of the protein bar wrappers echoing in the silence.

This new guard, though shorter than mine, is powerfully built. His black uniform and mask adds to his imposing presence. His muscular figure fills out the long-sleeved black shirt, the material clinging tightly, revealing the definition of his muscles.

As I take the bar, I look up at him, his face a mask of indifference.

His uniquely pale gray eyes held a distant, almost vacant stare, revealing little of what was within. I've felt this unease before.

"How do I know it's not poisoned?" I ask, arching my brow.

He rolls his eyes, his body language shifting as he leans in, a low chuckle rumbling in his chest.

"Drugging would be a simple escape for you." I swear there's a twinge of Irish as he speaks. Almost as if he's hiding it beneath the American accent.

He dishes out the rest of the bottles and snacks before returning to me with sterilizer fluid and a cloth. My mind races—did I hear Irish?

Do I recognize those eyes? Or are these games fucking with my head? All this thinking about Jimmy could be playing tricks on me.

"It might sting a bit." I can hear the menace in his tone as I shrug, pushing back my chair.

The Irish twang is no longer there.

"Go ahead," I tell him, keeping my voice neutral.

I swear he laughs as I let out a hiss of air.

"Told you."

I keep my face straight. I don't flinch, I just stay seated and let him do what he needs to do.

"Nice cuts. Very precise."

Grabbing my water, I drink the entire bottle in one go.

Three more rooms to go, I guess…

Or, one room closer to my endgame.

CHAPTER 44

DECLAN

Watching Finn tend to Ebony makes my blood boil. He wipes away the blood, and he says something that makes her smile.

That smile is a kick to my gut.

I look down at the balaclava on my desk. It's taunting me.

I could go in, undetected.

I wonder if she smells the same? Or if she's changed her perfume?

As soon as Finn exits the room, I click on the screen, ready for the next room. I'm fascinated.

Within a minute, he's opening up my door and ripping off his mask, ruffling out his hair with his fingers.

"I'm worried," he blurts out, pouring himself a scotch.

"Why?" I spin my chair to assess him. He's rattled.

He knocks it back and pours another. I was wondering what his thoughts were about her arrival. He kept quiet up until now.

"She's dangerous, Declan."

I nod.

"We gathered that. But I saw her struggling in the last game."

I quickly grab the remote I was using on her and toss it in my drawer.

"Not that kind of dangerous. As in, violent. A lack of emotion and reaction to pain. Probably a complete disregard for her own life. She is broken, brother."

A sharp pain shoots through my chest as I rub it.

It's a similar assessment I made five years ago, but I coaxed life out of her. She was there, hiding beneath the pain.

"What are you saying?" I press.

He claps his hands together.

"Once that light goes out in someone, probably in desperation, they'll do anything. Kill anyone. We don't know her motives."

The rhythmic tap-tap-tap of my fingers on the desk punctuates my contemplation of his words.

"We won't get answers until she wins. We own her now, remember that."

Finn shakes his head.

"You think interrogation will work on someone that doesn't flinch, cutting themselves?"

I flick my eyes back to my screen, watching as she enters the "take a sweet" room.

"I'll find her weakness."

He follows my gaze and leans over.

"Like she found yours, hmm?" His lips form a thin line as he watches her.

"She's fascinating. Needs studying, really," Finn whispers, and I push him away.

"Get back down there and monitor her."

He nods and slides the mask over his head.

"I mean. She could have stabbed the guards in the last game and didn't. Dangerous. She has a game plan, I'm telling you." He taps the side of his head.

I trust his gut.

But I also trust mine.

I won't let her beat me again.

There's more of us than there is of her. If anything, this shows me she has a plan and she won't fuck it up. I see the determination in her eyes.

We are starting a battle, one I intend to win.

CHAPTER 45
CHARLOTTE

As I step into the next room, it's like every kid's dream.

The air is thick with the sweet smell of candy. A deep breath fills my lungs with the sugary scent of various treats.

Ignoring the rules, I look up, and my stomach rumbles. Every single inch of this wall is decorated with candy. It's like a rainbow threw up in here. Pinks, reds, purples. A six-foot lollipop, impossibly tall and shimmering with an unnatural sugary gleam, towers before me. I'd never seen anything like it.

As I look down, the soft, pink, sand-like clouds of sugar surrounds my feet.

Wow.

But as I glance to the far left, the stark reality of the situation hits me with full force.

The table is covered in dildos and other mysterious devices whose names escape me.

We're led into the center of the room, the silence amplifying the thud of our footsteps. Only four of us remain. As I glimpse over at the bitchy blonde, she scowls at me.

I'm sure she has no sense of reality. Everything has probably been dished to her on a silver platter.

To her, this is a game. Not for survival because she doesn't believe she can lose.

We stand in silence, the only sound the frantic drumming of my heart against my ribs as each second ticks by.

Until the now familiar robotic voice booms through the speaker.

I straighten my spine, the tension easing out of my shoulders, and then slowly drop my head, my hair brushing against my chest.

"Welcome to the room of dreams. A little treat for completing the first two games."

I suck in a shaky breath.

This is not a reward. It will still be a test.

"There is no challenge here."

Interesting.

"I'm sure you have seen the array of candy, but some of you should have noticed the table of other delicacies. Pick your weapon wisely. You'll be needing it for the next game. Once you've chosen, you have fifteen minutes to treat yourselves. Everything is edible. Enjoy."

It cuts off and the blonde girl rushes over to the table. The other girls follow behind her.

I glance at Richard. With a quick flick of his eyes, he gives me a silent command to "go".

"That's huge!" the red-haired girl says in horror to the blonde, who is proudly holding up a gigantic dildo with a shit-eating grin.

"I'm not an amateur," she spits back and glares at me with her dark amber eyes.

"I hope the next game involves anal," I whisper to myself; she will split her ass in half with that.

The other two girls look at each other warily and pick their 'weapons'. As they move out of the way, I stand in front of the table.

Okay, why do they all look kinda scary?

There's a black one that stands out to me in the middle. It has a hook shape on the top; so I pick it up. It has one button, which I press, and it buzzes to life, stopping the girls chatting behind me.

"Need instructions with that one?"

The blonde girl's squeaky voice has me squeezing the toy and it vibrates my hand.

Spinning to face her, I arch my brow.

"What's your name?" I ask. I need a name to this annoying voice.

"Tara."

I don't offer her mine in return.

"Tara, what?"

"Renegade. Why?"

I bite back my laugh. I've never heard of them, but it gives me an insight into her high-class life.

"What's yours then?" She shoves her hand on her hip.

I ignore her and turn it off, but as I press the button again, it vibrates harder. And again. After the fourth one, it stops.

As embarrassment heats my cheeks, I move away from the table.

The other two girls are now ripping candy off the wall.

"They really shouldn't eat all that sugar. They keep up with that, they'll be bulging out of these." Tara pulls on her leather straps over her pink bra.

"Why does it matter what they eat? Now of all times? It isn't going to matter in a grave," I say coolly.

She shrugs, and I step away from her and head to the back wall that's covered in jelly sweets. Picking one off, I shove it in my mouth.

If I'm going to die here, I'll eat what I want.

Damn, that's amazing.

God, I needed the sugar. So I grab another one, this time a red and green gummy worm.

Just as I take the last bite, I notice the guards position themselves in a line in front of the wooden door that's arched with purple flowers.

"It's now time for the third game to begin," the deep voice tells us as the door is opened by Richard.

Tara confidently steps forward with her huge dildo proudly in hand.

I fall in line behind her and the two remaining girls behind me.

I look down at my device and close my eyes for a second.

I can do this.

If anything, to beat Tara and wipe that smug grin off her face.

CHAPTER 46

DECLAN

A low, genuine laugh rumbles in my chest as I catch Ebony's muttered curse.

Anal.

Fuck. That would've been perfect.

A sly smile curves my mouth as the girls are led into the cream room—walls painted a bland, sterile shade. But there's nothing neutral about what's coming next. The game here isn't about color. It's about control. About breaking through that final layer of resistance and watching it crack.

Ebony holds the best weapon in the room, and she doesn't even realize it.

That curve on the tip is designed to shatter a woman from the inside out.

But only if she lets go long enough to use it right.

That's her problem.

She's always calculating.

Always locked in her head, planning an escape no one's offering.

But the look on her face right now... the confusion twisting those sharp features...

It's fucking beautiful.

I can't wait for the realization to hit her.

A thrill runs down my spine as she's guided to the bed. Four of them line the room, spaced evenly apart, each bolted with worn leather restraints, stiff from use. Heavy chains coil from the head-boards to steel collars, waiting to wrap around soft throats.

If they jerk forward, try to rise; they choke.

It's that simple.

Surrender or suffocate.

Once the guards finish strapping them down, it's my turn to stir the pot.

I clear my throat, press the speaker button, and let my voice slide across the room like silk pulled tight over a blade.

"Welcome to Room Three, ladies. It's called the Cream Room. Not because of the bland-ass walls, though."

Ebony's right leg twitches. She's trying not to squirm, squeezing her thighs like they're the only things holding her together.

"This room may actually give you a little… relief."

Tara, the one with the absurdly large dildo, grins.

She has no idea.

No fucking clue what's at stake here.

But my girl does.

She's still. Focused. Ready.

That's why she's behaving so goddamn well.

Because she understands the cost of failure.

And whether she knows it or not, she's already mine.

"I'll put you out of your misery," I continue, eyes locked on the screen. "The game is simple. You're going to make it rain for me. Using your toy, your fingers…whatever you need. The only way into the next room is by setting your mind free."

Ebony stiffens like I've cracked her spine with those words.

Then she turns her head, avoiding the camera.

My jaw ticks.

No.

I want her eyes.

I want her defiance, her arousal, her fear—all of it.

Her eyes tell me what she won't say.

"And by rain," I drawl, slow and sharp, "I mean you have to make yourself squirt for your Master. You should be thanking me—for allowing you to come as many times as it takes. The first three women to complete the task move on."

The guards step back, placing themselves behind the girls' heads.

They'll need the illusion of privacy to surrender fully.

To let go enough to come that hard, that loud.

"Time to show me how well you know yourselves. How far you're willing to go for a golden ticket to freedom. Show me what you can do."

My finger hovers over the button for just a second longer.

"Have fun. Let me hear you."

I cut the feed and lean back in my chair, the ache in my chest twisting into hunger.

I zoom in.

Her.

Always her.

I'm itching to get my hands on that body.

That mouth. That fire and fury she tries so damn hard to suppress.

But for that to happen—

She has to win.

CHAPTER 47
CHARLOTTE

Squirt?

How the hell do I do that?

Fuck.

Lifting my head with my thighs spread, the sudden movement causes my collar to press against my windpipe, triggering a cough.

Instead, I lay my head back down and take a deep, calming breath, the silence pressing in on me.

I've never done this before.

Can everyone even do it?

I close my eyes and hit the button on my vibrator.

Hearing Tara's fake and dramatic moans next to me is really fucking off-putting.

This whole damn room is.

Opening my thighs, I graze the tip of the cool object against my clit and imagine the sound of the waves in Italy.

Jimmy's sandalwood aftershave.

His eyes.

His tongue.

All of it.

If I have any chance of this, it's his memory.

I completely zone out of the room and transport myself to five years ago.

Almost like a torture technique, but this time I'm immersed in pleasure and sin.

Picturing his handsome face between my legs.

As I slide the toy towards my entrance, I slowly sink it inside me and let out a gasp.

Its deep vibrations make my legs shake instantly.

With every gentle thrust in and out, I replay that earth-shattering night.

The way my pussy stretched around his cock.

How he tended to every inch of me.

My entire body trembles as I up the pace. I switch my brain off from everything else other than this.

Each thrust makes me jerk on the bed, which squeezes the collar on my throat.

My head swims, and I throw my arm over my face, biting down hard enough to taste blood as I try to block out the noise.

I'm so fucking close to falling apart.

Everything is tingling. Something I've not experienced in five years.

An orgasm.

"Oh my god," I whisper and bite into my shaking arm.

I shatter with intensity as I tremble on the leather bed, the sensation almost violent as it courses through me.

The damp heat of my skin makes the fabric stick.

As I come down from my high, I rub my hand over my face and let out a long exhale.

I turn to my right; the dark-haired girl, contestant six, has already been released.

My breathing is shallow and my heart almost races out of my chest.

No one has released me.

"Fuck," I whisper.

I can't go again. How the hell do I even do this?

The weight of the world suddenly falls on my chest.

It's like I can't breathe. I don't have the option to fail. Not now when I'm so close to the end.

The cries of the red-haired girl rip through the room, almost animalistic, and my heart sinks as the guard walks over to her table.

I shake my head and slide the vibrator along my slit again.

Nothing. My brain is racing too fast.

It's almost painful more than anything, and so sensitive. It's weird.

Tara screams out in frustration, and I can't help but find it amusing. The big fat dildo isn't doing quite what she wanted.

Come on, Charlotte. Think. How would you squirt?

It can't be impossible for me.

I slide the vibrator back inside me and leave it for a few seconds to adjust to it again.

This time I use my imagination for a different scenario. One like I would write. Our "what if?"

Perhaps up against a bookshelf, with his hand around my throat as he whispers in my ear what a good girl I am for him.

Using his fingers like an expert to melt me into a puddle for him.

"Mmmm." I let the sensations wash over me as I imagine him licking his warm tongue along my jaw before kissing me.

It's almost like he's with me now. I can smell that strong aftershave.

"That's it, good girl, keep going," a deep Irish voice whispers in my ear.

I freeze.

It's just like Jimmy. Husky and delicious.

"Keep your brain wherever it was. Go back there and use the hook on your toy as deep as you can. Find that spot and keep hitting it. Put pressure on your lower stomach if you need to. Let it consume you, don't fight it. Run with it. Let it take over you."

Holy fuck, his voice.

I open my eyes, and he tuts.

"Close them. Go back there and do as I say."

The commanding nature of his voice reminds me of him. So I do as he says.

I push in the toy as far as it will go and I jump when it hits that spot, deep in my core.

"That's a good girl. Keep going," he whispers so softly.

Biting down on my lip, I keep going.

"Mmm, look at you." His voice comes from behind my bed, right at the top of my head, where I can feel his hot breath on my scalp.

I press down my free hand on my lower stomach as I think about Jimmy eating me out, using his fingers and tongue. Telling me how good I am. How decadent I taste.

"Fuck, fuck," I pant out.

"Ride the wave and make it rain, baby."

I'm shaking like crazy as I pull the toy out and go again.

A heavy pressure builds up in my core, almost like I'm going to explode.

Liquid drips over my hands, and I keep going. Playing out the scene in my head.

"Good fucking girl," he tells me, and that sets off the fireworks.

I ride it out completely, focusing on only that, as warmth gushes out of me, all down my thighs. I cry out, almost like a feral animal. As my back arches off the bed, my throat is squeezed, and my head fucking spins.

Every muscle screams in victory as I win, a wave of exhaustion and triumph washing over me.

I pull out the toy and hide my face in my arms, trying to regain my breath.

"Congratulations," he says in a low, deep voice.

My heart fucking stops.

Now I'm coming down from my high. It really fucking sounds just like him.

My mind is playing tricks on me.

It can't be, can it?

CHAPTER 48

DECLAN

My cock is throbbing so hard I can't see straight.

The effect my voice had on her.

That was fucking stupid of me.

The way she fell apart. She even smells as perfect as I remember.

Watching her shatter almost released some of my hatred. For those few minutes, all I could remember was her smile.

Or the way her lips parted when she came.

Fuck.

"Give her five minutes and take Tara out," I tell Reggie under my breath.

Ebony was right, Tara picked the wrong toy.

I don't even let him respond before I dart out of the room and straight down the hall to my office.

The second I walk in, I tear the mask off my face and throw it on my desk.

Locking the door behind me, I rip open my belt and open my pants, releasing my aching dick.

"Fuck!" I shout as I stroke myself, sitting on the couch.

I'm on fire.

Her screams replay in my mind and I tug harder, imagining her tight cunt clamping down on me. Her heat smothering me. Her perfect lips devouring me.

In this moment, I don't care; I just have an unrelenting need for her.

It doesn't take long before my thighs are tense and I toss my head back, letting my own orgasm take over, and I spill all over my hand.

"What the hell are you doing to me, heartbreaker?" I mutter, grabbing a tissue to clean myself up and heading into the bathroom.

As I wash my hands, I look at my red eyes in the mirror.

She's right in my grasp. The answers I've been longing for are near.

Yet, this pain that takes over still doesn't leave me.

Taking my seat back at my desk, I sigh as I watch her get helped up off the bed.

She almost seems vulnerable like this.

Way out of her comfort zone as she rubs the black cuffs on her wrists with a nervous disposition.

She keeps her head down as she walks to the fourth room.

Rolling up my sleeve, I look at my Rolex as my stomach rumbles. My mind is spinning. I need a break and my brothers to knock me back into sense.

Dialing Finn, he answers straight away.

"We're taking a break for a few hours. Meet me at Inferno."

"Copy that. Girls to their rooms?"

"Yep. Make sure Reggie stands guard in Ebony's room."

There's a slight pause.

"I'll send Rowan and Reggie," he tells me.

She's really rattled my brother.

"See you in ten." I cut the call, pull out my cigarette packet, and grab my mask.

Air. I need some air.

I can't be behaving like this over her. She is the enemy, the one who betrayed me.

CHAPTER 49

It's a long drag back down the purple hallway.

I'd rather get this over and done with than delay it any further. More time to ponder. And after the last game, my mind is reeling.

Was that Richard helping me again? Why did his words have such an impact on me?

It's like he knew how to control me, how to enjoy me.

The problem is, I'm starting to doubt my own mind. I need to end this, not take a nap.

I stop before the guard closes the door. Richard has a friend this time to escort me. It's like looking into identical sets of eyes.

"Why are there two of you?" I ask as we stop outside my door.

"Less contestants to look after now," Richard replies flatly.

"How long have I got?" I ask.

He scratches his jaw and looks behind him.

"A few hours. I'll bring you some lunch up soon."

I give him a sweet smile. You never know who can save your life. Or who I could sacrifice to save my life.

"Thank you."

As the door softly closes and locks with a gentle click, I flop onto the bed and bury my face in the cloud-like softness of the lush pillows, their scent a comforting blend of lavender and cotton.

Two rooms to go.

And I doubt we've hit the worst yet.

As my eyes flutter closed, all I can hear is the Irish voice from the last room.

I'm not losing my mind. He called me a good girl, and it was exactly how I remember.

A coincidence?

A high? The sweet room. I could have been drugged, possibly.

I pinch the skin of my arms; I'm fine.

His presence sparked me to life.

And he has a link to Enzo, I've seen it with my own eyes in Italy. My heart starts to pound. What if?

Shaking my head. There is no damn way fate can do this to me.

And what are the chances of him being in Pennsylvania?

Or are they lying to me? I could be anywhere. I was knocked the hell out.

Jumping out of bed, I pace the room, hearing the guards mumbling outside my door. Heading over, I quietly lean in and rest my ear on the door.

"Dangerous. Right." One lets out a deep chuckle.

Are they talking about me?

I think about Jimmy, that soothing, deep voice.

I hope one day I can find him and tell him how his memory kept me alive all these years. Although I'm not sure how the hell I explain my participation in the games.

If I lose, I'll never get a chance to tell a soul anyway.

This time the monsters are waiting behind a locked door for me, rather than sleeping beside me.

For now, I can rest.

When I rise, I finish this.

I fight to get my life back. And I guess, come face to face with ghosts.

CHAPTER 50

DECLAN

I prowl the dimly lit bar inside Inferno, the stale smell of beer and sweat clinging to the air, feeling like a caged beast.

The private bar inside is on the top floor and requires an extensive security check that Enzo has installed. Fingerprints, retina, the works.

This is where the business happens.

The fun happens below us.

Finally the doors open. A perplexed Finn and a relaxed Conan stroll through. Conan beelines towards the bar and starts pouring our drinks.

"Talk, Dec." Finn presses, taking a seat at the bar.

I shake my head and hold up my finger, downing my scotch first.

"Reggie said you broke your own rules. Twice." Finn says harshly, sipping his own drink.

"I had to," I reply, lighting up my third cigarette in half an hour.

"Explain. You've never once entered a game. You've outright refused even Conan's ideas. Why now? Why her?"

His jaw ticks. Finn himself is probably diagnosable as a true psychopath. Perhaps it takes one to spot one?

She's under his skin, for entirely different reasons than me.

"We want her to win. She needed help. I knew she did." I swallow the burning lump in my throat.

It's a half-truth.

Even if she lost, I can intercept her and interrogate her, regardless. It's my fucking game. My factory.

A chuckle escapes Finn's lips, and Conan stares at me, his confusion evident in his wide eyes.

"I told him to have fun," Conan tells Finn.

I don't need defending.

Pulling out my cigarette packet, I offer one to Finn, who accepts and pulls out his Zippo.

"You losing your head over her, brother? If so, I can step in and finish the games," he tells me, exhaling the smoke into my direction.

"No. I'm fine. I just need a break. So do the girls."

Conan lets out a low chuckle.

"You're too nice to them," he tells me.

"I don't want my potential sub to be scared to death every time I breathe near them, Con," I snap back.

I've read enough books now to know exactly how to create the perfect submissive.

Balancing fear and pleasure. Learning exactly what gets them going. How to turn their minds off.

And what better way to learn how to be a dominant than by the words of a woman.

"Fair enough. I do." Conan walks round to our side of the bar and takes a seat next to Finn.

"So what exactly is your plan?" Finn asks, and I take another drag.

"Please fucking tell me you have one." Finn rubs his hands over his face and lets out a huff. Patience has never been his strong suit.

Except he can operate on someone for hours on end without breaking a sweat, but hits the roof if we don't answer a question in seconds.

Psychopath.

A brilliant one.

"Of course I fucking have one. She wins the games. We hold her in the last room and interrogate her."

"And then?" he presses, tilting his head to study me.

"She has to go, Declan," Conan tells me.

I shoot him a look, dread pitting in my stomach.

"We will have to assess once we get there, who knows her motive or how we can use her. And we need to speak to Enzo." The words just keep tumbling out.

"You're stalling. Don't let her get to you. That's her plan." Finn taps his finger to his temple.

"Crazy. Remember that. You could still be in jail or fucking dead because of her."

I nod, and the anger flows through my veins as I clench my fist.

Finn pulls out some paper from inside his gray trench coat and hands it out to me.

I take it and I crumple it. It's her application.

"What?" I ask.

"I had another look at the files Enzo sent. This was his late addition."

I gathered that.

"Russian links. Already screwed you over. The same trip you met Enzo. This isn't a coincidence."

My mind spins. Finn doesn't trust Enzo. Never has. Believes someone with that much power at his fingers can turn at any moment.

That's why we have minimal help from him. We avoid interventions. We run our games. Enzo helps from a distance.

But would he fuck us over?

Whatever he has going on in Russia is spilling into my territory.

No. We're an important asset. The games are too. We purposely created this to become too hard to lose.

"With everything going on in Russia, the unrest after Ivan's death, and Mikhail not wanting to lead the Volkov family there? Yeah, Enzo probably does have another motive. But it won't be against us, brother."

I rub the back of my neck, trying to relieve some of the tension. I hope I'm right.

"Fine. I trust you. Maybe speak to him before you reconvene the games? He's holding his cards, and you fucking need to see them."

Finn straightens, leaning heavily on the bar, the scent of old wood and stale alcohol heavy in the air, and takes down the bottle of our father's whiskey.

A constant reminder of how we got here. The empire we've built is on the foundations of his sacrifice.

Blood is everything, even in death.

No one takes that from us.

Not even her.

CHAPTER 51

There's a knock at my door the second I finish my sandwiches. I had to start with the chocolate-covered strawberries and champagne.

This all seems extreme to find a submissive for a year.

Especially when none of us seem to be willing participants. That isn't the vibe I get from any of them.

Something doesn't add up.

I bet Drago could have worked this out sooner. That last game has thrown me off. I don't want to believe it's him. Maybe I don't want to face my past.

From the small interactions I've had with the girls, none of us are part of the BDSM world.

So why on earth would the 'Master' want us here to compete?

But there is one key between us all. One that Tara gave away. You can just tell by the way she carries herself and looks down on all of us.

Money.

This isn't about us. This is about our families. That way in for them into Inferno as the contract stated.

I think we all come from powerful families, and I bet we've all been forced to sign these contracts.

And why are they putting us up in luxury rooms and providing three-course fucking lunches with champagne?

Even Richard is nice to me.

If this was Vlad, I'd be being dragged around by my hair.

Power has the potential to make men evil, especially over a woman.

Yet, here, that isn't the case.

It's all very orchestrated.

The guards haven't touched us without consent inside the games.

This game had the potential to be ruthless. There are no laws or rules.

They could have done anything with us.

But we do it all to ourselves?

It. Makes. No. Sense.

Yet, I bet it makes perfect fucking sense to those who know the truth.

I finish the last bite and check myself in the mirror.

At least I look less exhausted after the nap. I freshen up fast and brush my hair. My hands are trembling, but I force them still.

They don't hurt us.

But the losers... they're shot.

The first time it happened, I flinched. Now, I flinch remembering it. That sharp crack of the gun. No hesitation. Just death.

This is the first time in my career I truly have no idea what I'm walking into. And somehow, that terrifies me more than any enemy I've ever faced.

Yet there's power in surviving this long. A fucked-up kind of pride.

The door opens. I drop my gaze as Richard steps in.

I wonder what his real name is.

"It's time for the next game. You ready?" he asks, voice smooth and low.

"I am," I whisper.

He wasn't the one who helped me in the last round.

I offer my wrist. He clips the strap onto the cuff, right over the scars. They're raw and aching. The metal irritates them, but I ignore it.

He leads me down the corridor. My eyes dart over the floor, the walls. No blood. Clean. Sanitized. That doesn't mean it's safe.

Where do they take the bodies?

I don't want to know. But I do have an educated guess.

Incinerators. It's a fucking factory.

Clever.

Adrenaline surges, but it's cold. Not the kind that sharpens. The kind that tightens your chest and clogs your lungs.

We enter the room. The door slams shut behind us.

Pitch black is what I'm greeted with.

My breath hitches. I can hear the girl next to me breathing, sharp and shallow.

"Welcome to hell," the distorted voice crackles through the speaker.

Blinding lights slam on. I blink, then I freeze.

The walls are black. Splattered with red. Thick, dark paint, or blood? I'm not sure. I don't want to be.

Three benches sit in the center. Each with a mounted saddle. A dildo rises from the middle—large, slick, and of course, purple.

Chains dangle from the ceiling.

The back wall is a gallery of torment. Whips, paddles, floggers. I want to throw up.

This isn't just another game.

It's a violation waiting to happen.

The girl beside me gasps. I want to comfort her. Tell her to breathe. But I can't afford that right now.

Empathy gets you killed in here.

They made it this far for a reason. They're survivors too. Sweet faces can still hide steel.

Tara should've been one of them. She was strong, extremely annoying, but strong. And now she's gone.

The voice cuts through the heavy silence again.

"This room is your nightmares brought to life. A test of resilience in many forms. You will be pushed to your very limit. Over and over again. How much can you endure?"

My stomach knots. I swallow back the bile.

"This game has no set time. It goes on for as long as it takes for one of you to tap out."

A tremor racks my body. My chest tightens. Breathe, Charlotte.

I force myself to remember my training. My instincts. But that old, soft version of me—she's clawing at the edges.

I need the ruthless one now.

The one who killed to survive.

But the darkness, the restraints, the fucking dildo beneath me— it's overwhelming.

Focus.

Remember why you're here.

"The guards will help you into position. And then they will start the games. Remember, you need to survive hell to get a taste of heaven. The golden ticket is so close you can almost touch it. Two more rooms to survive. I'll be seeing one of you very soon."

The speaker cuts off. Silence follows like a scream muffled beneath a pillow.

The girl beside me yelps as she's dragged to her bench.

Then Richard moves to me.

"Position yourself," he says, motioning to the saddle.

I hesitate. But I climb up. Slowly. My arms do the work, my legs trembling. I lower myself onto the dildo, gritting my teeth. It's slick, at least.

"Hold up your arms."

I obey.

The cuffs snap onto the chains above, yanking my arms high. Cold metal bites my wrists. My shoulders scream in protest.

Pain radiates with every breath.

I am completely restrained.

Powerless.

Exposed.

There is no escape.

Just the hope that one of the others taps out before I break.

I won't look at them. I can't.

That's how they get in. How you lose your edge. You make it personal.

The lights cut out again. The darkness swallows us whole.

I close my eyes.

Two more rooms…

Just two more.

CHAPTER 52

DECLAN

The night vision on these cameras is top of the line, providing crystal-clear images even in near-total darkness.

In that moment, before her eyes fluttered shut, I felt the culmination of five years of anticipation.

Terror.

Her demons are in this room, and I intend to hunt them out.

I will find them and use every means at my disposal to extract the truth.

With a grin, I press the on button to all three of the Sybian Saddles, anticipating the buzzing sound that will soon fill the room.

Noticing her wince, I immediately turn hers all the way up.

"Let's go demon hunting, shall we, heartbreaker?" I whisper to her.

She tried to break me.

Now it's my turn to break her soul.

She squirms on the hard bench, her legs dangling over each side, swinging gently back and forth. Her arms tense, but she's careful not to move them too much.

It won't be long before they're dead anyway.

Soon the only sensation she'll know is a wave of intense, sensual pleasure washing over her.

Over and over again.

That is when the balance of pleasure and pain tips, possibly torturously.

But this time, it's not just physical pain to endure.

It's mental.

The process of degradation, harsh and unforgiving, weeds out the weak with brutal efficiency.

For some, it turns them on.

For others, it will make them crack.

Find their weakness and use it. Just how our father taught us. Although probably not with the intention of this.

And I'll be watching every second to find hers, ready to use on her later.

The illusion of being the villain must remain intact. We've helped her twice.

She's on her own now.

I'm out of her spell.

It's almost time to come face to face with my heartbreaker.

CHAPTER 53
CHARLOTTE

Song- How Villains Are Made, Madalen Duke

"How does that feel, you dirty whore?" A deep voice whispers in my ear.

I let out a whimper as my brain spirals to the place I never want to go to.

The place that will destroy me if I go too deep.

My survival is attributed to my refusal to ever open that door.

Ten years I've been numb. Molded into this woman I no longer recognize.

I'm angry. I'm hurt.

I can't let myself feel the pain. That won't keep me alive, and it won't save my daughter.

One day the time will come, and I'll process my past.

But now I'm fueled by hatred and the thought of revenge.

I've never been allowed a moment to be soft.

I am simply a vessel. I cannot open that door.

I cannot let the monster in.

"Filthy. Fucking. Slut." Each word is said with venom, and it's a punch to the gut.

Winding me and closing in my chest.

No.

I push Vlad out of my brain. He won't be the end of me.

"Is that what you like? A big dick using you? Huh? Is that what you need?"

I shake my head as my eyes burn from holding back the tears. I won't cry, they won't break me.

The girl next to me moans loudly, having the opposite experience to me, and it sets off panic.

My hands go numb above my head, the cold seeping into my bones as I shake them, and a searing pain rips into my wrists from the raw, angry red scars.

The nights tossing and turning, trapped in my bed with the devil.

"Fuck," I cry out.

My throat closes in; I can't swallow. It's like he's breathing heavily in my ear. His stale cigarette breath. His offensive aftershave.

"Whore."

This time, the taunt is in a Russian accent. Well, to me it is.

The line between reality and my nightmares is blurring, the chilling sounds of my dreams now echoing in my waking hours, a terrifying fusion I can't seem to break free from.

I squeeze my eyes shut and shake my head, trying to breathe. But the more I try, the harder my chest tightens.

My heart has never raced so fast.

Blood is everywhere when I close my eyes.

Dead body after dead body.

My mom. My dad.

Isabella.

"Slut. Whore. Cheat."

This isn't real. I keep telling myself over and over.

My heart hammers against my chest, a frantic bird trapped in my ribs, its rhythm so strong I feel it pulsing in my neck. It's all I can hear.

Vlad's dark brown eyes bore into mine, and a scream escapes my lips as he violently tears open his belt.

With a cruel smirk he taunts, "You want this, don't you, you dirty bitch? You deserve this."

The blood rushes from my head to my toes, leaving a dizzying, tingling numbness.

While the dildo vibrates, I feel a mix of pleasure and desperation, my body reacting with involuntary twitches and trembling movements. I can't. I can't fucking do this.

I gasp for air, a burning sensation in my lungs, bile rising in my throat, a bitter taste coating my tongue.

A searing inferno consumes my body, while simultaneously, a glacial shard of ice impales my heart, creating a contrast of unbearable heat and bone-deep cold.

"No. No. No," I cry out in desperation.

I hear Vlad's deep chuckle echo through the room. Taunting me.

"Help me," I whimper.

Visions of Vlad grabbing Isabella spring into my mind. The more I fight, the weaker my body feels.

A flash of light blinds me before it fades to black again.

I try to speak.

Begging for help, but my body won't let me as I fall limp.

CHAPTER 54

DECLAN

"Finn. Get in there and get her out. Now!" I scream through my headset.

Abruptly I stand, watching Conan and Finn rush into the room. The guard's rough movements as they remove her restraints are audible before her body flops heavily into Conan's arms.

"Be careful. This could be a trick." I tell them.

I don't believe my own words.

Whatever demons she came face-to-face with knocked her the fuck out.

The agony as she cried out for help was almost haunting.

In that moment, her fierceness subsided, and her true vulnerability came out. I'd expect that to excite me, but it didn't. It made me feel sick.

"The games are over for now. Put the remaining two in the holding room. Finn, check over Ebony and let me know the verdict."

I tug at the hem of my black T-shirt and rest my hands on the desk.

They carry her into the third room and lay her down on the bed as Reggie brings in some of Finn's supplies that we keep nearby.

He uses a stethoscope to check her heart rate and takes her blood pressure, the cuff tightening around her arm.

Relief washes over me as she blinks her eyes open. They're red, and she's confused as she looks around.

"W-what happened?" Her voice is soft, almost innocent.

Relief, that is all I feel.

"You passed out," Finn replies bluntly, not shifting focus from his task.

A masked Conan, a mountain of a man, stands arms crossed, his broad shoulders blocking the doorway completely.

"Drink this." Finn passes her a bottle and helps her sit up.

She downs it almost in one go, and he takes it straight from her, tossing it on the floor beside him.

"Anything hurt?" he asks.

She rubs her shoulder but shakes her head.

"No." She frowns as she looks at him.

"You're Irish?" she asks.

"Now is no time for questions, Ebony. You lost the games," he says flatly.

I swear she's about to cry. But it also appears as if she's sizing up the number of men in the room as Finn removes the blood pressure cuff from her arm.

"Why save me? Why look after me and ask how I am? I should be dead."

Is she worried?

It sounds like it.

But this could, as Finn said, be a plot.

I hit the button for that room's speaker.

"Contestant three. Your time in Decadence has come to an end. Which is a shame, I had high hopes for you."

Her head snaps up to the camera.

"You are aware of the rules."

She looks up at Conan in the doorway and Finn next to her. Looking at his belt area for a weapon, I presume.

"Before you meet your end, I'd like to introduce you to someone."

"Who?"

I tut.

"Remember the contract. No speaking back and do as you are told. We're extending your life momentarily. Follow the guards, and we will return for you later. Your time in Decadence has been extended. For now."

Finn scowls, his brow furrows in a deep frown, and shakes his head, his dark hair swaying slightly.

He needs to learn to trust. I press the button on my comms.

"Let's play a new game. Put her in the holding cell."

That gets Conan's attention as he sends a questioning look at the camera.

It's time to get our answers and get rid of our enemy.

Enzo might be holding his cards close, but this girl might have all the answers I need.

He can wait.

As they escort her to the cell, I shake my head, rewinding the footage of her passing out.

Her face pales as she tugs on the chains on her wrist.

I pause just as she looks at the camera.

That pain behind her eyes, the same as it was in Italy.

It hits me right in the chest, almost pushing my anger away.

"Who is hurting you, heartbreaker?" I whisper. Tapping play on the mouse, I watch again.

I zoom in on her and stop on her tattooed arm, squinting to watch her movements.

I close my eyes when I see it. Those angry red scars under the cuffs as they move.

They aren't fresh. My fists clench, and I step away.

I need to find out why she's here and what she wants, using my head, not my heart.

Coincidences like this don't exist.

She isn't a true Decadence contestant. Her body isn't to be used and abused.

It's to be worshipped. Just like I did that night.

But that is just a dream. A fantasy that can never be reality.

We are in our nightmare.

A fresh hell neither of us can escape.

I flick over to the footage from the holding room. Rhett has his hand on her bicep, and I want to rip his head from his shoulders for touching her.

I hold my breath as I watch the footage, changing to the inside angle as he lightly pushes her inside.

I can't help but smirk at the confusion on her pretty little face as she realizes her first truth about the games.

"What's your next move, heartbreaker?" I tap my desk and wait.

Time will reveal her true intentions.

But for now, I know her weakness.

CHAPTER 55
CHARLOTTE

The door slams shut with a loud bang. The girls huddle in the corner, pressed to the cold, hard floor, faces pale with fear.

What. The. Fuck?

My head's still fuzzy, and the world blurs as I stumble farther into the room.

"I—I thought…"

Tara looks up at me, a cruel smile twisting her lips. "Not so confident now?" she spits.

I raise a brow. I could kill this lanky bitch in seconds.

"Because we're all in such a fantastic position now," I mutter, gesturing at the pokey room around us.

"We need to figure a way out," I tell them, met only with blank stares.

Even when I feel like shit, I still have fight left in me.

"Hello? Did you not just go through the same hell I did? This place is fucked up. We need to get out. Did you read the contract?"

I want to bash their stupid heads against the wall.

"None of this is real," the redhead whispers nervously.

Wait.

The two at the back.

"Shouldn't you be in the final room? You won the last game. I tapped out."

A shrug. A look of pure terror. A visible shiver.

"The guards said the games were over and brought us here," one of them whispers.

Confusion coils in my gut.

"The gunshot was fake. To make you think we were dead. But they didn't kill us," Tara says.

"Yet," I snap.

I've dealt with assholes like this my whole life. We're probably just fucking lab rats now.

"Is that what you want? To be owned like a fucking slave? Because I don't see them ever letting us out."

The words hit hard. Property of Decadence. It's what the contract said.

The contestant from the second room starts crying, bottom lip trembling. I almost feel sorry for her.

Almost.

There's no room for sympathy. Only survival.

I'm not leaving Isabella behind. Not like this.

"Maybe… it'd be better than living at home." Her voice is barely a whisper, but her face says everything. Broken. Familiar.

I see myself in her pain.

"Who made you sign the contract?" I ask, taking a step forward.

"My stepdad."

I swallow the rising lump in my throat as she looks away.

I crouch down beside her. Dignity left the second we stepped through those gates.

"If we work together and get out, we can escape them. Your family. I can make that happen."

Her hand trembles as she wipes away tears. I clasp it, grounding her.

"We can do this. Just trust me."

I scan the others. Tara's face flushes with rage.

"Daddy wouldn't hurt me. This is just a game. You're going to ruin it for us!" She stomps like a toddler.

I ignore her.

Then one of the girls from the last room steps forward—dark-haired, eyes downcast.

"My husband sent me. If I won, he'd get more money and power. I thought if I got the money, I could run and never look back."

A sad shrug. "But clearly, I didn't read the contract properly."

I nod. Makes sense.

"What's your name?"

"Emma."

I pause, remembering the cameras. "Ebony," I say with a smile that doesn't reach my eyes.

I turn to the rest of them.

"Jess," the redhead says.

"Rebecca," the blonde adds.

"Okay. So you all read what happens to the losers, right?"

Jess chews her lip and nods.

"That's illegal. Daddy would never do that to me!" Tara whines.

Perfect. Delusion makes her dangerous.

"Well, news flash. He did. And now we deal with it. Your daddy is a power-hungry monster who sacrificed his own daughter. Get your head out of the clouds."

Her face twists. "What? Your daddy didn't love you?"

Rage blinds me.

I lunge.

My hand wraps around her throat as I slam her against the wall. The others gasp.

"Keep talking, and I'll end you before they get the chance."

She gasps, clawing at my hand. I squeeze harder.

"Now sit down. Shut up. And do what I say."

I release her, letting her crumple. She whines, hands to her neck like a child.

Before I speak, the door bursts open.

A masked man stands there. Different from the others.

"You." His deep voice makes my heart stutter.

"Who, me?" I ask, all innocence.

The games didn't work.

Now I play my own.

One chance left.

Survive.

"Yeah," he grunts.

He steps closer, and I assess. Pistol on his right. Knife at his waist. Handcuffs clipped to his belt.

I let him get close. Close enough to smell the cigarettes on his breath.

He's wary of me, I can see it in his stance. His hand lashes out, fingers splayed, but I anticipate his move and swerve, the rush of his movement brushing against my arm. I can feel the heat of his anger. Driving my heel into the back of his knee with every ounce of strength I possess, the impact sends him sprawling onto the hard ground.

With my right arm wrapped around his throat, I secure it in place with my left hand, applying pressure to the right spot on his neck.

"Grab the fucking key!" I scream.

Emma scrambles forward, trying to grab the key, but this asshole reaches out, violently tugging on her hair, easily throwing her to one side. Jess reacts instantly, claws extended, and scratches his face. My muscles scream at me as I tighten my grip. As Jess holds up the key, I grab him by the hair and push him down on his front, sitting on his back, digging my knee into his spine.

"Cuffs," I shout, and Emma's shaky hands find them and hand them to me.

"He's too strong," Jess whispers through gritted teeth.

I pull back his head.

"You fucking bitch," he seethes.

I need to speed this up, so I smash his face into the concrete, hard enough to knock him out. He goes limp beneath me, and the girls get to work.

Jumping off him, I roll him over with a grunt, swiping the gun first, then the blade and chain of keys.

Making a run for the door, I stop as I swing it open.

"You coming?" I ask them.

Emma shakes her head. Tara is a shaking mess in the corner. Visions of Isabella flood my mind.

I don't have time for this. But they need some sort of weapon; they helped me.

"Here."

I toss the gun at Emma's feet, slam the door closed, and stop at the first corner.

I look up as the red dot flashes on the camera.

Maybe he will come to me.

As I reach the door, I stop, remembering the way we got in.

With a grunt, I roll this guy over and flick open the knife.

"Emma. Hold his palm down hard," I order.

Despite trembling, she manages to maintain her composure as I open the flick knife and begin cutting through his thumb.

"You're a fucking psycho," Tara cries out.

To make the task easier, I snap the bone before finally grasping his thumb in my hand.

"I'll cut yours off if you want." I grin at her.

She shakes her head and backs off.

If these girls don't want freedom, that's fine. I will not sit here and wait for my death.

I head back to the door and close it as I exit.

Survive hell and find The Master.

Although, I very much expect he's already on his way to me.

CHAPTER 56

DECLAN

"Fuck!" I roar, punching my fist into the wall beside me. I shake out the throbbing, fiery pain in my forearm, a dull ache that makes my hand tremble.

"Ebony has escaped the holding room. She's armed and dangerous." I pause. "Extremely fucking dangerous."

"What do you want us to do with her?" Finn asks through the earpiece.

I rub my crotch. I should not be so turned on right now, watching the enemy take down one of my men with such ease.

But I am.

She's a clever girl who took note of the thumbprint security system. I'm impressed and furious.

She has that effect on me. Like a witch casting a spell on my soul. I am at her mercy. That was always my fucking fear.

She is my weakness.

"Don't hurt her."

The words come out of my mouth before I can stop myself.

"It's your chance to get your girl, brother." Conan blurts out, and I clench my jaw.

"Unharmed and straight to my office. The rules have changed.

305

Defend yourselves as required. But keep her alive or I'll fucking end you," I seethe.

I'm not angry at my men.

She's mine to punish.

"We're on our way," Finn replies.

I tap my fingers on my desk as I watch her on the screen.

"There is nowhere to hide, heartbreaker."

A smile breaks out on my lips.

I watch her sliding against the wall, the blade in her right hand, Asher's thumb in the other.

The more I watch her, the more I realize I had an effect on her earlier.

I am her weakness, too.

Tapping my comms, I change my mind. There is only one way this is meant to go down.

"Change of plans. Stay back, everyone out. I'll get her myself," I tell them.

Sliding open the top drawer of my desk, I take my father's blade and holster my gun. Not forgetting the special ingredient that I shove in my pocket. I might need it.

I won't be played twice by her.

Clicking on the screen, I watch as she heads down the hallway and stops outside the door to the office. I pull up the control center and turn off the lights and the security footage, and my screen goes dark.

"It's time to play, baby." I run my hand over the warm screen and grin.

My heart hammers against my ribs as I jog towards the door, the cold air biting at my face.

I need to get to her before she finds the hidden door behind the bookshelf.

It's time to play the real game.

And end it this time…

CHAPTER 57
CHARLOTTE

The room is swallowed by darkness, and the girls' high-pitched screams slice through the silence, echoes rattling down the hallway and bleeding through the closed door.

Before the lights cut, I saw this was an office.

"Shit," I hiss, thigh slamming into the edge of a desk.

The thumb slips from my grip.

I drop to my hands, feeling around. I can't see a damn thing.

It's silent.

Too silent. I expected his men to be on my tail.

I'm trained in a lot of things. Operating blind in pitch black wasn't one of them.

He's been watching me through the cameras. He knows I'm here. He knows I'm armed.

My heart pounds as I find the wall, sliding along it with one hand. The knife rests between my teeth. I feel for a switch.

A slow, agonizing creak breaks the silence.

The door opens.

I flatten against the wall, the rough plaster scraping my skin as I suck in a shaky breath.

Not a fucking sound.

Then, footsteps. Heavy. Slow. Measured.

The scent hits me—sandalwood. Rich. Clean. Familiar.

No.

No. No.

Another step. The air crackles. It's like my body remembers.

My eyes shut. This isn't real.

"I know you're in here."

My eyes fly open. My heart slams against my ribs like a war drum.

That voice.

Him.

His fist hits the wall, an earth-shattering thud that vibrates through my bones.

"There's nowhere to hide. Nowhere to run."

His Irish lilt is rougher now. Darker. Still laced with the power that once melted me.

The footsteps stop.

Silence wraps around us.

This is the last thing I wanted, not him. I wanted to be wrong so badly.

I draw the blade from my mouth, grip it tight in my fist.

I know where the door is. He took six steps.

I could run.

"You smell just like I remember," he breathes in, deep, almost reverent.

My stomach knots. Every nerve flares.

"Decadent."

The word drips from his lips like poison.

Jimmy.

A choked yelp slips out. I freeze.

I swear I hear him smile.

He's alive. Not rotting in some Italian cell. I didn't ruin him.

But it appears he became the devil. Or was he already that? Was everything in Italy just one big fucking lie?

Anger consumes me. Trust no one.

It all happens fast.

A blur of motion. Instinct takes over.

I run.

Blind toward the door. Just one second of grace. One miracle.

Only one of us leaves through those gates.

I reach for the handle—

But a force slams into me, launching me backward. My head cracks against the wall.

Familiar hands wrap around my throat.

Not like that night.

Harder. Controlled. Deadly.

My lungs scream. I thrash, every limb fighting for breath, for air, for anything.

With a snarl, I yank my blade, but he's faster. He slams my arm into the wall, bones screaming.

The knife clatters to the floor.

He chuckles. That same laugh that once made me alive is now slowly killing me. My hopes and dreams dying with each second.

He feels bigger. Stronger. Crueler.

"Quite the escape artist, aren't you, sweetheart?"

His voice burns. My skull throbs.

I brace.

Then slam my head into his nose.

Crack.

Pain explodes across my forehead, but he lets go.

I hit the ground hard, gasping, clawing at my throat.

Desperately crawling to the exit, but I'm stopped when his legs pin me down.

He steps over me, looming, weight pressing into the floor beside me.

"Oh, now you want to act like a fucking animal?" he growls, grabbing my hair and yanking my head back.

"Maybe that's exactly how I'll treat you."

"I—I can explain," I gasp.

If he only knew. About Isabella. About everything.

Maybe if I stop fighting… maybe that's my way in.

His hands grip my hips, rough and controlling. He drags me up like I weigh nothing.

His nose brushes my cheek, breath hot and cruel against my skin.

"I've been waiting a long time for you to join me in hell, heartbreaker," he whispers.

"Welcome to Decadence."

My blood runs cold.

Jimmy was never just Jimmy.

To meet Enzo in Italy, he had to be someone. Someone powerful. Connected.

Of course.

He lied as much as I did. Five years ago, we were both pretending. It's a hard pill to swallow.

The Prince was never coming to save the Queen. It seems he wants to destroy her too.

I guess now it's time to learn who we really are.

His hand clamps over my mouth with a cloth. My scream is swallowed.

My eyes plead with him. I need one chance to talk. Perhaps he has a shred of humanity left to listen.

He doesn't let up, his hand smothering me, and each breath is now burning.

"Sweet dreams, baby. We have a lot of catching up to do."

The last thing I hear before the dark takes me—

A soft, eerie melody. Ringing like a lullaby in hell.

CHAPTER 58

DECLAN

Carefully laying her on her side, I turn on the lights. And then I see her there, her breathing shallow, her eyes closed. Peaceful.

Beautiful.

Mine.

I instinctively clutch at my chest, a searing, familiar pain lancing through me. The same agonizing stab that always accompanies the memory of her.

The way she screamed for me.

The way she betrayed me.

I tap on the headset, and Finn's voice comes through.

"Office," I say.

Folding my arms over my chest, I get down on one knee, brushing her hair from her pretty face. She still has the deep purple running through the ends of her hair, throwing my mind straight back to Italy.

"It didn't have to go this way," I tell her.

The door opens behind me, and I back away from her.

"Tell me she ain't dead?" Finn asks as I turn to face him.

"No, just knocked out for a bit. You should know, you're a doctor."

I point at her chest, clearly moving.

"What's your plan?" he asks.

I resist the urge to roll my eyes.

"To use her weakness against her to get her to speak." I tap my nose and grin.

Her weakness is me.

As she is mine.

"Take her to the final room."

I watch the color drain from his face, and he slowly shakes his head.

"So that's it? She wins?"

I step in front of him and look down.

"I'm The Master of the Inferno, correct? I am positioned to maintain power. You—" I jab him in the chest. "—your role is to execute. Maintain the order behind the scenes."

He swallows and looks down at my finger pressing against his ribs.

"Yea, boss." The sarcasm rolls off his tongue as he bats away my hand.

"You want whoever the hell entered her into the games to be welcomed into Inferno?" he asks.

My jaw ticks.

Something isn't adding up.

I shake my head.

"We make no announcements to the families of the contestants' results until I get the answers from her." I look down at my heart-breaker, and my anger sizzles.

"Right. We can hold off a few days. I guess."

"Have the remaining girls held in the cabin until it's resolved. Let's see if she makes it out of the next room alive first."

I swallow the lump in my throat.

Could I?

I grit my teeth. She's made me into this man. She betrayed me, and in that very moment, I swore never to trust anyone outside my small circle.

"I don't like this, Dec. Something's up, and I bet Enzo knows all about it."

"Perhaps. But we're the Quinn brothers."

I clasp his shoulder firmly.

"And no one fucks us over and gets away with it. Not her. Her family. Nor Enzo. He relies on us now. Our games, our order. Our kills."

A faint cough leaves her lips and we both look at her.

"Let's get her set up before she can kill us both."

Finn laughs, but I don't join him.

I'm not even sure our first encounter was fate now. But twice.

This is fate in a twisted kind of way.

She was sent here to me.

But the shock she was in when she realized it was me, that wasn't fake.

Whether she knew it or not, she was after me.

And I intend to do whatever it takes to get the truth.

As Conan steps through the door, I step out of the way.

"Take her to room five."

My cock twitches. Fuck.

"You got it. Enzo is on his way, Dec. He just called me." I look up at the blinking monitor in the right corner of the room.

He's known as the best hacker in the country for a reason.

I wave at him through the camera and smile.

He knows something, or he wants to know something.

She has his attention as much as she has mine.

Finn looks at me warily as Conan lifts her into his arms.

"Careful," I grit out, and Finn shakes his head.

"I don't know what spell her pussy put you under for five years, but keep your fucking head. No cunt is worth our empire, brother," Finn tells me, and I clench my fists.

We lost our father for this.

We lost ourselves along the road.

Selling our souls to the devil gave us a one-way ticket to hell.

CHAPTER 59

CHARLOTTE

Song. F E R A L. Bad Omens

The soft drizzle of the melted chocolate dripping from the fountain in front of me only reminds me of the consequences of losing.

Like everything else here, it's extravagant. A fountain, which settles on a pool of chocolate, could probably fit six people. I wonder what the purpose of this room is for?

It smells delicious, a dark chocolate, and yet, I don't have an appetite. Fear of death usually takes that away.

The chair scrapes along the floor, and he turns the back towards me and straddles it.

I don't react as he tilts his head, his gaze roaming over my body.

Our silence hangs heavy in the air.

When his eyes meet mine, it's a blade through the heart.

There is only one man that walks this earth who I could never destroy.

The man who altered my life with one night. He was the light to my darkness, a memory that's kept me from being six feet under.

Except, as I stare into his striking blue eyes now, the light has gone out.

It's funny, this man has every right to kill me. In fact, he's glaring at me as if he wants to do just that.

Yet, being in the same room as him is the most relaxed I've been in five years.

I suppose if anyone is going to end my life, I want it to be the man whose memory has kept me alive.

He's become another monster in my life, wanting to drag me back to hell with him.

But that's exactly where I want to be. He owns my heart, mind, and soul.

They say once you enter the game of decadence, you don't come back out.

What if I don't want to? What if I am willing to sell the remains of my soul to this devil.

He clears his throat and I look away.

"Eyes on me," he commands. Without thinking, I do.

As he smirks, my stomach flips.

"Cat got your tongue, heartbreaker?" He pulls out his flip knife and runs the blade along his fingers.

"Jimmy?" I whisper.

He chuckles. It's deep and menacing.

"Ebony? Brittany? Who are you today?" His tone lowers.

A shiver runs down my spine, and I bite down on my tongue until it stings.

Until I work out what the hell is going on here, he isn't getting a thing out of me.

Is he The Master?

I'm assuming so. It all clicks into place. The link to Enzo. This is even worse than I first thought.

"You know, I could just cut that tongue out of your pretty little mouth if it's not going to be of use to me."

My heart hammers as I look at the knife and smack my lips closed tight.

I'm seriously fucked.

I tug on my restraints as he leans in, running the cold blade along my throat.

"Come on, heartbreaker. Give it up. Who are you?" he whispers in my ear.

"No one," I reply.

He pulls back and frowns.

"Oh, come on. You're important to me." He grins.

My heart races.

"You, sweetheart, are the answer to a lot of my questions. So you have some importance. Don't be so hard on yourself."

"Fuck you," I spit out and regret it instantly.

He smiles, revealing his white teeth.

"Here we fucking go. She's arrived." He stands and pushes his chair out of the way as he steps in front of me, towering over me.

Gripping me by the chin, he tips my head up to him.

"This can go two ways. I'm sure you're well established with this lifestyle. Hard way or the easy one?" He clasps me tighter, his gaze not faltering.

"The hard way doesn't involve my dick this time either. By hard, I mean painful." He winks and releases me.

"Who are you?" I ask.

Confusion flashes across his face. "Who am I?" He points at his chest.

"Your master. Declan Quinn."

I nod slowly.

"Didn't think you looked like a 'Jimmy'." I hide my hurt.

Maybe nothing about that night was real. We're both two fucking liars.

"You're a bloody good actress, heartbreaker. You set me up for murder, I assume? Which poor guy did you kill in the end? The one you drugged or beat up? Jimmy was just your next victim."

I shake my head.

"No. That's not true," I whisper.

He paces the room, shaking his head, before turning to me and pointing.

"No. I'm not falling for your bullshit again. None of it was real," he shouts.

He rubs his chest, almost like he's in pain, yet a darkness flashes across his eyes, and I shudder.

It seems he doesn't know what to do with me. That only tells me one thing.

I have a chance to get through to him. If I can get him to see the Charlotte from that night.

Perhaps he will believe me.

But right now, he looks furious.

This is my last resort, my last chance to save my daughter.

"Easy way," I say.

He stops in his tracks; he's gripping the knife so tight in his fist, blood starts to drip onto the floor.

"You're bleeding," I stutter.

He glances down and raises his eyebrow at the drops on the white flooring.

"You can't feel pain when you're numb," he whispers, almost to himself.

"I know. Survival mode creates monsters."

"Is that what you are? Hmm?"

I swallow past the lump in my throat.

"I do what I have to do."

He shakes his head in disappointment.

"We all have a choice in life, heartbreaker. You chose to leave that knife in my suite. You chose to betray me. Use me. And now you're back? To finish the job?" He pauses for breath, his face reddening.

"Not this time. I won't let you get under my skin again. I won't let you."

"It's not what you—"

He lunges forward and grabs my throat, his warm blood now on my skin as he squeezes.

"I'm not the same man I was back then. You helped create this version, and now that's going to bite you in the ass, heartbreaker. And not in the good way, either."

He keeps squeezing tighter, my lungs start to burn.

"Because of you, while my father was sacrificing himself, I was trying to get out of fucking Italy, away from the cops. I couldn't save him. You. Did. That."

Tears burn in my eyes. The guilt swallows me whole. How can he forgive me for that? I had no idea. I was saving myself, and the consequences, it turns out, are horrifying.

"C-Charlotte," I manage to choke out.

I heave for air as he releases me.

"Charlotte. That suits you better. Last name?" He rubs his thumb along my jaw.

He's right, he has changed. I can't work him out.

"Kovalyov. But Novikov is my true surname."

He huffs.

"Russian. You don't sound it?"

"I moved to the States as a kid."

I know he's going to search this name up. I'm a ghost thanks to Drago. I'm a ghost in that house and to the rest of the world, and so is my little girl. We don't exist.

But that family name holds weight, especially in the mafia.

He steps away from me, and I'm not sure if that's comforting or not.

"Good girl." He says with venom and throws his knife down onto the ground before opening the door.

My mouth drops open, and my body gives me away.

He's seen the flush spreading up my chest.

CHAPTER 60

DECLAN

I almost beat down my office door to get inside. Air. I need fucking air away from her.

I fall for her every single time. She distracts me.

But I have a name. Potentially.

As I stumble into my office, I find Enzo reclined back on my chair.

"Quite something to watch between the two of you. You know her?" he asks, clasping his hands together on his thigh.

"Uh. Yea? She's the woman who set me up in Italy."

"Interesting. Five years ago?"

I nod.

He turns my screen around to face me. I'm not even going to question the fact he's hacked me.

"The name she gave you. You heard of that family?" he asks as I stare at a guy's mug shot on the screen.

He looks fucking evil. About my age, maybe older.

Enzo points to the screen.

"This right here is Mr. Vlad Kovalyov. One below the leader of the Kovalyov family. They're going for a Russian takeover. Well, he is, potentially against his family's wishes."

I scratch my head.

"And you invited him?" I ask. Enzo nods, his blue eyes burning into me.

"There is a lot I want to learn about that family."

A silent message I'm not getting. My head is spinning.

And then my heart fucking stops.

"He entered his—"

I can't finish the sentence.

"Wife. Declan. Charlotte is his wife."

I smash my fist against the wall beside me.

Wife.

She was never fucking mine.

"Did you know it was her?" I shout, heading straight for the drinks cabinet. I don't even bother with a glass, I just down it from the bottle.

"No. I wasn't sure who they would send here. Like I said, I'm figuring them out. I thought it would be a different ghost that ended up here." The disappointment in his voice is clear.

"Who?"

He shakes his head.

"It doesn't matter. We have Charlotte. She might have the answers we need."

I motion to the door.

"Have at it. Ask what you want. Take her." I dismiss him, returning to my whiskey.

He stands and laughs.

"She broke your heart, didn't she?"

I scoff as he approaches, swiping the bottle from my hands.

"It was one night. How could that break my heart?" I ask, looking up at him.

"Funny how the heart knows. We all have one person in this lifetime. You know when you find them, and you feel the pain for eternity when you lose them."

"Even if they betray you? If it wasn't real?" I ask.

He places the bottle back in the cabinet.

"If it wasn't real, it wouldn't hurt, Declan. I think that answers that. As for the betrayal. Maybe we hear her out. Vlad is evil. She said something in there about survival, correct?" He straightens his navy suit as he heads to the door.

"She did."

I think about the pain in her eyes.

The truth I hear in her words.

And shake my head, remembering that blade on the floor.

"She's married."

I rub that tattoo on my pec. I need the whiskey back.

"Like that matters. Plenty of ways to eliminate that problem, Declan," he says as he swings open the door.

He points to my computer.

"Watch and listen carefully. We might get answers without all the sexual tension boiling between the two of you."

Does it matter what she has to say? She can't take back trying to frame me. She can't give me those days back where I didn't save my father.

I sigh, leaning back. Would it have made any difference if I did make it back in time? My father knew what he was doing, and he was never a man to be stopped.

As the door closes, I let out a breath and study the monitor. She's managed to shuffle her chair. Now it's on its side, and she's on the floor.

What I don't like is the familiar look in her eyes when Enzo waltzes through the door.

"Charlotte," he greets her, heading to the chocolate fountain, leaving her on the floor.

He kicks the knife a few feet away from her and sits the chair back upright.

"Recognize me?" he asks, and she blinks at him.

"I don't know you."

He laughs and shakes his head.

"I am not the man to lie to." His Italian accent deepens.

She shivers, and suddenly, I'm nervous. I'm not sure I want to hear what he will drag out of her.

Chewing on my lip, I watch with apprehension. She's mine to interrogate.

To break.

Not his.

Cracking my knuckles, I lean in closer.

"We've never met," she whispers.

He pulls out my chair and takes a seat in front of her, resting his hands on his thighs.

"Correct. Not officially on my end." He holds out a hand to her and chuckles.

"Oops. Bit tied up, aren't you?"

She scowls at him and I can't help but smile.

"I'm Enzo. I'm sure your husband knows me."

Her eyes widen. There it is. That horror. The pain.

Inside, I'm pleading with the universe for her to say he isn't her husband.

"My husband doesn't divulge business with me. That's not my job." She looks down, disgust on her face as she said those first two words.

As she looks up at the camera, my heart races.

I'm not sure what I feel.

Hatred. Anger. Betrayal. Hurt?

Sympathy?

It's something. Yet deep inside me, I want to rush down there and throw Enzo out of the room to get my real answer.

I don't even hear my door, as Conan is behind me clasping me on the shoulder.

"You okay, bro?" he asks.

"Not fucking really." I nod to the screen.

I thought it would be easier than it was to let my anger out on her.

Yet one look in those pools of blue and I was lost. Transported back to a time where life was easier.

To a time I felt alive.

I've lived in a hard shell for five years, doing anything to chase that high she gave me, with no success.

"Tell me, Charlotte."

Enzo leans in closer, and I clench my jaw.

"Who runs the family you work for? I assume you aren't just married for love?"

My heartbeat is so erratic my chest burns.

Her shoulders slump, but I see her mind racing as she stares into Enzo's eyes.

"Tatiana is the head of the family. Vlad and Emil are her brothers. I'm married to Vlad," she says harshly, like it's poison on her tongue.

"How much do you know of Tatiana?"

Enzo is almost flustered, patting down his suit.

"Her brothers fear her. She recently got shot, she's recovering." Charlotte looks deep in thought.

"I've come to the conclusion she isn't as evil as her brothers. She doesn't know me or—" She cuts herself off.

"She doesn't even know I exist."

"And who?" Enzo pushes.

"M-my handler."

Bullshit. She's hiding something.

And how would this woman not know that her brother's wife exists? How fucked up is this family?

"I find that hard to believe." Enzo leans back, studying Charlotte.

"She thinks I am a contract killer for Vlad. She has no idea I was forced to marry him. I'm under strict orders to not speak or even look at her. My guess is they are scared of what she will do to them if she knew what they had done to me."

"And they? Who is the other one?"

"Emil. Him and Vlad are the ones who stole me from my family, the ones who have trapped me."

My stomach drops.

She was fucking kidnapped.

Shit. That was close.

Opening up the daughter can of worms is not what I need right now.

Currently, I'm on the line of thought we have aligning enemies. Although, something about Tatiana has Enzo rattled. Which bugs me. I'd prefer his hatred to be aimed at my husband.

A sinking feeling settles in my stomach as I glance up at the camera.

I know Declan is listening. I've made that situation worse.

"I've been told to fear you," I tell Enzo. I'm trying to gauge how I can use this to my advantage.

I'll happily kill my husband if my daughter's safety is guaranteed.

"Your husband is a clever man."

I bite my tongue, I wish he'd stop saying it.

"His name is Vlad. Don't call him my husband."

His brow twitches, and he almost smirks.

"Noted. However—" He flicks his finger between us.

"—you are the one being interrogated here, not me. Remember that. We are not friends, Charlotte. We are enemies until I deem otherwise. Capisce?"

I nod, feeling like I've been told off by my parents as a kid.

"W-what do you want from me?"

He taps on his dark stubble.

"For me? I just need a list of every single name of those

surrounding Tatiana and how they link to her. Locations, jobs, and any information you have of her past. Other names she uses, perhaps."

"I can do that. Then I can go?"

He shakes his head and grins.

"That's just for me. You belong to Mr. Quinn now. I can't help you out of that situation. I assume you were sent here with another motive?"

He taps his fingers on his thigh.

"I was." I look down and sigh.

"They wanted me to interrogate whoever was running this to find out what you know about something they stole and then kill them."

His eyebrows shoot up and his eyes go wide. I've thrown him.

"Stole from me?"

"Yes. I assumed money. Drugs. Guns. I don't know."

He mutters something aggressively in Italian and abruptly stands.

"Once Declan is done with you, write down everything for me. Anything you can think of. Then you'll be free of my wrath."

A light goes off in my head.

"I have a notepad," I tell him.

He scratches his stubble. "Continue."

"Anything I heard in the last ten years I thought may be relevant for my escape. Dates, places, names, conversations. To me, a lot of it means nothing, but I guess to you…" I trail off.

"To me it's a fucking gold mine."

I swallow. I'm unsure what he wants with Tatiana. My gut tells me it's deeper than I could ever imagine.

"Where is it?"

I look down.

"Safe. Hidden. At his home."

"Fuck." He kicks the chair across the room. I don't flinch. I'm used to this.

"For now, write what you remember. Then, I'll be back."

I blow out a breath when he kicks the knife back towards me, but then his eyes light up and he grins.

That's never good.

Turning, he bends down and retrieves the knife, and walks towards me.

"N-no. Don't. I'll get you the names."

Fear courses through me as he stops in front of me. I squeeze my eyes shut as his strong aftershave wafts up my nostrils.

"Let's make it more fun for him," he whispers, and the tension in my wrists is gone. I try to wriggle my fingers, but they're tingling.

"Play this clever and you might be able to win him over. Play it dumb, you'll end up six feet under once we're done with you."

The seriousness in his tone makes me gulp. To look at, he's less scary than Vlad.

But the sense I get is, actually, the men here are far more dangerous.

They're smart. Thorough and deadly. The worst combination.

I keep my arms where they are behind my chair.

I give him a curt nod as he steps back, shoving the rope and knife in his pocket. He doesn't even look back as he slams the door shut behind him.

Being out of Enzo's wrath is only one part of the war.

My future, and our daughter's, hangs on the man who will next walk through.

I know how to play this smart. If I can bring back the light in his eyes, I might win.

Win what? I'm not sure.

So I sit still—and I wait.

CHAPTER 62

DECLAN

My mind is reeling from the information Enzo gathered. To me, it makes no sense.

Tatiana? Other names? Russia? It's meaningless to me and my empire.

My office door swings open, and Enzo pours himself a neat vodka.

"Do not, under any circumstances, kill her." He points at me and knocks back his drink.

"Who is Tatiana?" I ask.

"A fucking ghost. My concern. I'll deal with it."

He shrugs, pouring another.

"My interrogation is done; get that information to me, then do whatever with her. Alive, obviously. I may need more answers. Do not let her free either. I have to go. And we are getting that fucking notepad."

"And the other girls? We usually have a couple more days to organize plans."

He pulls out his phone.

"I'll sort it out. Romeo will send the details and transportation. Everything is in place. They will all be safe, and Finn can get to work on the elimination process. Charlotte is your priority now."

By the time he's finished the shot, he's already halfway to the door, pulling out his phone and calling someone.

Perfect.

Don't kill her.

Don't let her go.

So, I guess, hold her hostage and get her to beg for forgiveness.

A smirk tugs on my lips. That doesn't sound half bad.

For now, I'll let her stew.

Instead, I get the monitor feed up on my phone and head down to the holding rooms with Finn.

By the time I arrive, he's got all the girls clothed again and all sitting in a line on the back wall.

The angry red marks catch my eye on Tara's throat, and I bite back my grin.

"All set?" I whisper, leaning in to my brother.

"For what? What's the fucking plan?"

Rubbing my hands over my face, I nod to Reggie to step in as Finn leaves the room.

"You killed your girl yet?" he asks as the door shuts behind us.

"I won't be. She's staying with me until further notice."

His jaw ticks, and he shoves his hands in his pockets.

"Right. Let me guess, Enzo wants her alive?" His voice deepens.

"Yeah. She has information he needs. Lot of background here, he needs to fill in some gaps, but I trust him."

"Hmm. So she gets the golden ticket, I assume?"

I nod slowly.

"Yea. Games are over. I've got my sub."

I suppose she does. I can make her life hell for as long as I want.

"So, now what?" Finn questions.

"You work with Enzo to complete phase two."

Now that makes him smile.

"We might have an issue persuading one of the girls."

"The strangled blonde with a daddy fetish?"

When he chuckles, I start to relax.

"Yeah. How'd you guess? What if we let your girl loose in a room with her? Might solve the headache for us."

As fun as that would be, it's not who we are.

We steal them away from the real danger.

We've never come up against a contestant who refuses to start a new life and leave their old behind.

"Looks like her father is first on your list. She can't go running to him then. She will come around; Enzo will know where to place her to keep her safe, even if it is from herself for a while until she realizes."

Finn tuts.

"Of course he does."

I clasp his shoulder and look at him in his pale gray eyes.

"Get it done. This has been a fucking mess, yes. But we're the Quinn brothers. We deal with it and move on. This is just a little blip, okay? Once I've dealt with Charlotte."

His eyes go wide.

"Charlotte. Sure suits her better."

"She's married," I reply deadpan.

"Easily resolved."

I laugh.

"You and Enzo are more alike than you think." I wink at him, and he scowls.

"Let's sort this shit show out and let me get my hands dirty. I'll calm down once I start that."

"Keep the hands clean, brother," I warn.

Surgeon by day, fucking serial killer by night. A psycho with a killer grin.

"You got it, boss. Go get your girl."

I huff and step back.

"I don't want her, not like that. I just want the truth."

He shakes his head and rolls up his sleeve, looking at his silver watch.

"I give it maybe six hours before she's etched under your skin again. I saw the way you looked at her in Italy. I can see how riled up you are now. Husband or not. I know when you want something, you go after it and take no prisoners. Just don't fucking let her tear our empire down." He pauses and frowns.

"Or tear your heart out," he finishes quietly.

"I've got this. Heart is shielded." I knock my fist over my chest.

"Better be reinforced."

"Catch up later. Have fun." I wave before turning on my heel and heading down the hallway.

Stopping outside her door, I pull out my phone to see what she's up to.

I wish I could shut off my feelings when I look at her. But even now, my breath catches in my throat.

My hand hovers over the keypad. I know the next interaction seals our fate.

Which version of her will I get?

Which version of her is the real Charlotte?

Who is she, and why is she lodged in my fucking heart like the blade she drew?

CHAPTER 63

CHARLOTTE

Song- Silver Swarm, Thornhill

The door opens and goosebumps erupt over my skin.

I know without looking up it's him.

Slowly, I tip my head up, and I'm met with his scowl. The whites of his eyes are red, his tattooed hands clench by his side.

I need him to hear me out. How I do that, I need to figure out, really fast.

I stay silent as he approaches, wishing the pounding in my ears would shut up.

"I think it's about time I got answers, don't you, Mrs. Kovalyov?"

I keep my gaze fixed on him, ignoring the ache I get hearing him say my last name.

"Ask away."

He sucks in a deep breath and tips his head back.

"I like you like this." His tone lowers as he steps forward.

"Scared?"

"Just ask what you need to ask so I can go."

I keep my arms as still as I can.

"Is that what you want? To get as far away from me as possible, again? Are you going to leave the knife in my damn back this time?" He tilts his head, assessing me.

"No knives. Just words."

"Let's keep it simple, shall we? Yes and no. I don't want a conversation. I just want my answers, then I'm done with you."

A sinking feeling pits in my stomach. I don't know why I expected anything else.

"Were you married when we fucked?"

He almost sounds disgusted.

I flinch, and my leg starts to bounce.

"Yes."

He scoffs, looking away from me for a split second.

"Were you in Italy to set me up?"

"No."

"Did you know I was your mark when we had sex?"

"No," I reply firmly.

He opens his mouth and closes it again.

"Are you here to kill me?"

I close my eyes.

"Look at me, heartbreaker. Are you here to fucking end me?" he says calmly, and I open up my eyes.

"Y-yes."

He slams his palm against the wall and rests there.

"Do you fuck men on all your little missions?" He glares at me.

"Was I just your prey to play with? Huh?"

I blink at him and shake my head.

"No."

A smile tugs at his lips.

"You're a mighty fine liar, Charlotte. You played a good game, though. I fell for it, hook, line, and sinker. I bet you and Vlad had a laugh about it. Didn't you? Oh, how easy it was to trick me into believing you were real. That you were hiding pain and needed to be set free."

His nostrils flare as he pushes himself off the wall.

"N-no." My breath hitches.

He crouches down in front of me.

"Liar," he spits out.

I need a new tactic. He isn't going to sympathize with me. Nor listen to me.

My mind flashes back to Italy. I got under his skin by being me. The sassy version.

"Whatever helps you sleep better at night, knowing you lost to me and you've clearly been thinking about me for years. Decadent? You named a whole factory after my pussy," I laugh.

Rage fills his pretty face, so I keep going.

"I got under your skin, and you hate it." I grin at him and cough as his hand shoots out and grips my throat.

"You did not get to me," he seethes in my ear.

Fuck it.

I swing my arm forward and squeeze his neck.

His heart races against my palm and his eyes go wide. But this time, there's a spark in them.

He lifts me up and slams me against the wall. It vibrates through me.

"You wanna play, sweetheart?" He leans in and my breath hitches.

"Yes. Because I know I'll win again."

His gaze rapidly flicks between my lips and my eyes. He's torn, and I need to make the decision.

"You fucking—"

I cut him off by slamming my lips over his. I need him to hear me. To feel me.

Understand that the woman sent here to kill him is not me. Not really.

I am the Charlotte he brought out.

He deepens the kiss and runs his hands through my hair before pulling so damn hard it feels like it's being ripped from my scalp.

"Your spells won't work on me this time," he pants out.

I lick my swollen lips as he presses his body tighter against mine.

"Tell that to your brain." I look down at his crotch.

"My brain is up here, heartbreaker. You just wanted a look at the last decent dick you had, didn't you?" He smirks.

I bat my lashes at him.

"Maybe. Or maybe I was distracting you so I can do this."

His frown deepens as I quickly seize his biceps; with a surge of strength, I push him back, using his body to leverage my own and pull my legs up. In one forceful move, I kick out into his gut, sending him stumbling backwards onto his ass.

He splutters a cough as he gets up on one knee. I plaster myself against the wall, trying to regain my balance.

"Proposing already? Why are you so obsessed with me, Mr.

Quinn?" I step forward as he grabs hold of his stomach, getting his breath back.

Digging my fingers into the pressure points between his neck and shoulder, I look down at him.

"Not a fucking clue, sweetheart." His voice is gravelly, that Irish twang makes my body heat.

"But trust me, I'm nowhere near my full potential of psycho with you just yet."

His eyes darken as he lunges for my waist, dragging me down to the floor.

We tumble around, I grab hold of his shirt and it rips open the top few buttons. As he extends to snatch my wrist, I roll out of the way.

"You think I don't know how to deal with psychos?" I shout as I crawl away.

He snatches one of the leather bands around my waist and drags me across the floor. Swinging my leg back, I smash it into his ribs.

I make it over to the edge of the chocolate fountain.

"You have no fucking idea what I've been through or why I do what I do. I'm asking you to listen, Declan."

He grunts behind me. As he approaches, I turn around and dip my hand in the warm pool of chocolate, splashing it all over his face.

"Decadent? Right?" I mock.

My lungs heave as I look at his chocolate-splattered face. He slowly licks his lips, and I stop before splashing again.

"Pretty much. Try it for yourself." His tone is icy.

I gasp as he grabs the back of my head and shoves me forward, right into the stream of melted chocolate flowing.

I try doing everything I can to get out of his grip, but the more I try, the harder he squeezes my neck. Just as my lungs burn, he pulls me out.

This is not going the way I want.

But I don't have a damn plan other than to fight it out.

CHAPTER 64
DECLAN

I release her as she gasps for air, wiping the chocolate out of her face.

Even like this she's fucking beautiful.

She wants me to listen? To more bullshit excuses?

She's doing what she does best. Playing me.

Except that fucking nagging feeling is gnawing at me to hear her out.

Not yet. I'm having far too much fun with her.

"Well? Is it decadent?" I wipe my own face.

She shrugs and sticks her finger back into the chocolate and licks it.

Her full lips wrapping around it as she sucks it clean.

I lied. I didn't reinforce my heart.

"Pretty decent, I guess," she shrugs.

A growl erupts from my chest as I step closer.

Bad fucking move.

The closer she is in my proximity, the easier it is for her to penetrate my walls.

There's only one thing on this earth that is truly decadent.

Her pussy.

The air crackles around us.

I have so many questions for her. Yet, part of me doesn't want to hear it.

Call it self-preservation. What if all of these years of anger have been misplaced?

And as I look into the depths of her eyes, I know the truth.

That woman who opened up to me is the real her.

"Please. Hear me out," she whispers.

This whole façade, everything behind the gates of Decadence is a game.

I should know, I'm the fucking master of it all.

My eyes lock onto her lips.

No. Not again.

When she kissed me back there, everything melted away, and she was all I could think about.

My weakness. Just like I knew she would be.

"Why should I? You'd say anything to keep yourself alive. You came here to kill me, heartbreaker. I guess your name really was right?"

I step back, creating some needed space between us.

"Nothing I did was personal. I don't have a choice. I had no idea you were my hit until I saw you meet Enzo. I tried to keep you away from me. I warned you. You. Didn't. Listen. You kept pushing and pushing until we both caved. Maybe I am the enemy in your story, but trust me, I am in my own story too."

She shakes her head and turns away from me. I can't help but reach out and spin her to face me.

"Hate me all you want. I have my reasons. What's your excuse? The games, the women, all of this!" She throws her hands up.

"You are just as shitty of a person as I am, and in my position, you would have done the same thing." She pokes me right in the chest where her tattoo rests.

Wrapping my fingers around hers, I squeeze.

"Remember who you're talking to. I get to decide your fate now. My property," I say in a low tone.

She looks up with defiance in her eyes.

"No, Declan. You'll have to kill me before I become another man's property."

She rips her hand away, and that pain etched on her face is like a slap.

She might be able to get a read on me, but I can on her too.

This concerning connection between us goes both ways.

Wrapping my arm around her waist, I drag her body flush against mine.

As she looks up, I push her hair away from her face.

Her features soften. I'm not done with her.

"It wasn't a request, it was a statement. You belong to me, whether you like it or not. That ink on the dotted line still stands. Congratulations, you're the third winner of the Decadence Games. Rules have changed. You don't get money and freedom. You get a whole different kind of prize. One of my men will show you to your new prison." I clear my throat and release her.

"I mean home."

I flash her my best smile as I back away. If this interaction has shown me anything, it's that she is my weakness, and I need to keep my distance until we are done gaining information.

Then she needs to leave and get far, far away from me and never return.

I've hunted down my ghost, and now I need to sage my soul.

"Welcome to hell, heartbreaker."

I slam the door shut behind me and don't look back. I can't.

Resting my back on the closed door, I hear the heavy footsteps of Conan approaching.

"When's the wedding?" he jokes.

I scowl at him.

"Not in this lifetime." I push myself off the door and face him.

He rolls his eyes and I resist the urge to slap him.

"Escort her to my home." I shove my hand in my pocket and pull out my keys, holding the gold one up to him.

"Lock her inside her room. The one next to the master suite."

He nods and takes the keys.

"You got it. Sure you don't want her in with you? Celebrate her win? Get reacquainted with her?" He smirks, and I want to smack it off his face.

"No." I dismiss him.

If I sink in that sweet pussy one more time, I'm done for.

"Grab a notepad and pen and put that in with her. Enzo wants information."

"Anything else, sir?"

"Don't push me. Not today. Just get it done and meet me and Finn at your cabin after."

He frowns.

"Ruin any more of my furniture, and I'll beat your ass."

I chuckle and pat him on the shoulder. There's no doubt he would.

"No shootings. Just scheming."

Conan pulls out his mask and shoots me a questioning look.

"No need. She knows who I am."

"Cool." He shoves it in his pocket and this time retrieves his gun.

"Yeah. Take that. I still have no fucking idea how dangerous she is. But she's unarmed."

"I'll keep her away from the chocolate fountain too, looking at the state of you," he chuckles.

I rub some of the dried chocolate off my forehead.

"She's violent." I shrug.

He claps his gun between his hands.

"Ah, a menace. The best kind of sub."

"Take her," I brush him off.

"You don't mean that. Now go and shower, I'll get her sorted."

No. I don't mean it. Not one bit.

"Great."

With that I take off down the hall and head to the cabin. As soon as the fresh air hits me, I tip my head back and soak in the sun.

What in the fuck is happening?

CHAPTER 65
CHARLOTTE

"Ah. The brother," I say as the beast steps through the door. He's unmistakable without the mask and same cut-glass jawline and unsettling charm the brothers all share. Something magnetic, even when you're trying not to look.

He nods, flashing me a cheeky grin. But my eyes go to the pistol in his right hand.

"Don't even think about pulling that karate shit on me. I'll shoot you. I'm not my brother. I've got no feelings toward you."

My mouth falls open.

"Doesn't count if it's hate," I counter.

He shrugs.

"Feelings are feelings. If he felt nothing, that'd be worse for you." He pulls a pair of cuffs from his jacket. "I don't trust you, and I've gotta escort you to your room. Make it easy—hands behind your back." He taps the barrel against the metal. "Quicker you do it, the quicker you can shower."

God. I must look feral. And I cannot wait to scrub this melted chocolate off me.

So I turn, letting him snap the cuffs into place.

"Damn. You do these yourself?"

He gestures with a nod to the angry marks on my wrists.

I chew my lip. "No. Years of being chained to a bed every night does a number on your skin."

"Jesus," he mutters. The cuffs aren't even tight. Sloppy.

Dumbass.

"Come on," he grunts, nudging me forward. We hang a sharp left down a sterile white hallway until we hit a set of locked double doors. He scans his prints and punches in a code.

The sunlight stuns me.

Air. Real air.

I breathe deep. Even the gravel under my bare feet feels like a gift.

"Bit of a walk. You good?" he asks, glancing down.

Should I mention the mile I once hiked barefoot through snow on a mission?

Probably not.

"I'll survive. I've made it this far."

"Fair enough."

We head toward the trees. No houses in sight. Just woods. Dense. Endless.

"How big is this place?" I ask. Conan seems like the type who'll talk.

Also, he doesn't seem to hate me. Yet.

"No clue. Fucking massive. We've got the factory, Inferno, a mansion each... and my sweet little cabin hidden in the woods. For my games."

He's practically bouncing.

"Right. Your games?"

I keep him talking. My left hand is almost free.

"Yeah. Mine's next, The Decadence Chase." He throws his arms wide like he's welcoming me to a theme park. "Perfect hunting ground, right?"

I nod, my pulse spiking.

Great. I'm up against the hunter.

With my wrist free, I match his pace. He's huge, muscle and menace, which might slow him down. Might.

But he's trained. I'll get one shot at this.

We plunge deeper into the trees. The birds are quiet. The air stills.

"Inferno? What's that?" I ask, slicing through the silence.

"Declan will tell you. You'll have fun."

A chill cuts through me. Fun sounds like a threat.

But I won't belong to Declan. Or Decadence. My heart wants to tell him everything. But if he won't listen? I run. I fight. I win.

There has to be an edge to this forest. A hole in the fence. Something.

"Not far now," Conan mutters.

I stop cold, wrists still behind my back.

He turns, scowling. "No fucking around." He steps toward me.

I glance at the gun, then smile.

"What are you gonna do about it?"

I hope I've read him right.

He lifts the pistol, aiming for my shoulder.

Gotcha. He won't shoot to kill.

"You're defenseless, and I've got a gun. Thought you were smarter than this."

I bite the inside of my cheek. Stay silent.

He flicks the safety off. "Move."

I shake my head.

"Make me."

His aim shifts to my forehead. That's when I move, snatching his wrist, twisting hard. The gun hits the ground. I dive for it and aim.

He doesn't fight me. Just smirks.

"Silly girl."

I fire. Or try to.

Click.

Nothing.

Shit.

His laugh echoes as I drop the gun and run.

Adrenaline explodes through me. I sprint, lungs screaming, heart pounding so loud it drowns everything else. Drago's voice is in my head:

Survive.

I don't get far before Conan's heavy steps start to get closer behind me.

Then roaring engines erupt, and two black 4x4s cut across the path, blocking me. I dart my head left and right, my body starting to head in one direction. But then Declan steps out, rage written all over him, and I freeze.

"Get in the fucking car, heartbreaker!" he roars.

I stop. A gunshot cracks, splintering the tree trunk inches from my head.

"Next time I won't miss. Get in. Now!"

Conan's breath rasps behind me.

Game over.

"Go with him. He's your safest option."

Reluctantly, I walk, avoiding his gaze. Declan throws open the door.

More cuffs.

I stare at the dirt as he locks them around my wrists.

"You really have a death wish, don't you?"

I shake my head, finally meeting his eyes.

"Quite the opposite," I say.

He'll understand.

Soon.

CHAPTER 66

DECLAN

We drive to my house in complete silence.

I'm furious.

When Conan called through on the headset, I just knew.

We cannot underestimate her skill.

I look up in the rearview mirror and find her blue eyes staring back at me.

Entering the code in my gates, I pull up past the fountain and switch off the engine.

Her mouth falls open as she looks at my home.

As she goes to speak, I hold up my hand to silence her.

"I don't want to hear a single word that comes out of your mouth. We're done talking," I tell her harshly.

Sliding out of the driver's side, I open up her door, and she shuffles out. Extending my arm to help her, I loop it around her waist so she can drop down to the ground.

My hand on her bare skin sends electricity up my arm and I jolt back.

"Ladies first." I nod to the steps to my mansion.

I keep my eyes off her ass as she struts up them. But I can't resist.

Damn, it's perfect.

Sliding out my keys, I open it up and allow her to walk in.

"Up the stairs, first on your right. Go."

She doesn't falter. She's learning, perhaps, and heads straight up the stairs.

Unlocking her door, I push it open and she walks in.

"Clothes are in the wardrobe. Shower and get cleaned up. Emilia will be preparing dinner soon, she will bring it up. I'll get you a notepad and pen for Enzo's task. This will be your new home until he is done with you."

She doesn't look back at me, she just heads into the room towards the en-suite.

"Any questions?"

I tighten my grasp on the handle.

"You told me not to speak." Her voice is quiet.

"Speak when I ask questions. Better?"

"I guess."

I sigh. She was going to shoot my brother. She tried to escape.

The thought of her leaving me abruptly again hurt, more than I'd like to admit.

I open my mouth, intending to tell her I'll be in the next room, but I stop myself, leaving us in an awkward staring contest.

"I'll go shower then."

Closing the door and locking it, I head back down the stairs and pour a coffee, shooting a text to Finn for him and Con to meet me here. She's a flight risk, and I can't trust anyone with her.

Luckily, Conan unloaded his gun before he went in.

The man is smarter than he lets on, it's all part of his tactic.

It's really how the Quinn brothers all thrive.

"Everything okay, sir?" Emilia asks as she comes out from the laundry room.

"We have a guest staying for a while. She will be staying in her room, but will require meals and laundry."

She gives me a sweet smile, making her eyes wrinkle. She worked for my father for thirty-five years. I didn't think she would want to relocate to America, but after her own husband's passing, she chose to come with us.

"That wasn't my question, Declan." She shoves her hand on her hip and drops down the washing on the counter.

"Yes. Everything is fine, Mrs. Richards."

She steps forward and squints at me.

"Is that chocolate on your face?"

"Yes. Long story."

"You seem stressed. Is it to do with the girl upstairs?"

"Partially."

"Why's she here?"

The questions give me a headache. She was my mom's best friend over the years. Basically part of the family. She's watched us all grow up.

"She's a ghost from my past and causing me problems again."

She smiles like she knows something I don't.

"What?" I ask, grabbing a mug and pouring her a cup.

"She's the one, isn't she?"

"The one?"

She nods and takes the mug from me.

"The one who gets your blood flowing. Brings the light back in your eyes. I see past your anger, boy. Your mom and dad fought like cat and mouse at the start too, you know?"

The front door opens, and relief washes over me. My brothers can be my escape from this conversation.

"This is different. Mom never tried to kill dad."

Her mouth makes an 'o' and it's my turn to laugh.

"How many love stories start with attempted murder?" I say as a joke.

Her features soften, her eyes creasing as she looks at me.

"You never know. Fate works in mysterious ways, Declan. Keep your eyes and your heart open, you never know when it might try to kill you or give you the woman of your dreams."

"Noted." I hold up my mug to her and pull out my cigarettes.

"You good?" I ask a red-faced Conan.

"Are you impressed?" he replies, snatching my coffee out of my hand.

"With who? Me and Finn saved your ass."

"I was just about to snatch her!"

Finn slips onto the barstool. Mrs. Richards pours him and me another coffee.

"Thank you," I mouth, turning my attention back to Conan.

"Yes. I'm impressed you removed your bullets. Less so that you gave her room to try and escape. We're under orders to keep her held here."

"Look, I saw the marks over her wrists, and I probably didn't do the cuffs up tight enough. I felt bad, okay?"

I tilt my head.

"See. You aren't a monster, Con. But this time your heart was misplaced." I keep my voice stern, but his words trigger my brain.

Those marks, her pain, it has an effect over me that I want to swallow down.

"Wait. Here?" Finn pipes up behind me.

"Yes. Here I can keep an eye on her."

He taps his rings against his mug and I turn to him.

"Inferno is much more secure." He arches his brow.

"We've all seen what she's capable of. She's my responsibility, she stays here."

He nods and takes a slow sip of his coffee.

"She might kill you in your sleep."

"She won't."

"She did try and shoot me, Dec." Conan appears beside me.

"Where?"

"She aimed for the thigh."

I grin.

"So she wasn't aiming to kill. See? I'm safe. Don't worry about me."

Finn blows out a breath.

"I'm not worried about your safety. I'm now worried you'll let her in."

I roll my eyes and get a cigarette out of the packet.

"I won't let her get to me again. She's just here until Enzo gets the information he needs, then she will be gone and we can move on. I'll just spend a year without an official sub. I'll survive."

Sliding open my door, I head into the yard and light up.

Do I even want another sub?

She's here because she has to be, not because I want her in my home.

Perhaps if I keep gaslighting myself, I'll eventually believe my own lies.

I don't want her.

Chuckling to myself, I flick the ash from my cigarette onto the ground.

"Bullshit," I mutter out loud.

I'm fucked.

CHAPTER 67

CHARLOTTE

A sweet old lady delivered my food on a tray earlier. I expected it to be Declan.

There's plenty of things that could be a weapon in this room, but it's pointless.

The only way now I can survive is by getting him to listen to me.

To tell the truth and hope he believes me.

I keep scribbling in the notepad. Pages and pages of names and locations.

I've kept Drago out of it, he's the final trick up my sleeve if I can somehow make contact.

For now, I withhold. I need to protect him, just like he does me. Until I know of their intentions with this list.

If I can get in Enzo's good books, my chances of survival are higher.

Once he's done with me, my life is in Declan's hands.

And so is his daughter's.

Every day that passes, a part of me dies that I'm away from my little girl.

Running my hands through my damp curls, with a sigh, I place the pad down beside me and stretch my legs out.

Every conversation I've heard over the last ten years replays in my head.

Tatiana is a lost soul. Drago told me this, and it has confused me ever since; perhaps Enzo will make sense of it. So I quickly write that down. Seeing as she seems to be the interest of Enzo.

A pain stabs through my chest, thinking about Isabella being trapped there.

What if Enzo sends an army to the house?

Fuck.

"Drago will protect her," I whisper to myself, over and over.

I need her back, and I need Declan to listen.

Jumping up from the bed, I frantically beat my fists on the wood to get his attention.

When I hear the lock click, I step back.

"What?" he asks dismissively as he swings open the door.

He doesn't look directly at me.

"We need to talk."

His gaze lands on the notepad on the bed, and he walks over to collect it.

Opening it up, he flips through the pages.

"You've got quite the memory, it seems. Enzo will be happy." His voice is flat as he slams the book shut.

"I'm not done with it."

He flippantly throws it back on the bed. As he brushes past me, I grab his wrist.

"Please. Listen to me. There's someone at home I need to get."

He snatches his arm back and doesn't turn around.

"Your husband?" Venom drips from his tone and he swings the door open.

"No. Someone I actually love."

"You don't strike me as someone who knows what love is. Grab me again; I'll have you restrained, and one of my men will take notes for you. Understand?"

My lips snap shut as he faces me, his eyes darkening.

He's pissed, so I nod. Now isn't the time.

"Don't disturb me again until you're done writing."

He scoffs and slams the door shut behind him. Tears burn in my eyes.

This is my final shot and the man can't stand to be in the same room as me.

CHAPTER 68

DECLAN

"Fuck," I hiss, spilling my whiskey on the counter as I pour it.

Replaying the game footage doesn't show me anything.

Nor does her application form.

Instead I sit here staring at her husband's evil eyes.

Is he the one causing her pain? I'd put my money on it. I hit replay on the footage from Enzo's questioning of Charlotte.

There it is. That fear when his name is mentioned.

I squeeze the glass in my hands and pull up a search, typing in his name.

As expected, nothing. They're all ghosts.

I tap my rings on my father's old oak desk that I had shipped here.

"What would you do, Dad?" I whisper, tipping my head back in pure exhaustion.

Sometimes it feels like he's right here with me. No matter how many years pass, I often wake up, and for a split second, I forget he's gone. I half expect him to be downstairs pouring a whiskey for breakfast.

That pain never leaves me when I remember that he's never coming back.

Some days I mask it, I drown out the world and carry on with the duties he left me with.

All in the hopes that he will be proud of me.

That's all I can do now. Live my life in honor of him.

I lost my father that night, but I also lost a piece of myself.

Yet, seeing Charlotte again and losing myself in her eyes is the first time since his death that I've felt truly alive.

My brothers keep telling me to listen to her. Listen to what?

More lies? She will do anything to survive. Even the damn games.

There's a knock at the door and I rub my hands over my face.

"Come in."

Reggie's bulky frame fills the space and I gesture for him to come in.

"Boss, Arthur Bowen is on the phone for you," he tells me, and my blood fucking boils.

The Bowens are lucky I've not returned back to home soil.

The second I do, I'm coming for all of them. We've got the manpower, the ammunition, and enough will for revenge to set their empire into flames.

And right now, I'm angry enough to declare war.

I shake my head.

"Now isn't a good time. Tell him he will hear from me when I'm ready to talk to the scum that murdered my father."

"Okay. He sounded pissed."

"Speaking to me will only make it worse. He needs to stay on that side of the pond."

"You got it."

As the door clicks shut, I knock back my whiskey and pull up a text to Finn.

ME

I need to get some anger out. I'll come with you tonight.

FINN

What about your girlfriend?

ME

I'll knock you on your ass instead if you carry on.

ME

I'll have Conan stay here tonight.

FINN

yeah… cause he coped so well with her the first time. Get some rest, use your home gym, and let Con knock some sense into you. I don't need help.

ME

fine.

I drop my phone onto the desk and sigh, cracking my knuckles.
Me: Meet me at my home gym when you're free.
Conan replies instantly.

C

Frustrated?

ME

Pissed off…

I see the bubbles keep popping up, he's probably laughing to himself as he texts.

C

you know, there's a woman in your house who could resolve all your tension, rather than letting me beat the shit outta you.

M

ha ha. Shut it.

C

just saying.

I could just head to Inferno and fuck my frustrations away. There's plenty of women ready and will be on their knees the second I snap my fingers. But with Charlotte in my home… it will be a useless attempt.

My cock only wants to be in one hole.

Unfortunately for me, it belongs to the woman who betrayed me, who has lied to me at every turn.

Yet, she's the only one who plagues my mind.

Another text pops up from Conan.

C

I'm busy tonight. I promised Scarlett a night to
remember in the woods ;)

Fuck it. Looks like I'm getting drunk tonight. At least then I can
stop the swirling thoughts in my head.

CHAPTER 69

CHARLOTTE

My eyes burn, the weight of exhaustion dragging me under.

I don't deserve sleep. Not the peaceful kind, anyway.

I should be planning my escape. Calculating every step. But right now?

Nothing.

No plan. No exit. Just silence pressing in.

I heard Declan half an hour ago, doors slamming, boots storming. He's close. Probably asleep in the next room. I'd be a fool to think there aren't guards stationed nearby, fingers itching on triggers.

They don't trust me. None of them do. Not after what happened with Conan.

I'm boxed in.

I need to reach Drago. I need to know my little girl is okay.

The thought alone almost breaks me. I clutch the pillow tighter, as if it can anchor me to something soft in this place that's all sharp corners and locked doors.

Tomorrow. Tomorrow is a new day.

Maybe Declan will be less furious. Or, Enzo will show up for the notepad.

I always find a way. I've survived this long. I can keep going.

As my eyes flutter shut, I can't tell which is worse—my reality or the things that chase me through sleep.

CHAPTER 70

DECLAN

Song. Sleepyhead. Jutes.

I leap out of bed the second her screams tear through the wall.

Agony. Pure, bloodcurdling agony.

I don't think, I don't even breathe, I just move.

Still in nothing but my boxers and a black t-shirt, I sprint across the hall and shove her door open.

"Don't hurt my baby, please. Please."

Her voice is wrecked, and it shreds through the room. She thrashes in her sheets, soaked in sweat, her body twisted in panic, as if she's trying to fight something invisible.

"Take me. Not her. Don't do this to her."

Her words slice through me.

I said I'd be her nightmare. But right now, I'm not sure that's something I can live with.

Her agony is too real. Too raw.

I reach toward her, hovering over her flushed skin. My fingers tremble as they graze her cheek.

"Shhh, heartbreaker. It's me."

She recoils sharply, knocking my hand away, her nails digging so hard into her wrists that blood starts to well, a crimson stain against her pale skin.

"Fuck."

I lunge for her hands, wrapping mine gently around them, trying to stop her from doing more damage.

"Charlotte. It's Declan. You're safe. No one's going to hurt you."

Her eyes snap open, almost black in the dark.

"Isabella," she breathes. "Save her."

The name hits me like a fist to the gut.

I scoop her up and hold her close, cradling her like she might shatter in my arms. Her tears streak across my chest, her sobs tearing into the quiet.

"It's okay," I whisper, my hand finding her hair, smoothing it back. "It's okay. I've got you."

"Save who, baby?"

She doesn't answer at first, she just clings to me tighter, sobbing like her soul is collapsing.

"Talk to me, heartbreaker. You said you wanted me to hear you out. This is your moment."

Her voice is barely audible. "I—I can't. You can't."

She shifts, straddling my lap, arms wrapped around my neck like I'm the only thing tethering her to earth. My heart hammers against my ribs.

"Who is Isabella?" I press. "Who's hurting her?"

Please, let this be the moment. Please tell me.

She swallows, trembling.

"My daughter," she says. "And my husband."

I still.

Everything in me stills.

Daughter.

Husband.

I feel like I've been hit by a truck.

Her body shakes in my arms. Her tears soak through my shirt, and I can barely breathe through the pressure in my chest.

"Your daughter," I echo. "Vlad hurts her?"

The thought alone ignites something murderous in me.

She shakes her head. "Not yet. I need to go home. Please. Let me go home."

She clutches me like she's drowning.

"Does he hurt you?" I whisper.

She pauses, then nods. Just once.

"Yes."

I pull back and gently lift her chin. I need to see her. I need to see her eyes.

"Is he the one who haunts you?"

Another nod. Slower. Her lips quiver like she's trying not to fall apart all over again.

And suddenly, I don't know what the hell I'm doing anymore.

I've seen her fierce. I've seen her break bones and spill blood. I've seen the chaos inside her.

But this. This shattered version of her, raw and exposed and trembling in my arms, is my undoing.

How can someone be so powerful and so broken at the same time?

I trace her cheek with my finger, then down to the curve of her neck, settling my palm over the center of her chest.

Her heartbeat is erratic. Wild. Like it's trying to escape her ribcage.

And her eyes... that spark is gone.

She's fading right in front of me.

I should let her. I should break her all the way. That's what I wanted? But I can't. I don't think I ever would have.

For the first time in a long time, I follow my heart.

I study her face, her breathing, every tremor in her muscles. I need to bring her back, quiet the storm inside her.

I need to understand.

Because whether I like it or not, my soul is tied to this woman.

And I don't think I could sever that bond even if I wanted to.

"Do you trust me?" I whisper, brushing the damp hair from her forehead.

Her eyes narrow.

"No. I trust no one."

A small, dark smile tugs at my lips.

"There she is," I murmur. "Good girl."

She shudders.

I could offer her sleep. I could offer her warmth. I don't think either of those will work for my girl.

I believe we are cut from the same cloth. And that maybe, just maybe—

She needs pain.

CHAPTER 71
CHARLOTTE

Song, the crown, take luck
https://takeluck.komi.io

"W—where are you taking me?" I ask, my voice barely above a whisper, as he links his fingers through mine and leads me out of the room on shaking legs.

I hate feeling weak. I hate that he's the one holding me up. And worse…I hate that it feels right.

"Well, we either fuck it out or fight it out. I'm using my brain for once and going for option two."

I freeze.

He chuckles. "What? You prefer the first option, heartbreaker?"

Electricity shoots up my arm, and I swear he feels it too by the way he looks down at our hands.

His thumb brushes mine. It shouldn't feel this way. I pull in a breath.

"Beating you on your ass is fine."

Not that I'm in any shape to. But I've trained for this. I can always fight. No matter what.

He leads me down the stairs and into a long hallway. At the end, he pushes open two double doors, revealing an indoor gym.

It's all state-of-the-art. Sleek equipment. Floor-to-ceiling mirrors. And a fucking cage in the center of the room.

Figures. These guys probably all fight like pros. Especially the big one.

Declan finally lets go of my hand, and the skin still tingles where his fingers were. He tosses the gloves to me. I catch one. The other falls to the ground with a soft thud.

Suddenly, I'm hyper aware I'm wearing only a tank top and tight black shorts. Great. Bending down, I snatch up the glove and pull both on, securing the Velcro with my teeth.

"Mats or cage?" he asks.

I scan the space. "Cage rules?"

His white teeth flash as he grins. "No rules. I can take it."

"I'll be gentle with you," I say, smiling before I can stop myself.

For a second, it's like we're somewhere else. Another time. Just me and him.

"I don't do gentle, sweetheart," he replies, his deep Irish lilt dropping an octave. Butterflies erupt in my stomach.

I tighten my ponytail and climb into the cage. He follows and shuts the door behind him with a solid clang.

As I turn to face him, he raises the mitts to shield his face.

"I wasn't going straight for the face!" I laugh.

"With you, I never know where you'll aim." He drops one mitt to cover his crotch.

I throw a soft right jab into his shoulder. "See? Gentle."

Jogging in place to warm up, I wait as he sets the position.

"Hit as hard as you want. Let it all out," he says, his voice calm and low.

"1–2–1 to start," I tell him, settling into stance. He nods.

The first few punches are light. Testing. Controlled.

"Come on. You can do better than this," he taunts.

So I land a harder shot.

"Good girl. Better. Keep going."

So I do.

Punch after punch, I hit harder. Faster. Sweat begins to bead on my forehead, dripping down the side of my face. My arms burn, lungs heaving.

"More!" he yells.

I give him more.

He shifts the mitts, changing placement, making me think, making my body work.

"Imagine it's him. Hurt him. Show me how much you hate him. Show me how fucking fierce you are."

And then I see them. Vlad's black eyes. That cold smirk. The monster in my nightmares.

A scream rips out of me as my fists take over.

I don't think. I don't hesitate. I just fight.

All I want is revenge. My baby safe. And my husband buried in the fucking ground.

CHAPTER 72

DECLAN

The switch that went off in her eyes tells me I pushed her over the edge.

I duck as her flying fist aims directly for my jaw.

She's powerful, and her punches fucking hurt.

But she craves this and I need to know the truth.

She's not lying to me.

When the day comes and Vlad feels her wrath, he's in for it.

"Charlotte!" I shout, trying to snap her out of it.

A punch lands in my gut and winds me.

Ripping off my pads as she lunges at me, I grab her biceps and spin her, pressing her back against the cage.

She kicks and screams, but I hold her still.

"Fuck you!" she shouts, getting an arm free and clocking me straight in the mouth.

Stars fill my vision, and I hiss out in pain, wrapping my hand around her throat as I wipe away the warm blood dripping from my lip.

"Enough," I tell her firmly.

She blinks at me, looking like she's just coming back to reality.

Squeezing her throat, I remind her who I am.

I am not him.

Her chest heaves and I watch the rise and fall of her breasts as I lean in.

"God, you're fucking beautiful when you're angry," I whisper, trying to calm her.

"You've got a great right hook on you." I smile against her hot skin.

Holy fuck, fighting with her has left me feeling like I could throw her down right here and fuck her until she forgets the pain of her past.

She turns her head, her lips are a breath away from mine.

I can almost taste her.

I loosen my grip on her bicep with my left hand, which allows her to drag her fingers up my t-shirt, and her hand settles around my throat.

As I stare into her eyes, a feeling of completeness washes over me. Even if I'm radiating pain all over from her attack, I'm on fire from within.

For her and because of her.

She is my inferno.

My gaze flicks between her bright eyes and her plump lips, and as they part, the last shred of restraint I was grasping hold of is shattered.

"Kiss me," I whisper.

She squeezes my throat tighter in response. So, I repay the favor right back at her, pushing her harder into the metal bars by the neck.

"Kiss me and make me forget why I ever hated you, heartbreaker."

Her breathing quickens and her heart races under my palm. Without wasting another second, she drags me down to her and crashes her lips over mine.

A sinful heaven.

Five years of torture washes away, replaced only by a feral need to claim her.

Sliding her back up the metal, I wrap her legs around my waist and deepen the kiss, moving my hand up to grip each side of her jaw.

When she moans into my mouth, I almost lose it.

"Fuck, yeah. Give me more, baby. Earn your forgiveness," I say against her lips before going in for another kiss, smothering her and stealing all the air from her lungs.

She belongs to me. All of her.

Her hips start to roll, her hot pussy rubs against my cock.

"That's it, sweetheart. Keep moving your hips like that, show me how desperate you are for my dick. Beg me to make you feel good, and I might just think about it."

"Please, Declan," she gasps as I sink my teeth into her throat.

Digging my fingers into her ass, my other hand strokes the side of her face before sliding behind her head, to the roots of her hair.

Grabbing a handful, I yank her back and devour her neck.

"You like that? It hurts good, right?"

I groan as a little moan escapes her as I tug on her hair again.

"The deeper I sink my teeth in you, the more soaked your pussy is for me. Fucking beautiful, heartbreaker."

I'm sure she was made just for me.

Mine to bend, to break, to train.

Just all mine.

Her hands run up the back of my head and she grabs my hair, pushing it towards her.

I capture her lips and let my tongue explore.

Letting my fingers play with the top of her tight Lycra shorts, she shivers under my touch, and I grin.

I hiss as I slide them under her panties. She's drenched for me. Circling her clit, her hips buck against me.

"Mmm, good girl. Nice and wet for me, aren't you?" I bite on her bottom lip and slide my fingers back to her entrance, and they glide right in.

I let out a hiss as her pussy squeezes me. My dick is aching to be inside of her again.

Her moans grow louder with each thrust, her wetness dripping down my fingers onto my palm.

Sliding in a second digit, she gasps, and I kiss her.

So deep, so passionately.

Desperate for her. She yanks at my hair, her body quivering against me as I up the pace.

"Fuck," I groan.

"I need to taste you, baby," I tell her.

And the desire in her eyes gives me all the answers I need. But I don't take. I wait.

"Words." I keep my voice firm.

"Do it." She grins.

In one swift move, I hold her by the waist, and her legs tighten around me as I spin us and lower myself to my knees on the canvas.

Laying her on her back, I yank off her shorts and panties in one go, gripping her thighs and spreading them apart, revealing her glistening, pink pussy on display for me.

I hold onto her hips and raise her up to my face, while she uses her hands on the ground for balance.

I need her to fuck my face more than I need air to breathe.

CHAPTER 73

CHARLOTTE

Song- GODDESS, Written by Wolves

"**E**yes on me. Watch what you do to me," he commands with a dangerous edge to his tone.

I open my eyes back up and wrap my legs around his neck.

He licks all the way up to my clit, so slowly with the tip of his tongue that I shiver.

That raw hunger in his bright blue eyes sets me alight.

"I-I need to come." My voice shakes.

I suck in a breath when he slides his fingers inside me and sucks on my clit.

"I'm not done eating you out yet, sweetheart."

Squeezing my core muscles tight to keep me still, I let my orgasm build. With each swipe of his tongue, I can't help but moan.

"Declan, oh my god."

I stretch around him as he inserts another finger. I try to grip the floor, but it's no use. My hips buck against his face on their own accord.

"So desperate for me, aren't you?" he growls.

I nod. I've been dreaming of this moment for so long it almost doesn't feel possible.

But then he curls his fingers inside me and I jolt in his grip.

Oh, he's real. Very real.

And there's just as much hunger between us as there was five years ago.

Burning for each other until we explode.

"Y-yes. I need you, Declan."

His eyes soften as he plants kisses on my throbbing pussy.

"How much? Hmm?"

I let out a scream as he spanks my ass.

"How much?" He raises his voice before slapping again.

"So. Much. Fuck!" I cry out.

He feasts on my pussy again, and I melt against the canvas. He has no idea how much I need him.

Sliding his rough hands up my thighs, he grips them hard and maneuvers himself onto the ground, pulling me upright at the same time, so I'm sitting on his face.

I look down at him, my skin flushing and his fingers dig into my ass.

"Sit."

A simple instruction, yet my body ignores him.

"Sit on my fucking face and let a man eat. Ride my tongue like the good slut I know you can be for me."

Leaning forward, I hook my fingers through the metal cage and lower myself down.

"Ah, that's better. Your cunt smothering my face is exactly how I wanna die one day."

He slaps my ass and I roll my hips as he fucks me with his tongue.

"Oh my god," I cry out.

His hand slides up my front and he grabs my boob and squeezes.

The way he's groaning against my pussy only turns me on more.

Tipping my head back, I close my eyes and ride the wave of pleasure only he can give me.

"So good," I whisper.

Just as I'm close to the edge, he lifts me by the waist and slides me down his body, I shuffle further so I'm resting on his hard cock.

"Come here." He grabs my throat and pulls me down, slamming his lips over mine, while his other hand wraps around my waist, holding me in place.

"Still decadent." He pulls back and grins.

I blink a few times and his deep chuckle makes me tingle.

"I need to be inside you, heartbreaker."

His eyes sparkle with life, and I smile.

"I need you, Declan. Fuck me hard enough I can forget."

He tilts his head and cups my cheek. With him, my brain goes quiet. He starts to heal the broken parts of me.

"Forget what?"

"Everything. Except that night with you in Italy. Take me back there, to the last time I was alive."

He swallows and I rest my head against his.

"You too, huh?" It's so quiet I barely hear him.

Brushing his nose along my cheek, he steals another kiss.

"Ride me. Time to prove how much you missed me, baby." He winks, and I find the hem of his black t-shirt.

I pull his top over his head and run my nails over his six-pack.

"So hot," I tell him, lifting my hips a touch so he has room to pull out his dick from his shorts.

"Take a seat." He taps my ass, lining his cock up with my entrance. I slowly sink down onto him while digging my nails into his shoulders.

It burns as I stretch around him.

"Keep going, I'm a big boy, remember? But if I recall correctly, you take me perfectly," he tells me, gripping my waist and gently pushing me down onto him.

"Huge. Not just big," I pant out.

"Good girl, take it all."

Closing my eyes, I feel his palm on my cheek. Then I wrap my arms around his neck once I'm at the base.

"Fuck, you feel so good," he hisses in my ear.

His hands slide down my sides, and he grabs my waist, lifting me up and pushing me down onto him.

"Fuck!" I cry out.

I take over. I can't get enough of him. He hits that spot that has me gushing all over him.

"I'm so close."

"Good. Because in a few more thrusts I'm going to fill you up."

He grits his teeth as he pounds up into me. Nuzzling my face into his neck, I press a kiss there.

I cry out when he holds me in place tight and slams into me.

Biting down on his throat, I let him ruin me.

"That's it. Leave teeth marks on the deepest parts of my soul, heartbreaker."

I let out a scream as he yanks my head up by my hair; his fingers grip my throat, and he studies me.

Watching me as he fucks me into oblivion.

"Come."

One word shatters me.

Explosions erupt inside me as I climax, to the point I'm shaking as he fucks me through it.

My name comes out like an animalistic roar from his chest as he spills inside me. Hearing him scream my real name knocks down another wall to my heart.

"Holy fuck."

I collapse against him, our sweaty skin sticking together. Our erratic breaths mirror each other.

"Feel better?" he whispers in my ear.

I sit up straight, and my eyes trail down his body.

That's when I see it.

"Is that…" I press my finger over the ink.

"It certainly is, heartbreaker."

The design I drew him on our "date" in Italy is now etched across his chest.

"It's beautiful," I gush, emotions taking over me, leaving me almost speechless.

"I'm a man of my word. I said I'd get it tattooed," he tells me quietly.

That hits me right in the chest.

I'm the liar here. The backstabber.

I am the dagger through his heart, and I really wish I wasn't.

"Even after what I did?" I say quietly, and he lowers his head to look at me, wrapping his hand around mine.

"Especially after what you did. The beautiful, deadly dagger through my heart. A true heartbreaker. It was my reminder to never, ever, let anyone in again. It's served me well."

"I'm sorry."

It's all I can say. I have so much to say, and yet, nothing more comes out.

All these years, his memory has kept me alive, yet it seems I had an adverse effect on him.

"I don't want your apology. Now, we sleep. Tomorrow, we talk. And then I can decide what I do with you."

My heart sinks, and I tip my chin down, only for Declan to tilt it back up to him.

"You've got a lot of explaining to do, yes. But—" He rubs his thumb along my cheek.

"You don't get to run this time. You've been sent to me twice. You were meant to find me in this lifetime, heartbreaker. My father always taught us to believe in fate, and he's landed you in my lap again. I'm not letting this go. I just want the truth, then, as crazy as this sounds, we find a way to make it right."

I'm pretty sure I forget how to breathe.

"Whatever is causing that pain behind your eyes, we hunt. Whatever has you chained, we break them. Whatever stands in our way, we defeat. Alright?"

"How can you ever trust me? I've been sent to kill you... twice!"

His dick twitches inside me and he twists my nipple between his fingers, causing my back to arch.

"That word there. Sent. You didn't want me dead? Did you?"

I shake my head as he leans in and licks along my collarbones.

"The woman I fell for in Italy, she was the real Charlotte, correct?"

"Y-yes. I wasn't trying to trick you. I tried to keep you away."

He nods and bites my neck.

"I'm starting to piece you together. I understand this life. We all have choices, but sometimes we have to do shit to simply survive. Tonight, you've let down your walls and shown me exactly what I needed to see."

He pulls back and stares into my eyes.

"What's that?"

He blinks, and then a smile spreads across his lips.

"You. The real, raw, fierce, kinky, you. My heartbreaker. The beautiful dagger lodged in my heart."

My breath catches in my throat. When his face softens, he reminds me so much of Isabella.

"I-I have more to tell you."

He places a finger over my lips to silence me.

"Not tonight. We've fought. We've fucked. Tomorrow, we talk and we plan. It can wait, we need to rest."

My eyes flutter closed as he presses a kiss on my forehead.

A simple act that means everything to me.

For the first time in ten years. I don't feel alone in this world.

I just wonder how long it will take to come crumbling down.

CHAPTER 74

DECLAN

I hover by the door, watching as she tucks the comforter under her neck and snuggles into the pillow.

My hand tightens on the handle as her eyes lock with mine.

I want her to ask me to stay. Earlier was a lot. For both of us.

Her nightmare sparked something deep inside of me. This need to protect her. Not save her, because she does a damn good job of that herself.

No, I just want her. That's why her betrayal hurt so much. Because she was the first and only woman I've connected deeply with. I was angry—at her, at the world—and placed my hatred onto her.

When actually, like me, she's a product of this lifestyle. We don't ask to be who we are, we are created and molded to be.

The Charlotte that I met in Italy, she captivated me. And now, even more so.

I'd be a dumbass to let her go when I know there isn't someone else out there for me. No one comes close. I know it deep in my bones.

"Night, heartbreaker," I whisper.

She pouts, throwing back the blanket, revealing those slender legs.

"There's, umm, room for two in here," she says quietly.

That's enough.

Ripping off my clothes until I'm down to my boxers, I get in behind her.

"Thank you. I didn't really want to be alone," she says quietly.

Sliding my arm under her body, I pull her closer so my dick is pressing into her ass.

"Oh, I see. I'm just a piece of ass in bed with you?"

She giggles and my chest flutters. That sound is perfect.

"You know, I've spent the last four years chained up to my bed as I slept."

I close my eyes as the burning rage floods me. Instinctively I rub her wrist lightly. Those marks. It all clicks together in my head as to why she passed out in that game.

Chains, degradation. It must have triggered a trauma response. Fuck.

I feel terrible.

Once I get my hands on this man, I'll chain him up and torture him until he's begging for death.

"I'm sorry, baby." I kiss her head.

I want to learn about her past, but part of me is dreading what horrors she will tell me.

Knowing all this time I was resenting her, she has been living in hell.

"Don't apologize, it isn't your fault."

I sigh and rest my head on hers.

"Sure you don't want to be the little spoon?" she giggles, wriggling her ass, and I laugh.

A flash of a memory of a similar conversation in Italy makes me smile.

Cuddling her with my arm over her waist, I rub small circles on her toned stomach.

"Careful, sweetheart, or you might wake up with my dick in your ass," I whisper against her hair.

"Maybe if you're lucky I'll let you be the first and only man in there."

My heart jumps, and so does my cock.

"Absolutely I will be the first and last one."

Fuck, just thinking about her ass strangling my cock has my blood pounding.

"Now get some sleep before I do just that."

I stroke her hair as her breathing steadies and close my own eyes.

And just like that, the weight of the world that was resting on my shoulders is lighter.

Because she is in my arms.

In this moment, everything feels right again.

This is exactly where we were meant to be.

CHAPTER 75

CHARLOTTE

Song- everything i wanted, Billie Eilish

By the time I wake up, I'm alone. Sitting up, noticing how my body aches all over.

How long have I been asleep?

As I get out of bed, the first thing I do is head to the door. I wonder...

Pulling down the handle, to my surprise, it opens.

Is this another test? I have no idea where I stand.

If it is, it's one I'm desperate to pass. because I need this man.

I'm done being part of everyone else's games. Now we enter mine.

The one where I get my daughter back. *Our daughter.*

I step back and let it click shut, instead deciding to shower and freshen up. By the time I do that, I rub the towel over my hair to get rid of the dampness.

As I open the door, I stop in my tracks as I come face to face with a casually dressed Declan.

Black jeans with a black sweater. pushed enough up his forearms to reveal his tatted skin.

"Morning." He looks down at his Rolex.

"Well, afternoon, I suppose."

Jesus. I don't know the last time I've slept that long.

He flashes me a grin and steps aside so I can go past him.

"You look pretty," he tells me.

"In this?" I point at my modest outfit of leggings and a sports bra, finished off with a camel knitted cardigan.

"Yes. In that. In anything."

He holds out his hand and I stare at it blankly.

"Come on, I've made breakfast."

Linking my fingers through his, we head downstairs and the sweet essence of pancakes fills my nose, and my stomach rumbles on cue.

He directs us into the kitchen and pulls out a chair for me at his dining table.

There's two placemats laid out, in the center a stack of pancakes and just about every assortment of toppings you could want. Sweet and savory. He's done it all.

I take a seat as he rushes over to the refrigerator.

"I forgot the most important ingredient."

I arch an eyebrow and cover my mouth with my hand to muffle my laugh.

A whole jug of it. As I study the purple packaging closer, it reads, Decadent Milkshake.

He pours two champagne glasses and hands one to me.

"Cheers. I guess?" I say.

Taking a sip, I moan. It's the best I've ever had.

"Wow. That tastes like… an actual chocolate bar?"

He nods.

"We've been working on the recipe for a year now. I had to get it perfect." He winks, holding up his own glass and knocks it back.

"You did a good job."

He really did. It's delicious.

"Thank you. Although, it would probably taste better if I was drinking it out of your cunt."

I nearly spit my drink out, and he chuckles.

"What? That's the only way you can get the full experience of a Decadent Milkshake. No glasses required, just a sweet pussy. Specifically yours, heartbreaker."

I'm speechless. But undeniably turned on.

"It would probably taste good being sucked off your cock too."

As soon as the words leave my mouth, my face is on fire. Where the hell did that come from?

He runs his hands across his neat stubble.

"Damn. I've never been this hard at breakfast before."

Good.

"Eat. Before I throw it all off the table and spread you out on it instead."

Chewing on my lip, knowing not to push it with him, I take a pancake and a spoonful of strawberries, pouring the chocolate sauce over the top.

"Thank you," I tell him as I look up.

"No need to thank me. We're here to talk, the food is a distraction."

I look down, and suddenly, the crashing impact of my reality settles over me.

"How do you want to do this? Me just talk, or do you have questions?"

"Eat first. Then yes, tell me what you deem relevant for me to know. And then if I do have questions, I'll ask them."

I nod and cut a chunk out of the pancake. It's yummy, but my appetite has gone.

So I force it in as quickly as I can, washing it down with the milkshake.

I take a deep breath and hold my hands under the table.

"Ready?"

"As I'll ever be."

I blow out a breath and start from the top.

"I was taken by Vlad and his brother on my eighteenth birthday. I watched them murder my mom and kidnap my father. We were married that month. He kept me hidden from everyone for the first month, until Drago found me. He managed to cut a deal to get me out of that captivity, but honestly, even if I was out of a locked room, I was still in a cage. I was a good fighter. So he made me a better one. A useful asset to Vlad. If I did that, I kept my father alive. While Drago and I tried to find a way to escape."

My hands start to shake. I've never really grieved my father's death. I never get a chance to stop and reflect on the past.

My only thought every day is to simply survive and fight to find a way out.

"So, in Italy. I was sent on a mission with my handler, Misha. He was a complete asshole. Our job was to take and interrogate whoever Enzo was meeting. And then kill them. Vlad wanted to know what Enzo was doing and what he knew.”

Declan nods, fiddling with the rings on his fingers.

“But, Misha recognized you from the hotel. He knew more than I thought about my movements. He threatened to tell Vlad about us, and I couldn’t risk that.” I run my hand over the tattoos on my arm.

“I killed him. And that knife I planted, that was the knife I used. It was a panicked decision between me and Drago. I didn’t want to, but ultimately I had to save myself and make it look believable to Vlad that you had killed Misha. Otherwise, my life would have been over, Declan. And maybe yours too.”

I can’t look at him.

“Charlotte. Look at me.”

I shake my head.

“Now.” His tone is firm, and I snap my head up.

“I would do anything to save my father’s life. Anything. I understand. If he were still here and I was in your situation, I would have done the same thing.”

I blink at him, processing his words.

“I’m sorry my actions stopped you,” I say quietly, the weight of my guilt hurting.

“Maybe that was exactly how it was meant to go. My father died to protect Conan, to stop a war, and ultimately, probably save all of his sons. Perhaps I was never meant to stop that from happening. As shit as it is, I think we can both confirm that fate works in funny ways.”

Fuck.

Tears well in my eyes.

“I’m so sorry, Declan. I wish I could turn back time.”

He shakes his head.

“I don’t. Because we wouldn’t be here, right now, putting our past to rest. Continue.”

I blow out a breath.

“After I returned home, Vlad believed our story. Except, another thing happened.”

I swallow the lump in my throat.

“I was pregnant.”

“Isabella? That’s your daughter who you cried out for?”

I nod.

I’m waiting for him to realize.

"I tried to escape; it was my last chance before she was born, but it didn't work. He killed my father as punishment, and I've lived in nothing short of hell since. I do everything I can to shield her. Thanks to Drago, Isabella is kept a secret from the rest of the family, she's safe. I take the brunt of it all for her."

Tears free fall down my face and Declan jumps out of his chair and rounds the table, taking the seat next to me.

When his arms wrap around me and I'm buried in his chest, a sense of calm washes over me.

"Shhhh. It's okay, baby. Let it out."

And I do. For the first time I let my emotions crash over me like a tidal wave, because I am safe here.

CHAPTER 76

DECLAN

Holy shit. I'm furious, but I'm not letting it take over.

She deserves better.

"Does he hurt his own daughter?" I ask and hold my breath, waiting for her answer.

If it's yes, I'll go there myself and burn his fucking home down to ashes.

She sniffles and pulls back, searching my eyes.

Fear lies beneath them, and I straighten my spine.

"She isn't his."

Frowning, I sit back, endless possibilities running through my head. That all seems to come to the same conclusion.

"How old is Isabella?"

I rub my hands on my pants as she looks away from me.

"No." I use my index finger to guide her gaze back to me.

"Four."

"Birthday?" I snap.

"May the tenth."

"Fuck." I run my hands over my face, all the blood draining from me as I stand up, holding onto the table for support.

"Does he hurt my daughter?" I spit the words out.

As soon as I say them, I regret it as she flinches.

She stands, and her chair goes flying across the room.

"No, he doesn't fucking hurt her, because I sacrifice myself every day to that man. I let him chain me up. Beat me. Fuck me.

Everything. I am his property to keep him away from her!" she screams, pushing against my chest, knocking me backwards.

"I don't fucking matter anymore. And I'll keep doing it until the day I die. Because I won't be leaving this earth without that bastard. And then she will be safe. So don't 'my daughter' me. I've done all I can. He hasn't touched a hair on her head."

Her nostrils flare and her chest heaves.

I still haven't fully processed.

My daughter.

"Fuck!" she shouts, slamming her fist on the table.

"You need to let me leave. Please. Let me out of here. I can't do this anymore. Just take the notepad for Enzo and let me finish this."

As she tries to step past me, I grab her face to silence her.

"Enough, Charlotte." I deepen my tone to let her know I'm not fucking around.

Releasing her, she bats my hand away.

"Get off me."

"I'm not done talking." I pull out a chair and maneuver her to it. She reluctantly sits.

Picking up the one from the floor, I place it next to her and sit facing her.

Reaching out, I place her hands in mine on her lap.

"I have a little girl?" I say softly.

I ignore the sharp pain in my chest. Four years I've missed.

Enough time for her to know her daddy is a piece of shit who hasn't saved her.

Long enough for her to have her own personality now.

"You do."

Her chin starts to quiver, and I squeeze her hands to reassure her.

"What's she like?"

Her eyes snap to mine. That darkness that lies behind them, with that switch just like Conan has, is tempered for now.

"She's perfect, Declan. Bright as a button. Loves to fight and draw. And stories. She loves me telling her stories."

Rubbing my thumb on the back of her hand, I bite back the tears.

"She looks just like you. Those eyes. Every time I look at her, I see you."

Letting out a hiss, I can't help but scoot forward and wrap my arms around her.

"I'm not there to protect her, Declan. I need to go home."

The thought of my baby girl being in that house with that monster makes my skin crawl.

"No, baby. That's not how this happens. Not anymore."

This changes everything and nothing.

Charlotte was destined to be part of my life. Now that just cements it.

"That is not your home and never should have been. You belong here, with me."

"Not without Isabella."

God, that knife in my chest twists.

"I'm a dad," I whisper, resting my head on top of hers.

I hope I can be half the man my father was for her.

Starting now.

"Let me get her back, Declan."

That fire in her voice returns, and I pull back, cupping her beautiful face in my hands.

"How I see it is we have two options. One, we keep inflicting the hurt on each other. Or, we flip the script. We take our suffering and use it to go after the people who did this to us."

I will raise hell for this.

For everything they've done to her.

For keeping me from my daughter.

"There's no way we can win. We won't last a day in Russia. They're powerful, Declan."

The fear returns. For someone so fierce, they've broken her— yet created the most powerful woman I've ever met.

"Sweetheart, who do you think you're talking to here?"

I arch my brow.

"I don't run this empire by being weak, Charlotte. I've made some very powerful allies. We're ready."

Tearing down the Bowens can wait. This is far more important.

"That comes with a price, Declan. A big one."

"Are you ready to sell what's left of our souls to Mr. Volkov?"

Her eyes go wide, and a familiarity washes over her face.

"Ivan's dead."

I nod.

"I wouldn't work with that piece of shit anyway. His son, Mikhail. He will be our ticket into Russia."

I watch as the cogs in her head turn.

"I have a contact inside. We need to reach him."

"Him?"

Jealousy rages through me.

"Drago. He's why I'm alive and why Isabella doesn't have a clue how awful these people are. He keeps her sheltered."

"Yet sends you into Decadence."

Running my hands through my hair. What are the chances Vlad knew I ran this game? Or that I'm her father?

Not many people know until they are entered into Inferno that the Quinn brothers run it. But I don't see this being a coincidence.

I need Enzo. And I need my brothers.

Holy fuck, they are going to lose their minds over this.

Stepping forward, I run my fingers through her soft curls.

"I've got you, baby." I lean in to kiss her and she turns her cheek.

"What?"

"I'm not some weak little princess that needs saving. Don't treat me like that. Equals or nothing. She's my daughter. He's my husband—and my kill. I've saved a space for him on my arm already."

A smirk tugs at my lips as I glance at the flowers delicately wrapping her arm.

"Ah. So that's what they are." I trace them with my finger.

"That's a lot of kills. You naughty girl."

She freezes, and I lean in, pressing a soft kiss on her shoulder.

"A warrior is never embarrassed or ashamed of their kills. Wear them with pride, not remorse. Every flower is a reminder you fought."

"What if I'm always this monster?" she says quietly.

"You aren't one. Not really. I see past you, just as you do me. Deep in here is the woman you truly are." I press my finger in the center of her chest.

"But right now, we need that fighter in you to take the stage. For our little girl."

Taking her face in my hands, I press a kiss on her plump lips.

"Thank you," I whisper.

"What for?"

"For beating the truth into me. For protecting our daughter. I'm so fucking proud of you." I kiss the tip of her nose and wipe away her tears.

"I'd die for her, Declan."

A breath catches in my throat, and I go cold.

"No. You've done enough. It's my turn to step up now."

I've never met my daughter, but that doesn't mean I wouldn't lay down my life for them both.

It's the least I could do.

"Now, I need to make some calls. We need backup on this plan."

"Can you get me access to my emails? Preferably something untraceable. I can make contact with Drago."

"Consider it done. I'll be back."

I drop another kiss to her lips, this time deeper.

Running my hands into her hair and holding her in place as her hands wrap around my waist.

Looks like Finn was right. Kill the husband just became top of my to-do list.

CHAPTER 77

CHARLOTTE

I check the laptop again.

It's the hundredth time in an hour, and I still don't have a reply.

Each second that ticks by claws at my nerves, whispering something's wrong. My fingernails are chewed down to nothing, and when the television dares to make noise, I kill it with a sharp jab of the remote.

"Here. Eat something." Declan appears from the kitchen, holding out a sandwich.

"I'm not hungry." I mutter, my stomach growling like a traitor.

His brow lifts, and he pushes it closer. "Don't lie to me."

That voice, it's not angry. It's just truth. Hard, clean, undeniable.

"Eat. You need your strength."

My fingers twitch. I cave, taking a bite. Fresh greens and turkey hit my tongue, and I moan.

"He's always on his damn phone. Dec." My nails tap an angry rhythm on the table.

"Maybe he's busy," he says, leaning back. "Didn't you say he's got ten jobs?"

"He does. Lawyer. He's helping Tatiana recover. Homeschooling Isabella. Training me. Security for Vlad. You name it, he does it." I pause, jaw tightening. "He always replies. This silence? It's not him."

His eyes narrow. "You look up to him."

"You could say that." I reach out and squeeze his shoulder. "But there's only one man I've ever wanted. And I'm looking at him."

That earns me a wicked curve of his mouth.

"Is that right?" he murmurs, stealing a bite of my sandwich before holding it back up. "Eat."

I obey.

"Good girl."

Heat shoots through me. My cheeks betray me and go warm.

"Is there a way I can log into my personal emails?" I ask, wiping my hands. "There's something I want to download."

"Yeah. Secure server. Go ahead." He nods, pushing the laptop back in front of me.

As I log in, my pulse spikes. The second the inbox loads, I go straight for the email I sent myself, backup files. Insurance. Proof that she's real, safe, loved.

I click on the photo.

There she is. My girl.

Isabella.

Tears race down my cheeks before I can stop them. My thumb hovers over her face on the screen.

"Is that—?"

Declan sucks in a slow, shaking breath.

I nod.

He moves in behind me, hands gripping my waist, eyes locked on the screen like it holds salvation.

"My little girl." His voice is gravel. "She's beautiful. Just like her momma."

I reach up and touch his jaw, soft and slow.

"Did you ever want kids?" I whisper, flicking to the next picture. Isabella is surrounded by her army of teddies, beaming so big it makes my chest ache.

"I hadn't thought about it," he says, voice rough. "In this life, you don't plan. You just survive."

I know that truth better than anyone.

"Sometimes, I'd just sit at night and watch her sleep," I admit, the words catching in my throat. "And I'd wonder where you were. If you'd moved on. If you had your own kids. If you were happy."

He closes his eyes.

"One of my biggest regrets in life will always be the fact I never came for you."

"We can live our *what if*," I say quietly. "Just... delayed."

The next photo loads. A selfie of me kissing her cheek, her little face scrunched in a perfect pout. I remember Drago letting me take all of these in her nursery on his phone.

"She pulls the same faces as you," I say, smiling through the tears.

Declan sniffles and tightens his arms around me.

"She looks happy. Healthy. You've done an incredible job, heartbreaker."

He pulls me into his lap, and I curl into him like it's the only place I still make sense.

Ping.

The laptop lights up with a new email.

My breath lodges in my throat.

I hesitate. Just one word. That's all I sent him.

Voitelnitsa. *Warrior.*

His reply slams through me like a gunshot.

"Two hours."

Beneath it, a secured email. One contact number.

"Do you trust him?" Declan asks, his fingers sweeping my hair aside like silk.

"With my life," I answer, no hesitation.

He nods. "Everyone's meeting us in Inferno in an hour. Finn. Conan. Even Enzo and Mikhail are flying in."

I turn in his lap and straddle him, nerves coiling tight.

"You want me there? When you explain?"

"You think I'm facing this storm without you?" he says, one brow raised.

"But your brothers—"

"Conan is less mad, more amused. Just don't pull a gun on him again."

I grin. "Promise." I cross my heart, and he grabs it, kissing the spot like sealing a vow.

"Want the grand tour first?" he asks, voice low.

I shake my head, biting the inside of my cheek.

"Can I see all of Inferno... *master*?" My voice dips, teasing.

He smirks, eyes gleaming.

"I don't see a golden ticket."

"I won by default. Why the Decadence Games?"

That's the question that's been burning in my throat since this all began.

"So many questions," he says, leaning in, brushing his lips against mine. "Let me show you."

"Okay," I breathe.

And this time, I let him kiss me like we've got a war to win. But tonight, we're still allowed to feel alive.

I squeeze Declan's hand as he unlocks the golden doors to Inferno.

At first glance, it's impressive, but not shocking—just another exclusive club with a sleek circular bar at its center. Suited men cluster around it, their conversations dying the moment Declan steps in. The energy shifts. Heavy. Electric.

"This is our bar area. A waiting room, let's call it," he murmurs, leaning in.

"Want a drink?"

I shake my head. "No, thank you."

I need my focus sharp.

As we move on, I catch a cluster of women tucked in the corner. They're all flawless—curves, lingerie, expertly done hair and faces. One of them, a blonde with piercing green eyes, giggles and flutters her fingers at Declan.

He doesn't blink. Just tightens his grip on my hand and keeps walking.

He scans his thumbprint on the next set of golden doors. The hallway beyond is lined with black doors, each with ornate gold handles and names etched above them.

"These?" I ask, nodding toward them.

"Private rooms. Each one tailored to a particular... taste."

I pause at one called *Retribution*, raising a brow.

He tugs me in close, slaps my ass. "For the naughty ones. Like you."

Heat rushes to my cheeks.

"What other rooms are there?" I whisper.

He smirks. "Everything you could imagine."

I slide my arms around his waist. "Even a milkshake one?"

"No. That one's just for us." He winks and gives my ass another squeeze.

As we walk, I can't help but wonder how many people are behind these doors right now.

"Do you spend a lot of time here?" I ask.

"Sometimes. Depends. Work brings me in more than anything."

I bite my tongue. Our worlds are still so different. Can I really give him everything he needs?

"Stop it." His voice is stern.

I freeze. "What?"

In a flash, I'm backed against a door, his fingers wrapped around my throat.

"Don't you dare doubt yourself," he growls. "Or what I want with you."

His mouth hovers over mine, teeth grazing my bottom lip.

"You and me? We're not like the others. Your past? It doesn't matter. Your confidence? That's what I'll work on. Because Charlotte, you're fucking everything. Inside and outside of this bedroom. You just need to be worshipped. Trained. And that, sweetheart, I can handle."

His grip tightens, and I shiver.

"You think you can handle me?" I whisper.

"Handle?" His smirk is feral. "I'll *own* you."

He steps back. "Open your legs."

I glance around.

His hand snaps up, tilting my chin.

"Lesson one. Listen. Follow orders. Trust."

I part my legs and gasp as his hand slides beneath my jeans.

"Good girl," he praises. "Five years I've waited to feel this pretty cunt again."

"More, sir. Please."

His mouth crushes mine. My hands tangle in his hair, desperate for more of him, of this.

"You want me to give you more?"

I nod. "Please."

He nips my lip. "I'm not here to give you pleasure, heartbreaker.

Giving you an orgasm implies they are yours. That isn't the case. I take them from you. Because they are mine, just as you are. I own every inch of you. Every climax, every moan, every fucking drop of you belongs to me."

He slips a finger inside me and a sound escapes my lips.

"That moan?" His voice drops. "All. Fucking. Mine."

Just as my legs begin to tremble, he pulls away. I sag against the door, breathless.

He licks his fingers clean and smirks. "Mine."

Grabbing my hand, he presses it to the hard bulge in his jeans.

"This is what you do to me. Don't you *ever* doubt yourself again, heartbreaker."

I nod and squeeze him through his jeans.

"I'm glad I never killed you," I whisper.

He chuckles and strokes my cheek. "Me too, sweetheart. Now let's go hunt down the bastards who tore us apart."

We climb the stairs, a massive chandelier glittering above us. Another secure door, another layer of secrecy. We step into a room warmed by a glowing fire.

"What's behind that other door?" I ask, eyeing it.

"I'll show you after."

We head through the left, and conversation halts instantly. Conan and Finn are the first faces I see.

Finn watches me, gray eyes unreadable, hands clasped beneath his chin. Conan grins when he sees Declan holding my hand.

Enzo stands with his usual icy composure, and beside him, a man in a black balaclava, built like Conan. His dark brown eyes flick to me, intense but not cruel. Tattoos lace his hands like armor.

"Come on." Declan tugs me to the head of the table. Two chairs. He pulls one out.

"Equals or nothing, right? Now sit."

I sit. He joins me.

Declan clears his throat. His hand finds my thigh.

"I'd like to formally introduce Charlotte."

They nod. Even Enzo offers a flicker of a smile.

"Conan, Finn, you've met her already."

Finn scoffs. "You need assessing, brother? I can have Hallie pencil you in."

Conan nudges him.

Declan shoots him a look. "I'm fine. You might need it after I knock you out, though."

"Brotherly love," Mikhail rumbles with a laugh. "Me and Nikolai are the same."

Declan chuckles. "Charlotte, this is Mr. Volkov."

A chill ripples down my spine as I meet Mikhail's gaze.

"Charlotte," he says, voice like cold thunder. "I heard it was you who eliminated the last of my father's men?"

Declan tenses beside me.

"Yes," I say.

Mikhail nods once. "Good work."

Enzo clears his throat, flipping open my notes.

"Excellent intel. But one name is missing."

My chest tightens.

"Drago," Enzo says.

I glance at Declan. He nods.

"Drago," I repeat, louder.

"Why exclude him?"

I bounce my leg and Declan clamps down on it.

"Because he's the only one in there I trust. I won't let anything happen to him."

Enzo trades a look with Mikhail.

"Seems we share a contact."

Mikhail's tone drops. "Be very careful owing that man a debt."

My jaw tightens. Drago's complicated, yes. But he's protected me for a decade. He's not the enemy.

"For me, there is no debt," I say quietly.

Enzo doesn't look convinced. "We'll see."

"We need Drago," Declan jumps in. "He's the only way to get to Vlad."

Finn frowns. "Why?"

Conan cracks his knuckles. "We talking bombs? Guns? Knives?"

"No!" I slam my hands on the table. The room stills.

Declan just smirks like this is normal.

"My daughter is in that house," I say, voice steady. "She is our mission. Get her out. Safely."

"Our daughter," Declan corrects, softly.

The way Conan's mouth drops open would be funny if this weren't life and death.

Enzo sighs. "This just got complicated."

"Are you sure she's yours?" Finn asks Declan, his voice tight.

"Yes."

Enzo turns to Declan. "Do you have Drago's contact?"

Declan slides over his phone.

"What time?"

"Now."

"I'll speak to him," Mikhail says, reaching out.

I look him dead in the eyes, pulse racing. The next words out of my mouth might blow up everything.

CHAPTER 79

DECLAN

"I'm sorry, Charlotte. Say that again." My voice is gravel, low and laced with disbelief.

No. I must've misheard.

Because the words she just said… they don't make sense.

"The only way to ensure Isabella's safety is to offer me over to Vlad. A swap."

She says it calm and casual, like she's ordering coffee.

"I know how that man's sick brain works. He'll want to punish me. He won't be able to turn that down."

My blood turns to fire. The room tilts. Charlotte, my Charlotte, offering herself to the monster that shattered her.

"No." The word claws out of me like a beast.

Mikhail shifts, scratching his jaw through his mask. Silent. Watching. But all I see is her.

My fists clench so tight I feel bone grind. My chest is a pressure cooker.

"Not fucking happening." The finality in my tone doesn't even make her blink.

"Declan, it's an option," Enzo says, and I turn on him like I could kill.

"You think I'd risk her?" I growl.

"This isn't about me." Charlotte cuts in, firm. "It's about Isabella. My life for hers? That's an easy deal. No one else gets hurt."

She won't even meet my gaze. Good. Because if she saw the

hellstorm in my eyes, she'd know I'm two seconds from burning the world down.

"You think she thrives without a mother?"

That lands. She jerks, spine straightening like I slapped her. "Don't you dare."

Venom drips from her voice.

"Hold up." Finn cuts through the tension, casual like it's just strategy, not the fucking air I breathe we're gambling with. "We offer a deal. Doesn't mean we actually follow through."

My gaze snaps to him. "A setup?"

Mikhail nods once. "We have locations. Resources. People. Between Moscow, Vegas, New York…"

My mind races. She's not going back to that man. Not on my watch.

And if this goes sideways, I know her. She'll sacrifice herself without hesitation.

"I'm not risking Charlotte."

She's already pushing back her chair. That spark in her eyes of pure rage, the kind of fight that both infuriates and seduces me.

"I'm not staying here."

"You think I can't make you?" I speak it low. Deadly.

She stiffens.

"You wouldn't dare." Her voice shakes, but not from fear. From fury.

I stand, towering over her, every inch of me ready to dominate.

"Oh, I fucking would."

Her breath catches. And just like that, she's seconds away from throwing a punch or tearing my clothes off. Probably both.

"Enough eye-fucking," Conan snaps.

We pull apart. Barely. I'm still burning.

"I'll call Drago. We plan this right."

"Who's at the complex?" Enzo asks.

"Vlad, Emil, and Emil's son," Charlotte replies. Her tone is all business.

"And Tatiana?" Enzo questions.

She shakes her head.

"No. I'm kept away from her. She lives in her own compound somewhere hidden."

Enzo hums, deep in thought.

"Too risky." Enzo shakes his head. "Two innocent kids. And the off chance of hurting Tatiana? That's a suicide pact."

He looks at Charlotte. "We fake the deal. A clean swap. Then we intercept. Can you do it?"

I want to rip his tongue out for asking. But she says yes. Of course she does.

My heart cracks, the sound of it loud in my own head. Finn nudges my shoulder. "Let's get Drago in. Hang tight, brother."

"Your daughter must come first. Listen to Charlotte. You can't cage a mother's spirit. We need her," Mikhail says coolly. Before I can reply, he's already on the phone and walking towards the door.

I know that. Doesn't mean I'll accept it.

What eats me alive isn't just the plan. It's how quickly she was willing to walk away from us.

To leave. Like I'm just a chapter she's ready to close.

"Finn. Conan. Take her home."

The door opens and Mikhail steps back in, phone on speaker.

"He needs proof of life."

Charlotte steps up, brushing right past me, and takes the phone.

"Voitelnitsa."

A pause.

"Are you okay?" Drago's voice is deep.

"Yes. This was my idea. We need to talk."

"How's she?"

That cracks Charlotte's calm. "Keeping you on your toes?"

He chuckles.

Her breath hitches. My heart clenches.

"She doesn't know me," I whisper to Finn.

"You okay?"

"No."

"You trust her?"

I nod.

"I don't want to lose her, Finn. I can't."

"You won't."

His voice is convincing. His hand grips my arm.

"We've got this. Like always."

"Tell her mommy loves her. I'll see her soon."

Her voice breaks. I move, pulling her into me, arms locked around her waist like I'll never let go.

"I will. I tell her every night," Drago replies softly.

Charlotte's still holding the phone. "Is this really it?"

"It is," Drago answers. "You understand the danger?"

I grip her tighter. I like this guy. He gives a damn.

"Yes. But I've spent ten years planning my escape. This was always the endgame. Only now, I'm not alone."

Drago sighs. "I'll do what I can on this end. I'll keep Tatiana out of this. She doesn't need to know."

Enzo steps in. "Good. Keep it that way."

"No debts. Let me speak to Mikhail."

"Thank you," Charlotte whispers.

"I'll see you soon, Voitelnitsa. Remember your training."

Plan's in motion. But she doesn't realize—*it's my turn now.*

I'm not letting her fight this alone. The others file out, and Charlotte spins in my arms.

"Didn't realize you had such a death wish, heartbreaker. Should've said so sooner."

Her eyes flicker with pain. I hate myself for saying that.

"I've trained for this. I know how to kill. You don't get to make me weak just because you love me. I will save our daughter. With or without you."

She tips her chin up, daring me to fight her on it.

"Oh, really?" I grab her cheeks.

"You want another punch to the dick?" she teases.

"No, but you can get down on your knees and suck it," I murmur, voice dropping an octave as I unbuckle my belt.

She drops. Instantly.

And fuck me, she's never been more perfect. A killer. A queen. And still all mine.

"You were made for me," I growl. "And I'll punish you for your recklessness later."

She doesn't flinch. She *thrives* under it.

And that? That's why we'll win. There is no other outcome to this.

We haven't gone through hell, not to get a taste of heaven.

I step past her, heading for the door.

"What—where are you going?" She stands, breathless.

I smirk. "We're going home."

It's time she realizes… she's not fighting this war alone anymore.

CHAPTER 80

CHARLOTTE

"Declan?" I call out, knocking on the last door.

I've not ventured this far through his mansion. It has two damn wings. As soon as we got home, he headed to his office, and I've not heard from him since.

I understand why he's annoyed. Once he meets Isabella, he'll realize why I'd give my life for hers. Swallowing the lump in my throat, I try not to think too much. Vlad won't go down easy, and he trusts no one. Let alone me. He's many things, but stupid isn't one of them.

"In here," he shouts back.

Pushing on the wood, I see him sprawled out, book in his lap, glasses hanging from his hand, and a smirk that could level cities. Fuck, he looks fine.

One foot rests on his knee, the red-bottom boots on full display. His black suit is unbuttoned just enough to reveal the intricate ink crawling up his throat. He clears his throat. I close my mouth before I start drooling.

"Hi." I smile. He quirks a brow and the room shifts. Thick with heat as he watches me.

I force myself to look away, taking in the space around him.

An enormous glass window towers behind him, throwing fractured beams of light across the dark wooden floor. To the left, a full wall of books. Floor to ceiling. All matte black shelves.

"Damn. A rolling ladder?" I ask, almost in disbelief.

I step closer, letting the scent of old pages fill my lungs. Running my fingers along the spines, I pause.

"Take one out." His voice is laced with amusement.

"Okay." I slide a book free where my hand rests.

Every cover is black or gray. My brows knit. "All the same author?"

He chuckles. "No, these are custom covers to fit the aesthetic… and perhaps hide my tastes."

My pulse picks up.

"Go on. Open it up," he commands.

I flip to a random page.

"Read it."

Scanning, my eyes go wide.

"Lots of cock and spanking, sir." I bite my lip, heat flooding my face.

But I keep reading. Goddamn, it's hot.

I might need to borrow a few lines, hell, it might help me finish my book if I ever make it back.

A sharp gasp leaves me as I look up. He's right in front of me. Towering over me.

"You read a lot?" I ask, peeking over the book. Obvious answer, dumb question.

He nods, rolling up his sleeves. "Helps with some of my other interests."

"Oh, yeah?"

A stupid flicker of jealousy twists in my gut. Him. Other women. I hate it.

"What better way to learn how a woman likes to be pleasured than by reading the spicy words of one? These books are like instructions for me."

My breath stutters as he leans in, brushing his lips against my cheek.

"They're also incredibly helpful for coming up with creative ideas to punish a naughty, reckless sub."

His hands are on me before I can think. He's grabbing my ass, lifting me like I weigh nothing. My back hits the shelf and his mouth finds my neck. I gasp; my legs locking around his hips, his cock is already hard against me.

"Am I in trouble? Is that why you're ignoring me?"

His hand wraps around my throat.

"No. I'm ignoring you because I'm trying to behave and not fuck some sense into you. You don't see it, do you?"

His eyes bore into mine. Unrelenting.

"I told you I'd do anything to get my girl out safely. I wasn't joking, and you won't change my mind."

"Goddamn it, Charlotte. I'm not losing you. Not after I just got you back. Isabella needs her mom, and so do I."

His words gut me.

He doesn't want to lose me. Not just for our daughter—but for him.

It's… terrifying. To be wanted this much. To be respected. Safe. No hidden motive. No trap.

Just him.

"But—"

He crushes his mouth to mine.

"It's about time you learned your place, baby. I'm done being nice. You need more to understand, don't you?"

My eyes widen as he rips off my panties and tosses them behind him.

"Pain and pleasure. That's what you're desperate for, isn't it? Clearly you want to be hurt. Punished, even."

His pupils darken as he tears open my blouse, buttons clattering to the floor like shrapnel.

"So fucking sexy."

He licks his lips, hikes up my skirt, and drops to his knees.

The book slips from my fingers, hitting the floor as he licks my pussy and a moan escapes my lips.

"The real question is, do you deserve more?" His voice rasps against my thighs.

"I do. Please, sir," I plead.

He flicks his tongue over my clit. I start to shake, and as I do, he pulls his mouth away.

"Remember how nice that feels. Chase it."

In one motion he's up, gripping my throat, yanking me from the shelf.

"Kneel."

I drop. As easy as that. It's like I was made to do this, just for him. My body just knows.

His fingers glide through my hair, the other hand unzipping his pants, freeing his cock. I lick my lips, watching the pre-cum bead at the tip.

But he backs away, smirking as he strolls to his desk and picks up his glass of whiskey, dipping his finger into it.

"Open."

I obey, and he slips his finger into my mouth.

"Mmm."

He pulls away, grabbing something from his pocket. A lighter. He flicks it on and I watch the flame grow in his hand.

"Even if this room was on fucking fire, I still wouldn't let you leave until you finished sucking my cock."

His voice is gravel and flame as he lowers the lighter toward my face.

"That's bullshit and you know it. You just told me you don't want me to leave."

He licks his lips and takes a slow sip of whiskey.

"Hmm. No. Perhaps I'd change it up. You can't leave until you come on my face. Just think, you're watching the flames tear this place apart, creeping closer and closer. You're battling fear and pleasure. But there is no escape. In that moment your only choice is to be consumed by one or the other. Pain or pleasure. And that will decide if you fall apart for me... or you fucking burn for me."

His words ripple down my spine like ice.

"That's what you want, isn't it? To walk into your own death? You don't seem to care if you live or die."

I breathe, barely able to find my voice. "And what about you? Because if I go, it looks like you're not too far behind."

He doesn't speak. Doesn't blink. Instead, he walks back to his desk. Papers everywhere, and he pours whiskey over them without breaking eye contact.

I freeze.

"I'll burn with you and because of you. You are the blaze in my life, my mind, and my fucking heart. We are the flame, sweetheart. Together, we can destroy everything in our wake. But if we're separated? We extinguish. There is no me without you. So yes. If you want to burn... I'll burn right beside you."

He tips the last of the bottle out, the amber liquid soaking through the sheets.

My heart pounds as he approaches again, the flame dancing in his hand.

"What do you say, heartbreaker? Burn with me?"

I don't know why, but I nod.

And I swear I've never felt more alive.

CHAPTER 81

DECLAN

Song- Who I Was, Y.I.P.N

A spark dances in her eyes.

"Say it."

"I'll burn with you."

Pulling her lip back with my thumb, her eyes go wide as I toss the lighter over my shoulder and directly towards the desk.

"You better come quick, sweetheart." I tell her, picking her up and slamming her back into the bookcase.

My lips crash over hers, and with one hard thrust, my dick glides all the way in.

"Watch the flames, baby. Feel the heat and come for me."

With my fingers squeezing her throat, I sink in her hot pussy, each thrust earning me a moan.

Louder and louder.

"Declan!" she screams, nuzzling her face into my neck.

Yanking her head back by her hair, I see the fire dancing in her eyes. I don't look behind.

I can feel the heat on my back.

I can hear the roar of the flames as it tears apart my desk.

"Come on, baby. Focus." I grunt out as her pussy clenches around me.

"How good does it feel?" I whisper. She gasps as I pound into her.

"So good," she moans.

"Fuck. You're perfect, heartbreaker," I mutter against her lips before stealing a kiss.

Letting her consume me the way the fire engulfs this room.

Pushing her thigh up towards her chest, I use that to push in deeper, harder. Enough to get her screaming.

I don't have long.

"I'm about to explode inside you. Come with me or don't come at all," I hiss, feeling every muscle in my body tense.

"Now!" I roar, fucking her relentlessly, until I violently erupt.

I let her cries rip free through the room as I sink my teeth into her neck.

As I close my eyes, succumbing to the pleasure, the sprinkler system turns on.

Sprays of cold water smother us, but it doesn't cool us down.

Our fire is from within.

Grabbing her face I kiss her with everything I have. Proving to her that she is mine.

I won't lose her. I can't.

I meant what I said.

I will burn with her.

"Oh my god, Declan." She's breathless as I stroke her damp face.

"Are you insane?" She blinks at me, the flush on her cheeks turning me on again.

Wiping away the water dripping down my forehead, I shake my head.

"Crazy for you. Or perhaps, because of you."

As the sprinklers start to ease off, I lift her into my arms and sit her down on the couch. My cock already twitching to be back inside of her.

"Spread your legs," I command.

She inches open her trembling legs and I get on my knees.

"Mine," I growl, my head is between her legs, and I begin cleaning her up with my tongue.

"Declan!"

"You want me to stop?" I question, and she grins.

"Never."

I smile, and my heart races.

"Be a good girl for daddy and ride my face. Help me clean up all the mess you made. And if you behave, I'll let you suck my dick clean after."

I wink at her, and she blushes, spreading her legs wider for me.

As soon as I start to feel her get close, I sit back on my heels.

"I think it's time you paid for me wasting a perfectly good bottle of whiskey, baby. Turn over and get that ass in the air, daddy needs to punish his naughty girl properly."

She bites down on her lip and I dig my fingers into her thigh.

"Each second you hesitate is another spanking. One... Two... Three..."

Before I can get to four, she scrambles around and rests her body on the couch, and her ass is now in front of my face.

"I'll start easy. Ten."

"What?" she exclaims.

I run my hands over the globes of her ass.

"Don't pretend like you don't love it."

Sliding my hand between her legs, she's dripping down her thighs, I thrust in two fingers. As she gasps, I spank her hard.

"Count," I order her.

"O-one."

"Good fucking girl."

Adding my thumb circling her clit, I smack down again, admiring the red welts beginning to form.

"Two."

My cock begs to be inside her.

By the time we get to seven, I'm almost panting as she squirms under my grip.

"What have you learned today?" I ask, rubbing her tender cheeks.

"That you'll burn down a building to prove a point."

She jolts forward as I slap her ass again.

"Eight. And wrong."

"That I need to not be reckless. That we belong together. That I don't want to ever leave you." She cries out as I add a third finger inside her, stretching her nicely.

"Almost."

Retrieving my fingers, I groan as I suck them clean.

"The lesson is, we burn together. We tear this fucking world down with our inferno. But that only works if we're a team. No sacrifices. Let me in and let me help. We won't make each other weaker, baby; it's the opposite. We light each other's flames."

I land one more spank and spin her to face me.

"This is petrifying. I know. But I promise you, I won't let you down." I look into her eyes and pour out my soul to her.

"You don't need to pretend with me, Charlotte. I see you. I hear you. I won't hurt you, I am not him."

She nods and reaches out to cup my face.

"I never thought you made me weak. I just didn't want you caught in the crossfire with Vlad. This isn't your battle."

Resting my hand over hers on my cheek, I close my eyes.

"The minute you walked into my life in Italy was the minute it became my battle."

CHAPTER 82

CHARLOTTE

I come to a halt as Declan taps in the code to Decadence.

Being back here makes my body shiver.

"You okay?" He holds out his hand behind him and wiggles his fingers for me to grab.

"The games. They were a lot."

On one hand, they set me free. They brought me back to Declan, which is right where I'm meant to be.

I don't need a savior. But a partner who will stand by my side and hold my hand as we take down the man who tried to break me? That is everything.

"That's the idea. We weed out the scum in our world and give the girls a lease of new life. But to form a new life, one must shed the remains of their last one. That's where the games come in. Survival brings out a side no one knew they had," he tells me as the doors open.

As we walk past the first room, I look inside at the dildos on the wall.

"Why kinky games?" I ask.

I know he's grinning without even looking.

"How else do I find a submissive perfect for me? There had to be a prize."

I look down at my sneakers.

"But I didn't win. I actually quite catastrophically lost, Declan."

He pushes me back into the room and shuts the door.

"You won. You won me five fucking years ago. The winners of the games, they're temporary. A year, and then they move on. You? You're for life. The ultimate prize."

A smile tugs at my lips as he steps towards me.

"Once I'm finished, you'll be the best damn submissive I've ever had. And my last one."

Goosebumps erupt over my skin as he traces along my collarbone.

"You have a lot to learn and a lot to forget. Your new life will begin, Charlotte. I promise you."

"And the other girls in your life?" I ask.

I knew Vlad fucked around, a lot. He made no secret of his infidelity. I didn't care, if he was entertained elsewhere, it meant I didn't need to do it.

But Declan, he's different.

"When I have you in front of me, why the hell would I be looking elsewhere? Five years I've tried to fill the void you left. No one can. Only you."

He leans in and my eyes flutter closed as he kisses me.

My brain is still trying to catch up with everything.

"I still can't believe it is all an illusion. That was pretty believable. The gunshots. Very good." I wink at him.

"Thank you. All part of the grand plan. See, the families have to believe the women are dead. So that way, they can form whole new identities."

I shake my head.

"And people do this to their daughters? And come here and look you in the eyes after?"

I clench my fists, thinking about Isabella. I could never. Ever. Hurt my baby.

"Not only that, they'll thank me and shake my hand." His jaw ticks. I'm glad he feels the same anger I do.

"They deserve to die."

He taps the side of his head and smirks.

"Great minds, baby."

My mouth falls open. Weeding out the scum.

"But shh. It's our little secret. It's even better for the girls if no one comes looking for them too."

I pretend to zip my mouth closed.

"You're one of the good ones really, aren't you?" I lean forward and stroke his cheek.

"I'm a balance. Evil when the time requires, but a good heart thanks to my mom."

"Now, come on. We've got scheming to do." He taps my ass and leads me to the door.

CHAPTER 83

DECLAN

Conan and Finn have been working tirelessly for the last two days with Mikhail, Drago, and Enzo.

Apparently they've mastered a plan.

Giving a mission to Conan is like giving candy to a kid. He gets all giddy and obsesses over it.

Finn, he's the details guy. The one who assesses the risks and thinks of things no one else would.

And me? I oversee the madness. Keep them in check.

Finn requested Charlotte joins us, as she knows Vlad best to predict his actions.

In an ideal world, I don't want her in the same country as that cunt. But reality says she has to be.

"Glad you could finally join us," Finn grunts, looking up from his computer.

Conan greets us with a smile and ushers us inside my office.

"Take a seat, this is a good one," Conan tells us.

So I sit down on the leather couch and pull Charlotte onto my lap.

My eyes go wide, and I jump up, taking Charlotte with me as Conan swipes every damn item off my desk and onto the floor.

Glass smashes, whiskey pours out onto the ground, and my blood fucking boils.

He pulls out a map that spans the entire desk and finally makes eye contact with me.

"Why the fuck did you just do that?" I shout, throwing up my hands.

Conan steps back and grins like a little kid. Except it ain't cute on a six-foot-six beast, covered in tattoos.

I've seen him cave enough skulls in with his bare hands that I can't see him as my *little* brother anymore.

At this point, I'm lucky the bloodthirsty maniac is on my side.

"I've always wanted to dramatically clear a desk and make a plan using a map. You know, like in the films."

I look at Finn, who is just as clueless as me, and I glance down at the shards of glass near my feet.

"Most people want to clear one to fuck. Not for maps." I keep my tone serious, despite dying on the inside looking at the confusion on his face.

"No. I disagree. Keep the fucking out in the woods and the maps on here. Much cleaner."

That gets Finn, who bursts out into a fit of laughter.

"I'll bring you back some sanitizer from the hospital, Con. Didn't realize you had a thing for cleanliness."

"Shut up. The map." Conan jabs his finger on the wood.

"You're lucky I don't stab you with that glass, brother," I tell Conan, letting the shards crunch under my boot as I step towards him.

Finn pushes between us and jabs his finger to Russia on the map, right where the red circle is.

"Don't suppose you have a pen ready for this, Conan?" I bite back a grin.

I can't let him know right now that I actually find him funny. I need him to engage the survival part of his brain rather than the clown.

"Don't need one. All up here." He jabs a thick finger into his temple.

"Great."

Looking down on the map, I'm distracted as I see Charlotte intently studying it.

"So, he lives about an hour out from that location." She presses her finger down on an area south, and Finn marks a cross.

"Good," Finn replies.

"This location suggested, do you know of any ties? Drago didn't."

She chews on her lip.

"No. Closest I've been is about twenty miles west. But that was to take down the remaining men of Ivan."

"Volkov?" I ask.

"Yup."

"How active are they?" Finn asks.

"Pretty much all dead."

Snaking my arm around her waist, I nestle her into my side, a sense of pride in my chest.

"Who owns this location?" she asks.

"Technically, Mikhail now. But it's no one's really. Just an empty warehouse used to store arms once upon a time."

Conan rolls out another sheet.

This time blueprints to the warehouse.

"We will have men surrounding the building, hiding in the woods."

"He will no doubt do the same," Charlotte says warily.

"He has a big unit."

"That is where Drago comes in. He knows where each is positioned."

She nods.

"Is the plan bringing my daughter to a war zone?" She taps her finger on her forearm.

Conan looks to me for help.

"Well, we will allow him to enter with Isabella; we will not make a shot until she's out of harm's way.

"And if he makes a shot?" she counters.

"It's a risk. We can't plan for every eventuality, but we are all on the same page. You and Declan go in, we surround the area, and I'll be the sniper. Drago will let us know Isabella's location for the swap. In an ideal world, it's a clean swap, and we simply follow your tracker to the location and gun the place down, all while Isabella is taken to safety. Right?" Conan finishes, almost out of breath.

Finn nods.

"Yeah, that's the plan. Secure parameter, clean swap, and a tracker. To put it simply. Getting Isabella out is our main priority."

Charlotte gives them a sharp, approving nod.

"When?" she asks.

I hug her tighter.

"Waiting on the go-ahead from Drago. Any day. Mikhail and his men with Enzo will meet us there. We need them to keep us safe with the general unrest since Ivan's death. Plus, he has safe houses dotted around."

"Good."

I'm proud of them. Vlad won't be getting anywhere with either of my girls.

I don't have a good feeling about this, and looking at Charlotte's blank expression, neither does she.

"What do you think, baby?" I whisper in her ear and feel her shiver against me.

"If we're smart, have the manpower, and Drago protecting Isabella, I can't see why it wouldn't work."

"See. Told you. Awesome plan." Conan proudly picks up his blueprints.

"Make sure we arrive before Vlad does," I tell them as Charlotte and Finn study the blueprint.

"There looks like only one way in and one way out. I say me and Declan head in there and wait for Vlad so we have the advantage if he does come in guns blazing for me." She points on the table.

I squeeze her shoulder.

"Vlad will be heavily armed for this," she says sternly.

"And so will we," I reassure her.

"Mikhail has guys going over there now to check it out, Jax and Alexei. They'll report back tomorrow and can lay anything out we need before we even confirm with Vlad," Finn informs us.

"We've got this." I hug Charlotte tight to reassure her.

The pressure I feel must be nothing in comparison to her.

"We will catch up with you later," I tell my brothers, leading Charlotte out.

"What are you thinking?" I ask her, guiding her by the lower back.

"I need to get some training in. I'm feeling weaker than usual." She spins to face me with a grin.

"You got any throwing knives? Machetes?" she asks.

That glimmer in her eyes makes my cock throb.

"Let's head to the cabin. Conan has everything. Can even throw some axes if you want."

"I'd love to."

She nudges into my side and grabs my hand.

"That's what gets you going? Violence?" I chuckle, and she stops.

"I suppose so. It's who I am now."

"I like you just how you are. Never change. Just no throwing knives at me."

She nods and giggles, making my heart swell.

"If you behave, Mr. Quinn. You won't become another flower tattoo."

I let out a groan as she takes off into a jog towards the woods. I speed up to match her.

"Your next flower can be your last, if that's what you want."

She rubs a hand over her forearm and slows her pace.

"I have a special spot saved especially for that asshole. I'm ready. This is the closest I've gotten to ending it since I ran before."

I stop and rub my face.

"What happened when you tried to leave?"

"I was five months pregnant. I knew it was only a matter of time before he realized she wasn't his. I'd been protecting my father for years by staying, but then I had something more important to fight for. But it wasn't successful. I managed to take out the guards and get out of the compound; he always had one over on me. He stopped me in my tracks. I lost my father, and I lost my freedom completely, but Isabella, she was free from harm, so that is all that mattered. I never saw a way out, not with the threat he put on her life."

She takes in a shaky breath, and I squeeze her shoulders, pulling her into my embrace.

"Until now."

I'm fucking murderous, he threatened my baby.

Oh, he's going to die a slow and painful death.

Stepping forward, I stroke her cheek.

"No matter what, our little girl will be safe. Okay?"

It's strange, having never even met her, I love her so fiercely.

She is a piece of me, and she deserves everything I can do to save her.

"I know."

"Let's go throw shit, ay?" I kiss her forehead.

"You think Conan and Finn want to join us? I might be able to teach them a thing or two."

Hmm. It would be nice for my brothers to get to know her. See what I see, rather than a threat.

"I like that."

Plus, I'd love to see her wipe the smugness off them. I have no doubt my girl has the skill.

CHAPTER 84
CHARLOTTE

The old cabin, set behind Conan's, creaks as the wind cuts through the trees. Weapons line the walls: blades, axes, even a row of throwing stars. It's a playground for killers. I'm impressed.

I can't help myself but pick up the first knife that speaks to me. My eyes fix on the target and I throw. The blade sings through the air and buries itself deep in the center of the post with a sharp, satisfying thunk. My heart's not pounding, it's steady.

Here I am free again.

Declan's behind me, close enough I can feel the weight of his stare between my shoulder blades. I don't need to turn around to know he's watching every twitch of muscle, every breath I take.

"Looking good, heartbreaker."

I grab another knife from the table, heavier than the last. I like the way it settles in my palm, like it belongs there.

"I'm not here to play," I snap, testing the balance before lifting my gaze to the target. "This isn't for show. I need to be ready. For him. For her."

Declan steps closer.

"You're ready, you know you are," he says, but there's a catch in his voice. Like he doesn't quite believe it. Like he's trying to convince himself, too.

I whip the knife through the air, harder this time. It slams into the wood, right beside the first. Not perfect, but deadly enough.

"Not ready," I hiss. "Not yet."

His hand brushes mine, like he's trying to ground me. I yank away. I don't want grounding. I want fire. I want rage.

"Don't," I say, spinning to face him. "This isn't a fucking therapy session."

His jaw tics. "And what is it, then?"

"It's war."

He doesn't flinch as I snatch another blade and throw it with enough force to rattle the post. This time, I don't look away from him.

"That one was for Vlad."

His eyes darken.

"And this one?" he asks.

I grab a fourth and press the tip to my palm, feeling the sharp kiss of metal, just enough to sting.

"This one's for me," I whisper. "For every time I flinched. Every time I begged. Every time I stayed quiet while he broke me."

I hurl it with everything I've got. It slams dead center, splitting the wood slightly.

Declan's breathing hard now. Matching mine. There's no air between us, just heat and tension and the throb of something violent.

He reaches for my waist.

"This time will be different. You're not the same woman who escaped before, are you?" he murmurs.

"No," I say, eyes locked on the knives. "I'm the one who's going to make him bleed. I'm angrier now than I ever have been."

I feel his fingers slide up my side. "Show me. Teach me how to throw like that."

I smile and pick up a blade and press the hilt into his hand.

"I'll show you," I whisper, stepping in until we're chest to chest. "But you better keep up, soldier. I don't train soft."

His grip tightens on the knife.

"Good. Because I don't want soft. I only like it hard." He winks, and my stomach flips.

I guide his hand, pressing the blade against my thigh, not hard, but enough to feel it.

"Then don't flinch," I say, my voice dripping with challenge. "Because if you do, I win."

CHAPTER 85

DECLAN

She takes a step back with a naughty glimmer in her eye. The blade, now in my grasp, ready and waiting for me to throw.

"Show me what I'm working with," she orders with her hand firmly on her hip.

Sizing up the target, I throw it, and it hits, the blade digging into the wall, but quite a few inches from her attempts.

"Hmm."

She taps her finger against her lips, her eyes roaming my body.

"Take your shirt off."

I don't move; instead, I tilt my head with an amused smirk.

"Now."

The command in her voice does something to me, something primal. I pull the shirt over my head and drop it to the floor. The cabin air is cold, but her gaze on my skin is fire. It always is.

She steps into my space, close enough that her breath grazes my throat. She presses the tip of the knife just beneath my collarbone, and I suck in a breath.

"You think I won't bleed for you, sweetheart?" I look down at her.

"Trust me?" she asks, but it's not sweet. It's a threat. A dare.

"I'd let you cut my fucking heart out," I say.

She drags the blade downward, slow and shallow, tracing the line of my sternum. I watch her the whole time. She doesn't blink. Doesn't hesitate. The pain is sharp but clean.

She's not cutting me because she wants to hurt me.

She's cutting me because she wants to own me.

And I fucking love it.

"I could carve my name into you," she whispers. "Brand you. A bit like the one I marked my own skin with for you in the games."

"I'm already yours. It's even there in ink, baby. But go ahead, mark me some more."

She stops. Eyes flicker up to mine. There's a crack in her armor now; it's small, but there. I reach for her wrist and gently guide the blade down until the tip rests against my abdomen.

"Do it," I murmur. "Whatever you need to take back control, do it with me. Right fucking here. Let it out."

Her breathing stutters. She looks down, then back up, and something shifts. Her control splinters and shatters. She drops the knife and forcefully grabs my face in both hands and kisses me like she's drowning and I'm the only air she has.

Enough to make us become the fire.

We crash to the floor in a tangle of limbs and teeth. She claws at my chest, dragging her nails through the blood she drew. I pull her hips against me, grind her down until she moans into my mouth.

"Take your pants off," I growl. "Now."

She obeys without a word, kicking them away. I grab the knife from the floor, press the flat of it to the inside of her thigh, dragging it slow, deliberate.

She gasps. Her legs shake, but her eyes glisten with mischief.

"You like that?" I murmur. "You want more?"

"Yes," she pants. "I want it all."

I flip her onto her stomach, press a hand between her shoulder blades to keep her there. Her ass is already red from earlier. I grab her hips and pull her back against me.

"Good girl. Now don't flinch, remember. Or you lose," I whisper, gripping onto the knife.

She is frozen in place as I run the flat edge of the blade along her ass cheek; before I take it any further, I pull my hand back and launch it at the target, this time hitting between her last two.

"I throw better when I'm turned on," I tell her, and she laughs.

"Good shot. Now, you need target practice. Your dick inside my pussy. Go," she orders.

Now that is one instruction I won't get wrong. I fuck her like I'm trying to bury myself inside her forever.

She screams into the floor, and I cover her mouth with one hand.

I pound into her relentlessly, until I start to see stars in my vision. Everything about this moment is raw, and it's fucking electric.

"Give it to me," I shout as I almost reach my own peak.

Releasing my hand from her mouth, she screams out my name, and that is my undoing. I violently shudder as I spill inside her.

She sobs into the wood, shaking beneath me. I collapse on top of her, arms wrapping around her, holding her so fucking tight.

"I've got you," I whisper, brushing her hair from her face. "No matter how dark it gets—I've fucking got you."

And when she turns her face to look at me, eyes glassy but fierce, I know.

This woman has my heart.

We're each other's weapons. And there's no one I'd rather bleed with.

"Can we… go home, Declan?"

Home. I don't believe that is a single place anymore.

It's simply wherever my heartbreaker is.

CHAPTER 86
CHARLOTTE

Song, Scream My Name, Thomas LaRosa

I roll over to face him as he rests his muscular arm behind his head.

I can hear the cogs turning in his brain, so I trace my finger along the ink up his neck, watching the smile twitch on his lips as I touch him.

Tomorrow is the day we fly out to Russia. We've spent the last four days training, planning, and, well, fucking. But he can now toss a knife like a pro.

"What's up?" I whisper, leaning in to press a kiss on his sharp jaw.

"I'm nervous," he admits, looking up at the ceiling, so I sit up and cup his cheek.

"You, nervous, why? We can take down Vlad." I tell him.

With Enzo and Drago on our side, there is no other option than to win. At least, that's what I'm making myself believe.

He sighs and shakes his head.

"Not that. I will meet my daughter for the first time. What if she thinks her daddy is an asshole? She's already nearly five. I've missed five whole years. Enough time for her brain to learn her daddy wasn't there for her."

My heart hurts for him.

"Isabella is a beautiful, kind soul, Declan. She knew her daddy couldn't come for her, not wouldn't. I told her stories about you her whole life."

He blinks a few times and turns to look at me.

"She knows about me?"

I nod, chewing on my lip.

"She knows you as the prince in my story. The one I promised to find her one day after I'd saved us both."

I close my eyes thinking about her sweet little face.

"I bet she's a warrior just like her momma. Ay?" It's his turn to sit himself up and brush a stray tear from my cheek.

"I hope she's nothing like me," I say quietly.

He tuts and shakes his head.

Pushing me onto my back, he clambers on top, nudging my knees open with his thighs and holding my wrists loosely above my head.

"I hope our daughter is just like you. A woman who will burn the world down for those she loves. A woman who is so fierce she can't see how powerful she truly is. A force with a kind heart and beautiful soul. Who never fucking gives up. I hope our daughter sees how hard her mom loves her. And I hope one day, our baby girl can see how much her daddy loves her and her mommy. I hope both of you can see what it's like to be truly cherished. My girls will have the world, baby. I will not stop until I deliver it."

I suck in a breath as the hot tears stream down my cheek.

"She is going to be obsessed with you, Declan. She deserves a daddy who will show her true love."

"You both deserve that, heartbreaker," he whispers as he presses his lips to mine.

As I go to return the kiss, he pulls back, holding my hands in one hand, the other trails along my face and down my chest.

"It's our last night just the two of us," he mutters, peppering kisses along my throat.

That sounds perfect. No more fighting and surviving, finally I can live and bring Isabella up the way she deserves. Safely and as part of a family. That's all I've ever wanted for her.

"Hmm, mmm." My eyes flutter closed and I tip my head back to give him better access to me.

As his hand slides south, I wiggle my hips and try to shimmy out of his grip.

"What. Are. You. Doing?" he growls.

Oh God.

As his fingers go under my panties, I freeze, and he stops.

"Words."

"I've just come on my period," I confess.

I was so pissed off when I went to the bathroom earlier, I'd completely lost track of my cycle. Talk about ruining the moment, I can feel his cock pressing against me, and I want it. So bad.

"And?" He smirks, dipping his hand lower.

I shake my head.

"It'll make a mess." I nod to the bright white sheets that we are lying on top of, and he chuckles, but his grip on my wrists tightens. He's still careful not to hurt my scars there.

And that makes my heart pound. Knowing I am safe with this man in every way.

"Look, I can get you off if that's what you need. We don't have to waste tonight," I tell him, and his eyes darken.

"You think I just want you to get me off? You don't think your pleasure is as valuable as mine? Hmm? I get off on you getting off, sweetheart. This doesn't work one way."

My cheeks heat, and my pussy throbs for him.

"Spread your legs wider or you won't come for the rest of the month."

My mouth snaps shut and my legs open for him.

"Good girl."

He lightly circles my clit and a moan escapes me.

"Look how responsive you are. Good fucking girl, baby."

He runs his tongue up my throat, keeping a light pressure on my clit.

"What I need, more than anything, is to hear you scream my name while you come all over my fucking face."

I let out a gasp at his filthy words, and he nips at my skin.

"Yes. You heard me right. Nothing can stop me from making my girl feel better. Not tonight, not ever."

Before I can respond, he crashes his lips over mine and steals my breath away.

"Just relax," he whispers, and I open my legs wider for him.

I can't deny it. It does feel good.

His hips grind against me as he expertly makes me forget everything else, other than how incredible he makes me feel.

"Such a good little slut for daddy, aren't you?"

I let out a whimper as he slides off my panties and tosses them on the floor.

"Don't move," he whispers.

He jumps off the bed, I hear his heavy feet down the stairs and swiftly back up. Time seems to stand frozen as I wait for him.

That mischievous glint in his eye makes me nervous, yet he's excited as he reappears in the doorway.

"Close your eyes."

I let them close and hold my breath.

"And breathe, baby. The only pain I will ever inflict from now on will be to aid your pleasure."

His voice gets louder as he approaches and the bed dips as he rejoins me, pushing back open my legs wider and settling between them.

A tiny whimper escapes me as he pulls on the string of my tampon.

"You are safe with me," he whispers, as it pops out and tosses it in the trash.

He slides in two fingers as he continues to circle my clit with his thumb, adding enough pressure to have sparks flying as he leans in closer and sucks on my throat.

"God, you're beautiful at my mercy."

I gasp as the freezing cold block connects to my clit while his fingers pump in and out of me.

"Declan." I arch my back, just as he laces his fingers around my neck.

"Feel everything, Charlotte. Let go. Just like you did in Italy. Be mine." His deep Irish accent soothes me and turns me on something crazy.

"Y-yes, sir."

I discreetly open my eyes as he repositions himself lower down, almost in a sniper position between my legs. In a slow motion he runs the ice along my slit, and I shiver in response. I'm so close to the edge I'm almost shaking.

"Fuck," I cry out as the icy cool is replaced by the heat of his tongue.

"Good girl, see how good I can make you feel?"

I nod and snap my eyes closed, but I desperately want to see him enjoy me.

"I want to watch, sir," I beg, and he chuckles.

"Open those beautiful eyes then."

I blink them open, and he's staring up at me, his eyes full of raw hunger for me. He places the ice back in his hand and offers it to me.

"Play with this on your nipples," he orders, and I take the cube between my index finger and thumb.

My nipples tingle as he licks me slowly and sensually.

"Just like that, baby. Pinch them, show me what you want me to do to them."

A shock runs through me, a sharp pain against the cool, balanced against the warmth from his tongue on my pussy.

His rough hand reaches up, and he steals the ice, popping it in his mouth and giving me a wink that electrifies me.

Propping myself up on my elbows, I watch intently as he uses his mouth to run the ice along my core.

"Oh, my god," I cry out.

He pushes my thighs up, spreading me wider and holds me firmly in place. I'm panting, my head almost spinning from all the sensations.

"I need to be inside you, fuck," he grunts as he sits back, spitting the remaining ice cube on the floor.

I let out a squeal as he picks me up and throws me over his shoulder, rushing us to the en-suite.

"Declan!" I giggle, kicking my legs as he strides into the walk-in rainfall shower and turns it on. Sliding my body down his front, he slams my back against the tiles and I pull on the collar of his shirt as the water heats up, cascading over us.

"You have too many clothes on," I say against his lips before he slams them over mine. I grip his throat and squeeze my legs around his waist tighter.

"I. Don't. Care. I just need you," he grunts, and I roll my hips against the bulge in his pants.

A spark lights his eyes as he pulls back, using one hand to free his cock.

He leans back and rips his shirt over his head, tossing it behind him before grabbing my face and coming back in for ferocious kisses.

His dick rubs against my entrance, and I moan in anticipation.

"Please," I say between kisses.

"I love it when you beg for my cock. Now do it louder, so I'll never forget how it sounds. Etch yourself in my memories, heartbreaker."

"Please, daddy. Fuck me, fill me up with your massive cock. I'm begging you. Please."

It's like a spark goes off, and he violently thrusts into me, sliding me up the wall with the force.

"Is that what you need?" he says, squeezing my throat.

"Yes," I choke out.

The water freefalls over us, and I claw at his neck to hold on as he pounds into me. Stealing my breath with every kiss.

"I'm fucking obsessed," he mutters between kisses.

"Me too."

I've obsessed over him for so many years, this feels so right, so natural. Like I'm finally home. There's just one piece of our puzzle missing.

"Are you going to come for me, sweetheart?" he growls in my ear before nipping the lobe.

"Can I? Now?" I whisper.

"Fuck yeah," he groans out as my pussy clenches around his dick.

With a few final thrusts and his hands squeezing my neck, my nails digging into his muscular shoulders, I fall apart for him.

Except I'm not falling apart; I'm being put back together, day by day, by him.

My name erupts from his lips and he tips his head back, so I lean in and bite into his throat.

"Fuck, heartbreaker!"

He's breathless as he spills inside of me, and a wave of ecstasy washes over me, my body shakes and stars fill my vision, and I scream out his name.

As I orgasm, his hands cup my face and he kisses me through it.

"Such a good fucking girl for me, aren't you?" he whispers against my lips and I melt.

Brushing my hair away from my face, he slowly puts me on my feet and leads me directly under the spray.

"Now let me take care of my girl." He smiles, grabbing the pink shampoo from the holder behind me.

"Turn around."

I do as he says, closing my eyes, and a moan escapes my lips as he begins massaging my scalp.

"Fuck, that feels good," I moan.

He thrusts his hips and his dick presses into my ass.

"Keep moaning and I'll bend you over."

By the time he washes out the soap, he gets to work on rubbing shower gel all over my body. His touch is light as he runs his palms over me.

"I need to fuck these," he whispers in my ear from behind, cupping my breasts in his hands.

As he runs down my body, I open my legs as he cleans between them, his finger brushing over my clit.

"Declan," I hiss out.

His hands roam to the back and he grabs my ass with both hands.

"Such an amazing ass. I'm going to train you to take me perfectly here."

My eyes shoot open as he parts my cheeks and rubs my back entrance with the tip of his finger.

"Wow."

So different. Yet so hot.

"Will be good, this time of the month," he tells me, sliding in his finger just a tiny bit more.

"Fuck, so tight."

His breath hitches as he grabs the back of my neck and bends me over.

"More?" he asks and I nod.

"Words, baby."

"Yes. Please," I cry out as he pushes in a little more.

"Perfect. Good girl."

I sag forward and hold myself up against the wall.

Looking behind, I watch him drop to his knees.

"Declan!" I cry out as his tongue circles there, his fingers digging into my ass.

I jolt forward abruptly as his palm cracks down on my cheek, the pain searing through my body.

It's all a blur as he is back on his feet and spins me to face him, I look up through my lashes as he towers over me.

"Can I clean you now, sir?" I ask and pout my lips.

He nods and pulls back my bottom lip.

"Yes. You can start on your knees, baby," he tells me, pushing me down to the ground by my shoulders.

"Once this is over, we can explore each other every damn day."

My heart flutters and I smile, taking his cock in my hand.

"I like that plan," I tell him.

It sets a fire inside me, one I need to keep hold of until I get Isabella back.

Only then can we really start planning our future.

Because right now, there's a chance I won't be in it.

CHAPTER 87

CHARLOTTE

My leg bounces erratically as we drive through the woodlands.

After a long flight and a few hours of sleep in Mikhail's safe house, the time is finally here.

Being back in Russia heightens my fears. I'm back in hell, and I'm about to come face to face with my tormentor.

Squeezing my fists as I aimlessly watch the trees go past, Declan clamps his strong hand on my jolting leg and holds it still.

"Everything is going to be fine, baby. Mikhail's men have been patrolling the warehouse for days, they're already in position. We have the upper hand," he whispers, leaning into my side.

Visions of my first escape attempt flood my memories. This time, he has my little girl.

My worst fear has come to life, and I have one opportunity to fix this. So he's not wrong, everything will be okay—for Isabella at least.

"We don't know that, Declan. I need you to understand something."

I grab both of his hands in mine.

"What, sweetheart?"

"That if there is a choice between saving me or Isabella. You chose her, Declan. I need you to promise me that you will save our daughter over me."

I blurt the words out, and it's like a weight lifts off my chest.

He blinks at me a few times, and I squeeze his hand.

I know how hard this is, asking him to pick a daughter he's never met over me. But the second he lays eyes on her and that shock goes to his heart, he will understand.

She is a true Quinn.

"I give you my word, heartbreaker. Not because I want to, but because I understand. And I want you to know something too…"

Fuck, this is awful.

I've just found him again, and now there's a chance that if shit goes south, I won't make it out of here.

"What?" I fight back the tears.

"That if it comes down to it, I will die to protect my girls. I don't give a fuck if I've never met her. I am her dad. She has my blood. She is my legacy. And I love her with my whole heart."

I suck in a breath.

"But it's not going to come down to that, Charlotte. We're fighters. Life has been cruel and sent us here. But we're stronger together. Maybe life has thrown everything at us so we can be the strength she needs."

I stroke my thumb along his knuckles.

"What if this one is running out of fight?"

Ten years is a long time.

I'm not the fighter I was a few years ago.

"That's why we go in as a team, sweetheart. You've fought for a long time. This is the last one. I promise you, once we get our baby girl back, it's going to be different."

I love his positive outlook.

But he hasn't lived my life. Deep down, there's only one way this is going to go.

The way it has to go.

Vlad told me I'd never escape him, not even in death, and that thought races through my mind every day.

I will never be free of him, but she can be.

Declan saved me five years ago with that one night. The idea of him kept me sane for the next five.

Now, I have everything I ever wanted in my grasp.

It's always my husband, my monster, that stands in the way.

You have to burn those kinds of vermin and watch their souls get ripped from their bodies.

The only way Isabella is safe and can live a normal life is by ripping that man's heart from his chest and watching him take his last breath on this earth.

He isn't walking away from this. I'm going to make sure of it.

"I know. And I know we have a plan. I just needed to hear you say the words for my own sanity. Her over me. Okay?"

Declan closes his eyes and rests his forehead against mine.

"I hate this. But yes. Our baby first. But bet your ass if it comes down to it, I'll be burning the world down for you too. You're important to me." He swipes his thumb along my cheek.

"Thank you," I breathe out, trying to keep my emotions in check.

"Look at me," he commands as my eyes flutter closed.

"There is a lot of fight left in you." He pauses, rubbing his nose against mine, but his eyes are burning into mine.

"Scorch the earth if you have to. Let your fire burn their souls, heartbreaker. It's time to make them pay for all the years they've tried to destroy you. Now you need to become their nightmare, baby. I don't care if you take me down too. You are the flame, and not just a flicker, you're the fucking inferno."

He blows out a long breath before slamming his lips over mine.

My heart melts at his words. A real man empowers his woman, he doesn't tear her down.

I'm his equal, and that in itself gives me the strength I need to win this.

"Then stick to the plan, Declan. Don't let your heart get in the way here. Vlad is coming to this on the pretense he gets me." My fingers toy with the broken heart necklace, the one wired with a tracker and a heart-rate monitor. The lifeline if things go bad.

We've got an army outside the warehouse. But this is his turf.

Vlad's a malicious bastard, and he's not going down easy.

"I know the plan," Declan says, jaw tight. "And I'm sticking to it."

I stroke his cheek, catching the fire behind his eyes. He hates that I'm the bait. But he's smart. He gets why it has to be this way.

"There's one more thing," I whisper against his lips.

"What's that, sweetheart?" he asks, twirling his finger through my ponytail.

"If the worst happens… There's something I want you to read. It's saved on the laptop you gave me."

He raises a brow.

"You make me a naughty video?" His voice dips, playful and sinful.

I laugh, patting his hard chest. "No. Well, maybe *word porn*. I started a book. Based on us. Or… what I wished for us if we were different people."

His expression shifts, brows drawing together. "Why different people? Why not us?"

"I never thought I'd see you again. I wrote it as a dream. In that world, I was free. I never betrayed you. It's our *what if*."

He's quiet, processing. "And how does it end?"

I shrug, sliding my hands up his chest. "I don't know. I never got that far."

He grabs my neck and kisses me like he's claiming my soul.

"You're going to finish it. And then we're going to reenact every spicy, dirty, kinky scene you write. Hell, I'll help inspire you," he growls.

"Oh, yeah? You want to help write our future?"

His eyes lock on mine. "More than anything."

A grin tugs at my lips as I whisper, "I'll hold you to that… Jimmy."

CHAPTER 88

DECLAN

The car comes to a halt outside the warehouse unit, its tires crunching over gravel and frozen dirt.

"Still no signs of Vlad or his men." Mikhail huffs through the comm in my ear, his voice clipped, tension rippling beneath every word.

Charlotte glances at me, eyes flashing with unease, a subtle tremor in her jaw betraying the storm she's holding at bay.

"Nothing on this side either," Conan confirms, his voice low but steady.

We've got the place surrounded. Conan's stationed with his sniper rifle in the woods to the left, nestled beneath the pines like a ghost. He's got eyes on the main entrance. Mikhail and Frankie's men are scattered in tight formation, blanketing every approach with ruthless efficiency.

"We'll go in and get in position," I say, the words grounding me. Stick to the plan. Don't let the adrenaline pull me under.

"Any contact from Drago?" I ask, glancing at Charlotte. I know her mind is half on this mission and half on the man who risked everything to protect our daughter.

"No," Enzo replies sharply.

He's our tech and our drones in the sky, cameras hacked, tracker active around Charlotte's neck. If she's scared of Vlad, I'm taking no damn chances.

"All units on standby," Enzo calls out. "Looks like we've got ourselves an ambush. Vehicles incoming in multiple directions. You've got five minutes. Get ready."

His words send an icy bolt through my spine.

"Copy," I respond, voice grim.

"Fuck yeah, let's get this party started," Conan whoops in the background, the anticipation getting to him.

"Ignore my brother," Finn mutters dryly. "He gets a little trigger-happy."

I turn to Charlotte and slide my hands slowly up her tattooed arm, feeling the tension beneath her skin, the fire simmering just under the surface.

"Come on, heartbreaker. It's time."

She slides on her jacket and zips it up; it's almost distracting, pinching her in at the waist.

"What's he done?" she asks, biting her lip as her fingers hover over the butt of her pistol.

"Just a few of his men approaching. Nothing we can't handle. We stick to the plan and get inside the warehouse."

"Drago?" she asks again, quieter this time.

I shake my head. Her sigh is heavy and full of things she won't say out loud.

"We got this, baby. It'll be over soon." I lean in and press a soft, lingering kiss to her lips, one I don't want to end, but know it has to.

Three words are on the tip of my tongue, pressing hard against the back of my teeth. But I swallow them down. She deserves to hear them when we've both made it out alive. When we're free.

I step out of the car. The cold air slaps me in the face, sharp and biting. The world around us stills, it's almost unnaturally quiet.

Straightening my suit jacket, I adjust the vest strapped to my chest, already itching to rip the damn thing off. Rounding the vehicle, I open her door and offer my hand. Her palm slides into mine. She laces our fingers together, grounding us both.

"Ready?" I ask.

She nods once, jaw tight as she looks up at the hulking steel structure before us.

"Yep," she replies, her voice strong despite the nerves dancing in her eyes. She lifts her chin defiantly.

Gunshots echo in the distance, and we pause.

"Ten armed, east side. We've got it covered," a Russian voice crackles through the comms.

"About the same approaching from the north," Enzo confirms.

Let's hope these fuckers are as incompetent as Charlotte says. Mikhail's men are savages. So are mine.

I reach for the black wooden door, fingers curling around the cold metal handle, and push it open. The scent of aging wood and grease hits me, rising from crates stacked like barricades to the ceiling.

"Damn," Charlotte mutters, scanning the rows. "What the hell are we storing here?"

"Guns and drugs, probably," I reply, sliding my hand inside my trench coat and pulling on the brass knuckles that have been itching to taste blood.

She lets go of my hand, and I hate it.

"We're sitting ducks here, Declan. I don't like it." Her voice is low, but her steps are measured as she starts pacing the aisle, her gaze scanning for weak points.

"They confirmed it's just one exit, right?" she calls.

"One way in. One way out."

"Declan. Prepare. Black truck approaching the driveway. Getting closer now," Enzo's voice cuts through.

"He's on his way, Charlotte."

She swallows, her breath stalling as she turns to the light bleeding in from the door.

She beckons me forward and pulls me behind a stack of crates. There's a perfect gap to watch the entry. Her mind is always five steps ahead.

"Do not fire first. Let's see what his play is. See where Isabella is."

"It's Vlad and a second driver. Back's blacked out. No sign of Isabella," Enzo confirms, and my gut twists.

"Enzo confirmed it's him."

She nods, eyes locked on the open doorway. The tension in the air is thick, almost tangible.

"Isabella?"

"Not in view."

She pinches the bridge of her nose, breath trembling as she crouches, sliding the blade from the hidden pocket in her boot.

"God, that's hot," I murmur, trying to slice the tension.

"Not now," she hisses, and I grab her hips with a grin.

"So fiery. Keep it that way."

She slaps my arm, just as gravel crunches outside.

"They're here," she whispers, the words almost lost beneath the sound of footsteps.

My heart thunders. Adrenaline floods my veins like gasoline.

"East side secured," Frankie confirms through my earpiece.

"I've got eyes on Vlad," Conan chimes in.

"Declan, five men, armed, coming out the back of the truck," Enzo warns.

"We've got five to kill," I tell her.

She shakes her head, a dark smirk playing on her lips.

"He should know me better than that by now," she mutters.

I screw on the silencer, and wait.

"Make that four. I got one," Conan confirms.

The first two masked men storm inside, weapons drawn, followed by two more. The lead guy gestures for them to split, two veer off while he comes straight toward us.

"You take the two right. I'll take the others," she whispers.

I nod, motioning for silence as the lead guy steps into our row.

I slip between the crates. The second he's in my sights, I squeeze the trigger. The bullet tears into his temple and he drops like a rag doll.

The man behind him fires wildly, splinters of wood explode around me. I duck low, heart hammering.

Then silence.

I peer out.

He's on his knees, gasping. Charlotte's blade slides clean across his throat, her eyes sharp and unflinching.

A grin curves my lips as I step forward and shoot him clean in the skull.

"Two down," she breathes, wiping blood on her thigh.

She grabs my hand, pulling me down the aisle toward the next two.

"One each?" she offers. That deadly glint in her eyes reigniting something primal in me.

I glance at her blood-slick fingers.

"You got it." I wink. "These are your kills."

"Two more incoming, Declan," Enzo warns.

"We got two more, baby."

She rolls her eyes, but the smile is there.

"Let's get this done and go get our girl."

I grab her face and kiss her hard. If this is the last time, she needs to know what she means to me.

"I'm fucking proud of you," I say. "Now let's finish this."

She smiles, then her eyes go wide.

"Down!" she shouts, shoving me backward.

A bullet whistles past. She spins, fires, and nails the asshole in the chest.

Two more rush us. I fire fast, catching one in the shoulder, then drop to a knee and shoot the second in the thigh. He screams as he falls.

Charlotte approaches without hesitation, pistol raised, and plants one in his skull.

"One left," I mutter.

I step forward, and pain explodes against the side of my head.

The cold steel of a gun presses into my temple, and I suck in a breath, remaining as still and calm as I can.

"Drop the weapon," a thick Russian accent growls.

"One more inside. Vlad's out of the van," Conan says with urgency in his voice.

I drop the gun, and the bastard kicks it away.

"Give us the girl, and you live."

"Where's my daughter?"

"You'll get her... once we have Charlotte."

"That wasn't the fucking deal," I growl, tightening the brass knuckles.

He cocks the safety.

Bad move.

I twist, grab his wrist, shove it up, and slam my metal fist into his jaw. The gun fires wide. I hit him again, this time blood splattering from his mouth. His wrist snaps under my grip, and the gun falls. I grab his throat, slamming him into the crates, and beat him senseless.

Letting out all of my rage until his face is unrecognizable, as he's gasping for air, I squeeze his throat. I only stop when I hear Charlotte's cry rip through the warehouse.

Everything inside me ignites.

I squeeze harder, crushing his windpipe, watching life leave his eyes.

When he goes limp, I drop him and bolt for the door.

I come to a halt as I find her smashing a man's face into the crates and tossing him onto the ground.

"Fuck you!" she screams, stomping his skull until it caves.

She looks up at me with blood on her brow and a beautiful fire in her eyes.

"You good?" she pants.

"Yeah, baby. You?"

She nods. "Felt good. He was an asshole. Better than the others though. Drago probably trained him."

Jesus. This woman.

Her rage is a thing of beauty.

"Any more?" I ask.

"Negative. Just Vlad and the driver. They haven't moved," Conan replies.

"You think you can take on two more?" I ask, already knowing the answer.

"We need backup west side!" Reggie shouts through the comm.

"We're coming," Mikhail grunts.

It's time to end this.

CHAPTER 89
CHARLOTTE

"Is she outside?" I ask, my voice raw and scraping against my throat.

Declan chews his lip, the tension in his jaw pulsing. "We have no sightings, baby. We gotta go out there."

This is exactly what the bastard wanted. Sending his men in was never the plan, just another way to stir the pot, to rattle us, to test the waters. A distraction. A twisted little appetizer before the main course of his chaos. This isn't even close to how dark Vlad's mind runs.

"Remember what you promised me, Declan," I whisper, more steel than plea. "He came here for me."

He rubs the back of his neck, eyes clouded, darker than I've seen them in days.

"I'm not letting you go without a fight, heartbreaker."

A chill rides down my spine. He laces our fingers together, grounding me, and presses a cool, heavy gun into my palm. I stare into his eyes—those eyes that have seen too much but still look at me like I'm something worth saving. A heat blooms in my chest, fierce and aching.

He is my safety. He is my future. But I'd give it all up, this love, this fierce devotion, for one thing. My daughter.

He can be her protector now. He's already proven himself worthy of that.

We walk to the doors in silence, the only sound our joined breaths. Declan cracks the door open, sunlight slashing across the dusty floor like a blade. He leads, positioning his body as a barrier between me and the world.

The distant echo of slow and deliberate claps pulls my heart into my throat.

My fate is already sealed. It was the second I left that compound five years ago.

Vlad always has something else up his sleeve. He always plays the long game.

Declan stops suddenly, his breath catching. I step beside him, heart thundering.

"Wasn't that a bit of fun?" Vlad's voice slithers into the air, thick with mockery.

A growl rips from Declan's chest.

"Yes, very," Declan bites out. "Although I'm not sure why you're so amused that your army is dropping like flies, Vlad."

Vlad shrugs, his smugness unshakable. "It's easy to regrow an army, Mr. Quinn. The world is a lot bigger than that tiny island you crawled from."

He pushes off the black truck, like a villain in an old western. Declan lifts his gun in response, steady and cold.

"Doesn't my wife look beautiful today?" Vlad coos, gesturing to me like I'm a prize at an auction.

Declan's jaw ticks, the tendons twitching under the skin.

"Oh, come on, Declan. I can call you that, right? Since you and I are on such friendly terms now." Vlad smirks, teeth flashing like a wolf.

I shift closer to Declan, my voice low. "He's up to something. Keep your cool."

"Declan is fine," he replies stiffly.

A sudden gust of cold wind lashes my face, sending goosebumps down my arms.

"Where is my daughter?" Declan demands, voice gravel.

"Patience," Vlad croons. "Pleasure first. Then business. Move over and let me see my pretty wife."

Vlad waves at Declan like he's instructing a waiter, arrogant to his core. Declan doesn't move.

"Do it," I whisper. "I think she's in the van."

"Listen to the whore. She's quite bright," Vlad mutters, tapping his temple like he's making some grand gesture of admiration.

Declan steps slightly to the side, exposing me fully to Vlad's gaze.

"That's close enough, Vlad," Declan growls.

"Oh, look at you," Vlad sighs. "Fresh-faced and glowing. So happy. So in love." He wipes imaginary dirt off his pristine shirt. "I'm itching to get my hands on you, printessa."

A violent shiver crawls up my spine. Declan inches closer, sensing it.

"Fuck you. Give us our daughter, and I won't shoot you," I snap at him, and he laughs.

"That wasn't the deal," Vlad hits back, his jaw clenching.

"Give. Me. My. Wife. Back." He spits on the ground between us. Disgust crawls over my skin.

"Not until I see my daughter," Declan bites out.

Vlad shifts his gaze to Declan, a twisted grin forming on his face. "You think you've won, don't you? With your snipers, your Russian friends, and what's this… a little Italian flavor?"

He steps closer. Declan doesn't flinch.

"Wow. Déjà vu, right, princess?"

He pulls a small black device from his pocket. My stomach knots.

"I don't need games anymore," Vlad sneers. "No chocolate factories. No riddles. I've got the one thing that still makes her kneel locked in that van."

His lips curl, finger twirling in the air like he's spinning fate itself. "Rigged to explode. I press this button, it all goes boom. Then you two can share what's left of her."

"You motherfucker," I scream, lunging at him, but Declan's arm shoots out, steel-strong, holding me back.

"And if I kill you?" Declan challenges. "What good are your bombs then?"

Vlad chuckles, the sound pure poison. "Emil's got a switch, too. Eyes on everything. One wrong move, she's ash. But I'm reasonable. Let's make a clean trade. I get my wife, you get your daughter. No one else dies."

I clench my fists behind my back to hide the tremble.

"Let me see my daughter," I say, voice calm, razor-sharp. My insides quake. But he ignores me, setting his sights only on Declan.

"Declan, do we have an agreement?"

I look up at him. His throat bobs as he swallows hard. His eyes meet mine, I can see he's torn. He doesn't want to do this. But he knows what needs to happen. So do I.

"Please, Declan. Our promise." My voice breaks.

Vlad will sleep just fine if he murders Isabella. I won't survive that.

Declan closes his eyes and inhales slowly. I can tell it's cutting him apart.

"Thermal confirms she's there, baby," he whispers.

"Do it, Declan."

"This isn't how our story ends, heartbreaker," he whispers.

I slide my hand into his and squeeze tight.

"I know," I whisper. "The prince is coming to save the queen."

His brow furrows in confusion.

"Ask Isabella to tell you the story."

One last squeeze, and I let go. The worst kind of letting go.

I turn to Vlad with fury in my eyes. I will never let him see my fear.

"Well?" he barks.

"Yes, deal," Declan replies.

"Enzo can't cut Emil's feed. Can't trace him," Declan mutters, leaning into me.

"Fuck." My breath hitches.

"This is how we do it," Vlad declares. "Charlotte walks into the van. Isabella walks out. We're both within blast range, so you know I'm not bluffing."

Declan nods, jaw like iron. "Fine."

Vlad gestures, his smirk a brand on my soul. I force my feet forward, my rage a leash that keeps me from launching at him.

He opens the van doors, and my world shatters.

There she is.

Isabella, curled into the corner, arms wrapped around her legs, sobs shaking her tiny frame. My heart dies a little more.

"Baby," I croak. "It's Mommy."

She lifts her head, those blue eyes just like Declan's, locking on mine.

"I need you to go to Daddy. He's here to save you, baby. Just like in the story. He'll keep you safe."

She shakes her head, tears slipping silently.

"Awww. Sweet little reunion. I gave you a minute. I'm generous like that," Vlad mocks.

"Fuck you," I hiss.

He wags a finger in my face and I want to bite it clean off.

"I'm going to have so much fun with you, princess."

I turn away from him, bile rising.

"In the truck you go. Get your brat out here." He clicks his fingers like she's nothing.

I climb in, arms wrapping around Isabella. She clings to me like I'm her whole world, just as she is to me. The reality sets in that this could be our last time. We never anticipated a van rigged with explosives. We're off track now, and I have to find a way to keep myself alive.

"Shhh, baby, it's okay," I whisper, my voice cracking. "Daddy's going to save you. And then, just like in our story, come back and save the Queen. He's my prince, remember?"

Tears fall, and so do mine.

"Declan," I choke, "please… take her."

Even if it tears me in half.

Even if I never see the sun again.

Her life over mine. Always.

CHAPTER 90

DECLAN

Enzo's voice crackles in my ear, low and emotionless. "I repeat, do not shoot. The drone is showing that the van is rigged to the heavens. Stick to the plan."

His calm doesn't soothe the fire tearing through my chest.

Watching this unfold is a special kind of torture.

Charlotte's tears streak down her cheeks. The pain in her eyes will haunt me for the rest of my life.

Broken. Shattered.

Absolutely heartbroken.

Isabella's scream cuts through the silence like a blade.

"Mommy! I want my mommy!"

Her voice is so small, so desperate, and it makes a sob catch in my throat.

Charlotte peels our daughter off her neck, every movement a new kind of agony. I step forward, one arm out. The second Isabella's within reach, I cradle her close, tucking her into my side like I was born to do it.

She fits there like she always belonged. But she was always meant to have her mommy by her side, not just me. This isn't right.

Her warm tears soak through my shirt as I keep my gun trained on Vlad's skull.

Charlotte wipes her face and steps backward into the van.

"Good work," Vlad mutters, then slams the doors shut like he's closing a coffin.

The last image burned into my brain is her face, twisted in grief and fury and love.

She doesn't deserve this. She never did. And I'm going to do everything in my power to make this right.

I'll stick to the plan, for now.

I step back, holding Isabella like the world depends on it. Because it does. She is my world now.

Vlad opens his mouth to say something else, but the sound of tires crunching gravel shuts him up fast. Conan barrels into the scene in an armored truck.

Vlad doesn't even flinch. He lifts the detonator, calm as ever, like this is a game of poker instead of lives on the line.

"If you try to intercept the car, I'll blow it up with her in it," he says, smiling like the devil himself. "I'm always happy to go to hell if I'm dragging her with me."

My jaw ticks. My finger trembles on the trigger.

"Get Isabella to safety, Declan." Enzo again. Still calm. Still cold.

But Isabella's sobs tug me back from the edge.

"You have my word," I grit out to Vlad.

For now.

Because I'm going to kill him. There's not a universe where that doesn't happen.

Vlad hops in the truck and turns the key. Conan rushes toward me, shielding me and Isabella as gravel sprays under the tires.

"This is part of the plan, brother. It will be okay," Conan says, placing a heavy hand on my shoulder.

I don't answer. I just hold her tighter.

"I want Mommy," Isabella cries.

I run my fingers through her soft curls, kissing the crown of her head.

"I'll get Mommy back, baby girl. I promise. Daddy is going to fix this."

I open the truck door, heart heavy, chest caving in. She pulls back just slightly, and when I look into her face, it hits me like a freight train.

My eyes. Charlotte's button nose. That pouty lip quivering with heartbreak. A perfect mix of us.

"You're really my daddy?" she whispers.

"I am, baby. I am."

I keep her on my lap as we slide into the truck.

"Who is he?" she asks softly, nodding to Conan.

"That's your Uncle Conan," I say.

"I'm the fun one," he adds with a wink.

A faint smile ghosts across her lips. It wrecks me. I nod to my brother and hold her a little tighter.

All I can think about is Charlotte.

She should be sitting here, not me. I don't give a fuck if this was how it had to go, I hate every part of it.

And I won't stop until I make this right.

I slide my phone out of my pocket and pull up Charlotte's tracking device app. My heart sinks when I see the high heartbeat pulsing in the top corner.

But I watch that little red dot moving, and it gives me hope.

We have her, and we will get her back.

CHAPTER 91

I sabella's screams echo in my ears.

I feel like a terrible mom. I hope one day she understands. My hand clasps my necklace, knowing I have people watching over me helps.

I've come up against Vlad before, and he let me live.

This time, I won't be so lucky.

But I know he won't offer me a quick way out. The asshole thrives off feeling powerful. Perhaps because he's so under his sister's thumb in their empire. I was there to feed his male ego.

There is a reason he kept me hidden from her. He is scared.

I'll endure the pain while Declan gets Isabella to safety. I owe them both.

And if I am wrong about Vlad's motives, I won't go down without a fight.

I will see my daughter grow up.

I will prove to Declan he can trust me.

And I will end my husband.

He thinks he's won, but he has no idea how far a mother will go to protect her child.

He crossed his final line by putting my baby in a rigged-up car.

No matter what, Vlad will die today.

If I go with him, so be it. At least I'll leave this earth knowing the two people I love are safe.

CHAPTER 92

DECLAN

"Hey, baby. Would you like to go and do some coloring with Uncle Conan while Daddy does some work?" I ask, crouching down to her eye level.

I read online that this position makes me less of a threat to her. I have no idea what she's seen growing up. Or how Vlad has treated her.

She nods and chews on her lip, just like Charlotte.

"Jax brought some of his daughter's toys and coloring sets, they're in the back bedroom." Mikhail says from behind.

"Wow. That's cool." Her eyes light up, and my heart melts.

I'll do anything to keep a smile on her face.

Conan holds out his gigantic hand and she places her tiny one inside.

"You wanna walk or fly there?" he asks.

"Umm…" She looks at me, and I smile.

"Fly?"

"You got it, kiddo." He picks her up, and she lets out the cutest giggle as he carries her through the safe house.

"Declan. In here," Enzo's distinctive voice booms from one of the rooms.

Heading in there with Finn on my tail, I push open the glowing room, and as I step through, I see the wall filled with monitors.

"Where is she?"

He points to the middle screen and I focus on the red dot.

"Still on the road. I've done some digging, I think I have an idea where they're heading." Enzo spins his laptop on the desk to face me.

Scratching my head, I frown at the screen.

"A farm?"

He clicks the pad and pulls up a document.

"Looks like he's a co-owner. And then—" He pauses, changing tabs.

This time, he zooms out of the map, pointing to the top right of the screen.

"They've passed his house and any other notable stops. But to me, it seems Charlotte's tracker is heading that direction. Coincidence? I think not."

Finn steps closer and clears his throat.

"And if we guess wrong? Getting this a even just few minutes out could be life or death?" Finn questions.

I clench my fist at my sides.

"I say we head on the road, does Mikhail have any other contacts here?"

Enzo shakes his head.

"Not in this territory. He's taken a risk being here already."

I swallow.

"This is what you'll be dealing with." He pulls up a picture of a large barn with a straw roof.

And pigs. So many fucking pigs outside.

"Probably uses them to eat his bodies," Finn says matter-of-factly.

"Quite clever. Although, dumb registering any business in his real name," he continues, and Enzo nods.

"Looks like we're going pig farming." I clap Finn on the shoulder.

"Our men are loading up the armored trucks now. Although, for speed, Mikhail managed to source a Bugatti Veyron. You'll get there first in that. In the meantime, I'll continue hacking into what I can. Keep the comms in."

He ferociously begins typing, and I take that as my cue to vacate.

As Finn stops by the front door, I pause, looking to the room where Isabella is.

"I need to see her before I go. Help them load up, I'll send Conan down," I tell him.

"You got it."

A sinking feeling resonates in me. Saying goodbye hurts. How Charlotte had found the strength to do this, I don't know. But I will forever admire her.

As I approach the door, I hear her little giggles, and I wipe my hands over my face.

Fuck.

I need Charlotte back.

CHAPTER 93
CHARLOTTE

The door swings open, and my instinct is to lunge at him. Before my feet leave the ground, I come to a halt, staring at the detonator in his hand.

"Out," he commands.

"Now!" he screams, and I jolt back.

Doing as he says, I need to waste time, drag this out long enough to be rescued if I can't find myself an opening.

So I slowly make my way to the doors and drop onto the ground; as I do, two men grab my arms, holding me tightly in place.

"Tie her wrists and make sure she can't get out," he tells his men.

They force me to my knees on the dirt, and I pull up my nose as the foul pig smell assaults me. Yanking my arms behind my back, I hiss through the pain as the rough rope cuts into my wrists.

I kick my legs into the floor as they drag me away from the van, and they hold me still once I'm upright.

Vlad's hands connect to my ribs, and I cry out.

"I love it when you fight me," he whispers, and I shiver.

"Fuck. You." I spit in his face.

He harshly grips the back of my neck and presses a gun to my temple as his men head off into the barn before us.

"Walk," he hisses.

So I do, taking the smallest steps I can.

"The longer it takes, the longer your friend suffers." That menacing tone in his voice makes me come to a halt.

"Friend?"

"Patience, princess. It's a surprise, just so you don't feel lonely."

I close my eyes, and my heart sinks.

Drago.

That's why he wasn't at the meet. Why we couldn't contact him.

He shoves me through the first set of wooden double doors, filled with haystacks and wooden poles. Making a sharp right, with force he pushes me into the next room so hard I fall on my face into the straw.

"Dumb bitch, get up," he yells, grabbing my ponytail and yanking me to my feet.

"Look who it is," he whispers, his breath hitting my cheek, and my nose wrinkles.

I tip my chin up, and tears burn in my eyes as I look across the room.

I hardly recognize Drago, blood pours from his face, all bruised and swollen. He's chained by his wrists and ankles, spread out, between two poles.

"Fuck!" he groans as one of Vlad's men lays his fist into his ribs.

"Let him go, Vlad. You have me." It's worth a shot.

Vlad chuckles, spinning me to face him and grabbing my neck.

"What, so he can help you escape from me again? You think I don't know. I've had quite the revelation these past couple of weeks."

"Tatiana will kill you for this. Drago hasn't done anything wrong," I lie, testing to see if my theory is correct.

He squeezes my windpipe harder and lifts me off the ground.

"If I kill him, she won't know a damn thing. Because you'll be dead too. And guess who will be getting the blame? Or perhaps I'll force you to kill him as punishment." He wiggles his finger in my face.

"I won't do it." I pull my head back and launch it into his nose.

"Bitch."

He tosses me to the ground; as he swings back his boot, I instinctively brace for the impact into my ribs.

I scream out in pain as he connects his foot.

"You don't have to. But now that I've said it, I like the sound of that. Maybe after our games. Get up. Whore." His spit connects to my cheek.

Pain radiates through my torso and the wind is kicked out of me. Each breath in is agonizing.

Hooking my legs back, I tense my body, rolling and sitting myself upright onto my knees, and manage to get up one leg at a time.

His fingers dig into my shoulder as he drags me towards a beam in the center of the room, facing Drago.

"Back against it." He points to the beam, and I shuffle back until I hit against the splintering wood.

Drago looks up at me, blood dripping down his face.

"Be brave," he mouths, and I nod.

Vlad gets to work tying rope around my middle so tightly I yelp. Even through my thin jacket, it burns through. He starts at my waist and goes all the way up to my biceps, my wrists still bound behind my back.

"That feel comfortable? Bet you wish you could have the chains back from the bed. That must seem like heaven in comparison," Vlad mutters, and I bite my tongue.

"Any time I'm in your presence is hell," I tell him.

"I'm just preparing you for where you're heading. You belong in hell. You aren't worthy of anything else." His dark eyes bore into mine, and he smirks.

"If you had just behaved and not been a whore, we could have lived a nice life. Your dad would still be alive. Maybe we could have had a kid. Some dogs? But no. You had to spoil it."

"I would have never. I am not yours, and I never will be."

My head flies to the side as his hand connects with my cheek.

"You will always be mine, printessa," he hisses.

I shake my head.

"You've abused me in every way possible for ten fucking years. Do you honestly believe there is anything left you can do to me that would actually hurt? Kill me? Fine. End this nightmare. But just know, even in my death, that isn't the end, that is the beginning of your purgatory. And that, asshole, will be worse than anything you could ever do to me. I'm not alone in this world anymore. You think you're evil? You have no idea how bad he is. The man who truly owns every single part of me. You are not the devil. He is. And I'll be happy to burn in hell knowing you'll be following me soon. Then, I'll torture you just like you have me for eternity." I'm almost breathless as I finish my speech.

"You think he gives a shit now he's got his daughter back? Why would he want a useless mother like you back to fuck her up? He is a clever man, he won't start a war for you. Worthless. Bitch."

His words hurt worse than anything else he could do to me.

I would die for my daughter. I've done everything I could under the circumstances. Yet, that guilt eats away at me every day.

Could I have been a better mom?

Did I really do everything to protect her?

Would she really be better off without me?

A tear rolls down my cheek. I wish I could wipe it away. Just how I wish I could cleanse myself of my sins.

Be the mom that she truly deserves.

Not this monster constantly fighting to survive.

"Ah, interesting. My words hurt you, don't they? Your little soft spot."

Drago cries out, and I look over, and my eyes close, feeling his pain.

"Oh, and watching people you love get hurt. You're giving yourself away, Charlotte. Having Isabella made you weak."

It made me weak so I could open my heart, and I will never feel guilty about that.

Vlad's eyes darken as he backs away from me towards the shelves on the wall.

"What do you think, princess, would this hurt?"

He picks up a carving knife and runs his finger along the flat edge of the blade.

I keep silent.

"Come on, play the game. Would this hurt?"

"Yes! You fucking know it will," I shout.

He laughs, and my anger continues to brew. I expect him to walk back towards me, but instead, his sights shift to Drago.

I can't look.

The sound of fabric ripping fills the empty barn.

"Charlotte, it's no fun you looking at the floor, is it? Come on, eyes on your husband. Watch how good I am at slicing up meat. That's why I got the farm. To practice."

I feel physically sick.

Drago's nostrils flare as Vlad slowly draws the knife from between his pecs, all the way down to his belly button.

A trail of blood follows the silver.

Drago hisses, his face reddening. If he could get out of those chains, he would stomp Vlad into the ground.

He's bigger and stronger than him, and far more trained.

How the hell did he land up here?

"You're a fucking asshole, Vlad. You will pay for this," Drago warns, his eyes full of fury.

"By who? Huh? I answer to no one," Vlad replies smugly.

"Your sister. You, like all of us, are under her control. You can't deny it. You are nothing compared to her."

It's Drago's turn to smirk.

"Truth hurts, doesn't it? Asshole. Once Tatiana finds out the truth, you'll be a dead man. I should have told her years ago."

A growl erupts from Vlad's chest, and he fires his fist into Drago's gut, eliciting an agonizing cry from Drago.

"So does my fist," Vlad spits back and backs away.

As Vlad's phone rings, he huffs and pulls it out of his pants pocket, his eyebrow twitching before he cuts it off.

It starts again immediately, and he shoves it back in his pocket, spinning to face me.

"Your turn, wife." He waves the knife in the air, and my body starts to shake.

I let out a hiss of air as he runs it along my jaw and settles it against my throat.

"Beg for your life."

I shake my head.

"No."

"Beg!" he screams in my face, his saliva coating my skin.

"Beg you, bitch! Beg for my mercy. Beg to become my whore. Tell me you belong to me. Tell me how fucking sorry you are."

My heart almost beats out of my ribs, his words cutting into me.

"Why? Why do you even want me, Vlad? Why not get a woman who doesn't find you repulsive?"

I doubt she exists. The man has the personality of a brick wall.

"Because we're married. I chose you, and I will never let you go." He presses the blade harder against my skin, and I swallow.

I have to kill time.

"Please don't kill me," I whisper.

He leans in closer, and I wince.

"Louder."

"Please, Vlad. Let me live. I don't want to die," I say louder.

"Keep going."

He runs the blade down my throat and shivers run down my spine.

"I."

I can't say it. It's not true in my heart. It never was.

"You, what?" he pushes.

"I belong to you."

The words are acid on my tongue, choking me. But it works, he removes the knife and grips my cheeks, making my lips pout.

"That's my good little wife."

He presses his lips against mine, almost suffocating me.

"I can't wait to taste the rest of you, one last time," he whispers against my lips, and I want to scream.

I want to lodge that blade through his heart.

CHAPTER 94
DECLAN

I feel her big blue eyes staring at me from across the table. My heart melts looking at her, she even frowns just like her mom.
"You finished drawing?" I ask her.
I'm way out of my depth here.
She taps the pen against her cheek and pouts.
"I have. When's Mommy coming home?"
I rub my chest.
"Soon. I promise. I'm going to get her now."
She nods, her brain processing.
"The bad man has her." That frown appears again.
I take a seat next to her and look at the stick people scribbles.
I point at the smallest drawing.
"Is that you? Awesome job," I praise her.
"It's me, you and Mommy," she gushes.
"Can you take it to her?"
I pick up the paper and hold it out in front of us.
"Mommy said that the Queen can save herself in her story, but she needs the Prince, doesn't she?"
I swallow the lump in my throat.
"Is this the story Mommy tells you?" I whisper, trying to stop my voice from breaking.

"Yea. You'll have to get her to tell you. It's the best story. But I make her change the ending so the prince saves her from the bad man, and they live happily ever after with their princess."

She snuggles up against my side, and I close my eyes, resting my head on top of hers.

"The Queen is the strongest woman on the planet, the Prince just needs to help her win, that's all. Not saving, just protecting her so she can be the powerful woman she is."

She nods against my arm and her fingers trace the tattoos on my hands as she lets out a yawn.

"You have no color on your tattoos? None of them?"

I shake my head and roll up my sleeves to show her more.

"Nope. No color in my life."

Well, until she and her mom arrived.

Fuck, I miss her more than anything in the world right now. She should be the one sitting here, not me.

I cannot do this without her.

"But we all need color in our life," Isabella says softly.

"That we do, Princess. Want to add some to mine?"

The smile that lights up her face makes me want to permanently get whatever drawings she picks inked into my skin.

I can't fucking do this without Charlotte.

I want to hate her for this, but I can't. Not when I saw the pain in her eyes.

That silent plea will haunt me forever.

I promised to break her, to ruin her, when all along that was never what I truly wanted.

I am alive because of her, but I've never felt more dead inside without her.

I watch silently as Isabella makes the skull pink and draws some new flowers.

"Show Mommy this. She loves flowers."

I stroke her hair.

"I know she does."

I can't even look at her. I feel awful, but all I see is Charlotte, and it's like I've been stabbed through the heart.

"Maybe I'll add some color just like you've drawn; I'll get it tattooed on. To represent what you've added to my life, baby girl."

She grins at me and my heart explodes.

I'll tattoo anything she draws on me if it means she smiles like that at me.

I turn away and wipe my tears.

I cuddle my daughter tight. I never want to let her go, not now that I have her.

"I love you," I whisper.

Guilt sits in my chest, suffocating me.

I never told Charlotte I love her. Even though I do, with all my damn heart.

Five years I spent hating her, when actually, I simply wanted her to heal those shattered pieces inside me. To just love me and remind me that I'm not a monster.

To look at me how she did in Italy.

I made her a promise to protect Isabella with my life, I'll honor that.

She needs her mom.

We both do.

"I'll be back soon, okay. I promise. Daddy is never leaving you."

"Okay, Daddy," she chirps.

That gives me a new sense of determination to give her the life she deserves.

Closing the door softly behind me, I head out to the rest of the guys loading up the trucks.

"We good to go?" I ask, checking my Rolex.

"You're with me, bro." Conan hits the hood of the all-black Bugatti with his palm.

"And Finn?" I question.

I need both of my brothers nearby. They're the two I truly trust with my fucking life.

"I'll be in the first truck behind. I've brought medical supplies, just in case," he tells me softly, and secures his flat cap.

"Enzo has already set the Bugatti up with the navigation to the tracker, we're good to go." Conan taps the metal before hopping in.

I do the same, and the engine roars to life.

"Let me guess, you'll be purchasing one of these to add to your collection?" I ask him.

My head almost hits the dash as he flies out of the driveway.

"Fuck. Yes. I'll get ten."

"Just watch out for ice," I tell him, keeping my eyes on the road.

"We got enough weapons in this thing?"

"Yeah, it's got a Frunk. I filled it with some goodies. Don't worry."

"A what?" I shake my head.

"Front trunk. Come on, brother. Get your head back."

I shoot him a look, and a laugh escapes me when I see his cheeky grin.

No matter what the situation, even when it feels like my entire life is falling to pieces, I can always rely on Conan to lighten the mood.

Even if it's for a few seconds.

"I can feel it in my gut, Dec. We're gonna storm in there, get your girl, and kill that motherfucker. I know it. He's played his game. Now it's our turn."

I hope he's right.

"Let's hope."

A seriousness washes over his face, and he looks at me.

"We got Dad watching over us; we will be just fine."

Rubbing my hands over my face, I know I can't lose her.

That heartache will be the end of me.

"Well, foot to the floor, brother. Get me to her."

CHAPTER 95

CHARLOTTE

Minutes feel like hours.

Every punch, every kick, every slice inflicted on Drago I can almost feel.

I don't know how much more he can take.

Drago tugs on the chains, screaming in pain as Vlad swipes the blade along his thigh, and I wince.

"Stop!" I scream.

I can't watch this.

"Shut the fuck up," Vlad snaps back.

The ringing starts up again, this is now the fifth time. Whoever is trying to contact him really isn't letting up.

He mutters under his breath, cutting the call yet again.

There isn't an inch of Drago that isn't smeared in blood. It's like witnessing a horror film. Both eyes are now closed up and purple. His blood soaks into the straw by our feet.

"Drago! Stay awake!" I cry.

He groans, moving his head as Vlad lands another punch.

The phone goes off again, this time, Vlad tips back his head, releasing a frustrated groan.

"With me," he orders his lackey.

"I won't be long, Charlotte. My sister is relentless. Although, I'll start dropping some seeds about your murdering ways." He winks at me and blows me a kiss, storming past me.

As the door slams shut, I let out a breath of relief.

"Drago!" I call out.

"Hmm?"

"Talk to me. Stay with me."

The amount of blood he's losing, he doesn't have long. I need Declan.

"W-where is Isabella?" he grits out.

"Safe. With Declan. It's okay."

He nods. I swear I see a tear rolling down his cheek.

"How did you end up here?" I ask him.

I need to keep his mind active.

"Got caught. Trying to defuse the bomb," he sputters, and blood flies out of his mouth.

His head drops and my own tears start to fall. As I erratically thrash in my ropes, it cuts deeper into my skin. He's spent the last ten years being responsible for my safety. He put himself in that position. I became his problem to lighten the wrath of Vlad on me. That was the deal. He keeps me in line and trained to go on jobs, we all stay alive.

"Drago!" I scream at the top of my lungs.

"Do not fucking leave me here on my own. Fight, goddamn it. Fight, please. We need you."

He grunts again.

"I'm sorry, Drago. I'm so sorry I landed you in this mess," I sob.

He shakes his head.

"I'd do it again. No regrets. Not for you two. We did it, warrior."

I shake my head.

"No. No. We both survive this."

He coughs again, this time heaving for air.

"I'm proud of you, Charlotte."

"Drago, don't do this. Please."

"It's my time," he says quietly.

The warm tears freefall down my face.

"Just hold on a while longer, Drago."

"Tell Tatiana," he hisses in pain and stops talking.

"Tell her what, Drago?"

"Remember who she is." Is the last thing he says.

"What does that mean?"

Would that save me if it came down to it?

His body slumps forward against the chains. Fuck, he's out.

I squeeze my eyes shut, hoping this is all one big nightmare and I'll wake up when I open my eyes.

We can't lose him.

CHAPTER 96
DECLAN

"Turn the headlights off." I order Conan as we approach the picket fence.

He comes to a stop before we enter the gravel at the entrance.

"Enzo, how far behind are the rest of the guys?" I ask.

"Around ten minutes."

I scoff.

"Conan, I told you it could go faster." I hiss.

"The ice, brother. You wanna flip this thing and die? That won't save your girl."

He has a point, so I shut my mouth.

Conan zooms in on the map on the screen and looks ahead.

"I have an idea. A really, really fucking reckless one. But an idea nonetheless."

"Carry on." I tell him.

I trust him.

"She's on the right hand side of the barn. Looking at this, this entrance is separate. That's where the guards will be. If I had to take an educated guess."

"Hmm." I scratch my stubble.

"Well, let's fucking see how fast this thing can go." He taps the steering wheel.

"Take 'em by surprise with one hell of a bang. And just hope we don't die."

He grins at me.

"You're suggesting driving through the doors?"

I blink at him, trying to fathom his idea.

"I don't have ten minutes to wait. She's in there. There are two of us, and we have no idea how many there are inside. But she's away from the car if the tracker is exact."

"It is exact," Enzo chimes in from my earpiece.

I look at the map and her tracker. But it's her heart rate that concerns me.

One hundred and ninety-five beats a minute.

"Fuck it. Let's do it."

He slams the gas, and the Bugatti lurches forward like it's hungry for blood. The gates splinter, exploding into jagged shrapnel. My head snaps back against the seat. The barn looms ahead.

"Hold on," he says.

No warning. No mercy.

We hit the doors full force.

Two guards don't even get a chance to turn around.

We barrel through like vengeance on wheels. Just how it was meant to be.

Because I'm not walking in for a rescue.

I'm walking in for a reckoning.

CHAPTER 97
CHARLOTTE

The wooden beam above me groans like it's about to give, and I barely get a second to brace before a shockwave slams through the space behind me. The floor shakes. Dust rains from the rafters.

Holy shit.

He's here. I don't need to see him to know it. I feel him in my lungs, in my ribs, in the way my blood suddenly knows how to run faster. Declan.

"Drago!" I shout. "Wake the hell up!"

Nothing. He's still out, blood slicking his side like a slow leak. His skin is too pale. Too still.

I swallow down the panic clawing up my throat.

Another gunshot cracks through the walls, and I flinch.

I need to be out there.

With him. In it. Fighting back.

I suck in a deep breath. I can't fall apart now. Not when we're this close to ending it.

CHAPTER 98

DECLAN

I duck behind the Bugatti's door as a bullet slams into the metal with a deafening thunk. It misses my head by inches.

Conan's behind me, wrestling a guard like he's done it a thousand times, but my focus is locked on the bastard across the room. Vlad. My finger twitches on the trigger.

I lean forward and fire twice, missing him by a hair.

"Fuck it," I hiss. Some twisted stroke of divine luck put Vlad right here as we crashed through the fucking doors. We damn near turned him into a hood ornament, but Conan pulled the brakes just in time.

Doesn't matter. He's not mine to kill. He belongs to her.

We just need to tear through him to get to the barn. To Charlotte.

"Why don't you come out here and fight me like a real man?" Vlad's voice slithers across the room.

I reach down into the floorboard and pull out the brass dusters and slide them on.

"Why?" I spit back. "You out of bullets?"

Another shot hammers the car door, and I flinch instinctively. Conan drops down beside me, breath ragged, blood on his jaw.

"Plan?" he growls.

I jerk my chin toward the side door. "You run. Get Charlotte. I'll keep him busy."

Conan's eyes flick to Vlad, hiding behind a beam. "On three?"

I nod once.

"One. Two—"

I rise like a fucking storm and unload in Vlad's direction, bullets ricocheting off wood and steel. Conan breaks for the door, his massive frame smashing through like it's paper.

I pivot to track him, but pain explodes through my skull, white-hot and blinding. Fuck. My vision flashes. I stagger backward, grabbing my head.

Vlad's fist swings again, but I catch his wrist mid-air with my metal grip. He swings a plank at me and I kick him in the shin, knocking it out of his hands.

Before he can recover, I crack my brass knuckles straight into his mouth. He flies back into the shelving like a ragdoll. I'm wheezing, bent over, but adrenaline roars through my veins like jet fuel. He stumbles, and that gives me time to grab the plank.

As I swing at him, he blocks it with a goddamn iron pole.

"Fuck you," I growl.

He slams the pole into my ribs and I see stars, but I don't go down. I lunge, headbutting him hard enough that he stumbles. His arms lock around my waist and shove me back until I slam into a support beam.

His hands go to my throat, squeezing, making my eyes bulge as I grapple to get him off.

"Not so clever now, are you, Mr. Quinn?" he spits. "Dying for that whore."

His breath is acid on my face. I jam my thumb into his eye, hard and deep, enough to make him scream and release me.

Spotting the gun nestled in the straw on the ground, I don't waste the moment, I dive to retrieve it.

His expression turns ghost-white as he sees what I'm reaching for.

The gun.

My hand wraps around it, just as his boot crashes into the back of my skull.

I roll, dizzy but focused, and sweep my leg out, catching his shin, and he drops with a grunt.

I rise with my gun raised, pointing at his head.

"Never fucking call her that again," I snarl.

He spits blood right by my boot. "Go on. Shoot me."

His teeth are painted red, and he's smiling like a devil that's already lost his soul.

I stare down at him.

My finger twitches.

And that grin. That fucking grin makes it too hard to not pull the trigger.

"Fine," I mutter.

I drop my aim and fire. Right into his kneecap.

He screams like a little bitch.

Good.

Because he isn't my kill. He's Charlotte's. And she's coming.

CHAPTER 99
CHARLOTTE

As a red faced Conan rushes over to me, a mixture of relief and disappointment washes over me.

"Where is he?" I ask, desperately needing the answer.

"Dealing with Vlad. Let me get you out."

He jogs over to the shelving and starts throwing objects across the floor, returning with a machete.

"Careful with that," I warn him and he frowns.

He gets to work on the other side of the beam, cutting at the ropes until I finally feel relief.

I look down at the burns all over my skin through the open cuts of my jacket.

"Help Drago. Please."

Conan's eyes go wide as he really takes in the scene before us.

"Is he?"

I shake my head. Drago can't be, I won't believe it.

"Save him, Conan," I almost sob, my legs trembling beneath me.

Conan thrusts a pistol into my numb hands.

"Go to my brother. Finn will be here any minute, he will fix him up good." His deep voice is full of sincerity and I almost believe him.

But as I glance over and see the blood and the color draining from Drago by the minute, I don't know.

My eyes snap to Conan as a gunshot rings out from the other room.

"Go!" he bellows, and I run through the pain.

Even on weak legs, I run to him as blind panic consumes me.

As I hear the cries of Vlad, I come to a halt at the door, and a smile creeps up on my lips when Declan twists his head.

Those eyes.

Nothing else matters.

They tell me everything I'll ever need to know.

I am safe. I am loved. I am worthy.

"Declan," I breathe out.

"Heartbreaker." His voice breaks, and I run to him, wrapping my arms around him as we collide.

He pulls back and holds my cheek.

"Are you okay?" he whispers, and I nod. His gaze glances down my body and he hisses, shaking his head. The fury is evident as his jaw ticks, and he spins to face Vlad.

"You left marks on my girl, Vlad. You left fucking marks!" he shouts.

Before Vlad can respond, Declan fires another bullet into his good knee.

The screams of his agony are a sweet symphony to me.

"I'm going to let her bring hell down on you, Vlad. And I'm going to enjoy watching every fucking minute," Declan grits out as Vlad rolls around the floor.

Declan slams his boot on Vlad's throat.

"Come here, baby." Declan motions to me and I step forward.

He wraps his arm around my waist and pulls me snug against his side. My breath hitches as he tips my chin up with his hand, covered in brass.

"Remember how I told you if you burn, I'll burn right beside you?"

I nod and slide my hands up his chest.

"Yes. How could I forget?"

He frowns, his head tipping to the side as he leans in and presses a kiss to my cheek.

"I was wrong. That isn't love. What I should have said is that I will push you out of the way of the flames and burn for you. Because I fucking love you, heartbreaker. So goddamn much. And that's what I realized. Love is burning for the other person. Not with them."

Tears well in my eyes as he strokes my cheek.

"Before we end this, once and for all, I need you to know that. I need you to know how much I adore you, just as you are. I'm going to tell you every single day for the rest of my life. My heart beats for you."

I grab his throat and drag his lips down to mine, pouring every ounce of me that I have left to give.

"I'm not sure how much of my heart I have left, but you and Isabella, you two own all of it. You saved me, Declan Quinn. Without even realizing it, you brought me back to life; you allowed me to survive. You gave me hope. I love you, Declan, and I will until the day I finally lose the fight. I will love you with everything I am and everything that I am yet to become."

Vlad's groans cause Declan to growl, so he stamps his boot down harder.

"Shut the fuck up, asshole. Don't ruin this beautiful moment," he spits out, and I can't help but giggle.

"This is exactly how our story should go," I whisper, and Declan shakes his head.

"I'll take any plot twist that means I get the woman of my dreams and our little girl. It doesn't matter how we got here, all that matters is the Queen is safe, and the bad man is about to lose his life in the most excruciating way to pay for his sins."

I nod, my hands beginning to tremble as I glance down at my tormentor.

Helpless and weak on the floor.

My eyes go wide and my heart stops as a swarm of men enter the door. It's soon replaced by relief as I recognize Finn, holding a black duffle bag in one hand and a fucking automatic rifle in the other.

"Where do you need me?" he asks.

A lightbulb goes off in my head.

"In the barn, Finn. Go help Drago. Please."

My body freezes, and I fight back the emotions threatening to spill out.

"Finn, in there, help Conan get Drago out. The rest of you, secure the area and wait. We need some time here," Declan commands his men.

Finn rushes off and the rest retreat, leaving just us three in the room.

"Drago?"

I look down, not even wanting to think about it.

"It's not good, Declan. I don't know if he will make it out of this one." I hiccup on a sob, and he nuzzles me against his chest.

"Finn is the best of the best. We will do everything we can, Charlotte. I promise you."

He pulls back and tips my chin up to him.

"He would want you to end this, right? He did everything to help you get to this moment."

I nod, a new burning rage taking over as I glance at Vlad on the floor.

"It's time for the Queen to take her revenge, heartbreaker. Let this motherfucker feel your agony, let it all out and leave it to burn with him in this barn."

A smile creeps up on my lips as he leans in for another kiss.

"Could you be any more perfect, Declan Quinn?" I say against his lips.

"Trust me, I'm nowhere near perfect. But for you, I'm going to try my damn hardest to be. Get ready to be worshipped, exactly how you should be."

He brings my hand up to his lips and presses a soft kiss, his blue eyes piercing into mine.

"Now how do you want this to go, baby? I'm just here to help, this is your kill. You earned this one." He winks, nodding down to my husband on the floor.

I pout. I've dreamed about this for ten years.

This is for my parents. For my years of suffering at his hand.

For every time he's hit me.

For every time he's chained me up.

For every time he's fucked me.

This is for the innocent eighteen-year old Charlotte, who lost her life to this man.

For the evil he created.

I want to torture him in every possible way just as he has done to me.

He made me a monster, and I will be that woman for one last time; only then can I evolve into the woman I truly want to be.

CHAPTER 100
DECLAN

Charlotte leads the way back into the barn, and I get a sight of Drago as Finn and Conan struggle to lift him out.

Finn's face tells me everything I need to know.

This is not good.

"I'll do what I can in the truck. Enzo has more supplies being delivered to the safe house," he says, keeping his tone neutral.

I nod, knowing not to press further.

I never got to shake Drago's hand for saving my girls. It only gives me the power I need to drag this squirming asshole across the ground.

"Chain him up where Drago was," Charlotte orders.

Now isn't the time for her sassiness to make my cock twitch, but God damn.

I catch the sadness in her eyes as Drago passes her, and I drop Vlad in a pile of Drago's blood.

I can't resist slamming my boot into his dick as I connect the metal to either wrist as tight as I can possibly do them.

Brushing my hands on my coat, I grab the end of the chain and heave to pull, and Charlotte does the same on her beam until we have him in an upright position with his arms spread.

"Good job, baby," I praise her with a wink.

That little smile makes my stomach flip.

It's even the small things that make her eyes light up.

I step back and allow Charlotte to rummage through the

shelving units for her weapon of choice. Crossing my arms across my chest, I glare at Vlad.

He disgusts me.

Her face beams as she returns to me with a small, rusty blade. Out of everything she had a choice of, this surprises me.

"Trust me, Declan. You might not want to look, though," she says cheekily.

I edge closer as she approaches Vlad and runs the blade along his jaw.

"Feel good, Vlad?" she mocks.

"Bitch," he shouts.

"Keep your mouth shut, or I'll rip out your teeth and slice your tongue with this rusty knife."

I bite back my smile. Fuck, I'm proud of her.

"Just fucking kill me, Charlotte. I don't need to listen to another minute of your bullshit."

Charlotte's menacing laugh fills the room.

"Pathetic man. Giving up already? You lost, Vlad. But I lost ten years of my life to you. You aren't getting away that easy. I know your weaknesses, and I intend to exploit every single one."

She jabs the tip of the blade into his jaw.

"I fucking hate you, Vlad."

Holy shit.

With a smile on her face, she steps back and shoves the blade right into his cock. I have never heard a man cry like this before.

My face scrunches up, just imagining the agony.

"I was worried there for a second I might miss such a small dick."

I blow out a breath to disguise my laughter.

My heartbreaker needs this moment, and I am enjoying every second of watching her thrive.

CHAPTER 101

Song- Vore, Sleep Token.

"Was that too mean?" I pout at Declan, who has his tattooed hand covering his mouth, tears streaming from his eyes.

"It was perfect. Keep going," he urges me.

I glance down at the knife still lodged in his dick.

"I think I'll leave it in. Let the rust marinate."

"Fuck. You," Vlad grunts, and I spin to face him.

"Is this the best you've got, Vlad? Come on, you used to be so creative with your insults."

"Emil will come after you for this."

I roll my eyes.

"I'll slice up Emil easily. Where is he now, huh?"

His eyes go wide, and a bit more color drains from his face.

"None of your family will come after Charlotte, Vlad. Because she has an entire army protecting her now. Men from Russia, Italy, New York—you name it. Your family can't step foot in our country. So your threats are meaningless," Declan tells him.

"Thanks, handsome." I wink at him, and he blows me a kiss.

"See, I wanted to cut your tongue out. But, actually. I want to hear you hate every second of what's next."

I tap his cheek and he hisses at me like a damn snake.

I waltz over to Declan and lace my fingers through his, watching Vlad's nostrils flare.

Gotcha.

"I think it's time we really showed Vlad who I belong to."

Declan wraps his arms around my waist.

"What are you suggesting, sweetheart?"

I spin in his arms. I know this man will do anything for me.

"I want you to fuck me in front of my husband. I want you to fuck me so hard that he can see with his own eyes that I never belonged to him. That I have always belonged to you, Declan. This man needs a lesson- that a woman only comes for a man who deserves it."

Declan's mouth drops open.

"Don't you dare!" Vlad screams. Declan smirks in response.

"You are mine, baby. All mine, and I'm here to serve you." He dips his head into my neck and runs his tongue along my skin.

"So tasty. Such a good girl for me, aren't you?"

A gasp escapes my lips as his hands dig into my ass and he lifts me up. As I link my arms around his neck, a possessive growl escapes his lips.

"This is your moment, but I have rules," he says in a low tone that only I can hear.

"Rules?" I tip my chin up to look at him.

He nods, his face stern.

"One. He doesn't get to see you, but he can hear what I'm doing to you."

I chew on my lip; even in this fucked-up situation, this man will do anything for me, yet still protect me.

"Agreed. Only you get to see and feel."

He squeezes my ass harder.

"Good girl," he growls.

"Two. If you change your mind, you want me to stop, you want this to end, you say Decadence. Okay?"

"Like a safeword?" I whisper.

"Exactly that. I'll do everything I can to switch your brain off so we can give him the grand finale he deserves before he dies. Let's show him how fucking powerful you are."

A vicious smirk grows on his beautiful face, and I smile.

"Not just how powerful I am, how I belong to you, Declan."

His hand cups my face as he leans in and steals my lips.

"I fucking love you, heartbreaker. Now you better be soaking for me. Are you?"

He keeps kissing me, walking us back towards the far wall until my spine beats against the wood.

His hand slides under the band of my leggings and panties, and I tighten my grip around his neck.

"Getting there. Hands above your head," he orders, and I do as he says, resting them on the wall.

"Good." He slides two fingers inside me and I gasp, my chest flushing with heat.

"Let me hear it. Who do you belong to, Charlotte?"

He pulls them out and thrusts them back in all the way to the knuckle, making me cry out.

"You," I pant.

He shakes his head and I bite my tongue.

"You can do better than that, sweetheart."

"Who." *thrust.* "Do." *thrust.* "You." *thrust.* "Belong to?"

This time he pushes inside and twists his fingers.

"Declan Quinn. I belong entirely to Declan Quinn. I always have, and I always will."

His lips crash over mine, our teeth clattering as a raw hunger takes over.

He withdraws his fingers and drags them up my slit. With a light slap on my clit, I scream out, arching my back and squeezing my eyes shut.

"Declan!" I scream.

He lightly circles my clit with his thumb and keeps the rhythm with his fingers, sending me into a needy frenzy for him.

"Please, sir. I need you."

With the adrenaline pounding through my veins and the heat of his touch as his free hand wraps around my throat, I'm so close to falling apart for him.

"What do you want, exactly, Charlotte?" he asks.

"I want you to make love to me. I want you to come inside me and not let a drop come back out. I want to be marked from the inside as yours."

His brow arches and he licks his bottom lip with a grin.

"You're close, aren't you? I can feel you clenching around my fingers. So needy for me. So fucking perfect," he groans as I roll my hips against him.

"Look at you, baby. Coming apart for me, and we haven't really started."

The admiration, laced with pure hunger, only fires me up further.

"You. Declan. Only ever you." I tell him, looking into those blue eyes.

He releases his grip on my neck and slides his hand up my arm, being careful of the rope burns as he laces his fingers through mine.

"Hold onto my shoulders, it's going to be fast, hard, and rough, baby. We need to get out of here. I'll worship you once we get home, I promise." He nips at my neck as my arms float down and I grip onto him.

"Deal," I whisper.

He chuckles and sinks his fingers in deeper; my eyes flutter closed and I suck in a breath.

"Good. Because it wasn't a question. Mine, remember?"

Butterflies erupt in my stomach. I am his. And soon, we can have the future I once dreamed about. The one I even started writing about.

Our *'what if'* is no longer a fantasy. It's our reality.

I glance over his shoulder and set my sights on Vlad. His black eyes glaring at me, the vein on his forehead pulsing as he grits his teeth.

"Slut," he screams, but his insult bounces off of me.

He can't get to me now. Not his words, his actions. He is dead to me, and soon to the rest of the world.

"Ignore him. You're my slut, though." Declan winks, and I giggle.

"I'll get you screaming and your blood pounding, you won't even be able to hear that fucker."

I nod, rolling my hips harder against his hand.

As he removes his fingers, he brings them up between our faces and rests two of them on my lips.

"Taste what daddy does to you," he whispers, and I melt, parting my lips for him.

He slides them on my tongue, and I close my mouth, sucking them clean.

"Fuck, I'm gonna come in my pants if you carry on. I've never been so goddamn turned on in my life," he groans as he withdraws them with a pop from my mouth.

I shake my head and grin mischievously.

"Not today, I want all of it in me."

He grunts as he gets to work unbuckling his belt frantically.

"Be careful, heartbreaker. Keep talking like that, I'll have no choice but to fuck a baby into you."

A spark lights up his eyes as he speaks, and he pulls down my leggings on one side, only revealing the leg that Vlad can't see.

My heart races as the thick head of his cock pushes against my entrance.

"Stretch around me, baby. Relax. You can take it. You've done it perfectly a lot of times. Let me in," he whispers, his fingers stroking my cheek as he inches his way inside of me.

"Fuck me, heartbreaker. So fucking tight and all mine."

My fingers dig into his shirt as he thrusts all the way in one swift motion. I scream out and his lips slam over mine.

"I want those for now," he tells me between kisses.

With one hand on my neck, the other on my ass holding me in place against the wall, he pounds into me.

Each one steals my breath. Our moans grow louder. Faintly, I can hear the grumbles of Vlad. I hope he's dying inside.

Because I'm not. I'm freefalling into heaven with Declan.

"My good girl," he praises, and sparks fly, igniting from my head to my toes.

He works his lips down my jaw and starts to nip at my skin.

"So, beautiful."

His words keep my head where it needs to be. Right with him.

"You feeling good, baby?" he asks, pulling back and studying me. I open my eyes and see that pure desire on his face, and I nod.

"Never better," I tell him.

"Good. Now, let the room hear who you belong to."

He relentlessly pounds into me, squeezing my throat and smothering me with praise and kisses.

"Fuck, Declan," I scream at the top of my lungs as my body explodes.

"I'm about thirty seconds away from spilling my load. Come for me, my gorgeous girl. Let me feel it."

With a few final thrusts and a hard slap on my ass, even through the leggings, the pain radiates through me. I dive off the edge and let the most violent orgasm I have ever encountered shatter me. My hips work on their own accord, my needy pussy taking what it needs from him.

"Open your eyes," he commands, and they fly open, looking directly into his as he grunts, his warmth filling me up.

My entire body shakes in his arms as I ride the wave of my climax. My gaze flicks over to Vlad, who has his eyes squeezed shut, almost painfully, and I smile.

Fuck him. I hope this hurt his ego as much as his dick hurts right now.

"Back with me." Declan grabs my cheek and presses his nose against mine.

"I am so proud of you, heartbreaker," he whispers, lightly stroking his thumb along my skin.

As he slowly pulls his dick out, he swiftly replaces it with his hand, cupping my throbbing pussy, and my eyes go wide.

"You wanted it all?"

My mouth drops open and a gasp of pleasure escapes me as he slides his warm fingers back inside me.

He leans in, pushing his chest against me, sinking them in as deep as they go.

"Be a good girl, go and kill your husband with my cum dripping down your thighs." His deep voice vibrates through me.

"Thank you." I grab his face and press a kiss to his lips.

I don't think he will ever realize just how much this means to me. To have him beside me, my fierce protector. Even if I am strong, I deserve to have someone with me to fight alongside me. To take some of the weight of the battle sometimes.

I don't need saving.

But I do need protecting, perhaps sometimes from myself.

I need him like I need air to breathe. He brings me to life and brings me hope for a future.

With him, I can take on the world.

He delicately slides back up my panties and leggings and places my feet down on the ground.

"I'll be right behind you. Do whatever you need to, no judgement here."

"I love you," I say with my whole chest.

"And I love you, heartbreaker. More than you could ever imagine."

"Enough!" Vlad cries out behind us.

We burst out into laughter.

"I can't wait to never hear that annoying fucking voice again," I mumble under my breath, and Declan steps out of my path.

"Go get him, heartbreaker."

He taps my ass as I walk past him and I jump. Wiping the tears from the corners of my eyes from my rough fucking against a barn wall.

"Whore," Vlad bellows, and I ignore his existence, breezing past him to the shelf filled with weapons.

Or pig gutting equipment and farm shit, I guess.

Humming to myself, I tap my chin.

I want this over with. A gun is too easy for all the pain he's caused me.

Swiping my finger over the big carving knife, I pause. He isn't worth my time gutting him alive.

I keep pondering over to the next shelf, and a light goes off in my brain as I stop in front of the fuel canister.

Picking it up, I turn back to Declan, who nods approvingly at my choice. That gives me a jolt of energy to get back over to Vlad. Placing it by my feet, I reach forward and rip out the rusty blade from his dick.

I can't help myself as my fingers twitch around the handle, but to let out my anger and drive the knife straight into his gut. As it pierces his flesh, a little bit of joy creeps back into me.

"Declan, can you help me pour this over his head."

Before I finish my sentence, he is beside me, his hand on my hip.

"Of course, I can." He presses a kiss to the side of my head before bending down to pick it up.

He easily flicks off the lid and gets to work dousing Vlad, splashing it in his face first, before continuing to ensure every inch of him is fueled for the fire.

"You will pay for this," Vlad seethes.

"Maybe." I shrug.

"Or maybe not. No one really gives a shit about you, you worthless piece of shit." I jab my fist as forcefully as I can into his nose, hard enough to feel the bone snap.

Shaking out my hand, I laugh to myself.

"Sorry, that felt good."

Declan smiles and kicks the canister away from us.

"You do whatever you have to. Can I have a go?" he asks.

"Only if you put those brass knuckles back on. I wanna see how many teeth you can get out this time."

I look up at Vlad's already swollen and bleeding face as Declan releases a punch that resonates with a thud around the barn.

"Damn. Good hit," I tell him, and he winks.

Vlad heaves for air, fresh blood dripping over his eyes as Declan removes the metal from his hands.

I pause, looking between the men.

The man who kept me caged, who abused me, and made me a monster.

And the other, the one who taught me how to live again, who opened my heart back up. He gave me light when no one else could. A daughter to protect and fight for.

Perhaps everything does happen for a reason.

And for us, it was to form a path that leads to each other.

"I'm ready," I tell Declan firmly.

He slides his hand in mine and squeezes, slowly retreating us away from my flailing husband. Declan digs inside his jacket pocket and holds out the lighter in front of me.

"You do the honors, heartbreaker."

Wiping my palms on my leggings, I take the cool metal in my palm. The same lighter he used to almost burn us in the library to prove a point, that I am his and we will burn together.

Flicking it open, I roll the flint wheel so the flame dances in front of my eyes.

It's time to do what I need to.

Burn the old Charlotte. The evil and the trapped.

Maybe Vlad is right, and one day I will end up in hell with him. But until then, I'll do my damn best to flip the script and redeem myself by being the best mom I can be to Isabella. And the best partner to Declan I can be.

For the first time in ten years, I can see the light at the end of the tunnel. But now, I need to burn down the fucking tunnel and make a new path.

Squeezing Declan's hand, I launch the lighter at Vlad's chest. It quickly consumes him, a blaze engulfing him.

His terrified and agonizing cries make me smile. I watch as he struggles, tugging frantically at the ropes as his skin is melted from his body.

Declan keeps walking us back towards the exit. With each step, Vlad gets weaker and weaker, and we wait in silence by the door for his body to go limp.

I need to know that asshole is dead so he can't haunt me any longer.

Turning to Declan, he studies me, and tears fill my eyes.

"Take me back to our baby, Declan," I whisper.

"Home, heartbreaker. We're all going home."

CHAPTER 102

DECLAN

With Charlotte nestled on my lap, I rub my hand in small circles on her back as Mikhail drives the truck back to the safehouse, while his team deals with the fire and cleans up at the barn.

"You good, heartbreaker?" I whisper softly on the top of her head, and she nods against my chest.

"I'm so proud of you," I tell her, and my chest swells with emotions.

Ones I never believed I could feel. Pure, electrifying love. With her in my arms, going home to our little girl, I have never been so full of love in my life.

Pure perfection.

"It's finally over." Her voice breaks as she presses her face harder into my chest and I hold her tight.

"Let it out, baby. You've been strong for ten years, you don't need to fight anymore. Just feel. Whatever it is, embrace it, and we deal with it together."

My heart breaks for her. Because no matter how she defeated Vlad, he still inflicted pain on her for ten years. She's dealt with so much bottled inside her, with no one to cry on or take any of the burden with her.

"I'll always be here, sweetheart. No matter what. You are not on your own anymore. You've got me to fight with you now."

Her warm tears soak into my shirt and I close my eyes, resting my head on top of hers.

"I-I don't even know who I am anymore," she sobs.

I suck in a breath, knowing that feeling well. After my father died, that dark hole in my life propelled me deeper into the mafia, yet my heart ached. It ached for who I once was, for losing Charlotte, for not being able to save my parents.

I can't even imagine how hurt she must be inside.

"We can figure it out together. Just know, whoever you decide Charlotte really is, I'll love every single version of her. It doesn't matter to me. I love you for exactly the woman you are now, and whoever you become. I'm here for the ride, heartbreaker, wherever it may take us."

She pulls back, and my eyes start to sting with emotion.

"I want you by my side every step of the way, Declan."

Leaning in, I close my eyes and press a soft kiss to her lips.

"I'm not perfect, baby. But I'm going to try my hardest for you and Isabella. My father always taught us to put our family first, and now, that's you two. No matter what, I'm here."

She cups my face in her dainty hands and sniffles.

"You will be the best dad there is. I can tell."

I take in a shaky breath, my one fear is letting them down.

"Hey, we do this together, remember?" She reminds me, and I chuckle.

"Forever." I brush a stray strand of hair from her face, admiring her beauty as the truck comes to a slow stop.

"We're here," Mikhail tells us, and I nod to him.

The door slams behind him as he leaves, and Charlotte wiggles on my lap, maneuvering to straddle me.

"I love you, Declan Quinn. Our story isn't over, and I can't wait to see how it unfolds."

Wiping away her tears, I bring her forehead to press against mine.

"I love you so much, heartbreaker. I think you were right, we needed this hurt and pain to lead us to this moment. Because now, nothing can ever fucking stop us."

We stay cuddled like this for a few minutes, just soaking in the silence. There is no fear, no panic. Just quiet and calm.

"Let's go see our girl." I whisper against her lips.

Her eyes immediately light up with pure adoration and the final wall of ice around my heart melts. That's it.

Those two completely own me now.

After I help her out of the car, she practically races up the steps and through the front door. I guide her past my men and nod to Enzo as we pass. There is a time to catch up on business, and now is not it.

Charlotte double takes up the stairs, and I'm swiftly behind her.

"Second door on the left, baby," I call out, watching as she quietly turns the handle and pushes it open.

She stops in the doorway as I approach behind her, wrapping my arms around her waist, pulling her close.

We both just stand there, looking at our baby girl sleeping peacefully, snuggled in blankets. As she starts to stir, my heart races.

"Mommy?" She rubs her eyes.

"Yes, baby."

I release Charlotte and she jumps on the bed, hugging Isabella in her arms.

"Mommy is here, and I'm never leaving you ever again."

The raw emotion in Charlotte's voice makes me choke up as I approach them.

"Daddy's here too?" Isabella's tired voice makes me smile as I sit on the bed next to them.

"I love you, princess," Charlotte whispers to her, kissing her cheek.

"Can I have a daddy hug too?" she asks, and Charlotte tries to hide her sobs.

Scooting over, I take them both in my arms and hold them tight, never wanting to let go.

"I love my girls so much," I tell them.

I look up and catch a glance of Charlotte looking at me with a smile on her face.

"This is the moment I always dreamed of," she tells me. I swallow the lump in my throat.

"It's not a dream anymore, sweetheart. This is our life now."

And I've never felt more at peace.

Wherever my girls are is wherever my heart lies.

CHAPTER 103
DECLAN

"Shh," Charlotte whispers behind me.

I'm trying to shut Isabella's door as quietly as possible. We fell asleep, all three of us cuddled up for hours, and she's still tired, so we managed to untangle ourselves.

Before I reach the stairs, I grip her hips and tug her to me, turning her so her back presses against the wall.

She runs a finger along the dried blood on my forehead.

"We really need to get cleaned up," she tells me sternly.

"I'm fine," I grunt.

She shakes her head, her hands grazing down my abs towards my belt.

Loud footsteps approach behind us, and she freezes, and I grab her hands.

As Enzo clears his throat behind us, she steps back. I can't hide my grin.

"We've got two hours until the jet is ready. Conan and Finn are already in the air with Drago. We didn't want him in a Russian hospital. Finn is trying to treat him in the jet."

Closing my eyes, I wrap my arm around Charlotte's shoulder. After everything that she's been through, he needs to pull through. Her life has been cruel enough.

"Try?" she asks.

"Yes. He's not dead yet," Enzo replies bluntly, and I clench my fists.

"Finn is the best of the best, baby," I reassure her and glare at Enzo.

Now isn't the time to upset her.

"We don't expect any retaliation on American soil. So, let's just get the hell out of here and do damage control back in the States."

As Enzo goes to step back, he stops and looks at Charlotte.

"You've done yourself proud. I hope you can find peace now that he's out of your life."

She nods and extends her hand. He grins and shakes it.

"Thank you. Your invite to Decadence saved mine and Isabella's life."

"Fate works in funny ways, Charlotte. You'll be of great use to us."

I raise a brow. Like fuck am I ever putting her in harm's way again.

As he goes to walk away, I stop him, leaving Charlotte on the landing.

"She's not working for us, Enzo. I'm not becoming him. She only does what she wants to. End of discussion," I tell him firmly.

"Oh, I know. I was just testing. She's helped me with information, I don't require her any further. Be good to her, Declan. She deserves it, and so do you."

He squeezes my shoulder.

"You have no idea how lucky you are having them back in your life."

A sadness creeps into his voice that makes me pause.

"Whoever it is you're searching for, let me know how I can help. I owe you," I tell him, and I mean it.

"You've already helped." He nods up to Charlotte, and I follow his gaze to my beautiful woman.

He's right. I am the luckiest man alive.

I'll never take that for granted.

Striding back over to her, I take her hands and study the angry welts on her wrists. It looks worse probably because it's on already scarred skin. But a burning rage still rips through my chest, and I take a breath.

"It will heal, and once it does, I'll make it look pretty with tattoos," she tells me, and I run my finger along her ink, stopping in the empty space around her elbow and her inner bicep.

"You also have another flower to add."

She looks down and smiles.

"I've been waiting forever to fill that gap."

"Can you add some color to mine?" I ask, and she tilts her head.

"I can. Why?"

"I want to make my daughter smile. Not everything has to be dark all the time. That's what you've taught me."

She tugs me closer and drapes her arms over my shoulders, so I grab her thigh and hoist it up, pressing my pulsating cock against her.

"I'd love to give you some ink, Declan. Have you ever had your tattoo artist suck you off mid-session?"

My mouth drops open, and she giggles.

"No. But I will be having that. Fuck."

I pick her up by the waist carefully but can't resist slapping her ass as I stride into another bedroom.

Gently, I lay her down on the mattress and climb on myself.

"Now, I promised to worship you. How about we clean each other up, and then I'll spend however long we have left doing just that."

She pouts and gives me a cheeky grin.

"You have an hour. Then we get Isabella up and ready for the flight. Daddy duties start now." She winks, and I let out a growl as I pin her into the mattress and kick open her thighs.

"No, baby. Daddy Declan duties start right here, right now, with you."

The blush on her cheeks sends all the blood to my dick.

"Yes, daddy. Clean me up and make me feel good."

Goddammit.

She is going to be the most beautiful death of me.

CHAPTER 104

CHARLOTTE

Two weeks later…

I glance at the time on my laptop and spin in my chair. Three hours. I haven't even stopped for a sip of water.

Living in Declan's mansion in Decadence has already started to feel like second nature. And Isabella? She's obsessed with the fact her daddy runs a chocolate factory. She's toured the place, already brainstorming wild ideas for new chocolate flavors.

But nothing compares to that chocolate milkshake he created. It's a game-changer.

We've been looking into schools for her, both of us agreeing we want her to have a safe but *normal* childhood. The kind I never got. Friends, parties, experiences. All the things I missed out on, we're determined she'll have a chance to enjoy everything.

Of course, she's also got an army protecting her at all times. I don't think Declan's protective instinct will ever change—and honestly? I love it. Not having to always be the sole protector, always in fight mode.

Here, with him, I can breathe. Which is why I've spent the last three hours in the library, glued to my laptop, trying to finish our book.

A soft knock interrupts my thoughts, and the door creaks open. I spin in my chair and spot Isabella first, holding a big plate of fruit. Then, Declan steps in right behind her, carrying a tray.

"We made you lunch, Mommy!" Isabella giggles, her voice bubbling with excitement.

"Careful with the plate, baby," Declan says gently, and Isabella watches her steps as she approaches, making sure not to spill a thing.

"Thank you, princess." I kiss the top of her head, and Declan leans in to steal a kiss from me.

"Hi, Momma. Get a lot of words done?" He sets the tray down in front of me—a feast of pancakes, chocolate sauce, and a milkshake.

"I did. The inspiration you gave me last night helped more than you know." I raise my brows playfully, and Declan grins in that way that makes my heart skip.

"I'll help you later." He winks, and I blush, my cheeks heating up.

"We thought we could join you for lunch," Declan says, his tone full of that quiet affection I've come to adore. I close my laptop.

"I'd love that. Lunch with my two favorite people in the world? How could I possibly say no?" I jump up, scooping Isabella into my arms and showering her with kisses until she bursts into giggles.

"Daddy! Tell her to stop!"

Declan leans in, brushing my hair off my shoulder, his lips grazing my ear.

"You heard her, sweetheart. Or I might have to spank you later for being naughty."

"Declan." The heat in my cheeks spikes.

"What? It's the truth, heartbreaker. Don't make me take you to Inferno again."

I bite the inside of my cheek, still feeling the ache from last night, but with Declan? I trust him completely.

He shakes his head, a mischievous glint lighting up his eyes.

"What do you have planned?"

"Not telling." He presses a soft, teasing kiss to the tip of my nose.

CHAPTER 105

DECLAN

"**A**nd then the Queen got married to the Prince and made him the King. And they lived happily ever after with their little princess in the chocolate factory. And the King finally gets to live in a world of color again, rather than darkness."

Isabella's bottom lip trembles, and I brush my fingers through her curls, swallowing the lump in my throat.

"What's making you sad, baby girl?"

Seeing my little girl sad makes my chest ache.

"I'm not sad. I'm happy. I like that version of Mommy's story."

"So do I, baby. So do I. Now get some sleep and we can have a super fun day tomorrow with Uncle Conan and Finn."

"Yay!" she squeals.

It hasn't taken her long at all to warm to my brothers, and they love her, too.

Seeing Finn play doctor with her is a particular highlight for us all.

Pressing a soft kiss to her forehead, her eyes flutter closed.

"Night, night, Daddy. Love you."

I close my eyes and let her words sink into my heart, which has never felt so full.

"Night, baby. Sweet dreams. I love you."

Words that haven't rolled off my tongue in years now freefall out for Isabella and Charlotte.

Closing the door softly behind me, I head to my room and grab Charlotte's surprise.

When I reach the home gym, I slide open the doors and find Charlotte in exactly the same position I left her in.

Blindfolded, arms behind her back and kneeling, with not a shred of clothing other than her black and gold thong.

My cock throbs at the sight.

"Have you been a good girl and not peeked?" I ask, stepping into the room and placing the box down on the table and chairs set up on the mats.

"I promise, I haven't, sir."

Positioning myself behind her, she shivers as I run my hands over her shoulders and start to massage her neck lightly.

"I believe you," I tell her, stepping around to face her, dragging my fingers along her collarbone and wrapping them around her neck.

"I think you've been good enough for daddy to have earned a reward."

She nods, and I pull back her blindfold, revealing those blue eyes I just love to get lost in.

"Please, sir."

She shuffles on her legs, displaying how desperate she is for relief. All damn day I've teased her. Every fleeting moment we catch together, I use it to my advantage to edge her.

"Oh, I love it when you're desperate for me, heartbreaker." I stroke her cheek, and she moans.

Taking a step back, I hold out my hand and lift her to her feet, spinning her to face the setup on the mats.

"What is that?"

Leading her over, I unzip the bag, and she gasps, staring at the tattoo gun and array of ink and supplies.

I bought everything I thought she may need. I know how important this is to her.

"That final flower needs its spot, sweetheart. And then, it's about time we added some color into my tattoos."

Her body crashes into mine as she leaps into my arms and I catch her.

"Thank you. Thank you. Thank you." She showers my face with kisses, and I chuckle.

"You're welcome, baby. Your reward isn't just this, though."

I place her down on her feet.

"Panties off and sit your perfect ass on that chair."

Within seconds she strips and takes her seat.

Rolling up my sleeves, I catch her eyeing up my arms and wink. I know her weakness.

"Start getting set up." I nod to the array of items in the bag.

As she takes out the gun and black ink, I unbutton my shirt, watching her concentrate on squeezing the ink onto the little tub.

"I've had this planned for so long I don't even need a stencil. It's all in my head, exactly every line, every detail."

She twists on the battery pack and it hums to life.

"How long will it take you?" I question.

"Hmm. Maybe an hour, it's a fine line, so it shouldn't take long. Why?"

I drop to my knees and spread her legs wide.

"That means I have an hour to feast while you work." I look up with a smirk from between her thighs, and her eyes are wide, her plump lips open.

"Pain and pleasure, sweetheart. I want you dripping all over this leather seat and soaking my face. Once you've finished with your art, I'll throw you down on the mat and fuck you senseless. Until then, I will enjoy you."

Her eyes flick between me and the tattoo gun in her hand, and the determination is clear in her eyes.

"Am I allowed to come, sir?"

I nod.

"As many fucking times as you wish. This isn't punishment, this is a reward," I tell her, and slowly lick along her center, with my fingers digging into her knees, holding her legs apart.

She props her arm on top of the cushion and dips the needle in the ink.

"You're a wicked man, Mr. Quinn," she tells me with a smile on her face that tells a different story.

So I suck on her clit in response.

"I'm just obsessed with finding all the different ways to make you come, Charlotte."

I have more planned for when she tattoos me.

I want to explore her in every possible way and allow her to find out what she loves and what she doesn't so much. That way, every single time is perfect for her.

"I like that about you, Declan. I like you obsessed."

She begins to freehand her tattoo, and I get to work, starting off slowly to work her up and let her adjust to both sensations.

Once she's starting to soak my face, I insert two fingers slowly.

"Jesus, fuck. Declan," she hisses, and I look up.

"Get on with the tattoo, don't worry about me, baby," I tell her, spanking her clit before she gets back to work, and so do I.

Making small circles, I let my fingers work their magic, bringing her close to the edge.

When I hear the machine turn off, her fingers lace through my hair and she rides my face.

"That's it, baby. Take what you need from me."

I feast on her like a man starved, working in the rhythm of her hips as she bucks against me.

"Declan!" she screams, and I nearly explode in my pants hearing her cry out for me.

I hook her trembling legs over my shoulders and curl my fingers; as soon as I hit that spot, her body shakes against me.

I lick up every drop of her. I seriously don't know how I will last a full hour without needing a release.

This woman has me with a constant hard on. I'm ready to explode any time of the day. As she pulls my hair tight, it burns my scalp. Her juices drip down my hand and wrist, and the floodgates have opened.

I am soaked with her pleasure, her screams fill the room and I lose it.

My thighs clench, and my body goes rigid as I come violently in my boxers while she rides out her climax on my tongue.

"Jesus. Fuck," I pant out.

Once we come down from our high, I press a kiss on the inside of her thigh and sit back on my knees.

"You need to come clean up the mess you made on my dick before you carry on, heartbreaker."

I see the confusion on her post-orgasmic blush, so I unbuckle my belt and show her my cum smeared all over my dick.

"You? You came just by going down on me?" The shock in her voice makes me smile.

"Yes, baby. Because you nearly drowned me, screamed my name, and rode my face like it was the last time I'll ever eat you out. How was I meant to not come? You have no idea how fucking sexy you are, do you? Just looking at you makes me hard. But that? That was spectacular."

She blinks at me and then looks at my twitching dick.

"I got you." She winks as she pushes herself off her chair.

"Your turn to take the seat of orgasms."

As we switch positions, she kneels before me, holding onto my thighs.

"Quite the mess you made here, sir. It's a shame it didn't go inside of me." She bats her dark lashes at me, and I groan.

"You do some crazy things to me, heartbreaker. Now suck me clean so I can go again on you."

"This is going to take way longer than an hour," she whispers.

"Good. We have all the time in the world together now."

And what a fucking life it is going to be.

CHAPTER 106

CHARLOTTE

With Isabella tucked safely in Declan's arms, he guides me through the long hospital corridors.

Every step closer to the door, visions of the last time I saw him flash through my head.

The blood. His agony breaks my heart.

Drago is a good man, stuck in a war he didn't ask for.

It was only his kind heart hidden in that big chest that landed him in this hospital bed.

I remember the day he found me locked away in Vlad's house.

No one knew I was there, other than his sadistic brother. A dirty little secret.

I often wonder what would happen if the elusive Tatiana found out what her brothers were up to.

She is the only person who incited fear into Vlad. A family of deceit. It wouldn't surprise me if it runs a lot deeper than just what they did to me.

I shake my head. That is no longer my war.

Drago is my only concern. The one who saved me from complete captivity.

His alliance was once with Vlad. But the moment he saw me, withering away in that room, he did everything he could to get me out of there.

To the rest of Vlad's family, I was just a contract killer. Not his wife. I owe Drago my life.

I open up the door and tears stream down my face as I find him sitting up in bed, even with a busted lip, he's trying to smile.

"Come here, warrior," he croaks.

Rushing to his bedside, I'm careful as I lean over and hug him.

"I'm so sorry, Drago," I sob.

He tuts.

"I always knew what I was doing. It was always my risk and my burden. I chose that day to protect you. I'm sorry I didn't do a better job."

I pull back and shake my head.

"You did everything you possibly could."

Drago's eyes light up as Declan follows in behind me.

"Uncle Drago!" Isabella excitedly squeals.

As Declan drops her to her feet, she stops, and her eyes well up as she studies a beaten and bruised Drago.

I usher her over.

"It's okay, baby. He's just a little bit hurt, but still the same man."

She tiptoes to my side and I pick her up.

"Here's my little superstar. I missed you." Drago holds out his hand to her, and she takes it.

"Uncle Drago, you should see where I'm living now! A chocolate factory and loads of woods. We will have so much fun there."

"We will, once I'm fit and healthy again," Drago confirms.

I frown and look back at Declan, who is now edging closer to the bed.

"Am I missing something?" I look between the two most important men in my life.

My love and my best friend.

Declan strides over to the opposite side of the bed and holds out his hand to Drago, who gives him a firm handshake.

"It's good to finally shake the hand of the man who protected my girls. A debt I can never repay, but I will try."

"No debt, Declan. Just look after them."

"I will. With my life," Declan replies sincerely.

I clear my throat to get their attention, and they both laugh.

"For the time being Drago, once he's signed out of here, will be moving into a property on the Decadence estate. It's no longer safe for him to be in Russia. We are still unsure of the fallout that will follow from Vlad's death."

"But I thought Tatiana needed you?"

Drago swallows.

"She will be deeply hurt. I lied to her all of these years by hiding you and Isabella from her. I won't be welcomed back, especially with Emil still alive. There's a lot of skeletons in that family's closet. I hoped, one day, to be in a position where I could tell Tatiana the truth, which would have saved both you and her. The risk against you and Isabella was too large for me to rely on her. And who knows what the brothers would have done to her. I've worked under Vlad for long enough to know the sincerity behind his threats. Perhaps one day I will see her again, and I can explain."

I nod. Tatiana is a mystery, that's for sure. I have no bad blood with her; how was she supposed to help me when she was also kept in the dark?

If anything, I feel sorry for her. Trapped in that family.

"We can't risk you going back there. I think we've both exhausted our time in Russia, don't you?"

He scoffs.

"I never believed I would ever say this. But yes. I believe that is true," Drago replies, a sadness filling his voice.

"So, you're really staying here?"

He nods.

"Well, I gotta see this damn chocolate factory, haven't I?" He grins at Isabella.

"And it tastes soooo good, Uncle Drago. Like, out of this world." She even claps with excitement.

"You think I could live the rest of my life not watching her grow up? Never." He shakes his head, and my heart swells.

Isabella has no idea how lucky she is.

"I think it will be good for all of us, and Drago is exactly the kind of man I want in my organization. A man who will risk his life for my family."

Wow.

"Thank you," I mouth to Declan.

"We have all the time in the world to catch up, Charlotte. I'm safe here, I'm getting stronger every day. It won't be long until I'm back. Then we can get back to training."

I offer him a soft smile.

"I don't think that's the Charlotte I want to be anymore, Drago. I think my fighting days are over."

He arches his brow.

"Fighting is in your blood. You lived and breathed it, even before Vlad. Don't let him destroy your memories and your passion. Even if it's to teach Isabella or other kids. Don't lose your skill. Let it be your outlet and your peace. It was never meant to be a weapon, Charlotte. It's an art."

I wipe away the tears, thinking about my teenage years. How free it made me feel.

"Okay. You convinced me."

"You are not evil, Charlotte. Your skill doesn't make you a monster, it was him. Don't let him steal any of the parts of you that you love."

I nod, and Declan is already by my side, wrapping his arm around my waist.

"Words of wisdom, Drago. I always needed those."

"I didn't initially think I'd say this, but I like this guy," Declan whispers, and I giggle.

"Me too."

It's good they don't see each other as any sort of competition or enemy. They both add different things to my life.

Mine and Drago's friendship will never die, and hopefully, he and Declan are at the beginning of starting something pretty cool.

"Now, let me get my rest. I'll be seeing you soon."

Isabella perches on the edge of the bed and carefully gives him a hug.

As I carry her to the door, Drago coughs, and I stop.

"And Declan, if you hurt her, I'll kill you with my bare hands."

Declan's jaw ticks, and he spins to face him again.

"Trust me, if I ever hurt her, I'll deserve your wrath, and I'll take it gladly."

Drago laughs, and I relax.

"Just teasing. I needed to gauge your reaction. You passed the test."

Declan chuckles, and I usher him out of the door in front of me.

"I think you two will get on just fine," I tell him as he picks Isabella out of my arms and she snuggles into his side.

"Finn and Conan actually suggested the idea. So with the three of you all being Team Drago, I knew he had to be a good guy. I knew that anyway, after all he's done for you, it's the least I can do."

I go up on my tiptoes and press a kiss on his jaw.

"I love you, Declan."

"I wanna see Uncle Finn and Conan." Isabella pouts, and my chest swells.

She's got everything she needs in this life.

She is safe and loved, and I couldn't ask for anything else.

And now, three uncles who won't ever leave her side.

A lucky girl.

And so am I.

CHAPTER 107

DECLAN

"Bye, Uncle Finn! Bye, Conan!" Isabella beams, waving like she's the star of her own show.

"Hey! You forgot something!" Conan shouts after her.

She pauses, lips puckering into a pout. Then her eyes go wide with mischief.

"Oh, Uncle Cool Conan."

"There you go."

He sticks out his tongue as Finn shoots him a glare. Charlotte grabs my face and plants a kiss right on my mouth, messy, unapologetic, hers.

"I'll put her to bed and meet you in the library. One hour?" she whispers, breath tickling my skin.

"Good girl. I need to read what you've been writing."

Her cheeks flush, the color rising up her neck. I let my hand rest on her ass, firm and familiar over the cling of that black and purple sundress. *Fuck*, I need her beneath me again. Bent over. Breathless.

"You do, sir."

One last kiss, slow and deliberate, and she's gone, walking Isabella back to our home, leaving me high on the scent of her and already counting down the minutes.

"Whiskey?" Finn calls, already cracking the bottle, three glasses in his grip like a man on a mission.

He pours heavily. We clink. We drink.

"So, no more Decadence Games for our big bro, huh?" Finn smirks, refilling without waiting.

I shake my head. I have a new life to build with my girls. If we need a third game, we have other men that would step up.

"Nope. You two are upholding the reputation now."

They both nod like eager devils.

"Don't worry." Conan grins. "Our games are more than enough."

He's already diving back into the twisted setup of his own game, The Decadence Chase. Feral. Brutal. So very *him*.

"Maybe Drago could take them over?" Conan suggests, eyebrow raised as he lights a cigarette.

"We'll see. Let's just help him settle back in before we throw him into that fire. Reggie and Rowan want to host too, don't forget."

Finn's mouth curls into a sharp grin, jaw tight with anticipation.

"Or we just do four a year. We've got the time."

I should be thinking logistics. Instead, all I can focus on is the black diamond burning a hole in my pocket.

"Speaking of games…" I start, pulling their attention back. "I need your help."

They exchange a glance, silent and solid.

"You know we'd never say no. Spill it," Finn says.

I pull the box from my pocket and pop it open. Their eyes go wide.

"Damn," Finn mutters, scratching at his stubble. "You don't waste time, do you?"

"Too soon?" I ask, even though I already know the answer.

I open the box wider, watching the way the light catches.

"Actually? I don't give a shit. I'm marrying this woman."

Conan slaps a heavy hand to my shoulder.

"I *told* you. I said you'd marry her. Maybe I'm a fucking witch. Or what's the word—clairvoyant?"

I laugh. I can't help it.

"Yes, Con. You're the family witch. Now cast a damn spell to make sure she says 'yes'."

Finn doubles over, wheezing with laughter.

"Don't encourage him, Dec. Next thing, he'll be dancing naked under the moon, summoning soulmates with crystals."

"Wait, does that work?" Conan deadpans. He wiggles his fingers in the air and closes his eyes.

"I'm calling in the woman of my dreams to the gates of my games."

I smack his shoulder. "No. Wrong spell. Focus."

Finn leans on the kitchen island, serious now.

"What do you need us for?"

"I need to bring back the Decadence Games. One last time." I grin, all teeth and tension.

"Fuck *yes*." Conan snaps back to reality like he's been electrified.

"I need to get back to Charlotte. But I'll give you the details now so you can start. I want this happening as soon as possible."

I tuck the ring box back into my pocket. Safe. Waiting. That ring is going on her finger by the end of the week.

I want to spend every damn day loving her. Tearing down the scars of her past. Replacing those ghosts with something beautiful. Starting with marriage.

After that, she can drag me through hell or heaven, I don't care.

As long as she's beside me, I'll follow.

And I'll never let go.

CHAPTER 108

CHARLOTTE

Song- Wicked Game, Chris Isaak

The bell of the front door rings and I pull myself away from my writing and pad down the hallway.

Conan has taken Isabella for some training in the gym today. She wanted him to teach her how to cage fight, of all things.

She's got my fighting blood, that's for sure.

I'd love to see how Conan copes with letting a four-year-old in a tutu kick him around the cage.

As I open the door, I look down and find a huge pile of black and purple roses next to a basket on the doorstep.

I look up, and no one is there.

Picking them up with a smile, I pluck out the envelope and open it up.

You are invited to the FINAL Decadence Game.
The Master of Inferno will meet you at the gates at 2pm.
You will find everything you need to play inside the basket.
This will be the last time the gates ever open for this Master.
Good luck.

A GIDDY EXCITEMENT radiates through me as I grab the basket and head into the kitchen. I shake my head with a laugh as I pull out the carton of Decadence Milkshake. Next out of the basket is a black lingerie set, this time a corset style covered in diamantes, attached to a matching collar.

And then the dreaded garter set, although, this one looks much easier to put on as the straps are attached to the corset.

"Wow." I hold it up and let it sparkle in the sunlight.

Last out is a pair of red sole heels, black leather, of course. As I go to close the basket, a note at the bottom catches my attention.

In Declan's scribbly handwriting, I read it, and a sob catches in my throat.

I WILL ALWAYS BURN for you, heartbreaker.
I love you, forever.
Your Declan.

AFTER SPENDING the next thirty minutes showering and shaving every hair on my body and getting my hair into a perfect curly ponytail, I'm ready.

Nerves pit in my stomach as I shove my arms in my black trench coat and do it up tight. Before I leave, I swipe up the chocolate milkshake.

As I open the front door, Declan's black Mercedes pulls up, and he gets out, opening up the back for me.

"I thought it might be best to give you a ride there." He winks, ushering me towards him.

"No handcuffs?" I ask, making my way down the steps and onto the gravel.

He leans inside the back seat and pulls out a diamante set, holding them up in front of his face with his finger.

"I didn't forget. Keep hold of them, you'll need them soon."

As I bend into the car, tossing the carton on the passenger side, he slaps my ass, and I squeal.

He jumps in the driver's seat and his eyes catch mine in the mirror.

"You look breathtaking."

I blush and look away from his burning gaze.

"And I haven't even seen what's underneath."

Any nerves I did have about returning back to Decadence are washed away with his words.

He makes me feel sexy and powerful.

"I prefer this way of getting me to the games."

He chews on his lip.

"I can only apologize for that. If I knew what I do now, I would have never," he says solemnly.

"I know, Declan. It's okay. We are way past that."

It's a short and quiet drive to the gates. When he comes to a stop, he hops out and opens my door for me, holding out his hand to help me out.

"So this is the last time you'll host a game?" I ask as I link my fingers through his.

"I have more important things to be doing with my time. They were there to fill a void, the one that could only ever be filled by you."

I smile and bat my lashes.

"Good. We can still play together in Inferno, though?" I pout.

"Maybe. If you behave." He teases and guides me up the stairs. The doors open for us, and just like the first time here, the chocolate factory workers ignore us.

But the smell makes my stomach rumble. Isabella is right, their chocolate is the best I've ever tasted.

As we descend deeper into Decadence, through the familiar thumb coded door, Declan stops and laughs.

"I still can't believe you cut one of my men's thumbs off."

My eyes go wide in horror. I kinda forgot about that one.

"I need to apologize for that, a bit awkward otherwise."

Declan shakes his head and taps my ass, walking me through.

"I paid him off, he's pretty useless to me now."

We keep walking on the purple marble tiles, my heels clicking against them until we reach the final room.

"What happened to the other girls? Where did they end up?" I ask before we go in.

"They all work for Enzo in some capacity. They're all safe and well and busy working. Depending on what their background and skill was, he has businesses in most industries across the globe at this point. We ensure they're safe from their families now. New lives, fresh starts."

"Even Tara?" I frown, I doubt she took any of this well.

"She was harder. Finn dealt with her family first to avoid her running back there," he says matter-of-factly, and I pause.

"Dealt with?" I question.

"Yes. That's Finn's role. The kind of scum that enters women into these games deserves to die. So that is exactly what happens."

"I like that."

"Good." He pulls me in and kisses me.

"That is why you are perfect," he mutters.

He opens up the door and that huge chocolate fountain is flowing, except this time, the room is smothered with purple and black roses, just like my bouquet.

"Are you ready to play for your golden ticket?" Declan's deep Irish accent sends pulses to my pussy.

"I am," I reply, taking a step inside the room.

"Do I get the million dollars? Or something else?" I bite back a grin.

The first thing I find is our contract pinned up on the wall amongst the flowers. Next to it, a shining golden ticket to Decadence.

"There are new terms and conditions for this game. Your first instruction is to retrieve the contract."

I walk over and snatch it from the wall. I spin round to face him and find him on one knee, a ring box in his hand and a smile on his handsome face.

"Declan…" I gasp.

"Rip that piece of paper up. I don't want you as my property. I need you as my wife."

In one swift move, I tear down the middle of the paper and throw it on the floor, and it lands right next to the Decadence Milkshake beside him.

"No games. No rules. I just want forever with you, heartbreaker. Will you please do me the honor of being my wife? Marry me, Charlotte."

My heart almost stops.

Vlad was never my husband. On paper, yes. In every other way? No.

This man down on one knee, this is my future.

Declan is the only man for me. Always will be.

"Yes. I'll marry you."

"Give me that hand then, sweetheart."

I hold out my left hand, and he slides on the stunning coffin-cut black diamond, surrounded by white gems on a gold band.

"That is just perfect, Declan," I whisper, watching it sparkle under the lights.

"A reminder that even the darkest times can have a sparkle."

Tears cascade down my face and he jumps up to his feet and lifts me into his arms, smothering me with kisses. My back crashes against the wall, the flowers a soft cushion, as his fingers thread through my ponytail.

"My wife," he growls.

I squeeze my legs tighter around him, feeling his dick press against me.

"B-but I didn't play the game?" I ask, batting my lashes.

"We are now."

He pulls out the diamante cuffs from the inside of his pocket and shrugs off his jacket, tossing it across the floor. Rolling up his sleeves, I look at how well the colored ink is healing on his forearm.

It was so sweet watching Isabella pick each color and where she wanted it to go.

He's become her own personal coloring pad.

He drops me down onto my feet, and I hold out my wrists.

"I've had extra padding put on these so it doesn't hurt your scars."

I smile looking up at him as my heart swells with love.

"Thank you."

"Anything for you."

He carefully secures them on each wrist.

"Now, let me see what's under that coat. Show me what's mine."

I slowly untie the belt and let it fall to the ground.

His mouth almost hits the floor as his eyes rake over my body.

"Mmm, I could come in my pants again just watching you, heartbreaker." His gravelly voice lights me up.

"Oh, yeah?" I do a three-sixty spin to show him every inch of me.

"God, your ass is so close to being ready for me," he groans as he speaks, and the air crackles around us as I face him again.

I clench my thighs together to try and relieve the pressure building in my core.

"Open your legs and bend over." He spanks my ass hard, and I do exactly as he tells me.

As he peels my thong away from me and rests it over my ass, I shiver under his touch as his wet finger slides along my pussy and towards my back entrance.

"Now, sweetheart. Today we're stepping up a size," he tells me, sliding a finger into my ass and his thumb into my pussy.

He thrusts them in and out at the exact same pace, and my body burns for more.

"Fuck, Declan."

My legs are straining as I hold myself in position and he removes his fingers slowly.

I hear the cap of a bottle open and the lube squirt out, and I start to tremble with anticipation.

"Breathe for me, heartbreaker."

I blow out a deep breath, and he slides the toy inside my ass.

"Oh, fuck." My eyes flick open at the intrusion, and I adjust to it.

"Yes, baby. You're doing so, so well. Next time, it will be my dick."

Excitement buzzes through me, and suddenly, something else begins to buzz inside me.

"W-what?" I almost jolt upright, but Declan's hand on my neck holds me in place.

"You like it?" he asks.

"I think so."

It's strange coming from there, but the gentle vibrations feel good. Just different.

"Good girl. Now stand."

He steps back as I bring my body upright.

"You need some more distracting, baby?" he asks, closing the distance between us, and I nod.

"I want to watch you, baby. Lay down and fuck yourself, just how you want me to do it."

I look away, almost doubting myself for a second.

"Trust me. Keep your eyes on me, you can watch what you do to me at the same time."

I lay down on the purple padded floor and rest my top half on my left arm, sliding my right hand under my panties and shove them to the side so he can see.

"Soaking, all for me."

Declan unbuckles his belt and pulls out his erect cock, already dripping at the tip for me. As I slide two fingers inside, he swipes his pre-cum from the head and strides towards me.

I open my mouth and he feeds me his fingers. I lick them clean.

"Mmm," I mumble.

"All for you and because of you," he tells me.

He gets back into position in front of me and starts to stroke his cock, his eyes fixated on my fingers thrusting inside of me.

"Good fucking girl. Add another one."

I do, and I cry out, tipping my head back.

"Spread them wider, let me see that beautiful cunt dripping for me."

I let my knees fall to the floor.

"What a sight, baby."

"Declan, please. I need to come."

He drops to his knees and crawls to me, completely feral as he rips off my panties with a growl erupting from his chest. He heaves my right leg over his shoulder and dips his head.

His tongue connects to my clit and I keep the pace of my fingers going.

Just as I reach my tipping point, he pulls away and stands.

"On your knees and hands behind your back," he commands. That dominant darkness flashing over his eyes.

My legs are like jelly as I maneuver myself into position kneeling for him.

I suck in a breath as he walks behind me, fastening the cuffs together by the chain.

Even when he has me chained, I have never been more free.

Because with him, he isn't there to break me or punish me for who I am.

Declan is there to worship and love me.

I am at his mercy because I choose to be.

And right here, on my knees before him, is exactly where I want to be.

CHAPTER 109

DECLAN

I'm certain of it now, this woman is transcendent. Not just beautiful. Not merely obedient. There's no other way to explain the way she owns my every thought, my every breath. She's got this invisible grip on my soul. And I don't want her to let go.

I trail my finger along her plush lips. She parts them instinctively. That single, silent gesture tells me everything. She's waiting. Willing. *Mine*.

"So obedient. So needy for me," I murmur, voice low and rough with heat. "Is this what you want?"

I stroke my cock in front of her in a slow and deliberate motion, an offering and a warning all at once. She nods, her eyes wide and lips trembling with anticipation.

"Please, sir."

That's all I need to hear.

Without breaking eye contact, I slip my hand into my pocket and press the hidden button, upping the vibration speed on the plug buried deep inside her. She thinks she can mask the reaction. But I see everything. The twitch of her thigh. The flicker in her lashes. The way her breath catches like she's been hit with lightning.

She's trying to be good for me. That only makes me want to ruin her more.

Wordlessly, I bend down to retrieve the Decadence Milkshake. She watches me, still and waiting, that shimmer in her eyes giving her away, she loves being under my control. That flicker of lust, of surrender, is gasoline to my fire.

I kick off my pants, but I don't rush my movements. I'm not letting her forget who's in charge.

"Time for you to have the real Decadence Experience," I growl, the corners of my mouth lifting into a wicked smile.

I pop the lid off the milkshake and pour it over my cock, watching her shiver as the liquid drips down my length. I step closer, until I'm so close she can feel the heat of me.

"A taste of heaven," I whisper, letting the final drops fall.

She doesn't wait for permission. She parts her lips and takes me all the way in, gagging around the thick head as I hit the back of her throat.

Her warm mouth wrapped around my cold, dripping cock makes me groan; the contrast is electric, making my muscles tighten, my control flicker.

"Fuck, baby."

I wind her hair tight around my fist, gripping hard enough to make her gasp. She's not going anywhere. Not until I say so.

I thrust my hips forward, burying myself deeper into her throat. She gags again, tears pricking at the corners of her eyes, but she takes it. Because she wants to take it.

Every sound, every wet, choked moan that slips from her mouth makes my body burn hotter. I'm close. Too fucking close.

Yanking her back by the hair, I look down at her, breath ragged, control barely holding.

"Lick it clean," I order.

Her eyes glisten as I pour more of the milkshake down my shaft, just a thin stream this time. She licks every drop, her tongue slow, making sure to clean me thoroughly like the good fucking girl she is.

"Charlotte," I growl, as she sucks the tip again, teasing the sensitive head.

"Fuck."

She doesn't stop. She worships me with her mouth, her tongue tracing every ridge, her lips slick and eager. When she dips lower and licks my balls, it nearly breaks me.

"Oh, fuck. Fuck!" I cry out, throwing my head back as the pleasure crashes through me like fire.

And when she takes me back in, deep and merciless, I lose the last threads of composure. I fuck her throat like I own it, because I do.

Tears run down her cheeks; her body twitches beneath me, but she stays in place. Stays open. Stays mine.

And just when I'm on the edge of spilling everything down her throat, I pull out. The sudden loss of warmth makes me groan.

I grab her face, pressing it to the floor, and she immediately lifts her ass for me, with her back arched and her thighs trembling. Desperate. Perfect.

"You gonna be a good girl and take it all for me?" I growl into her ear. "You gonna let Daddy fill this tight little pussy?"

"Y-yes. Please, sir," she whispers, her voice so wrecked with need it makes my cock twitch.

I don't hesitate. I drive into her in one long, punishing thrust. She's so tight, so wet, so fucking ready for me it's like her body was made for mine.

I grip her hips, keeping her in place as I slam into her over and over again. There's no finesse now, just raw, primal need.

Her screams echo through the room, and I roar right along with her. This is ours, this moment. What started as a game, ended chapters of our lives and brought us here. But now, there's no need to play anymore. Not when I have everything I'll ever need in life.

"Come for me. Let me fucking feel it."

And then she does, clenching hard around me as her whole body shudders. Her orgasm rips through her, strangling my cock in the best possible way.

I follow with a groan, spilling into her, emptying myself completely. Letting her take every drop of me. Because she can. Because she wants to. Because I own her.

I'm still heaving, breath ragged, when I scoop her up and shift her onto my lap. Her thighs shake as she wraps herself around me.

Gently, I pull the plug from her and set it vibrating uselessly on the floor. I don't even bother reaching for the remote. All I want is her.

I cup her face, brushing my thumb over her flushed cheek. And then I kiss her soft and savage. A kiss that speaks of everything I don't have the strength to say aloud.

"You good, sweetheart?" I ask, my voice hoarse, my heart still thundering.

"Very." She pouts, rocking her hips against me with a lazy kind of need.

I lean down and take one of her nipples into my mouth, sucking slow and deep until she arches with another soft moan.

"You're on fire, heartbreaker."

She smiles down at me. "I burn for you."

I shake my head, brushing my lips over hers. "We *are* the flame, baby."

I wrap my fingers gently but firmly around her throat and kiss her again, deeper this time, stealing her breath just as she takes mine.

Loving her isn't a choice. It's instinct. It's survival.

Two broken souls who scorched the earth just to find each other.

This was never a coincidence.

This was inevitable.

And now, there's no undoing it.

We are bound.

Burning.

Together, we are the inferno.

THE END.

EPILOGUE

With the wedding party in full swing out in the woodlands of Decadence, I sit back on the couch with Finn, watching Charlotte twirl around in her shimmering black dress with Isabella twirling around in her arms.

Both with beaming smiles, dancing the night away without a care in the world.

They don't see the armed guards surrounding the grounds.

They don't sense any fear. Because there is none, not anymore.

Charlotte catches a glimpse of me watching and waves, prompting Isabella to spin around and launch herself at me.

"Looks like someone wants their daddy," Finn says with a grin.

"They both do."

He spits out his drink.

"Declan, really?"

I wiggle my eyebrows and catch my daughter on my lap.

"Daddy! Daddy! Come dance with us."

"What if Daddy isn't good at dancing?"

She pouts, and she's won me over. I was never denying her anything anyway.

"Mommy will teach you, she's really good."

"Oh, is she now?" I ask, standing up, and she grabs my hand, dragging me across the grass to my beautiful wife.

"Someone told me that you could teach this useless man how to dance," I whisper, grabbing Charlotte's hips and tugging her close.

"I could, if he asks nicely."

"Is that right?" I growl.

"Maybe I'll withhold your treat tonight if that's the case."

She shakes her head, and I kiss her.

"Call me your wife again."

My hands frame her face, and in that moment, the rest of the world fades away. The music, the chatter of my men, everything. It's just her.

"My beautiful, courageous, powerful, sexy wife."

She grips my throat and drags me in for a ferocious kiss.

"I love you, Declan," she mutters against my lips with a smile.

We may have had a small ceremony with the handful of people who we love with all of our hearts.

But it means everything.

We started our life as we mean to go on, in our own safe haven.

"I love you, heartbreaker. Just like I said in my vows, now and forever."

We fall into a steady rhythm with the music, my hands on her hips as she leads the way.

I glance over and find Drago twirling around the makeshift dance floor as best he can with Isabella safely in his arms.

It's been three months, and he's recovering well and already proving to be an asset to my organization.

"More spinning!" she yells.

"In a minute, let me get rid of the stars in my eyes," Drago puffs out.

"She's going to be feisty, just like her mommy," I tell Charlotte, who rests her head on my chest.

"I hope so. In this world, she needs some spirit."

I hold her closer and rest my chin on her.

"Especially with all of the siblings that she's going to be bossing around."

Charlotte pulls back, her eyes wide and sparking.

"Maybe we can try properly after our honeymoon." She smiles.

"And you think the last four months wasn't me trying properly?" I smirk.

She shakes her head and presses her finger to my lips.

"No. Because you would have got it right the first month if you really tried. I know you, Mr. Quinn."

She's right.

I can't help but chuckle.

"You got me. I'm letting you decide when you're ready. It's your body, your health. Your decision. I'm happy with exactly what we have here, I don't need more."

She runs her hands down my chest and presses her lips against mine.

"Oh, Declan. You think I don't want to see Daddy Declan in full force with a newborn? That is going to turn me on so much that I'll probably keep popping them out. I can't wait to do it again with you this time. Isabella will love it, too. But you're right, I need some time to just figure myself out first."

"You got it, baby. And if it's any help, I think you're perfect just the way you are."

"And so are you," she whispers back.

Finn shouting behind me catches my attention.

"Conan! Can you hear me?"

I frown, turning to take a look.

Without asking, Charlotte has her hand laced in mine and is stomping over to Finn, who's shouting at his cell.

"Where are you?!" Finn hisses.

"Er. Let me get the sat-nav up. It fucking hurts," Conan whines down the speaker.

"What the hell has happened? He was here fifteen minutes ago?" I ask, rubbing my temple.

"Yeah, well, asshole decided he needed to go pick up his girlfriend."

"She is not my girlfriend. Just a friend that is a girl. Who I may stick my dick in later if she lets me," Conan shouts back.

I roll my eyes.

"And?"

"And in doing so, on his way there, had his car smashed into on the highway and somehow ended up with a shard of glass sticking out of his thigh."

"Oh shit."

Conan's face appears on the screen as the video call connects.

"Did you see who hit you?" I ask. Always assuming the worst.

"Nah, just some assholes who don't know how to brake. They drove off, but my car is fucked. And look!"

He flips the camera, and I wince, looking at his injury.

"Look, I've texted Hallie from my work phone, she's on her way to pick you up and take you to my ward. She will fix you up and bring you home," Finn tells Conan sternly.

"Oh, Hallie. Hot name. Is she?" he asks.

"Is she what?" Finn asks through gritted teeth.

"Hot?"

Finn swears under his breath. I look at Charlotte, who is fascinated watching us all interact.

"Carry on, I'll tell her to make it as painful as possible. Be nice to her, she's doing me a favor. I'm too drunk to drive right now."

"Fine," Conan huffs.

"It really fucking hurts though, Finn. Am I going to lose my leg?"

"If you shut your mouth, you won't," Finn snaps back. I lose it, breaking out into a fit of laughter.

"You all good, Con. It is my wedding after all, I've got to get back to my wife. But text me when you're patched up. Which car was it?"

I have to ask. Those cars are his damn children.

"The Ferrari."

There's a sadness in his voice.

"Look, now you have room for the Bugatti. Silver linings, brother," I tell him.

"True. I'll fix this one up anyway."

Finn continues to listen to Conan and I lead Charlotte back over to Drago and Isabella.

"It's time for bed, don't you think?" I crouch down to Isabella, and she pouts, shaking her head and throwing her arms across her chest.

"Come on, sweetie," Charlotte coos and picks her up into her arms.

She yawns and snuggles into Charlotte's chest.

"You need some rest too." She glares at Drago.

"Yeah, yeah. I'll have a drink with Finn first. I feel good today." He stretches out his arms.

"A beautiful day for a beautiful couple. Congratulations." He rubs Isabella's cheek and says his good nights before heading over to the bar.

"I have another present for you when we get home," Charlotte tells me, bumping into me.

"Oh, yeah?"

She presses her finger to her lips.

"A secret. Just wait."

IGNITE

The games are over, but the Decadence Chase is just beginning…

The next brother to host his version of the games is Conan.

A primal game of survival in the woods.

But what happens when Conan meets the fiery, street-racing nurse, Hallie?

There are lots of secrets and twists to come. But it is going to be feral and so so hot.

You can pre-order it here!

WANT A LITTLE BIT MORE DECLAN?

Sign up to my newsletter to receive a **BONUS SCENE.** I'll give you a little hint, it involves him helping her finish her spicy scene…
READ IT HERE: https://dl.bookfunnel.com/poyuvjb2e3

To stay up to date with exciting news and releases, the best place to find me is in my FB Group: **Luna Masons Mafia Queens.**

And if you want **signed books,** store exclusives and all the *naughty art,* you can purchase directly from my store:
www.lunamasonbookstore.com

MORE FROM THE 'BENEATH UNIVERSE'

Beneath The Mask series has been picked up by Kensington.

You can read all four online and they will be releasing in bookstores throughout 2025:

You can find all the details for Distance, Detonate, Devoted and Detained here!

https://www.kensingtonbooks.com/pages/beneaththemask/

Some of the characters from Beneath The Secrets made an appearance in Inferno. You can read their stories in Beneath The Secrets.

A Dark and spicy Russian mafia romance set in Vegas.

Chaos:
https://mybook.to/QaGijx

Caged:
https://mybook.to/Fc18uiK

Crave:
https://mybook.to/rTb4

Claim:
https://mybook.to/6Nyh